"May be Andrew M. Greeley's best effort yet."
—*Baltimore Sun*

"A real Irish stew, with a ghost or two tossed in for good measure."
—*San Francisco Chronicle*

"Piquant characters who are engulfed in delightful Irish mystery. Recommended."
—*Library Journal*

"A marvelous tale of love, war, passion, politics, and intrigue—and since the setting is Ireland, a good dose of tragedy."
—*Gannett Suburban Newspapers*

"A mystery as modern as the . . . peace talks between England and Ireland, and as old as the Troubles of the 1920s."
—*Atlanta Journal Constitution*

"A tale of young love and faith, as modern as U2 . . . yet those who have followed his works in the past will find the same storytelling mastery and the same understanding of the heart."
—*Chicago Tribune*

ALSO BY ANDREW M. GREELEY
FROM TOM DOHERTY ASSOCIATES

*forthcoming

IRISH LACE

A Nuala Anne McGrail Novel

ANDREW M. GREELEY

TOR®

A TOM DOHERTY ASSOCIATES BOOK
NEW YORK

This is a work of fiction. All the characters and events portrayed in this book are either products of the author's imagination or are used fictitiously.

IRISH LACE

Copyright © 1996 by Andrew M. Greeley Enterprises, Ltd.

Cover photo by Don Banks

A Tor Book
Published by Tom Doherty Associates, LLC
175 Fifth Avenue
New York, NY 10010

www.tor.com

Tor® is a registered trademark of Tom Doherty Associates, LLC.

ISBN: 0-812-55077-3
Library of Congress Catalog Card Number: 96-24519

First edition: November 1996
First mass market edition: October 1997

Printed in the United States of America

0 9 8 7 6 5 4 3

For Kelly Anne, Jack, Sean, and Liam

"DERMOT MICHAEL," Nuala screamed on Sunday afternoon as she dug her fingers into my arm, "Turn off here! There's terrible things happening! Men dying everywhere!"

I had been listening to the five o'clock radio news. Another art-gallery robbery in the River North area—this time at the Thalberg Gallery at Erie and Orleans. Third robbery this month. Police were speculating that the robbery might be linked to the opening of the Monet exhibit at the Art Institute. What nonsense!

I turned off the radio and left Lake Shore Drive at 31st Street as I had been instructed.

Nuala Anne McGrail (aka Marie Phinoulah Annagh McGriel) is fey. Or psychic. Depending on your perspective. She would rather say simply that she "sees things." She is a holdover, albeit a gorgeous one, from the mists and myths of Celtic antiquity, a woman who in olden times would have been honored as a seer, a prophetess, even a minor goddess. Or perhaps burned as a witch.

Now she's an accountant.

Incidentally, her name should be pronounced as though it were spelled "Noola." The double O must be drawn out and said with a certain touch of the bog and the mists and the rain and the sea about it, which is very hard to do, though my brother George the Priest got it right the first time.

She is not fey often, as least as far as I know. When she is in one of those—what should I call them, "conditions"—I take her seriously. Usually it means that we are going to be involved in solving a mystery from the past and maybe one in the present, too. I use the term "we" loosely. Nuala is not only fey, she is also a detective.

She buried her head against my chest.

"Make them stop it, Dermot Michael. Make them stop it."

I put an arm around her, always a pleasant experience.

"It will be all right, Nuala. Just hang on to me."

We turned into the Lake Meadows housing development, one of the first integrated middle- and upper-middle-class rental developments along the South Shore of Lake Michigan—high-rise glass and steel buildings à la Mies van der Rohe, elegantly landscaped and protected by high fences to keep the natives out. The people—men, women, and children—who were outside on the lawns enjoying the mild Memorial Day weather seemed a subtle mixture of white, black, and brown. Racial integration, as someone once said, against the poor.

"What is this place?" she demanded.

Nuala was wearing white tennis shorts and a dark red T-shirt which proclaimed "Galway Hooker."

"It's the Lake Meadows development," I said, "a well-maintained proof that you can have racial integration so long as you limit it to one social class and build big fences."

"Oh," she said meekly.

"Nothing more," I continued.

"You'll be thinking that I'm nothing but a frigging eejit, Dermot Michael."

She actually said "frigging," the word represented

her effort to clean her vocabulary from the Dublin street language which was the lingua franca of Trinity College of the University of Dublin.

"I'd never think that, Nuala." I cuddled her close and stroked her long black hair.

"You would, too." She began to sniffle. "Won't you be wanting to send me back to the bogs?"

"Woman, I will not!"

She continued to sniff.

I should also say a word about how she pronounces the English language, lest I drive you out of your frigging minds with attempts to reproduce the actual sounds. The Irish language generally lacks a "th" sound, no equivalent of the Greek "theta" of the Anglo-Saxon "thorn" (often spelled as "Y" as in "ye" olde taverne, but still pronounced "th"). So in all words involving a "th" you are likely to hear from someone Irish the sound "t" or a "d" or more likely a subtle mix of the two. Nuala might say, for example, "I'm not going to take off dis binkini ding just because you want a midnight swim. What would your moder dink if she found out?"

Actually, she never said anything like that to me, worse luck for me, perhaps. But if she had and I were reporting it, I would have substituted the "th" sound. Nuala resolutely refuses to try to put the "h" sound in the "th" words.

"I know that English has a frigging 'th' sound," she says, "but it ought not to have."

Paradoxically—and perhaps perversely—she pronounces the letter "h" as "haitch"—as do all the other Irish.

How can I describe this astonishing young woman to you?

Should I say that she is the most beautiful woman I have ever met and surely the most beautiful that I have ever held in my arms?

"What was this place," she said as she snuggled

closer to me, "before it was your frigging Lake Meadows?"

"Slums, I guess."

"Did anything terrible happen here?"

"Maybe the Fort Dearborn massacre, though I think that was a little farther north."

"What was that?"

"The first settlement in this city was at the mouth of the river—downtown, as we call it now. The army built a fort there to protect the settlers from the natives and from the Brits. They called it 'Fort Dearborn' after a town near Detroit. During the War of 1812, after the Brits had captured Detroit, the commander of the garrison most unwisely decided to abandon the fort and retreat to Vincennes, down on the Wabash River in Indiana; not the last tragic mistake the American military made. The Indians killed them all shortly after they left the fort. It's represented by one of the four stars in the Chicago city flag."

"How many people died?"

"About forty, I think."

"A lot more than that here."

"Oh."

Yesterday evening at Grand Beach, she whispered into my ear, "Isn't it nice that your sister-in-law Tessa is expecting another child and himself a boy, with them already having three girls!"

"Who told you that?"

"No one." She put a finger to her lips. " 'Tis a secret."

Right!

I once described her as looking like a pre-Christian Irish goddess—Bride or Bionna or Sionna or Erihu or Maeve or one of those gorgeous and terrifying women. I'd never met one of them, however, so that was my hyperactive fantasy. It's always hyperactive when Nuala Anne is present. The child—she isn't quite twenty-one yet—is strikingly beautiful. Her cream white face and breast-length black hair stop you first and make you want to see a lot more of this young woman. Her face, slender and fine-boned, is the sort that stares at you from the covers of women's magazines—except that the cover women don't usually have a haunting hint in their deep blue eyes of bogs and druids and old Irish poetry. The bottom half of her face is a sweeping, elegant curve which almost demands that male fingers caress it with reassurance and affection. However, the center of the curve is a solid chin which warns trespassing—or potentially trespassing—male fingers that they had better not offend this young woman, or they will be in deep trouble.

Her body is that of a beauty-contest entry. In a fairly modest bikini of the sort she had worn most of this weekend at Grand Beach, Nuala stopped traffic. Women as well as men gaped. But the bodies of bathing beauties usually lack Nuala's grace and intense athletic energy. Her body and her face are almost always in movement, so it is hard to say what she's like in those rare moments when she is at rest.

Except some adjective that she would probably furiously reject—like delicious.

As I was calming her down after her fey attack, I thought about reaching under the T-shirt and caressing the smooth, soft skin of her belly, a liberty I was permitted on occasion. On almost any occasion I wanted, as a matter of fact.

Lake Michigan is quite cold at the end of May. Although she'd been warned yesterday that the water temperature was in the high fifties, she had charged down the stairs, tossed off her robe, and dove into the water. We locals would have screamed and run out. She, however, had swum out maybe a hundred yards with a powerful crawl, turned around and swum back in. She emerged from the water triumphant, a tall, willowy hoyden.

"Dermot! Me robe!" she had ordered. "Sure, isn't

it refreshing now! A lot warmer than the Atlantic Ocean or the Irish Sea!"

She didn't add, since my family was standing around awestruck, that when she and her mother went swimming in the Atlantic, they often wore nothing at all, at all. "If the men can do it, why can't we?"

Nuala was the youngest of six children born in an Irish-speaking family in Cararoe, way out on the end of the Connemara peninsula. Her mother was in her very early sixties and still a quite attractive woman, promising that Nuala's beauty would change but not fade.

"Sure," I had said once, in a mood to make trouble, "if I came upon the two of you in that condition, wouldn't I want to look at your mother first. Anyone can be beautiful at nineteen."

"And wouldn't that show you had good taste?" she had said dismissing my dirty fantasy with a brisk sweep of her hand.

"Feeling better?" I asked her as we waited at 31st and Cottage Grove.

"It's fading now. . . . Don't I feel like such an amadon, and me with these crazy spells?"

"I don't think you're an amadon, Nuala Anne," I said, stroking her right arm tenderly.

"I don't care what you think," she said. "I think I'm a nine-fingered gobshite."

"Last time I counted, you had ten fingers."

She laughed and then I laughed with her.

She kissed me and pressed her body against mine, her marvelous breasts taunting my chest.

"Dermot Michael Coyne, aren't you the dearest, sweetest, most wonderful man in all the world!"

"I'll buy that," I agreed.

What is the nature of my relationship with Nuala Anne? Well, that's a fair question, isn't it now? Obviously I'm hopelessly in love with her and have been since I had first encountered her on a rainy night in

O'Neill's pub down the street from Trinity College.

I had heard her discussing me with a young woman on the beach earlier in the day.

"Live with Dermot Michael? Ah, don't be daft. I don't live with him, I don't sleep with him, we're not engaged, we're not about to be engaged, we're not courting, and we're not walking out. I'd say that we're half-keeping company."

I had thought that was a fair enough description of our relationship.

The other child had said something I didn't hear.

"Isn't he respecting me freedom, and meself a greenhorn here and almost a child?" she had replied.

The other young woman had laughed. But I couldn't tell whether Nuala was being ironic.

In fact, we love each other. I plan to marry her some day. Even though in Dublin she said she'd never marry anyone because as she had argued, marriage and family only meant more suffering and loss in your life. Still, as far as I can tell, she plans to marry me, too, though I never hear a word about that from her. She'd probably marry me next weekend if I asked her. But she's new in America and she has to get her feet on the ground and find out whether she wants to be an accountant or a singer or an actress. The young women I know in Chicago usually don't marry these days until they are in their late twenties, the men often in their early thirties. We have lots of time, I tell my family, all of whom fell in love with her at first sight. Maybe when she's twenty-five and I'm thirty or so, she'll be ready to make the kind of commitment that marriage requires.

They tell me that I'm an incorrigible Irish bachelor. How can you be an incorrigible bachelor at twenty-five? I ask them.

"She'll get you long before that, Derm," says my brother George the Priest, with whom Nuala often compares me, unfavorably.

"That will be as may be," I said, using one of Nuala's favorite lines.

I turned on the ignition, backed up the car, pulled out on 31st Street, and drove down Vernon, which is what Cottage Grove becomes in Lake Meadows. Then I turned around and went back to 31st and on to the Drive. I was driving her home on Sunday afternoon, instead of Monday, because Nuala was singing on Sunday and Wednesday nights at the Tricolor (pronounced Trickcolor), an Irish pub on Webster Avenue between Clybourn and the Chicago River and not far from Southport Avenue and Belden Place, near where Nuala lives. I didn't altogether approve of that because the crowd at the Tricolor was a little thuggish for me, and their republican sympathies a little too noisy.

Moreover, chances were that most of them were illegals. Immigration usually left the Irish alone because they were too busy ferreting out Hispanics and Asians and sometimes Poles. Still, sometimes they do try sweeps of the Irish. While Nuala was here quite legally on a Morrison visa she'd won in the lottery and had her own precious green card, I was afraid that the INS might deport her before we could stop them, especially since these days Americans are back into xenophobia.

By "republican," I don't mean as in Bob Dole or Newt Gingrich or Phil Gramm, or other such unspeakables. I mean as in the Irish Republican Army. There's a cease-fire now in Ireland, though the Brits look like they're going to mess it up again. Still, the loudmouths at the Tricolor, safely far away from Belfast or Derry, boast about blowing up Brits.

"Sure, aren't all those gobshites a bunch of eejits?" Nuala says, dismissing them. "Besides, Dermot Michael, you've seen me in a street brawl; you know I can take care of myself. And anyway, is it any of your frigging business where I sing?"

That was a gotcha.

I had no claim on her, she was telling me, none at all. Not yet anyway.

I didn't like the way some of the rough young men looked at her either. Still they all shut up when she sang.

I don't look like a thug. I'm blond, clean-shaven, and kind of bland looking, though Nuala says I'm a giant and dangerous hunk. The dark, hirsute punks at the pub would think I was a pushover, not realizing that I had been a linebacker and a wrestling champ at Fenwick High School. I once threw three such thugs into a plate-glass window on Pembroke Road in Dublin; and, to be candid, I was itching to do it again.

"None of your macho violence in me pub when I'm doing me singing," Nuala warns me in an authoritative tone that Pope John Paul II himself might envy. "Not unless I ask you to."

"Yes, ma'am," I say docilely. Still, when I go into that pub, I'm aching to punch someone. Testosterone, I suppose.

On the Drive we headed north towards the wondrous Chicago skyline, a pastel pink watercolor in the weakening glow of the spring sunlight.

"Will I ever get used to seeing that?" Nuala said. "Or will I be a greenhorn forever?"

In the canyons of the Loop, Nuala always looks up at the tall buildings, awestruck. I keep her out of trouble with the traffic, pedestrian and vehicular.

"I like you as a greenhorn, and I hope you never take the skyline for granted," I said.

"I don't know why those things happen to me," she said slowly. "I don't want them to happen, and they usually don't do any good."

"A touch of Neanderthal gene, maybe."

"Weren't they cavemen?" I didn't have to look·at her to know that she was ready for an argument.

"And women," I added. "They seemed to have co-existed with our kind for maybe a hundred thousand years. Some people say we interbred with them, and some say we didn't. They weren't quite as much into talking as we are. . . ."

"Then I can't be one of them."

"So some people think that they communicated by some sort of telepathy, which was very useful for them, but not so useful for us."

"Whatever happened to them?"

"You get a lot of theories. Some say we killed them off, though there's no trace of that. Others say that they died because they were not able to compete with us for resources, though we seem to have coexisted for at least tens of thousands of years. Others say we absorbed them through mating and that each of us has a touch of the Neanderthal in him. Or her. Neander, by the way, is the name of the river in Germany where they found the first remains of their kind."

"Wouldn't you hope it was love, not hate?"

"You would indeed."

"You know so much, Dermot Michael and yourself without an honest job."

I don't work, at all, at all, you see. Nuala is secretly proud of this, but she passes up no opportunity to needle me about the fact.

"Or maybe in our own earlier days we also had the telepathic trait, but since we haven't used it much in maybe ten thousand years, it's grown kind of rusty. You may simply have it in a highly developed form."

"So I'm not a witch?"

"If you are, you're the prettiest witch in the world."

"Go 'long with you," she said, hitting my arm with her fist, very gently.

I don't work because I'm not very good at anything and because I made a lot of money one day on the floor of the Chicago Mercantile Exchange because of a mistake (mine). I did the sensible thing and retired. I asked investors more skilled than I am or ever would be to take care of my money. So I really don't do anything at all except work out and swim at the East Bank Club, a place which, like everything else in Chicago, fascinates my Nuala.

I write, too. That's what I like to do and have always wanted to do. I've had some things published. Nuala is very proud of that fact and will brag about it when she thinks I'm not around to hear her.

As she had said to her newfound friend at Grand Beach, "Sure, isn't he a great writer?"

The other person must have asked if I would ever become famous because Nuala replied, "Isn't he famous already?"

Well, only in a very limited circle.

I had written what I thought was a lascivious, albeit comic, story in Dublin about the fantasies of a young man when he first met a young woman not unlike Nuala. The editor who published it told me that it was a fine example of lyrical and romantic eroticism. Nuala had found it on my hard disk while she was working for me and had been pleased by it ("Dead frigging bril"), though I had thought she would be deeply offended.

"Ah, if young men didn't think like that about young women, wouldn't our kind have died out long ago? Sure, wouldn't I be terrible flattered if some young man had those nice thoughts about me?"

"Would you now?"

"Can I show it to me ma?"

"She'll think I'm a dirty-minded man."

"No, she won't."

I should have realized that, given charge of my computer and my hard disk, Nuala Anne would explore every file on it.

"When did it happen?" I asked her as we approached the remodeled Navy Pier.

"You mean my vision, though I really didn't see anything? I don't know. It was like all in the present. That's the way I felt it anyway. But nothing was happening there. So it was sometime in the past. . . . And when, Dermot Michael Coyne, are you going to take me for the ride you promised on that frigging Ferriswheel thing that your man put up on the pier?"

I had made many excuses. The truth was that I was frightened of heights

"And the carousel, too?"

I become dizzy on merry-go-rounds.

"Wednesday night."

"I sing on Wednesday night, as you well know."

"So you do. Thursday?"

I'd have to do it eventually. Maybe I would earn myself some tender loving sympathy if I got sick on one or both.

"Grand!"

See what I mean? She was still a youthful hoyden and she had no business at all, at all, in permitting herself to be tied down by a lecherous old man of twenty-five.

I turned off at North Avenue so I could work my way through Lincoln Park on Stockton Drive (by the zoo) up to Webster.

Beside me, Nuala stiffened again.

"Dermot Michael, there's bodies all over the place," she murmured. "Look at them!"

I glanced around as we went into the underpass beneath the Drive.

"Nuala, that's North Avenue beach."

"I mean dead bodies. Look at them all floating on the water!"

The lake was still much too cold for anyone but greenhorns from County Galway. She was having another one of her experiences.

I turned into Lincoln Park and stopped short of Stockton, a drive that winds ingeniously through the park and by the zoo.

"Are you all right, Nuala?"

She was trembling, as though caught in a blast of cold winter air.

"Bodies coming out of their graves, washed out by the lake, on the beach and into the lake. A terrible storm claiming the dead."

It sounded scary—so scary that I almost imagined I saw what she was seeing.

A cop came by and pounded on the side of the car. "What the hell is a matter with you, buster?"

Cops have a habit of permitting themselves to be annoyed by a young punk like me (as they see it) driving a Mercedes. Who knows, maybe I'm pushing drugs. The Notre Dame and Marquette emblems which deface the back window help sometimes but not always. When they ask what I do for a living, I'm in a quandary. If I say "nothing," they'll be certain that I'm a pusher. If I tell them a "writer," they'll think maybe I'm gay and, alas, cops still bash gays. If I fudge a little and say I work at the Merc, these days, they still suspect I'm a pusher.

"The young woman has a chill, officer."

"Does she now?" he asked, glancing at Nuala and becoming instantly solicitous.

I had learned another thing about cops—a quite important one: You don't get tickets when you have Nuala in the car with you.

"Are you all right, young lady? Should we take you to the hospital? Northwestern is just down the street."

Nuala looked like hospital material, pale, drawn, and trembling.

"I'll be fine in a moment, officer. I get these spells every once in a while. They're not serious."

"From Galway, is it?" he asked.

Especially you don't get tickets when a cop hears her West of Ireland accent, may she never lose it.

"Cararoe."

He then said some words in Irish to her and she responded promptly in kind. They both laughed.

The frigging Yank (D. M. Coyne) was out of the loop.

"I'm much better now, officer," she said, forcing a smile. "Tell me, was there ever a cemetery here?"

The cop raised his eyebrows. "So that's the way of it? You're one of them dark ones, are you?"

"Not my choice."

"Ah it never is, is it? . . . Well you're right about one thing. There was a cemetery here. Chicago City Cemetery, they called it. When they built the park, they moved the bodies somewhere else. All of them, the city brass said. Only some of them, others say. So if that's what you're feeling, there's some reason for it."

"There always is, officer," I said.

"That's the way of it. . . . Well, now, sir, take good care of this young woman. She's a special one."

"I know that, officer."

Nuala seemed to have calmed down. She was still ashen, however. I started the car and eased our way up Stockton.

"How are you doing, Nuala Anne?"

"Better, Dermot Michael, better. But you see I'm not daft altogether. There once were graves here."

"If you said so, Nuala, I never doubted it."

She sighed.

"Why do people have to die, Dermot dear?"

"There are two answers, Nuala dear. The first is that we die because we're creatures, and all creatures die. The second is that death does not end our lives."

"Do you really believe that?"

Nuala has an odd relationship with the Deity and the Church. She goes to Mass every morning at St. Josephat's which is right across Southport from where she lives, its twin green towers dominating the neighborhood like benign hawks. (On Sundays she attends Mass with me at Old St. Patrick's over on Adams and Des Plaines.) Yet she's not absolutely sure that there is a God or more specifically whether "God gives a good frig about the likes of us, and ourselves being such little gobshites."

She goes to church, she says, just in case God actually does care for us, which may not after all be such a bad argument.

"I suppose you're right," she said that Sunday afternoon. " 'Tis the only answer that makes sense."

"Were they the same people who were dying down at Lake Meadows?"

"Who?"

"The bodies coming out of the graves."

I glanced at her. She was frowning, as if she were trying to puzzle something out.

"I think so," she said. "I'm not sure."

To tell you the truth, I was not happy about her apartment, either. She was living with four other greenhorns (all women, thank God) in a two-bedroom place that was at least as crowded as her apartment in Dublin when she was going to Trinity College (T.C.D., to the initiate). I knew they were paying her enough at Arthur Andersen to entitle her to something better. I suspected that she was paying most of the rent and had taken the others in, as she might once have taken in stray kittens.

Nor did I especially like her roommates, who were part of the crowd at the Tricolor. They were rough, noisy young women from Dublin, not at all like my shy child from the Galway Gaeltacht (Irish-speaking region). They were nannies or maids and were almost certainly in one degree of illegality or another. She put up with them, but I didn't think she enjoyed them all that much.

Again, it was none of my business. And maybe I was just being a snob. Either way, I kept my mouth shut.

We arrived at the wooden house on Southport which had yet to be blessed with the gentrification that was seeping through the neighborhood.

Nuala hugged me and then clung to me.

"I don't know why you put up with me, Dermot Michael, and meself dragging you away from your long weekend with your family at that wonderful place and then acting like a real gobshite on the drive in."

As I kissed her, I found the smooth flesh of her belly and the hard muscles that kept it in place. She sighed happily.

"I like being with you, Nuala," I said in lieu of more passionate words, at once more appropriate and more dangerous.

"Hmm," she said. "Well, you don't have to come and hear my singing tonight. Haven't you got better things to do than hang out in that shabby pub?"

"Nothing better to do if you're singing in it."

She eased out of my arms—reluctantly, I liked to think.

"I'm glad when you come, but you don't have to come."

"I know that."

"So maybe I'll see you then?"

"I'll call Prester George and see if he knows what happened where Lake Meadows is now."

"That would be grand," she said as she bounced out of the car and up the steps to her apartment, the second floor of a white frame house (with peeling paint) that had somehow escaped the Chicago fire of 1871. Like many buildings of that time, the entrance was on the second floor, up an outside wooden stairway, because the ground floor had once been awash in a sea of mud. The two floors had been split into two tiny apartments. The entrance of the ground floor, now six feet above the old ground level behind the house, was no longer threatened by the Chicago swamp. The stairway to her apartment might have been rebuilt once in the last century or so, but I would not have bet on it.

I drove back towards the Loop and to my apartment at the John Hancock Center with a feeling of unease.

I felt again that somehow I was missing a grand opportunity. Moreover I was worried about the two phenomena on the Drive. And about Nuala's singing and her pub and her roommates.

It might, I reasoned, be a very difficult summer.

That would turn out to be an understatement.

AS THE shadows of evening slipped in from the lake and over the city, I called our house at Grand Beach and found Prester George on phone duty.

"So you took herself home, did you?"

"You're beginning to talk like her, George."

"All I have to say to you on that subject, little brother, is that you better snatch her up before someone else does."

Should anyone else make such a pitch at my Nuala I would have become insanely jealous.

"I'm not so sure, George. She's a real shit-kicker, you know."

"And what do you mean by that?"

"Well, she knew that all of us played tennis, so she took up the sport before she came over so she could take us on despite the fact that we had more or less broken up in Dublin. Now she beats everyone, including you. She was spoiling for a fight."

"You don't like competitive women?"

"Well, there's a limit."

Secretly I was enormously proud of Nuala's athletic ability. I was sure the next step would be golf.

"She sure does attract notice on the tennis court."

"And that business with the T-shirt."

"The Galway Hooker one? I thought that was hilarious. So did the boss."

Well, it was, in a way. Nuala was flaunting it at the Grand Beach pious who had come to the Mass that the little bishop (for whom George works at the cathedral) says on the dune in front of his sister's house. There were a few raised eyebrows, to put it mildly. I had introduced her to the bishop, anyway. She had lost her nerve at the last minute and decided she didn't want to meet the bishop after all. I didn't let her escape from her folly.

"Did you crew on one of those craft, Nuala Anne?" he had asked her.

To be fair to her, there were some lines on the shirt which could have hinted at a sail.

"I did, milord," she had said shyly. "Last summer."

"And you won the race?"

"We did, milord," she had said more confidently, "though, as the Duke of Wellington said, it was a near thing."

"And the name comes from the Dutch word *hookuh,* which means fishing boat or something of the sort?"

"So they say, milord."

The bishop and Nuala had decided that they liked one another.

"Those that don't know the meaning would find perhaps some grounds for consternation in the word."

"They might, milord," she was now grinning broadly, "As my mother would say, however, to the pure all things are pure. Besides, isn't there a drawing of a boat on the shirt?"

"People might not notice that," I had said.

I did not add that what they might notice was the shape of the person beneath the shirt.

At the presentation of the gifts, the bishop asked herself and me to bring up the water and wine and bread. Herself beamed proudly.

"Yeah, George, but how many bishops would have known what a Galway Hooker is? She was just flaunting it to stir up trouble. That's the kind she is."

"You know that's not true, little brother. She's a shy child, and she was protecting her shyness with her outrageous wit."

George was absolutely right. Nuala arranges her layers of masks to protect her fundamental nature as a fragile bog flower. She also enjoys doing it.

"Funny kind of shyness," I said.

"Face it, little brother. She has your number."

"Maybe."

My family had fallen in love with Nuala at first sight. She had played the sweet, vulnerable West of Ireland child with a touch of whimsy, and they were charmed instantly. Not that the mask isn't revealing and transparent, but it doesn't tell the whole story. All the masks are transparent, which is why they are so ingenious.

As became apparent when she walked out on the tennis court and routed the whole lot of them. And along with myself, did the same thing at doubles. She had no compunction about beating me, either. Indeed she did it with considerable relish and much to the enjoyment of my parents and my various siblings.

It was assumed by everyone that I would marry her. Even such a stolid, dull bump on a log as me would not let Nuala Anne slip through my fingers. Well, I didn't intend to lose her. However, I did not like the whole family making common cause with her against me.

"Anyway," I got to the point of my phone call, "What was once where Lake Meadows is now?"

"Lake Meadows? Let me see, that's 31st and Cottage isn't it? The old Douglas Park, you know, after the Douglas in the Lincoln-Douglas debates."

"I thought Douglas Park was on the west side."

"That's another one. This one is older. The old University of Chicago was there before it folded and was reborn courtesy of the Rockefellers and the Northern Baptists. Somewhere on the campus they have a stone from the old place. There were also a lot of elegant old homes along there, not quite Prairie Avenue, but still pretty splendid. They turned into slums before the land was cleared."

None of that fit with Nuala's experience.

"Anything else?"

"Yeah, something jogs my memory.... Now I've got it. That's where Camp Douglas was."

"What was that?"

"It was a Union depot during the Civil War. Troops trained there. Most famous as the site of a prison camp for Confederate soldiers."

"People die there?"

"Yeah, it was no Andersonville or anything like that, but a lot of them died there during the war, mostly of disease and exposure. More men died of disease during the war than from enemy action."

"How many?"

"Thousands, as I remember."

"Yeah, OK."

"Why the interest?"

"I'll tell you some other time."

"Hey, one more thing, little bro. There was some kind of conspiracy there in the summer of either 1863 or 1864. A plot to free the prisoners, thousands of them, and burn Chicago to the ground, like we did to ourselves a few years later."

"Interesting . . . I'll let you know when I can let you know."

"Yeah. . . . Something else, little bro—can't quite remember what it was. Something kind of spooky. . . . Is your gorgeous little witch involved in this interest of yours?"

"Maybe," I said cautiously.

"Maybe that's what I'm thinking about. Some kind

of buried treasure involved with Camp Douglas. She has an affinity for buried treasure, doesn't she?"

"Once in a lifetime," I said.

After George let me go, I prayed fervently that we were not mixed up in another treasure hunt and that treasure hunting was not another one of herself's psychic specialties.

Nuala's fey instincts are highly specialized. She seems especially sensitive to incidents from the past about which the truth has yet to be told. Then she becomes a detective and solves the past mystery—and the present one too—like the detective in Josephine Tey's *The Daughter of Time.*

A lifetime of searches for buried treasure I did not need.

I was not about to let the family know about Nuala Anne's fey dimension. I don't know why. They adored her so much, they would simply add "that wonderful talent" to their litany of praise.

I just wanted to keep it to myself.

Since I would take a taxi up to the Tricolor—you don't try to park a Mercedes in that neighborhood—I poured myself a glass of cold Niersteiner eiswein and thought more about Nuala. She was easy to think about.

She could act and sing, the latter with a guitar or an Irish harp. I had given her one of the latter, a small, portable one, as a gift on her arrival in Amerca. She had received a little voice training at T.C.D. and would have improved greatly if she would get more in this country. But she was an accountant, and that was that.

"Sure, aren't there more than enough friggin' Irish sopranos?"

"Not like you."

"Go 'long with ya!"

She would not seek more training. She would not even allow me to help her to cut a CD. I asked a friend

of mine in the music business to come to the Tricolor
to listen to her.

"She's commercial already. The country is ready for
a sweet soprano with the lilt in her voice."

I introduced him to Nuala; she listened to his praise,
thanked him politely, and did absolutely nothing about
it.

"I'm an accountant who sings a couple of nights a
week at a grungy pub because she likes to sing," she
said to me.

That was that.

I couldn't even persuade her to sing at Mass or at
weddings at Old St. Pat's.

"I have no business at all, at all, singing pious
hymns."

When Nuala made up her mind, there was no arguing with her. Mind you, she was capable of changing
her mind, but always on her own terms. Indeed, she
would use my arguments to justify a decision of hers
as though she had thought up the arguments herself
and was trying to persuade me.

I had yet to figure out whether she knew what she
was doing in such shifts of position. She might. She
was, after all, and by her own admission, "a terrible,
frigging conniver altogether." It was this propensity of
hers to connive which led to my breaking up with her
in Dublin, one of the dumbest things I've ever done.

"Ah, well, weren't you terrible sick with pneumonia
when you said those eejit things."

Surely my adored grandmother was also a conniver,
a point which Nuala had made to me when she got
the last word in at the Dublin airport.

Still, her habit of scheming annoyed me.

"Damn it all, Nuala Anne, you don't have to scheme
with me."

"I do, Dermot Michael, I do. You're such a mystery,
I can never be sure how you will react."

I would insist that she was the mystery. She would

laugh and say that she was no mystery at all, at all. "Only a girl from the bogs of Connemara."

Both of us couldn't be right, could we?

The fight in Dublin was mostly my fault. No, that's not true. It was entirely my fault. We had been trying to discover whether my grandparents were responsible for the death of Michael Collins, the great Irish revolutionary hero. As it turned out, they weren't. I thought I was the detective who would solve the various mysteries we encountered and that Nuala was my able assistant. I was Holmes and she was Watson, right? Only as it turned out Nuala was Holmes and I was her spear carrier. That hurt my male ego considerably. I was also infuriated because she had schemed to hide her Holmesian role so as to protect my male ego.

"I didn't want you to know because you would become angry," she said not unreasonably. "And now you know, and you *are* angry."

That's when I told her that I never wanted to see her again. She defends me on the grounds that I was coming down with pneumonia at the time. That was true enough. Yet I think I would have behaved the same way if my temperature had been right on the 98.6 mark.

When I got out of the hospital in Chicago, I realized what a friggin eejit I had been. Nuala was worth it even if my male ego had to make adjustments. Why *not* be her spear carrier?

She has not taken on any mysteries in Chicago yet, but when she does I'll gladly collect my spears.

Some of my friends, men my age and a little older, say I'm a wimp because I haven't dragged Nuala off to bed. "Fuck the girl and get her out of your system," these chauvinists say.

I had indulged in a turbulent and foolish love affair with a young woman I thought I was going to marry, so I wasn't a stranger to the world of premarital sex.

In that particular relationship, however, I guess I was the seduced rather than the seducer. It all ended when I refused to go to work for her father.

I don't want to get Nuala out of my system. Moreover I don't know whether she would sleep with me if I asked her, and I don't want to know. My argument against marrying her now applies to trying to bed her now and a fortiori. I respect the child and her right to her freedom and her opportunity to mature.

"Someone else will take her first," my guys say.

"That's up to them and up to her. It'll not be on my conscience."

Do I mean that?

Well, partially, maybe.

I went back to my fridge and poured another glass of eiswein.

I have rehearsed this argument with Prester George. He says, "What makes you think you are the only gentleman left in the world? Even the only romantic gentleman?"

Fair play to him, as Nuala would say, but I never concede anything to George or another member of my family on the subject of Nuala. Or anything else.

"You love the girl, so you reverence her? What's wrong with that?"

"Nothing," I say.

"You should not listen to your immature friends, little bro."

"So you agree that I should give her five more years or so?"

"Not many men could do that, but I suppose you could," he replies, staring at me thoughtfully. "If she wants five years, which I doubt."

"That doesn't answer my question, George."

"There are no answers to those kind of questions, little bro. There's no paradigm for courtship."

"We're not courting!"

"Well, whatever you're doing . . . I might be able to

come close to an answer, if I were sure you're not afraid."

"Afraid of what?"

"Of commitment, of marriage, and of that young woman."

"I'm not afraid of her!" I protest loudly. "Not at all, at all."

The vehemence of my protest gave me away.

YES, YOU ARE, said the Adversary inside my head who harassed me frequently on such subjects. YOU'RE AFRAID TO PROPOSITION HER AND EVEN MORE AFRAID TO PROPOSE TO HER.

So I was afraid of Nuala Anne.

"There's nothing wrong with being afraid of her," Prester George, a frequent ally of the Adversary, persists. "Any man in his right mind would be afraid of that one. You might just as well hitch yourself to a shooting star, or maybe a comet."

I'm a writer. I should be able to sort these things out in my work. But so far my attempts to develop the relationship I had described between my fictional narrator and the fictional young woman in Dublin had ended in worse confusion.

I stared out the window at the lights of Chicago as they came on, nicely organized by the checkerboard of orange lights on the main streets.

It was time to go up to the Tricolor. The implicit rules of the game were that I should enter the place only after she had started to sing.

This night I didn't want to go.

Just the same, I'd be ill-advised not to.

So I put on chino slacks, a white shirt, and a brown sport coat. No tie, not on the Sunday night of the Memorial Day weekend. I can be as grungy as the best of them (and for most of them it is a pose and a sick one at that), but at the Tricolor I stubbornly did not want to be identified as one of the thugs. Not that I look much like a thug even when I want to.

I found a cab on Chestnut Street and rode up to Webster and Clybourn. The driver's radio reported more details of the robbery of the Thalberg Gallery. Thieves had stolen more than a $100,000 worth of precious objects. They had somehow disarmed the security mechanisms of the gallery and cut through a window late at night. Art dealers were talking about buying their own police cars to patrol River North at night. The Chicago Police Department insisted that they were watching River North closely. The thieves, they said, were both very clever and very quick.

Odd, I thought to myself. I presumed that the cops or the insurance companies were taking a close look at the finances of the galleries that had been robbed.

In recent years, gentrification had transformed Clybourn, not so long ago a diagonal street of small warehouses and factories with occasional strips of very old homes. The Clybourn glitz and glamour had yet to transform the stretch of Webster between Clybourn and the Chicago River. A few blocks east, Webster was a main street of the fashionable and expensive Lincoln Park area. As it approached the river, Webster turned dank and dark and dingy.

The dark, smelly grunginess of the Tricolor overwhelmed me as soon as I had entered it—booze, cigarette smoke, vomit, human bodies, urine, and few other mysterious aromas I could not identify.

I imagined the owners going around the place before it opened with spray cans of these odors on which their livelihood depended. Grunginess was fashionable. You have to have it. I even designed in my fantasy art for the spray cans and ads for the spray on television—ads featuring lovely young woman semidressed in grungy clothes.

O'Neill's pub in Dublin, where I had first encountered her, was a much more attractive place. The Tricolor was a valiant, though not quite successful, effort to imitate a working-class pub on the north side of Dublin.

I edged my way through the darkness and found an empty table. I told the slovenly boy who came to take my order that I wanted a "pint of the best."

"Whadayamean?" he asked with a scandalous lack of knowledge of the proper rhetoric.

"A jar of Guinness."

"It comes in glasses, not in jars."

"Fine."

The "glass" of Guinness was soon delivered. Stout on top of Niersteiner eiswein was hardly proper, but in Dublin I had learned how to nurse a "jar" all night long.

Someone turned on a single spotlight, just to the left of the bar. It revealed Nuala Anne in a white lace spring dress, suspended from her shoulders by thin white straps.

Irish lace over a white lining. The dress would come off very easily if there were a lover to take it off.

It was an inexpensive dress, off the rack from somewhere. Nuala Anne was hardly a consumerist. She had been raised frugally and lived frugally, even though she earned a good salary (especially by Irish standards). However, the frugality was always tasteful.

As I drank her in from head to toe—and everything in between—I told myself again that she was indeed the most beautiful woman in the world. Worse luck for me, as she would say.

"Nuala," some of the others cried out. "Give us a song!"

"Well, I might just do that, now that I'm up here," she responded.

They all laughed. She was a favorite, all right.

She began to sing a sad, Irish lullaby. Most Irish lullabies are sad. Nuala's sweet pure voice caressed the words as if she had the child in her arms instead of the small Irish harp I had commissioned for her. She filled the pub with her love for this nonexistent child. The obstreperous conversations around me diminished to hushed whispers. Even the thugs and their consorts.

"Will you look at them tits!" an unshaven youth near me enthused.

"Would I like to get my hands inside that dress!" his equally unshaven companion agreed.

By their accent, they were both Yanks. Underage Yanks who had no right to be inside the Tricolor at all, at all. Or, to use the proper terms, friggin' underage friggin' Yanks.

My fist tightened around my Guinness. I had a strong impulse to plunge it down their throats, first one, then the other.

I warned myself that this was nothing more than immature boy talk, of the sort I had once engaged in myself and that the sentiments the talk expressed were understandable enough and that in, I hope a more reverential context, I shared them. Moreover, I added to my warning, they did whisper and, like all the other thugs and thugesses, they were respectfully quiet now.

I began to get an idea for a story in which a slightly snobbish admirer of Nuala's came to a place like this and made a fool out of himself.

Comedy, that's what I needed.

The crowd exploded in cheers when she finished the song. Some of the thugesses were crying openly.

You snobbish jerk, I told myself, most of these kids are homesick. She recalls the cottages, and the stone fences, and the bogs and the green fields they all miss.

The waiters hustled around the room to distribute more booze. I shook my head as my waiter glanced at me.

"Give us 'Molly,' Nuala," someone shouted.

" 'Molly, Molly, Molly,' " they chanted.

"Well, if you'd shut up and give me a chance, I might just do that."

They shut up.

"As I always say, I sing this for a special young man who loves the song."

It was too dark for her to see, but maybe she sensed I was there. More likely that was merely her standard introduction to the song.

I took a sip of Guinness before she started.

It's a sad, sad song, but on Nuala's lips, it also took on an air of joy. Molly still lives. Somewhere.

> *In Dublin's fair city,*
> *Where the girls are so pretty*
> *I first set my eyes*
> *On sweet Molly Malone.*
> *She wheeled her wheelbarrow*
> *Through streets broad and narrow,*
> *Crying, "Cockles and mussels,*
> *Alive, alive, oh!"*
>
> *Alive, alive, oh!*
> *Alive, alive, oh!*
> *Crying "Cockles and mussels,*
> *Alive, alive, oh!"*
>
> *She was a fishmonger,*
> *But sure 'twas no wonder,*
> *For so was her father and mother before*
> *And they both wheeled their barrow*
> *Through streets broad and narrow*
> *Crying, "Cockles and mussels,*
> *Alive, alive, oh!"*
>
> *Alive, alive, oh!*
> *Alive, alive, oh!*
> *Crying, "Cockles and mussels,*
> *Alive, alive, oh!"*
>
> *She died of a fever*
> *And no one could relieve her,*

And that was the end of sweet Molly Malone,
But her ghost wheels her barrow
Through streets broad and narrow,
Crying, "Cockles and mussels,
Alive, alive, oh!"

Alive, alive, oh!
Alive, alive, oh!
Crying "Cockles and mussels,
Alive, alive, oh!"

There were more tears when she was finished, even a bit of salt in my own eyes.

Sensing that someone was standing over me, I glanced up.

The man was not a young thug, but a thirty-year-old. He could have been more than a thug, possibly a gunman. He was encased in tight-fitting jeans, an equally tight-fitting sweatshirt, and a battered black windbreaker. His hair was cut short and his face was stony and cold, his blue eyes, just barely visible in the half-light, innocent of emotion. He was wiry and his muscles looked taut and solid. He smelled of human sweat—real men don't use deodorant. He was nursing a stub of a cigarette as if it were the last one he possessed.

He's either a hard man, or wants to create the impression that he is, I thought. Maybe just a touch of the sociopath in him. He could be one of the IRA men one sees on television; though, to be fair, some of the gunmen look like angels. What is he doing here? There's a cease-fire, the lads wouldn't send one of their executioners to this city now, would they?

Uninvited, he sat down across from me and set his own jar of Guinness close to mine.

He stared at me, sizing me up. He didn't like what he saw—which is to say, he thought I would be a pushover.

"That your bird?" he demanded in a thin almost-reedlike voice.

North Side Dublin accent.

"I beg pardon?"

"Is that bird your bird?"

"I find the word offensive."

"Do you, now?" His narrow lips parted in what might have been a smile, though a cruel smile. "What I mean is, are you fucking that bird with the nice tits?"

"The whole question—indeed, this whole conversation—is offensive."

"I think she is your bird, and I'm going to take her away from you and fuck her myself. How do you like them apples?"

He had sized me up as a snob, a weakling, and a coward. I might have been the first, I was not the second, and I'd be the third only if I let him push me too far. I sized him up as an alley fighter, neither a boxer nor a wrestler. He probably carried a knife or a razor.

"I'll fuck her whether she wants to be fucked or not," he continued. "Most women enjoy a little rape when I'm the rapist."

"Really?"

"Are you going to stop me?"

He shoved me with his clenched fist.

"Would you mind leaving my table?" I said softly.

He pushed me with both hands.

"You want to come outside and settle this between ourselves?"

"Not in the least."

I deserve no points for restraint. Rather, I was playing the role he assigned me.

"Then I'll beat the shite out of you inside. Your bird can see the blood all over you."

He rose from his chair, grabbed me by the shirt, and pulled me up with him.

I sighed loudly, pretending as I had through the whole conversation that the testosterone was not surging through my blood. This is *my* cave, you frigging bastard.

"Very well, have it your way. But do let us go out into that good night, lest we disturb the singing."

He will try something dirty as soon as we get out the door, I warned myself. Some kind of sucker punch.

"The back door," he said edging me in that direction.

"As you wish."

Might he have friends in back? I kind of doubted it. His image would require that the fight be man to man, if hardly by the Marquess of Queensberry rules.

I stepped aside at the door. "You first."

"Get outside, you fucking gobshite!"

I permitted myself to be shoved out the door. A very dark and garbage-littered alley. A big Dumpster parked near the door. The river was a wide band of darkness in the background. No one else around.

Sucker punch in the back of my neck first, I thought.

I spun away and ducked it. Then I grabbed his arm and threw him against the wall.

He shook his head to clear away the stars that were circulating in his brain.

"I'm going to beat the living shite out of you," he said.

Then he ducked his head and charged at my stomach.

I spun away again, and instead of my gut, he banged into the side of the Dumpster. He wheeled around and leaned against the Dumpster, breathing heavily. No fear in his eyes yet. No hint that he was facing the possibility that he might lose.

The next charge ended in a kick at my sexual organs. At the last moment, I tripped him. He fell on his face.

"You're a dirty fighter!" he screamed at me.

"I didn't want the fight," I said. "I'm willing to end it now."

I was, but I knew a remark like that would pour gasoline on the fire of his bruised male ego.

He struggled to his feet and charged me again, this time aiming for my legs, a kind of clumsy open field tackle. I stuck out my knee so that his jaw collided with it.

He sank to the ground, gasping for air.

"This is getting boring," I said, immensely proud of myself. "Let's end it."

I pulled him off the ground, banged his head a couple of times—not too hard—against the Dumpster, then picked him up and threw him into it.

"Garbage into the garbage. This time you get off easily. If you bother Ms. McGrail, I will be much harder on you."

I dusted my hands off and returned to the pub, another triumph for the guys in the white hats.

Nuala was singing her medley of Irish revolutionary songs, to the accompaniment of the stamping feet of the crowd. This was about as violent as they could get, a long way from the real IRA.

Herself was something of a nationalist. She wanted the Brits out and thought the Ulster Orangemen were "horrible gobshites." But she hated the gunmen and despised terrorism. She understood, however, that the music made her crowd feel good and wasn't any threat to anyone.

I returned to my table and sipped some of my Guinness. I was ashamed of myself. I wanted that fight, I wanted to destroy that little bastard, I wanted blood and I got some. What the hell was wrong with me? Was sexual frustration turning me into a caveman? Was I any better than he was?

He had asked for the fight, but I didn't have to provide him with it, did I?

And what was he, anyway? The lads did not send fools on missions far from home. They were, in their most recent manifestations, far too sophisticated for that.

My heart was beating rapidly. Apparently there was still some adrenaline in my veins.

Frigging eejit, I told myself.

More applause for Nuala Anne.

"Now if you would give me time to catch my breath, I'll come back to sing some more."

She slipped through the crowd, responding politely to the praise, and came unerringly to my table.

She kissed me on the cheek, sat down, and said, "How did I do?"

"Weren't you as wonderful as ever?"

"I can answer a question with another question, Dermot Michael—" she slapped my hand playfully— "but you're not supposed to do that."

"Then I'll have to find another woman who doesn't give me the habit."

"Don't you dare!" She slapped my hand again. "But seriously, did those, uh, spells this afternoon have any effect on my singing?"

I could have said, "Is it the effect of the spells you're worrying about?"

That would be the appropriate Irish response. In the circumstances, it also might be dangerous.

"None at all. Do they still bother you?"

"It usually takes a day for them to wear off."

"How awful!"

"I told you I didn't like the frigging things. Well there's no help for it. . . . Did I see you sneaking out the back door with some eejit while I was singing?"

Even in the dark, this one didn't miss a thing.

"You did."

"Why?"

"The frigging amadon was determined to pick a fight with me. I believe his very words were that he'd beat the shite out of me. When I declined politely, as you know I normally do, he insisted on starting the fight in here while you were singing. So I accepted his suggestion that we go outside."

"No marks on you." She examined my face.

"No."

"Where's he?"

"The last time I saw him he was in the Dumpster—ah, the large dustbin outside."

"I'm still a greenhorn, Dermot Michael, but I know what a Dumpster is. . . . Did you really throw him in it? He looked like a hard man."

"Not as hard as he thought."

"Fluttered?"

"Not in the slightest."

"Odd . . . You know, Dermot Michael, you're an accident waiting to happen to someone else. They kind think you're a weakling, and then you beat the shite out of them."

"I'm not proud of myself, Nuala. I didn't have much choice."

"Would you ever let me have a sip of your pint?"

"Woman, I would." I moved the drink across the table in her direction.

Nuala was not much into the creature. Not only had I never seen her fluttered, I had never seen her finish her evening pint when we went to pubs back in Ireland.

The Irish, by the way, have the lowest per-capita alcohol consumption in Europe—and the lowest liver-infection rate, too. The reason that even they think they are such terrible drinkers is that so many of them can nurse a whole pint or even part of a pint all evening long.

"You bring memories of Ireland to them, Nuala, to heal their homesickness, don't you?"

She took another sip of my pint. "Sure I do, Dermot. That's the whole point, isn't it?"

(Point is pronounced "pint," by the way.)

"I guess so. And these poor thugs need those memories."

"Do they ever. . . . Will I be seeing you afterwards?" she asked anxiously, as though there were some nights I didn't wait for her.

The scenario was that she'd spend her first break with me and her second with her admirers in the audience.

"Well, I might just hang around," I said.

"You'd better." She jumped up, kissed me again, and hurried back to her harp.

Her voice was so lovely in her second interlude that I almost forgot about the hard man. Not quite, however. If he were someone from the lads, his plan might have been to pick a fight, beat up some hapless victim, and establish himself as a kind of hero. Then he might be able to talk a few of these poor kids into joining him in some crazy stunt. Even if he wasn't IRA, there would be nothing to prevent him from posing as one of them—nothing, except that the lads were known to take an exceedingly dim view of someone pretending to be one of them.

They shot off people's kneecaps for such behavior.

Odd. Probably just a storyteller's fantasy.

He came at me again just as Nuala's second break was ending. He entered through the same back door out of which we had exited an hour before. He charged through the crowd towards me, knocking aside those who blocked his path. He looked a bit the worse for wear from his time in the Dumpster. His eyes gleamed with manic hatred. He was holding a short but dangerous-looking knife in his left hand. People screamed as they saw him.

I felt a touch of fear in my gut. The man was just crazy enough to be very dangerous. What should I do?

For a moment of pure terror, I had no idea. Then, just as he was upon me, I picked up the table and smashed it in his face. He went down, screaming in pain.

Then he bounced up and, blood pouring from his face, charged me again. I barely stepped out of his way this time. Then, as a matter of pure instinct for survival, I grabbed his arm and twisted. I must have twisted too hard because I heard bones crack. He dropped the knife and doubled over in agony.

Now thoroughly frightened, I straightened up and, just in case the table hadn't done it, broke his nose with my fist. That usually stops them.

Blood gushed out and splattered his already-dirty T-shirt. He fell back against the wall, sobbing in wretchedness. I noticed that he smelled of Guinness, probably from his time in the Dumpster. As a precaution, I picked up his knife.

Only then did I notice Nuala standing behind him, a heavy tray in both hands.

I gently removed the tray from her hands. "I think he's out of action, Nuala Anne."

The manager of the bar appeared.

"Did this gobshite try to attack you, sir?" he asked.

The sports coat and the clean face and blond hair meant I was the good guy.

"He seemed to want to start a fight earlier in the evening," I said mildly. "I'm afraid I wouldn't oblige."

Nuala, grim and pale, was watching with a stony face, her chest moving up and down in rapid—and distracting—breathing. Kathleen ni Houlihan, I'd know you anywhere.

"We can't have that going on in here. This is a respectable pub."

That was a matter of terms.

"I quite agree."

"Do you want us to call the police, sir?"

"No, just throw him out and don't let him back in again."

A massive black-haired giant lifted the sobbing man

up, said, "Here we go now," carried him to the door, and dumped him unceremoniously into that good night.

"You're very handy in these contests, sir, aren't you, sir?"

"For some reason, people like him seem to want to start fights with me. I must look like a pushover."

Nuala smiled and relaxed. Smiled proudly, I thought.

The bouncer came back.

"That gobshite has been hanging around all week," he said. "Last week, too, according to some of the folks."

A warning bell went off in my head.

"I've seen him, too," Nuala said. "He has the look of the hard man about him."

"Only the look, it would seem," the manager said with a bow in my direction.

"The lads wouldn't send a gobshite like him," I suggested.

"Not the *real* lads, maybe," said the bouncer who, come to think of it, looked as if he might know. "But with the truce on and all, you can't tell who's likely to start pretending to be with the lads."

Having watched Gerry Adams and Martin McGuiness on television, I would have judged that they were much too sophisticated to get mixed up with someone like my friend.

"Well, please let us get on with the singing," I said. "I'm sure Ms. McGrail is far more entertaining than this little contretemps. . . . Oh, by the way, sir, that, er, gentlemen made some threats of sexual violence against Ms. Grail. You might want to have some extra security when she's performing."

A massive thunderhead appeared on Nuala's face. She reached for the tray again, and then put it back down reluctantly.

"That's a very good idea. Thank you for your suggestion. We can't have that sort of thing going on in a respectable pub."

"I quite agree."

"You don't have to continue, Nuala," he turned to her and said, "if you don't want to."

"I wouldn't let a frigging nine-fingered shite hawk like that stop me."

- Not in a thousand, million years.

As Nuala Anne sang some of the classic songs of Percy French, I thought about what had happened. I didn't like any of it. What was that guy—old, by the standards of the pub—doing hanging around here for a couple of weeks? Why did he want to take me on? Would he go after Nuala? Come at me again?

I decided I would order some discreet security for her. And for myself. Why not? What was there to lose?

With his broken arm, the guy would not be much good at a lone attack. But maybe he had a gang.

Tell herself about the security?

No way.

The security idea would turn out to be a very good one, a lucky decision for Dermot Michael.

Her last song was the famous plea for a certain Paddy Reilly to come back to Ballyjamesduff, sung with a rollicking enthusiasm and joined by the whole crowd in the chorus.

A grand performer she was. She knew instinctively how to deal with the audience. Instinctively, and doubtless with a lot of careful study.

After the crowd had drifted out, she put a white sweater on over her dress, stored the harp carefully in its case, and joined me at the doorway.

"Will you be walking me home now, Dermot Michael?"

"I might be able to work that into my schedule. . . . Give me the harp?"

"Be careful with that thing!" she warned me,

"Didn't it cost someone a lot of money!"

"And didn't he insure it?"

"Did he now?" she said. "And wasn't that clever of him?"

She brushed her lips against mine and then took my left hand (the right being encumbered by the "thing").

"You get homesick, too, don't you, Nuala Anne?"

"Something terrible, Dermot Michael! Frigging terrible! How sweet of you to think of that."

"Hmm."

"I miss the lakes and the bays and the painted houses and the whitewashed stone fences and the funny little donkey carts and the narrow roads and old men and the old women and the gossoons playing soccer in the fields and even the tour buses that come by for teas. And most of all, I miss me Ma and me Da. It was bad enough when I was in school in Dublin and knew I could go back on the odd weekend."

"It isn't easy to be an immigrant, is it?"

"My sister who is in San Francisco told me how hard it was, but I didn't believe her. . . . What a pissant gobshite I am, and meself feeling sorry for meself, as though I were the only immigrant to leave Ireland."

"Did your sister tell you that she got over it?"

"She said most of the time, but even after twenty years, there are some sad moments."

I remained silent as we walked in the gentle spring night down the streets of De Paul, as the neighborhood is now called after the university in the middle of it.

"The thing of it is," she continued, "that it's too late for me. I can't go back. I'm a Yank whether I want to be or not."

"Irish-American."

"Even if I'm still a greenhorn, this is where I belong now. I'd be a fish out of water if I tried to go home and stay there."

I thought about asking her why, but did not.

"You can fly home to visit often," I said.

"And won't I do that, as soon as I save up enough money to go home. But it'll be different. I'll be counting the days until I can come back home. *This* home, I mean. There's nothing in poor old Ireland for me anymore."

"Did you know it would be like this?"

"I half-knew the risk I was taking when I applied for a Morrison visa. After that there was no turning back."

Silence as we turned the corner of Southport and Webster and walked up towards Belden Place. Men and women were sitting out on the porches and the stoops and enjoying the soft evening air.

"I'm a real gobshite, Dermot Michael," she said, squeezing my hand harder. "Why am I complaining to you, and yourself and your family being so good to me?"

"You're not complaining."

"And me and me frigging independence. I have to disagree with you a lot, just so I think I'm free and meself knowing that you're practically always right."

"Only sometimes."

"I'm wrong about where I live, and I'm wrong about where I sing, and I'm wrong about cutting the disk and about taking voice training."

"If you say so."

It was not the right time to drive home my points on these subjects.

"I tell meself I sing there to cheer those kids up. What a friggin eejit. I just make them more homesick. I'm afraid to try anything better."

"As usual, Nuala, you're too hard on yourself."

"Well, I'll be following all those suggestions, and I won't guarantee that I won't ignore all the ones you make from now on. Do you understand me, Dermot Michael Coyne?"

"Woman, I do."

"And I'll pay for me own voice lessons!"

"Well, I'm not going to pay for them—that's for sure."

"But you can find me a teacher." She threw her arms around me and kissed me.

"I'll do my best," I said, struggling for breath.

It was a classic conversation with Nuala Anne McGrail, my shy child.

We arrived at her apartment. I had visions of her falling down the wobbly stairs.

"You can make recommendations about my new apartment when me lease expires."

"Which is?"

"The end of the year."

"OK. . . . One more thing, Nuala. I called Prester George and asked him about what was along the lakeshore before Lake Meadows. He said there were some elegant old homes turned into slums. Before that there was a place called Camp Douglas, which was a prisoner-of-war camp during the Civil War. A lot of men died there."

Her hand went to her throat.

"How long ago?"

"A hundred and thirty years, give or take."

"Were the men murdered?"

"I'm not sure. I don't think so. Most of them probably died of disease. During that war, there were more deaths from disease than from enemy action."

"Oh."

"One other thing. George says that there was some kind of conspiracy to seize the camp, free the prisoners, and burn the city down. Chicago was mostly wood. We managed to burn it down in 1871 all by ourselves."

"I see. . . . Dermot Michael, would you ever find out more about it for me? It's important that I know. I don't know why it's important, but it is."

"Sure. I have time on my hands, and you don't."

"I didn't say that!"

"I know you didn't. I did."

"I feel like a frigging eejit asking you to . . ."

"I'd be interested in learning more about it even if you weren't. I'll dig up what I can, put it into the form of notes towards a novel, and then report to you."

"Thank you, Dermot, I know it's very important."

We kissed each other good night. It started out as an ordinary kiss and then, kind of by mutual consent, it turned passionate. Extremely passionate.

When we finally parted, she sighed.

"Oh, Dermot," she gasped. "That was too much altogether."

"It was," I agreed.

"Not, mind you, that it wasn't nice."

She turned and ran up the steps.

Five years, I thought, is too long to wait.

I walked over to Clark Street to catch a cab. I had a vague sense I was being followed, but I could see no one.

Yeah, but you got to respect her freedom, let her mature into the woman she wants to be, not the one you want to possess.

Not quite the last of the gentleman. Nor the last of the romantics.

ONLY THE LAST OF THE IRISH CATHOLIC ROMANTIC GENTLEMEN, the Adversary sneered. PROPOSAL OR PROPOSITION, DERMOT. THAT'S THE ONLY CHOICE. YOU'RE GOING TO HAVE TO BED HER SOON, ONE WAY OR ANOTHER.

"What if she says no?"

THAT'S YOUR WHOLE PROBLEM, he said and slipped away again into the depths of my unconscious.

Back in my apartment, I poured the remains of the eiswein into a goblet and finished it off.

The Nuala whom I had escorted to her home was yet another version, honest about her homesickness, candid about her fear of becoming dependent on me, and passionate in my embrace. I liked this version, but then, I liked all the versions. Yet I wondered if a docile and passive Nuala would not become dull after a while.

No, I decided, no danger of that. Not as long as she would kiss like that. Besides, this new version would change soon.

I permitted myself some delicious fantasies about a naked Nuala Anne in bed with me. Well, despite the Adversary, I wouldn't dare proposition her because she'd probably say no. And I wouldn't dare propose to her just yet because she would probably say yes.

Then, even though it was late, I looked up the number of the Reliable Security Agency—mostly off-duty cops—whom my sister Cindy had recommended when I was worried about Nuala after she had left our house and moved into an apartment of her own. I hadn't used them, but I had talked to them.

Even though it was eleven o'clock, I called and told the woman dispatcher what had happened and what I wanted. Sure, I knew the usual terms. I mentioned my sister's name.

"No problem, Mr. Coyne. No problem at all. Now you go to bed and get a good night's sleep."

In other words, we're on the case: forget your worries, your sense of impending doom lurking out there somewhere in that mass of lights which is Chicago.

I went to bed, but I didn't have a good night's sleep.

In the morning while I was struggling to get my act in order for a trip up to the Chicago Historical Society, my brother the priest called me.

"I did some more checking about this Camp Douglas business, little bro."

"That was good of you."

"It was a big plot, according to my friend, who knows less about Chicago history than he thinks he does. Tens of thousands of men slipping into Chicago: Confederate agents working their way in from Canada; Butternuts—downstaters who sympathized with their southern neighbors across the Ohio and the Mississippi; local Copperheads—men and women on the side of the South; soldiers of fortune who expected to get rich off the loot. And get this: a lot of Chicago Irish Democrats who were fed up with the war in which their sons were dying."

"Our kind of people!"

"They had no particular love for the 'darkies,' as they were called then, and even less love for dying in what they thought was a foolish war. Apparently, there was a whole mob of conspirators armed to the teeth and ready, each for different reasons, to turn ten thousand Confederate prisoners on the city. Then they were to go off to Rock Island and free the prisoners there and wage guerrilla war all over the North."

"Wow!"

"It wasn't clear to anyone that the war would be over in less than a year. It might not have been if the conspiracy were successful."

"But it wasn't."

"Right! The local feds caught on to it, rounded up the leaders, tried them, and sentenced them to death. Otherwise maybe Bill Clinton would be President of the Confederate States of America and Mario Cuomo President of the United States."

"We wouldn't let them into NAFTA, either."

"And Newt would be a hanger-on at a Georgia courthouse, and Phil Gramm a crooked sheriff in Texas."

It was the kind of fantasy word game which the priest and I loved to play.

"Oh, yeah, one more thing." He became serious. "I know your winsome witch from Galway is involved."

"Yeah?"

"Right. There's buried treasure."

"What kind of buried treasure?"

"A lost letter from one A. Lincoln about the conspiracy. Probably worth millions to whomever finds it."

"One letter is buried treasure?"

"He wrote it late in the day on Good Friday 1865, just before he and the wife went over to Ford's Theater to see a play called *Our American Cousin* and keep a date with destiny in the person of John Wilkes Booth. They were the last words A. Lincoln ever wrote."

— 3 —

Nuala, my love,

Ever since the Ken Burns Civil War series on American television, I have thought of writing a novel about that horrific and probably unnecessary war. I would have made it a reflection on human folly and especially the folly of military leaders. Not that original an idea. I have not written it yet and probably never will because it exceeds my capabilities. I haven't even started the research for fear that if I did the research I would have no excuse for not writing it.

So now I'm doing the research. The Civil War is a fascinating and terrifying subject. I don't like it, and I can't leave it alone.

Anyway, here is my first report.

All my love,
Dermot

"All of it, is it now?" She looked up at me with a leprechaunish grin.

" 'Tis a convention," I said, "A rhetorical turn of phrase, if you take me meaning."

"Oh, I take your meaning, Dermot Michael," she continued to grin. "And I'll take all your love too."

I had proposed lunch at the Chicago Club, our most elegant eating club, just off Michigan Avenue. She argued that she couldn't take time off from work. I replied that she was entitled to a lunch hour. Reluctantly, she agreed to come.

The Nuala whom I greeted in the foyer was a dowdy professional woman: shapeless beige summer suit, hair in a bun, no jewelry or makeup, shoulders slumped, eyes downcast—the stenographer who was afraid of losing her job if she took too long a lunch hour. She glanced around at the dark green, plush red, and opulent oak club and the men with $1,500 suits and the women with $2,000 dresses, not counting the jewelry, blinked once as if she had entered a cathedral she had never seen before, and adjusted her image. In a twinkling of the eye that had blinked and without any change in costume or hairstyle, she became a high-powered woman executive, vice-president of a brokerage firm perhaps.

I was sure she made the change without any conscious reflection. She merely became the person that the scenery demanded.

We passed two senior partners from Arthur's in the grill-room lobby.

"Good afternoon Nuala," one of them said.

"Enjoy your lunch, Nuala," the other added.

"Good afternoon, gentlemen," she said with a radiant smile.

They both looked me over and decided that they approved, with reservations.

Despite her efforts to vanish into the woodwork, everyone at the firm knew her.

Part of the new image required that she flirt with me. I didn't mind.

"Well," she continued her discussion of "all my love," "I'm not the kind who rejects gifts, not even if anyone tries to take them back."

We ordered roast beef and a half-bottle of cabernet sauvignon.

I changed the subject as gracefully as I could, which wasn't very graceful.

"This is my first report, Nuala Anne. I thought I had to do some Chicago background first."

"Good. I must learn more about my new city. Don't interrupt me while I read it."

"It can wait."

"No, it can't."

So she read my report, distracted not even by the roast beef she wolfed down as she read.

I'm afraid I'll have to impose some Chicago history as background to the Camp Douglas story. I'll give you the background in this first report. Then, in the second, I'll write about life at Camp Douglas. Then I'll give you the information about the Conspiracy, which, it seems, is still a controversial mystery, and let you apply your skills to solving it.

The city was incorporated in the 1830s, twenty years after the Fort Dearborn massacre. At the beginning of the civil War, thirty years later, it was already the busiest shipping port in the world and the railroad center of America! In the space of a couple of decades, its population had increased from 5,000 to 100,000 (and would double again before the war was over).

It was a boomtown like the ones in the American westerns—raw, rough, disorderly, corrupt; but a boomtown with 100,000 people. It already had its red-light district at the south end of what we now call the Loop, its cheap hotels, its gambling dens, its brothels. Most of its buildings were of cheap wooden construction. Worst of all, Chicago was built on a swamp between two water systems: the Des Plaines, Fox, and Illinois rivers emptied eventually into the Mississippi and then the Gulf of Mexico, and the Chicago River emptied into Lake Michigan and eventually the Atlantic Ocean. A narrow portage, aided by a sometime body of water called Round Lake connected the two. Normally the Chicago River flowed into Lake Michigan; but, when the lake was high, the river reversed its course and flowed in the other direction.

The land between the two drainage systems was soggy at the best of times and a sea of mud at the worst. Just before the Civil War and for many years thereafter, Chicagoans coped with the mud by raising buildings off the ground level, sometimes as much as six feet, and filling in the land. Then they'd raise the levels of the streets and pave them with gravel. Maybe they'd add planked sidewalks, too. This process of jacking up the city—pulling it up by its own boot-straps, so to speak—would go on for decades.

The swamp and the mud made sanitation difficult, if not impossible. Sewer pipes had been laid before the war (and gas pipes for gaslights, too). The sewage drained either directly into the lake or into the river and thence into the lake—the same lake from which the city drew its water supply. Even more than most American cities at the time, Chicago was a cesspool (literally) of disease—typhoid, cholera, smallpox, measles, and scarlet fever. The worst of the cholera epidemics would come in later decades, until the city finally solved its sanitation problems by reversing the flow of the river permanently. But that's another story.

Another problem was the city's weather—too hot in the summer and too cold in the winter. You haven't lived through a Chicago winter yet, Nuala. I'm sure winter is worse in places like Moscow and Nome and Point Barrow. It's bad enough, however, in Chicago, especially if you are living in a cheap, uninsulated frame house with poor heat, inadequate clothing, and sickness. Many immigrants didn't make it through their first winter.

The city (governed by a "common council" made up of aldermen) was a city only in name. The government and the police had minimal authority. The civic elite, such as it was, made a lot of noise about crime and corruption, but had little power to do anything about it. Chicago was essentially a mob of people and a disorderly array of shacks, farms, animals, and muddy streets. Some of the people were rich, some were very poor (most of them immigrants and most of the immigrants Irish) and many schemers, operators, confidence men, and crooks determined to get rich quick. Some of the last group, men like Philip Armour and Potter Palmer and Marshall Field, would later become our most distinguished citizens. In a novel, Upton Sinclair would later call a Chicago neighborhood *The Jungle.* In 1860 the whole city was a jungle. The Board of Trade, that unique Chicago institution to which I must take you someday soon, was already up and running. Even then some men made a lot of money either through skill or crookedness or, as in my case, pure luck. Many men lost a lot of money.

To make matters worse for immigrants living in Chicago, the country was swept repeatedly by severe financial "panics"—a major one every twenty years or so, and minor ones more frequently. These were, in fact, severe economic depressions in which hundreds of thousands of men lost their jobs. In a boom city like Chicago, the impact of the "panics" was even worse. The one in 1857 just before the Civil War was particularly severe. It coincided, as panics usually did, with a bitter Chicago winter.

You have to understand this background if you're going to understand Camp Douglas—the swamp, the disease, the social disorder, the corruption, the winter weather, and the constant fear of fire.

I'm not making excuses for Camp Douglas. It was a terrible place. But I am trying to put into context. Many people in the city lived only a little better than those in the camp. The best estimate in the literature I'm reading is that between 4,000 and 6,000 of the 30,000 prisoners interned in Camp Douglas died—between 12 and 20 percent. In some of the cholera epidemics later in the century, between 12 and 17 percent of Chicagoans died. Before Camp Douglas became a prison camp in 1862, it was a training camp for Union soldiers. In four months, 42 men of a regiment of 600 died. A recruit wrote to his wife:

"The provisions they furnish us, Betty, is nothing special. I am so weak I can hardly hold my pencil." Life was tough and death was cheap, save for those who died or lost people they loved.

As she read, she passed the pages over to me. I stacked them in a neat pile.

" 'Tis hard to believe that this grand city is the same place. Sure, isn't it good for me that I was born when I was and came to Chicago now, instead of then?"

"Lucky for me too."

She actually blushed at the compliment.

I found some terrible letters in the archives of the Chicago Historical Society, written by an Irish immigrant from Galway to his brother—the fact that he could write made him different from many immigrants.

"October 14, 1858
"My dear brother Dan,

"America is not the place we thought it would be. I have not been able to find steady work. The cottage we live in is cold and drafty. Food is very dear. My dear Mary Anne is doing poorly, and the children are hungry all the time.

"Every night we pray to God that He will deliver us from our misery.

"Please write as soon as you can.

"Your loving brother,
Tim"

"November 10, 1858
"Dear Dan,

"The cold is terrible and the winter hasn't really come yet. We are all sick. I work one day a week for fifty cents a day. I'm so weak and so hungry, I can barely lift the shovel.

"The priests at St. Mary's help us a lot, but they have so many people to care for.

"I wonder if all of us won't soon be joining Ma and Pa in heaven.

> "Pray for us all,
> Tim"

"December 13, 1858
"Dear brother Dan,

"We lost our little Nan last night. She had a terrible chill and shivered for a couple of hours in Mary Anne's arms before she died. Only four years old. She knew she was going to die. Her last words were, "Good-bye, Ma, I love you."

"I can't help but thinking she's in a better place than we are. Only hell could be worse than Chicago.

"The priest at St. Mary's said a Mass for her and we buried her in a potter's field. It was so cold out at the cemetery that we all shivered like poor Nan when she was dying.

"Please pray for us all.

> "Your sorrowing brother,
> Tim"

"December 25, 1859
"Dear Danny,

"Mary Anne made it a nice Christmas with a tiny tree and some candles and a few bits of ribbon. We went to Mass at St. Mary's this morning, struggling through a foot of snow. Mary Anne and I wept in each other's arms after we put the children to bed. We know that we won't last the winter. It breaks my heart. She is so young and so brave.

"Tell everyone at home that we love them.

> "Your brother,
> Tim"

"January 18, 1860
"Dear brother Dan,

"I buried Paddy and Mary Anne this morning in the potter's field during a terrible snowstorm. The snow stung my face and the cold froze my tears. They both died of measles. The young priest cried with me. I don't know why I should feel that my suffering is different from so many others. I wonder if any of the Irish in this city will survive, other than the wealthy ones out in the West Division of the city.

"I don't know what Annie, our oldest and just six, and I will do. If we are to die of the measles, I hope she dies first. If I die first who will take care of her?

"It is so unbelievably cold that her soft skin is blue. Still she is very brave like her mother was and sings songs to me like her mother did.

"Good-bye Dan, I don't think I'll be writing again.

> *"Your brother,*
> *Tim"*

Nuala started to weep as she read Tim's first letter. She was sobbing at the end of them.

"I'll never feel sorry for myself ever again," she promised. "I've lived the life of a rich woman compared to those poor people."

"My guest is reading some very powerful material," I said to the concerned waiter.

"Yes, sir."

"Well," she said, "God took care of them all, I'm sure, and loved them very much, and they are all happy now."

I did not think it appropriate to remark on the sudden reappearance of her religious faith.

She dabbed at her eyes and returned to my report.

If he did write again, the archives don't have his letter. The tragedy of such deaths is that if Tim and his family had been able to survive another year, he would have been able to find steady work and a better home, and they might all have survived to become comfortable and even affluent Americans. Their descendants might still be with us. Can we pray that Annie did live and experienced a better America than the rest of her family ever knew?

She would die eventually, as we must all die eventually. Grim thoughts, eh, Nuala Anne?

I wonder if Dublin in the years after the famine was any better a place for poor people. I suppose it was not. Years later, Gerard Manley Hopkins, the great Jesuit poet, died at Newman House from typhoid fever. The people who write about him say that the disease was caused by inadequate drains in the building. Our cities have come a long way since then.

That's enough background about Chicago. Now about prisoner camps.

Neither side expected to have prisoners of war because they expected a short war, each underestimating the resolve of the enemy. Moreover, the few wars fought before in America were like many of the European wars in the seventeenth and eighteenth centuries, conflicts between small professional armies. Prisoners were exchanged almost as a matter of course if they gave their parole (their word) that they would not fight again, or in exchange for prisoners on the other side.

In the middle of the nineteenth century in Europe, the wars were usually short, settled in one decisive battle. But our Civil War was more like World War I in Europe, a long and bloody war fought by large armies with terrible casualties and large numbers of prisoners. Moreover, as the bitterness grew between the two sides, prisoner exchanges diminished. Both the Union and the Confederacy found themselves with large numbers of prisoners and little idea of what to do with them. Fort Donaldson in Tennessee fell to General Grant, and suddenly he had thousands of prisoners. What to do with them?

Someone made the decision to ship them upriver to Camp Douglas on flat-bottomed boats and on forced marches across the country. Suddenly Chicago had thousands of Confederates on its outskirts.

The troops assigned to guard prison camps were usually unfit for combat, or they would have been in combat. The officers were also not combat quality. Either they had failed in battle, or had been wounded, or were not deemed fit to lead troops. The prison commandants tended to be misfits, failures, schemers, ditherers, liars, and incompetents. They were also often ambitious careerists, more interested in pleasing superior officers than they were in protecting the lives and health of their prisoners.

All of this was clearly a recipe for disaster. The measure of how many men would die was usually the ability and the integrity of the officers. If more Union men died at Andersonville than Confederate men died at Camp Douglas, the reason was not that the Andersonville rebels were more vicious, but that the commander was utterly unable to cope with the chaos that had suddenly been dumped upon him. In all prisons there is some venality and corruption and cruelty. The prisoners become less human than their guards or captors. As the Civil War went on and the other side was demonized, hatred for the prisons increased. Thus, when a commandant asked a superior officer for money to build more efficient drains in Camp Douglas—and thus perhaps save many lives—he was rebuked sharply. The Union had better things to do with its money. Let the prisoners—many who could barely walk—do the work themselves.

Yet, as I read through the literature on the prison camps, I have to conclude that lack of preparation, stupidity, and incompetence account for most of the deaths.

One more bit of history, Nuala. The North was a lot more divided about the Civil War than our history textbooks in this country admit. War had never been declared, you see, never approved by Congress. The Rebs fired on Fort Sumter, Lincoln called for volunteers, and both sides stumbled into a gory mess that neither expected. Many Northerners—especially Democrats—hated President Lincoln as much as the Confederates did. They thought the war was a foolish and crazy business, that the Confederates had the right to leave the Union, and that Lincoln should have let them go. In retrospect, maybe they were right. Many Northerners, especially outside of New England, had no great love for the slaves and did not want to fight to free them. Even those who opposed slavery thought there had to be a better way to end it.

Most of the time, Lincoln had a thin majority of support in the North, but the size of that majority changed as did the fortunes of war. In the spring of 1864, it seemed that a war-weary Union would not reelect him. There was more support for the Union in Chicago than in other places (partially because of the incessant Union propaganda in the Tribune). Yet there were also many Confederate sympathizers in Chicago, perhaps one-third of the city. They had their own paper (the Times) and their own organizations, usually secret for fear of the Union police and their spies. The Union people were made nervous by the presence of so many rebel soldiers on the outskirts of their city and the Confederates were outraged at the cruel treatment of the prisoners.

By 1864 the city would be ripe for the "Great Camp Douglas Conspiracy."

— 4 —

NUALA REREAD the text of my first report as she sat next to me on the couch in
my apartment that faced west towards the
city, now washed in gold in one of our more
spectacular sunsets.

I had walked back to her office with her.

"I must read this again, Dermot Michael, and talk
about it with you. I don't dare read it at work," she
had informed me.

As we reached the entrance of the building, she re-
verted to her incompetent-stenographer image.

"You could come to my apartment this evening."

"To your apartment, is it? You wouldn't have any
etchings there, now would you?" She had never been
there before.

"Woman, you gotta be kidding!"

"Well, don't I know all about the morals of you rich
Yanks? . . . I should come right after work?"

"I might take you to dinner at the Cape Cod Room
afterwards. And you might bring a swimsuit along.
Don't we have a wonderful pool here?"

"A pool is it?"

"A pool it is, and the highest aboveground pool in
the world."

"As warm as Jury's in Dublin?"

"Even warmer."

"Won't I perish with the heat, now?"

"And I'll drive you home after supper."

"That's the least you can do. . . . I'm misbehaving again, Dermot, having you on. I'm sorry. I'll be happy to have supper with you tonight and to use your pool."

"I like you when you misbehave."

"Go 'long with ya."

She had appeared at the door of my apartment with a Marshall Field package in one hand and a dress bag folded over her other arm.

Poor child had spent a lot of her hard-earned money for a date with me. I was a dummy not to have thought of that.

SHE'S MAKING A GOOD SALARY, the Adversary informed me. STOP FEELING SORRY FOR HER.

"Didn't I have to buy a swimsuit?"

"I hope it's a modest one?"

"Would I buy anything else?"

" 'Tis a long ride up here," she had announced, "and meself afraid of heights. I see no etchings, Dermot Michael; you've lured me here under false pretenses. . . . And what a wondrous view! Sure, this is like a fairy-tale city! Hold me, Dermot, while I look out the window."

"The windows don't open, so you won't fall eighty-five stories."

With my protective arm around her, she approached the window cautiously. " 'Tis glorious," she sighed approvingly. "Don't you dare let me go!"

"I won't."

"Where is this Camp Douglas place?"

"Out there"—I pointed—"beyond the airport on the lake, where those high-rises are."

"Can you see Grand Beach from here?"

"On a clear day."

"You can let me go, Dermot. I'm not afraid anymore."

"And if I don't want to let you go?"

"That's another matter altogether. . . . Where can I hang me dress bag?"

COWARD, whispered the Adversary.

"In my mistress's suite."

I led her into the spare bedroom.

"Looks like you haven't had the mistress in here in a long time."

She hung up her dress bag in the empty closet and put the smaller bag and her purse on the bed.

"I usually clear out all the evidence before she leaves."

"Do you now?"

She removed my report from her purse.

"I do."

Before she started to read, she glanced around the apartment.

"Kind of a spartan place, isn't it, Dermot?"

" 'Tis. I don't need a lot to be comfortable here. . . . Would you like a drop of something? White wine, maybe?"

"A very wee drop," she said as she began to read.

I had opened another bottle of my prize eiswein, filled a goblet, and handed it to her.

"Not Waterford." She took it from me as she continued her reading.

"Nope. When I finally find a wife to bring into this place, I'll buy more elaborate stuff."

She had ignored my comment and replied, "Nice wine."

"Thank you."

She wept again at the letters from Tim to his brother Danny.

"Sure, Dermot, aren't you a wonderful clear teacher?" she said when she had finished. "And don't you make everything so interesting?"

It was still be-nice-to-Dermot week. I wouldn't fight it.

She gave the manuscript back.

"Why are we doing this, Dermot Michael?"

"Because you had a strange experience out there at 31st and Cottage and want to learn more about the place."

"It all seems kind of silly, doesn't it?"

"Not if you don't think it's silly."

"I know we should be trying to figure it all out, but I don't know why."

I told her about the "buried treasure."

"Why would a letter like that be so important?"

I filled her in on the myth of Abraham Lincoln as the great martyred president, a myth which told us much about those terrible times. She nodded at my story.

"I must learn more about this strange, sad, and wonderful country, Dermot Michael."

"I'll be happy to teach you."

"The letter was about the Camp Douglas conspiracy?"

She frowned as though she were reaching back in her memory of her Sunday-afternoon experience.

"That's the story. Or maybe I should say the legend. We don't know whether it was even mailed. There's no written record about it. Only rumors which became folklore. Some of the biographers mention it, but there are no citations of primary sources."

She nodded thoughtfully.

"You think we should continue our investigation."

Already talking like Sherlock Holmes.

"I learned in Dublin not to question your instincts. . . . Let's go swimming."

"Do you have a blower so I can dry me hair?"

"The apartment isn't *that* spartan. Now put on your swimsuit."

I gave her a white terry-cloth robe.

She emerged a few moments later from the spare room in a black maillot. The robe was conveniently open.

"Stop staring at me like you're imagining me without any clothes on," she ordered.

"I can't help it."

She snorted.

"You're not trying."

"And someday I won't imagine anymore."

"That will be as may be." She stuck her nose up in the air. "Now, are we going swimming?"

"We are."

Two of my neighbors were in the pool. They glanced up at Nuala, wondering if I had myself a bimbo. They took a second look and realized no way. On the third look, they saw her dive promptly into the water and kick into her crawl.

"The young woman is a splendid swimmer," said the man.

"Comes from swimming all year round in Galway Bay."

I dove in after her but did not try to compete. A pretty good writer and a fair alley fighter, I did not want to compete with that one in anything athletic.

" 'Twas grand," she said in the service elevator returning to the eighty-fifth. "Super, brilliant. I should swim more."

"Well, there's two ways to be able to swim every day. One is to join the East Bank Club. . . ."

"I'll never do that . . . wouldn't I have to pay a year's salary to buy the jewels those women dress in just to run?"

"The other is to move into an apartment in this building."

"If that were a serious offer"—she turned up her nose—"I might begin serious negotiating. Since it isn't, I won't."

A zinger right between Dermot Michael Coyne's eyes.

GOTCHA! said the Adversary.

"You want me in your apartment permanently," she

was saying in effect, "you'll have to marry me."

Well, didn't I half-know that already?

At least she hadn't flat-out said she wasn't going to marry anyone.

"Derm," she yelled from the mistress's room. "Where's your friggin' hair blower?"

I brought it to the door of her room.

"Here it is, Nuala."

Her head, wet hair sleek against it, and bare shoulders appeared around the door. She snatched the blower and ducked back behind the door.

"Thank you, Dermot," she called as the door closed.

"You're welcome."

I went back to my notes and tried to work over them as I fantasized about her alabaster shoulders.

She emerged a few minutes later, wearing heels and a slinky black sleeveless dress that barely reached to her thigh with a vee neck and a big scoop out of the back. She must have bought lingerie, too. She also had applied a tasteful touch of makeup.

I whistled.

"Well," she said with a pleased flush, "I can't go to this fancy Cape Cod Room looking like a dweeb, can I?"

After we had dumped her bags in my car, we crossed Delaware Street on the way to the Drake Hotel, my hand on her bare back. She returned to the subject of my report.

"I feel guilty, Dermot Michael."

"I know how you feel. I feel the same way."

"I have a good job, a friend with an apartment with a gorgeous view and a wonderful swimming pool, and I'm going to eat at a wonderful restaurant in a beautiful city. What right do I have to a better life than those poor people—not only that family, but all the men who were killed in your terrible war?"

"I asked myself the same question all day yesterday and today. Maybe more is expected of us."

"That's what I'm afraid of," she said grimly.

We entered the Drake's arcade from the Lake Shore Drive side because it was a pleasant walk to the Drive. Our table at the Cape Cod Room was waiting for us.

Nuala wanted some more of that "brilliant" wine I had served her. I told her that I didn't think they had it. I did not say how much eiswein costs. Not after our discussion of Chicago a century and a half ago.

"Well, get me something that tastes like it and order me dinner. I've never heard of any of these things."

So I ordered Bookbinder soup and crab Maryland and a sweet white wine.

She turned up her nose at the wine. "Nice, but not as good as yours, Dermot."

I may be creating a monster, I thought to myself.

She devoured the soup and the crab.

" 'Tis frigging good, Dermot Michael," she said. "Dead frigging good. I'll have to learn how to make them."

("Dead" is pronounced in such expressions as "did.")

"Any sightings of your man?" I asked her over the crab.

"Not by me; some of the others have seen him around, and his arm in a sling."

"We'll have to see if he turns up tomorrow night."

"Thursday night," she said. "I'll be singing on Mondays and Thursdays from now on. Your man was upset, but I told him that he'd make more on those nights."

This time "your man" was the manager of the Tricolor.

"Why the change?"

"Well," she considered me carefully, as she usually does when I might accuse her of scheming, "I thought that if I'm ever invited back to that Grand Beach place, you won't have to drive me in on Sunday afternoon."

"I don't know about inviting you back, Nuala, and yourself winning all those tennis matches and swimming in the cold lake and wearing a Galway Hooker shirt to Mass."

"I can have you on, Dermot Michael." She tilted her nose in the air. "But you can't have me on."

"Well, we don't really mind the swimming or the T-shirt. It's the tennis that puts us off. A guest shouldn't humiliate her hosts."

"I'll beat the shite out of you whenever I want, Dermot Michael Coyne!"

"I was afraid you'd say that."

"Besides, your mother said I was invited every Sunday of the summer."

Had she now? No doubt what Mom had in mind.

"Well, maybe you can ride up on the South Shore. It really is a nice train ride."

"And then tomorrow after work you can take me to meet me new voice teacher. I assume you've found one?"

"Woman, I have. A retired French opera singer who is a very lovely woman and a fine teacher."

"I'm afraid of her already."

"Madame is very nice, but you'd better practice or you'll be in trouble."

"I will, Dermot," she said grimly. "If I'm going to spend my money, wouldn't I be a frigging eejit if I didn't practice?"

"Woman, you would."

I didn't tell her—and I probably never would—that she'd be paying one-third of Madame's fees and I'd be paying the rest with secret checks.

"Can you get out of work an hour early tomorrow afternoon? I'd like to take you out to the site again and show you where things were, before you read my next report."

"Me boss thinks I'm a friggin' genius. I'll tell him I'm going to meet me new voice teacher that me young man has found for me."

This was the same woman who didn't dare read my essay at work.

"Am I your young man, Nuala?"

"Damn frigging right you are." She jabbed a finger at me. "And don't you ever forget it. I don't want to see you lollygagging around with anyone else."

Suddenly I was under suspicion of infidelity.

"I wouldn't risk my life doing that."

"Well, you'd better not . . . ah, sure, Dermot, I was only joking. I know you're not the lollygagging type. Would you maybe be better off if you were?"

"No."

"I don't think so either."

"Back to your man with the arm. He and a couple of guys like him were hanging around the Tricolor all last week, talking big."

"Were they, now? Three of them, is it?"

I wouldn't be enthusiastic about facing down three of those guys, even if one of them had an arm in a cast. I hoped the cops who were watching me were good at their work.

"They were hinting that they're from the lads, from your man himself."

That would be Gerry Adams.

"And what does he want?"

"They're saying that the Brits are going to break the truce and that Gerry needs the money to get ready to begin the campaign again."

"That's implausible, Nuala. The Brits wouldn't dare break the truce with Bill Clinton watching them."

"I don't believe it either, but they've got the kids at the pub all stirred up. Some of them might do crazy things."

"The young women you live with?"

"They're excited, but, sure, they wouldn't do a

thing, and themselves all being illegal. They have too much to lose."

I didn't like the sound of that, not at all, at all.

"Be careful, Nuala. That's dangerous talk."

"As I've told you before, Dermot Michael Coyne, I can take care of meself. Don't worry about me."

"Yes, ma'am."

"But I don't know about going back to that place again. It scared me."

"It's up to you."

She thought about it.

"Maybe I better go."

We both declined dessert but drank a very small glass of Bailey's, and I paid the check.

We walked over to the Hancock Center parking lot.

"Thank you, Dermot. It was a lovely dinner, even if they didn't have the right wine. . . . Where are you taking me tomorrow night?"

"Maybe to the Carlton Club at the Ritz-Carlton. If we get our work done, you can take another swim."

"You have to promise you'll stop undressing me in your mind."

"I can no more do that than you can stop beating me at tennis."

"Fair play to you!" she said with a vast laugh. "Ah, aren't you a tricky one with words, and yourself a Yank at that."

I drove her home and kissed her good night solidly, though by no means as passionately as the night before. She slipped quickly out of the car and bounded up the rickety stairs. Then near the top, she turned and bounded down again.

Careful, young woman, you could fall down those things, break your leg, and be out of tennis for the season.

"You let me forget me bags," she said, her face a cross frown.

"Did I now? Well I'll carry them upstairs for you."

I opened the trunk, lifted out the two bags, and walked towards the stairs.

"Careful with these stair things," she warned me, taking my arm in hers. "You could fall down and break a leg."

"And be out of tennis for the season."

She tightened her arm around mine as she laughed.

Actually, I slipped a couple of times on the stairs and was admonished in a fierce whisper to be careful and watch my step.

"I'm entitled to another kiss for carrying these up the steps."

"I don't know about that. . . ."

I started out with another very chaste contact of lips. Nuala, however, collapsed into my arms and pressed herself against me.

"I love you, Dermot Michael," she said fiercely. "I'll always love you."

"I love you too, Nuala," I stammered as she slipped away from me and into the house.

I turned to essay a walk down the stairs. They looked even more dangerous than they had on the way up. I eased my way down gingerly like a frigging old man.

The door opened and herself emerged, already in a robe.

"Don't break your friggin' skull on the stairs, Dermot Michael Coyne."

"It's my leg I'm worried about."

She watched till I was safely in the car.

I drove around the corner to get back on Webster. I saw a man lurking near a tree. It looked to me as if he had an arm in a sling. I picked up the phone to call her and then decided against it. I had told the security people to watch for a man with his arm in a sling. If I had seen him, surely they had too.

I didn't sleep well that night, either. I called Nuala at her office the first thing in the morning, allegedly to confirm when I could pick her up in front of her office.

"Three-thirty," she said. "I asked for three-thirty and got nary a word of protest."

Much later in the day, we were standing on the grounds of Prairie Shores again, poring over a map. Nuala this evening was wearing her dark blue work clothes, but at least she wasn't sporting the fake glasses.

It was a gray day with a chill in the wind off the lake, more like September than June.

"They built the place out here on Cottage Grove because they thought it far enough away from the city to be safe—four miles out. There actually was a cottage and a little grove of trees around it, one of those tiny islands of trees that dotted the prairie. A man named Graves owned the cottage and refused to sell it to the government, so the camp walls went around it. Stephen A. Douglas was a U.S. senator who had beaten Lincoln in a senatorial race and lost to him in the 1860 presidential election. He owned the land and donated it to the Union Army for the camp. He also donated the land on the other side of Cottage Grove to the University of Chicago, which folded in 1886. The university land was across Cottage Grove along the lake, where the approaches to the Drive are now. Douglas died in June of 1861 at the age of forty-eight. They say he ate too much, drank too much, and worked too hard. He did not live to see the war become terrible or the cruel use that was made of his land.

"Today Cottage stops at the entrance to Lake Meadows and feeds into Rhodes Avenue and then resumes south of Lake Meadows and goes out to the new university and beyond. Clear?"

"Uh-huh."

"Any vibrations?"

"Only a little. Left over from Sunday. I'm kind of anxious, though."

"The camp enclosed at least eighty acres and extended from 31st Street to 33d Street and from here to Martin Luther King Drive, four blocks in that direction; sometimes it might even have extended two blocks further. King Drive was called Kankakee Street in those days. It was surrounded by a wall of thick wooden planks twelve feet high. The main entrance was down in that direction at what would now be 32nd Street. The Illinois Central came by here and dropped off many of the prisoners. Still OK?"

"Go on."

"This parking lot here was the entrance to the Graves Cottage, the place that gave the street its name and whose people absolutely refused to leave during the war. White Oak Square, a horrible dungeon to punish prisoners, was on that grassy lawn in that direction. See it on the map?"

She tilted the map, glanced at it and then glanced in the direction I was pointing.

"The shopping center over there is where the smallpox hospital was. The dead were buried right behind the hospital until they were moved to Oakwood Cemetery. You can just see the children's playground. . . . That's where the university was."

"All gone now," she sighed.

"All gone by 1880. Not a trace on the ground and only a very few traces in the memory of Chicago—occasional scholarly articles, a book or two, some dissertations, maybe a commemoration on some Memorial Days. No one wants to remember it. It was, after all a disgrace to Chicago, and the men who died here were hardly heroes by Chicago standards. No one cares about them anymore. No one has cared for a hundred and twenty years, except some Confederate veterans and their families at the end of the last century; and they were concerned only about decent burial."

"How ugly."

"The war was over. The North was prosperous and wanted to forget the bloodshed of the war. The Union had been preserved. The slaves were free. What more was there to worry about? Besides, the Confederate prisons were worse, weren't they?"

"Was the war worth it?"

"Was the Irish Civil War worth it? Does your generation much care about it?"

"No."

"But the men that fought it thought it was worth it. So did the political leaders who led it."

"Eejits!"

"Eejitcy is pervasive in the human condition, Nuala Anne."

She nodded.

"You think it could have been settled without a war, that even the slaves would have been freed."

"I think so. I don't know for sure . . . again are you OK?"

"Just a little shaky. I'll be all right. It's not like last Sunday. I'm terrible sad, but I don't feel the suffering. . . . You say six thousand men died where this lovely high rise development is?"

"Yes . . . I'm sure you don't want to drive out to Oakwood Cemetery."

"I do, though, Derm. How far is it?"

"Ten, fifteen minutes at the most."

"Let's go, then."

She had been a very happy young woman when we left our audience with Madame at the Fine Arts Building (once the Studebaker Building) on Michigan Avenue. Madame's "studio" was on the fifth floor of the disheveled old rabbit warren of a building, looking out on Michigan Avenue and Grant Park. Her rooms—an office and a music room—were neat and elegant, with plants, oriental rugs, white walls lined with prints, and antique furniture. Madame, somewhere between sixty and seventy with rimless pince-nez and a large jeweled watch pinned on a flowing brown dress, had been a modest success as an opera singer and had invested wisely. She made it clear that she did not have to teach and would quickly dismiss a student who did not follow her instructions to the letter. Her long hair, pinned on the top of her head, had been dyed auburn, almost tastefully. She played with the watch constantly, gazing at the time during our "audition."

Nuala, as she had said later, "had gone all over shy."

"So, young woman, you want to be a singer?"

"Yes, ma'am," she had said, the Connemara accent thick.

"Did you attend university?"

"Yes, ma'am."

"Where?"

"Trinity College, ma'am. The one in Dublin."

"You had a voice teacher there?"

"Yes, ma'am."

"Who?"

"Mrs. Folly. She was professor of voice."

"Indeed! I believe I have heard of her. What did she say about your voice?"

"That I ought to have more training."

"What makes you think you can become a singer?"

"I don't think that I can, ma'am. I'd like to find out if I can."

"Very well. Sing something for me."

She had reached for the piano to give Nuala a note. It was unnecessary. Nuala had begun singing without the note. Madame had pulled back her hand and rolled her eyes at me. Perfect pitch.

"Molly Malone," naturally. With never a look at me.

I had heard herself sing that song many times. She had never sung it better. "All over shy" or not, she wasn't going to flub this "audition."

Madam had said nothing for a moment at the end of song. Had herself pulled on this woman's heartstrings as she always had on mine? Was there a tear in her eye, a memory of a young woman lost?

"I believe, young woman, in telling my students the truth at the very beginning. You have a lovely voice; very lovely, if I may say so. You do not quite have the talent to be an opera singer as I was. Few do. I think you have no illusions about that. However, I believe that you can be very successful as a singer of a certain kind of popular music, folk songs and standards, and religious hymns especially. People will be willing to pay to hear you, my child. Pay a lot, as a matter of fact. There is no doubt in my mind about that. Moreover, you are able to put just the right amount of emotion into a song. Would you sing something else for me?"

Nuala had tried her favorite lullaby.

"Hmm," Madame had mused. "Do you have a child of your own, my dear?"

"No, ma'am. I don't even have a husband."

"You acted at this university in Dublin?"

"Yes, ma'am. A little."

The lead in *The Playboy of the Western World,* but I wasn't going to say that.

"It will not be necessary to train you in the emotional interpretation of a song. However, you have much work to do. First of all, child, you do not know how to breathe."

"Breathe, is it now?" Nuala had begun to smile.

That had been a mistake.

"You have terrible breathing habits. You must improve your breathing. It is all coming from the throat."

She had wrapped her long, thin hand around Nuala's throat.

"No, the air must not come from here. You must use the diaphragm and lungs God gave you. Breathe from down here."

Then she had shoved herself's diaphragm.

"You breathe from here, child, from here. Take a deep breath now.

"Yes, ma'am."

"Now breathe from here and sing a couple of verses."

A fuller and richer voice emerged from Nuala. Its sound startled her.

" 'Tis not meself!"

Madame had permitted herself a small smile. They had agreed on a schedule of instruction, once a week for an hour. Madam had given her a typed list of instructions for breathing practice.

"If you don't practice, my dear, I will dismiss you."

"I'll practice, ma'am. I'd be a . . . an eejit if I didn't."

Herself sailed out of the Fine Arts Building several feet off the ground.

She had obviously suffered from the same doubts about her singing that I did (still) about my writing.

Now, as we stood in the gray light on the parking lot where the smallpox hospital had been, she was quiet and grim.

"We had our famine, didn't we?"

"And that killed more people than our civil war in a much smaller country."

"There weren't humans torturing other humans."

"No. But there were government policies that starved people to death."

"Aye, isn't that the truth?

I remained silent.

"And Auschwitz?"

"Infinitely worse than Camp Douglas."

"Didn't your man say he would not cry for the second child killed in a war, when the death of the first one was already an infinite tragedy?"

My "man" this time was George Orwell writing about the bombing of Guernica.

"He did."

" 'Tis a focking horrible world, Dermot Michael."

" 'Tis."

"Well, let's go out to that cemetery."

We drove down Cottage Grove to 65th Street and turned onto the old and tree-dense Oakwood Cemetery in which many famous Chicagoans had been buried. We found a custodian (African-American) in the cemetery office. He agreed (after I gave him twenty dollars) to show us the "Confederate" mound.

"Not many folks come out to see it anymore," he said. "I guess them folk are not fashionable. Not politically correct. I figure the Good Lord loved them just like he loved everyone else."

We stood in the semidarkness under the trees, staring at the single pillar with a roughly clad prisoner (presumably Confederate) on top and a cannon in front. Twelve tombstones in front of the pillar commemorated Federal soldiers buried here, too.

"The Union bought several acres of very swampy land here for the graves of the smallpox victims. Then, when the City Cemetery was removed to make way for Lincoln Park, they moved as many as they could find up here and buried them in trenches. There are 4,234 names on those bronze tablets—the low estimate of how many men died at Camp Douglas. But no one knows how many were actually buried here."

"Not much respect for the dead, was there?"

"The government tried. The land here was already below the level of the rest of the cemetery. The city and the cemetery filled in some of the cemetery land in the battle against the swamps. So all the drainage flowed into this plot. It sank even farther below the rest of the cemetery as the years went on. In 1902 Congress voted $3,850 to add more landfill and $250 per year for perpetual care. Oakwoods added six feet of fill above the plot. You can imagine how low it was."

"Do they still get the $250 a year?" she asked the custodian.

"Sure do, ma'am. Doesn't go far these days what with inflation."

"It is kind of peaceful, isn't it now?" she said.

"Yes, ma'am. God has given them peace and joy like he does to all of us eventually. Most folks who come to see this monument don't know they're walking over trenches filled with dead bodies."

Nuala shivered.

"I suspect it doesn't bother them much, since they're in the bosom of Abraham, aren't they?"

Good solid National Baptist piety. He'd get twenty more dollars when we left.

"Could you take us to the Leak marker?" I asked.

"Sure can."

At the edge of the grassy plot there was a single marker.

"It's the only marker still here. They left it to show where the trenches end," our Baptist friend observed.

"James W. Leak, 1st Alabama Infantry, February 10, 1865," Nuala read. "When did the war end, Derm?"

"Lee surrendered at Appomattox Courthouse less than two months later."

"If he had lived just two more months, he would have gone home to his mother and his wife and children."

"That's right."

"Folks tell me that the government got it wrong again," the custodian said. "Real name was Joseph and he died on February 11. Just like the government to do something like that."

We left Oakwood lost in our own thoughts.

When we turned back on the drive from the university, Nuala said, "It was nice of you to give that extra money to the man. He was very nice. Faith, just like me ma."

"You disagree with him?"

"No, Derm," she sighed. "He's right. Still, life is an awful mess. Or maybe I'm just growing up."

I turned on the car radio. Police were still unable to find the Art Heist gang, as the band of thieves were now being called. However, they had announced that there was no reason to suspect the art dealers themselves of being involved.

I turned off the radio.

It began to drizzle. More autumn weather.

"What could that frigging letter have to with that terrible cemetery?" Nuala Anne demanded suddenly.

I'd almost forgotten about Prester George's buried treasure.

"Probably not much."

"I *know* it has something to do with what I felt out here. I just *know* it, Dermot Michael!"

Neither of us said anything more till we pulled into the garage at the Hancock Center and I lifted her dress bag and sports bag out of the trunk.

"I don't think I want to swim or eat supper, Derm," she said slowly. "I hope you're not offended. I'll not be much fun."

"I'm not offended, Nuala. I understand."

"That's one of the troubles with you, Dermot Michael Coyne. You understand too friggin' much. You should insist that I swim. Make me have supper with you. Tell me that it will cheer me up."

"Wrong young man for that, Nuala."

"I know that!" she snapped.

She grabbed the dress bag.

"Come on, let's go swimming."

In the elevator, she sighed, as only the Irish can sigh.

"Why do you put up with a gobshite like me, Derm?"

"Can't find another woman!"

She laughed.

This time she wore the red bikini that had created

a sensation at Grand Beach. It was, as I said, relatively modest. We swam desperately for forty-five minutes.

Back inside the door of my apartment, something inside my head snapped. I grabbed Nuala, cast aside her robe, and kissed her still-moist body. She was stiff at first, then she melted. I kissed her neck, her shoulders, her chest, her belly, the tops of her breasts. She moaned but did not try to stop me.

I stopped myself, turned away, and sank into the couch in my parlor.

"Won't you get your couch wet with your swimsuit?"

"So what?"

I looked up at her. She had drawn the robe around herself and looked thoroughly rumpled.

"Why didn't you fuck me, Derm?"

"Did you want me to?"

"No. But yes. But really no."

"I feel the same way. I'm not going to violate you, Nuala Anne, not till our wedding night. And I won't do it that way. And if you say 'That will be as may be,' I'll put you over my knee and spank you."

"No, you won't do that, either. Though, mind you, it would be an interesting erotic experience."

"I'll have to try it someday."

She kissed the back of my neck.

"Come on, let's have supper. I'm in a mood to get slightly fluttered."

"All right."

This time Nuala appeared from my "mistress" room in a light blue dress with more bodice than the one she had worn the previous night, but less back. She seemed a little uncertain about it, as if she thought it might make more trouble. It didn't. I was beyond such things—for a while.

I whistled, she blushed, and we went off to dinner.

As we crossed Chestnut Street, she said, "The trouble with you, Dermot Michael Coyne, is that you're such a gentle man, and make it two words, and I trust your gentleness so much, that I put us in situations that are too much for us."

"Trust is in the nature of our relationship, Nuala."

"Mind you, I won't say it wasn't exciting."

"And, mind you, I won't say it won't happen again."

We both laughed.

"Not very often," I added.

At dinner, a special pasta, Nuala turned on her charm, chattered enthusiastically about her work and her singing, and exorcised the demons of death and lust. Most of them, anyway.

I resolved that there would be no more trysts in my apartment. If the woman wanted to swim, she could join the East Bank Club.

I drove her home after dinner.

"We've got to keep on this Camp Douglas thing," she said. "You know that, don't you Derm, me love?"

"I know. I'm not sure why, but we have to."

Prester George had told me that once—and well into this century—some of the Irish used to make love in the fields outside of a house where there was a wake.

"Sex defies death, little bro," he had said. "The life energies are stronger than the death energies. Nice sacramentality in that, isn't there?"

"Let's restore the custom and provide potato fields outside all the funeral homes in the city."

"Not a bad idea," he had agreed.

Not at all, at all.

I'd tell Nuala that some other time.

We arrived at her house.

"Now, don't try to climb them friggin' stairs," she said, kissing me lightly. "I'll see you tomorrow at the Tricolor."

I watched her dash up the steps, waited for her wave, imagined her glorious smile, put the car in gear, and pulled away from the old wooden building.

I saw no one lurking in the dark. There were, however, so many old trees in the neighborhood that the streetlights illuminated only small patches of sidewalk.

I didn't like that.

The next morning, late spring came back and chased away the rain clouds. Breathing properly from my diaphragm, I walked up to the Chicago Historical Society building at the edge of Lincoln Park and—come to think of it—not far from the site of the old Chicago City Cemetery, from which the bodies of Confederate soldiers were once washed out on the beach and into the lake.

I worked there till mid-afternoon, brought my notes back to my apartment, and decided that I would write up the second phase of my report the next day and give it to herself when I picked her up for the trip to Grand Beach.

Then I took a cab over to the East Bank Club and threw myself into a fury of exercise in the fatuous conviction that I would thereby exorcise the hormones from my bloodstream and the fantasies from my imagination.

As I showered, exhausted, sore, and confused, a man approached me who I vaguely recognized, even without his three-piece dark blue suit and his bifocal glasses, as a senior partner at Arthur Andersen.

"Do you know anything about Irish girls, uh, women, Coyne?"

"Them as say they do are 'round the bend altogether," I replied.

"We have a new junior accountant at our shop, a young Irish woman, who is an absolute crackerjack."

"Oh?"

Not exactly the word I would use to describe herself, but I let it pass.

"A certain Marie McGrail."

Marie, is it? And not even pronounced the correct way, as if it were "Moire."

"Hmm."

"We're very pleased with her, but she's as shy as a church mouse. Hardly ever says a word and never speaks above a whisper. Often we have to tell her to speak up so we can hear her."

So that was the mask we were wearing at Arthur's?

"Is that so?"

"Yes, we're sky-high on her. Best we've had in years. Very attractive, too, in a dowdy sort of way."

You should see her in a black dress. Or a swimsuit.

"You might want to consider the possibility that, like many of her kind, once she starts talking, she'll never stop."

"I think we could live with that. But she has to overcome her shyness to be really effective."

"She's probably very uncertain of herself in an environment that is quite different from anything she's ever known."

"Well, she's so good that we are really concerned about losing her."

"If she's that good, you might want to give her a big raise. And a promotion."

He winced, as accountants do when one talks about their money.

"Well, there's a six-month performance review coming up, and an annual one."

I turned off my shower and reached for a towel.

"Yeah. Well, you could think about that. If she's worth it in six months or a year, she's probably worth it now. As I say, I'm no expert of this variety of humankind and I never will be, but it's got a good chance of working."

And then, like Dr. Frankenstein, you may find that you have created a monster, a chattering, hoydenish monster.

"Maybe that's a good idea."

Riding back to the Hancock Center, I wondered if I had been involved in a conflict of interest.

Hell, he'd asked me, had he not?

Marie McGrail, indeed!

The two guys at the Chicago Club had called her "Nuala." So she was a different person for different people at Arthur's. Why be surprised at that?

I'd like to stick it to her about that, but that would have been plain crazy on several counts.

At the Tricolor herself, the so-called Marie McGrail was wearing the black dress she had worn when we went to the Cape Cod Room. She was rotating her four elegant summer dresses and if anyone at the Tricolor didn't like it, that was their problem.

Church mouse indeed!

She must have been practicing her breathing exercises all day, because her voice more often than not came from her diaphragm and filled the rafters of the dingy pub.

"Was I singing from me friggin' diaphragm?" she demanded the instant she sat at my table during her first break.

"Woman, you were! And didn't your voice fill the rafters of this frigging club?"

She then delivered an enthusiastic lecture about the bad things she had been doing when she was singing only from her throat and mouth, as if I had not been with her in Madame's studio.

"Do you hear anything about your man?"

Her face darkened.

"He's around talking awfully big, himself and those two gombeen men with him. Me friends and roommates asked me what I think. I tell them that he's like none of the lads I've ever seen."

"You've met the lads?"

"Now and again, they'd drop into O'Neill's; quiet, modest men, they were. Went to Mass every morning. And the more quiet, the more dangerous."

"Your roommates?"

"Aren't they all excited about something big? They

won't tell me about it because they know I don't like it. There's some kind of big meeting tonight, and they didn't ask me to come."

"Stay away from them?"

"Never fear, Dermot Michael. I may be an eejit but I'm not a frigging amadon. And don't ask me to explain the difference. You have to be real Irish to understand it."

"The guy threatened you, Nuala."

"I can take care of meself," she said, her nose going up into the air. "And, if you happen to be 'round, you can take care of me, too."

"As best I can."

"As best you can . . . Now I have to go back and exercise me diaphragm, lest Madame dismiss me."

She was wonderful.

MARRY THE GIRL, YOU FRIGGING AMADON, a familiar voice, with more than a touch of Galway brogue, inside my head shouted at me. SHE'S HOPELESSLY IN LOVE WITH YOU. MARRY HER BY CHRISTMAS.

The Adversary again.

"I've got to respect her freedom to mature," I replied. "She's too young and too new in America to make such decisions."

YOU COULD HAVE FUCKED HER THE OTHER NIGHT.

"I would have regretted it for the rest of my life."

STILL THE LAST OF THE IRISH CATHOLIC GENTLEMEN?

"Shut up!"

DO YOU THINK HER DECISION ABOUT YOU WOULD BE ANY DIFFERENT FIVE YEARS FROM NOW?

"No."

CAN'T SHE MATURE JUST AS WELL AS YOUR WIFE?

"Maybe."

WON'T YOU RESPECT HER FREEDOM BETTER THAN MOST MEN, EVEN IF YOU ARE A FRIGGING AMADON?

"I don't know that."

MIGHT SHE NOT BE FREER IF SHE HAD ALREADY SETTLED HER DERMOT QUESTION?

"We met too soon."

YOU'RE GOING TO FIGHT GOD'S PLANS? HASN'T PRESTER GEORGE WARNED YOU ABOUT THAT?

"I don't know."

SHE'S CRAZY ABOUT YOU, YOU EEJIT. CAN'T YOU TELL THAT? SHE WANTS YOU AS MUCH AS YOU WANT HER?

"Women don't desire the same way as men."

IT'S DIFFERENT, BUT THAT DOESN'T MEAN IT'S NOT AS STRONG. IT MIGHT EVEN BE STRONGER. SHE WANTS YOU AS HER MAN. SHE WANTS YOU IN HER BED AS MUCH AS YOU WANT HER IN YOURS. DON'T TORMENT HER BY MAKING HER WAIT.

"Leave me alone."

The Adversary took his leave.

Maybe he was right.

Then he sneaked back.

YOU'RE AFRAID OF HER; THAT'S THE PROBLEM.

"Up to a point."

TERRIFIED! YOU THINK SHE'S TOO MUCH WOMAN FOR YOU.

"She's a shy child." I used my last-ditch defense.

THAT MAKES HER ALL THE MORE POWERFUL WOMAN.

He was speaking in paradoxes. He must be a writer of some sort.

"She is a lot of woman," I admitted.

I'LL TELL YOU ONE THING. SHE'LL GET YOU EVENTUALLY. SHE'LL DRIVE YOU OUT OF YOUR MIND TILL YOU MARRY HER.

"That is altogether possible."

YOU'RE AFRAID OF HER AND YOU'RE AFRAID TO MAKE A COMMITMENT, JUST BECAUSE YOU'VE ALREADY LOST TWO WOMEN.

"Go to hell, you filthy bastard!"

He left again, this time for good.

I had engaged in dialogues like that many times before. He was more persuasive now then he had been. Since he was really part of me, I knew the argument was coming up from the depths of my soul. Or the depths of something.

Perhaps every young man who was enthralled by a young woman had experienced similar arguments.

But not many would contend that they were simply respecting the young woman's freedom. Maybe my quoting feminism was like the devil quoting scripture.

I tabled the discussion for the evening.

Later, when I was escorting her home, Nuala asked, "How much of Madame's fee are you paying, Dermot Michael?"

"What!"

"Am I such an eejit to think she comes that cheap?"

"Two-thirds."

I expected an explosion. Instead, she squeezed my hand even tighter.

"You're a sweet, generous, kind, and loving man, Dermot Michael Coyne. Thank you."

"I like taking care of you, Nuala Anne McGrail, as long as you let me."

"And haven't I come to like your taking care of me, even if I am usually too much of a gobshite to admit it?"

Or maybe too much of a church mouse.

I didn't tell her about the cops that were watching us at this very minute.

"You'll keep up with Madame?"

"Don't I have an extra reason now?"

Then as if struggling to avoid dependence, she added immediately, "I'll pay you back out of me recording royalties."

"What would your ma say about that remark?"

I heard a deep breath next to me.

"She'd say . . . she'd say that when someone gives you a gift, you should accept it graciously."

"So?"

"So I won't pay you back out of me royalties! . . . But I might, mind you, I said *might*, give you a free disk."

We laughed together.

"It would be this way all our lives together," I protested to the Adversary. "She'd drive a man out of his mind with her unpredictability."

YOU'RE SUCH A NINE-FINGERED SHITE HAWK THAT I WON'T EVEN TALK TO YOU ABOUT THE WOMAN.

The lights were not on in her apartment.

"No one home?"

"They're probably off at your man's strategy session."

"I'll walk up the stairs with you."

"You'll fall and break your neck."

"Woman, I will not!"

I took her arm firmly and guided her up the stairs.

"Well, at least you're not as clumsy as you were the last time."

"Open the door, woman."

"You're NOT coming in!"

"Yes, I am. I want to make sure there's no one there."

"The place is a frigging mess."

"That's all right. Open it."

She opened the door.

"Turn on the lights."

"You'll embarrass me altogether."

"I've done that before."

"I don't mean that way."

She turned on the light.

"It's a pile of shite, isn't it?"

" 'Tis indeed."

The three tiny rooms were certainly a pile of shite, meaning various womanly garments, intimate and less intimate, scattered in chaotic disorder. Since Nuala herself was always scrupulously neat, her friends must have created the mess.

"Satisfied that there's no one lurking here?"

"More or less."

"Don't think you're going to be staying here."

"No way."

"Good night, Dermot Michael."

She hung on my neck, kissed me, and then pushed me out the door.

"Won't I see you tomorrow afternoon?"

"You will."

As I walked down the steps, I saw three men waiting in the gloom at the corner, only faintly outlined in the streetlight. One of them had his arm in a sling.

I felt fear again in my gut, this time a whole lot of fear. I'd disposed of three thugs before, but these guys were older and more experienced. It could be a much more dangerous situation.

Nonetheless, I walked down the steps with all the aplomb I could muster.

I'd go for the big guy first.

They were closing in, so they'd be only a few feet away when I reached the bottom of the stairs.

Maybe I should jump and send them sprawling.

"We're going to get you, gobshite," said your man with the arm. "And a lot more than your arm will be broken."

Just then a black sedan pulled up on the street, the front door opened, and a man's voice said firmly, "Your car, Mr. Coyne."

The guys stopped dead in their tracks.

"Hi, guys, nice to see you again. I suspect I won't see you in hell, since I'm not planning on going there."

My heart pounding and my chest heaving, I climbed into the car.

"Well timed, gentlemen," I said.

"Those are mean-looking ones, Mr. Coyne."

"They are that."

"No wonder you want protection for yourself and the young woman."

"One of them had a broken arm," the other cop observed.

"Can you imagine that!"

"Happened before you called us, huh?"

"There was a fairly level playing field at that time."

I told them about our weekend plans.

"You don't want security over the weekend."

"Oh, yes, I do. I think we're pretty safe up there, but I don't want to take chances."

"We'll be around."

"You guys are good at what you do. Thank you."

The next morning, bright and early, I set to work on my notes. I didn't want to inundate herself with too much information. I finally figured out how to do it.

I finished just in time to throw a few things into a bag, dash down to my car, and drive over to her office. She emerged from the door just as I pulled up.

Good, I'd be in trouble if I were late.

She was not wearing her glasses, and her hair was down. They'd actually given her a raise or a promotion.

She threw her bag into the back, placed her harp carefully on the floor, jumped into the front seat, and kissed me vigorously.

"You're kind of loose today, young woman, for a respectable, hardworking accountant."

"Didn't I just get a raise and a promotion? Didn't they tell me that they were very pleased with my work?"

"Congratulations . . . I hope it was a big raise?"

"I almost lost me mind."

"Did you now?"

"And do you know what they said?"

She clung to my arm, squeezing it with happiness.

"Didn't they say they were worried about how shy I was?"

"Were you shy?"

"Well, sure. I was cautious, wasn't I?"

"Didn't say much, looked timid, barely whispered?"

"Well, not *that* bad."

"Are they going to be surprised on Monday morning when the real Nuala Anne McGrail comes bounding in."

"They also said that they hoped with the extra money I might buy some more stylish clothes. Isn't that mad?"

"On Tuesday, maybe you could come in with a beige sweater and not one that's a half-size too big."

"Go 'long with ya!" she said and slapped my arm very gently.

"They have sowed the wind; on Tuesday they'll reap the whirlwind."

I said Tuesday because I would drive Nuala into work on Monday. But Nuala wouldn't be working on Tuesday.

She guffawed. "Well, they'll see a slightly different persona."

Then, suddenly anxious, she added, "Do you think they'll mind?"

"Not a chance . . . Hey, why the harp?"

"Didn't your man ask me to sing at Mass?"

"Prester George?"

"His Lordship, the little bishop!"

She aimed her nose at the sky. Nuala Anne was an important person, doing business now with the hierarchy.

"I'm impressed altogether."

"Shouldn't you be?"

Traffic was slow because of the weekend rush. When we finally arrived at Grand Beach, it was after seven, and we were both starved. My mother was delighted to serve us huge roast-beef sandwiches with coleslaw and crab salad and listen to our adventures of the past week or more specifically to Nuala's adventures, since

I was deemed too much a sluggish Irish bachelor to have adventures.

Nuala babbled on happily about her job and her voice lessons, and the willingness of Arthur to send her to graduate school at the University of Chicago's riverside campus.

That was a new one on me. I didn't like it, though only for selfish reasons.

"Dermot Michael," she said to me after she had disposed of one of Mom's special Bailey's Irish Cream malted milks, "Would you ever come down on the beach with me while I have a bit of a swim. I have to run off some of me hoyden energy."

She should never forget my accusation that she was a hoyden.

"I will, but don't expect me to join you in the water."

"You'll freeze to death, dear," Mom warned her.

Until Nuala became a daughter-in-law, she would be treated like a very young daughter.

" 'Tis much warmer than the Irish Sea or the Atlantic. And I won't stay in it more than a few minutes."

So down the steps we went, Nuala bounding enthusiastically and meself trailing along behind.

I can bound, too. I'm not that old.

I had donned trunks, just in case there was some lifesaving to do, which was a pretty funny notion, come to think of it.

We walked to the edge of the quiet water. Only a touch of froth dabbed the beach. The air was pleasantly warm. I dipped a couple of toes tentatively in the water.

"Yipe!" I shouted. "It's freezing! It's no more than fifty-eight."

" 'Tis grand," Nuala said, after she had dipped a foot in the water. "Brilliant! Invigorating!"

The moon had taken its leave. Nuala and I were indistinct shadows against the stars, beyond the pane of light coming from the house up on the dune.

"You know what I'm going to do?" she asked.

"Woman, what are you going to do?"

"I'm going to take off this bikini thing and pretend that this is the Irish Sea."

"Nuala!" I said in shock. "I'm not your ma!"

"That's all right," she replied, as her outline discarded some cloth on the beach. "You can't see anything. It's too dark."

"That's what I object to."

"Have me robe ready when I come back," she shouted and dashed into the water till it might have been up to her waist, judging by the outline and then dove. Soon she was a phosphorescent splash ripping through the water.

All I had seen was the outline, worse luck for me. It was, however, a very lovely outline.

She was staying in too long. Why had I let her do it? Why did I tolerate such an awful chance?

The Adversary crept up to me.

BECAUSE, GOBSHITE, YOU HAD NO CHOICE!

"Yeah, but . . ."

NO BUTS. WOULD YOU LOOK AT YOURSELF, DERMOT MICHAEL COYNE, THE LAST PLAYBOY OF THE WESTERN WORLD, TO COIN A PHRASE—AND YOU SHOULD EXCUSE THE PUN—HAS TURNED INTO A WORRYWART. YOU WORRY MORE ABOUT HER THAN SHE WORRIES ABOUT YOU.

"Women are supposed to worry. That's one of the things they're for."

I WON'T DEBATE THE POINT. BUT I WANT TO MAKE THESE TWO POINTS.

Irish fashion, he said "pints."

"All right."

THE FIRST IS THAT YOU WORRY THAT WAY ONLY ABOUT SOMEONE YOU LOVE.

"I've never denied I love her."

YOU'VE ALWAYS SAID SHE HAS TO BE FREE TO BE

HERSELF. IF SHE'S NOT FREE TO DIVE NAKED INTO WHAT YOU THINK IS A COLD LAKE, THEN YOU'RE TRYING TO CHANGE HER FROM WHO SHE IS.

"What if someone comes down the beach?"

THAT LEADS TO ME SECOND POINT. YOU'RE ALREADY ACTING LIKE AN OLD MAN.

He was absolutely right.

I'd have to put a stop to that.

The speck of phosphorescence grew larger. I heard the splash of her strokes, then the delightful outline ran out of the water and up on the beach.

"Dermot!" she shrieked. "Me robe!"

Instead I folded her into my arms and pressed her against my body, exchanging my warmth for her cold.

She snuggled contentedly against me.

"Dermot Michael Coyne, whatever are you doing?"

"Warming you up, woman!"

"Och," she murmured softly. "You're sure doing that, aren't you now?"

We clung to each other—peacefully, happily, joyously.

"What's going on, Derm?"

"We're experiencing ecstasy."

"Is that it?" she sighed. "I like it."

Obviously, there was an erotic component in our embrace. You don't hold a wet and naked woman in your arms on a beach under the stars without some erotic reactions. But we felt more than that, much more. I would have to write it up to figure out what it was.

Finally, I picked up her robe off the sand and wrapped her in it.

We both giggled.

"You're a desperate man, Dermot Michael Coyne," she sighed.

"Am I now?"

She began to feel around the sand with her feet for her swimsuit.

"What did you do with me swimsuit?" she demanded. "I'll have to put it back on, or your ma will think I'm a terrible wicked woman altogether."

I gave it to her.

"No, she won't. In our family, Nuala, it has become a matter of definition that Nuala can do no wrong."

I guided her up the dark stairs to the dune, the two of us giggling all the way.

"What about that?" I asked the Adversary.

NOT BAD AT ALL, he replied. YOU KEEP THAT SORT OF THING UP AND YOU'LL BE A MARRIED MAN BY CHRISTMAS.

"Don't bet on it."

Most of the family was in the house when Nuala burst in, glowing from her swim, her hair trailing behind her.

" 'Twas glorious," she said. "Nothing like it! You can't beat it! Even if your man is afraid to swim in the dark."

She swept my delighted three-year-old nephew Brian into the air.

"What about it Brian, me lad? When you grow up, you won't be afraid of a bit of cold water, will you now?"

"No, Aunt Nuala," he lisped, "not if you're swimming with me."

General laughter from the family—at my expense.

Obviously, Nuala was going to put on a show. As much as I liked those shows, even when they were at my expense, I had something else to do.

I dashed up to my room, unpacked my sub-notebook computer, and set to work on a short story about the ecstatic experience of a somewhat-reluctant young man as he held the shivering, naked body of his true love in his arms after a midnight swim under the stars. It was a story about glory and hope.

In the story, he swam, too. Artistic license.

The point of the story was that the experience was

not of lust, but of love and grace and promise, none of which need ever end.

I finished it before midnight. I reread it. I was sure it would work. The editor would love it. It might also be the germ of a novel.

The plot would be simple: Boy meets girl. Boy and girl fall in love. Boy loses girl. Boy hesitates before he tries to reclaim girl. Boy may fail. Boy may succeed. What will happen?

Wait and see.

Outside, the lake continued to lap against the beach. I opened the door to my room. The house was quiet. Everyone had returned to their own places. Only Mom and Dad and Nuala and Prester George, if he had arrived yet, were in the house.

I'd wait till the morning to show it to her. After she read my Camp Douglas report.

Lust cures death.

So does love, even more.

IT WAS a glorious weekend. The whole summer is going to be like this I told myself: a delightful summer romance with my incomparable Nuala Anne.

I was wrong.

The *persona* Nuala donned that weekend was of the helpful, happy, singing servant. I struggled out of bed early because I wanted to see her every available minute of the day.

Dressed in white shorts and a black-and-gold T-shirt which celebrated the alleged 5000th anniversary of the County Mayo, she was already in the kitchen helping Mom with breakfast—raspberry pancakes and bacon. Rather, she was making breakfast, chattering away a mile a minute, while Mom sat at the kitchen table watching her new servant with undisguised bemusement.

"Ah, 'tis himself, is it now? Dermot Michael, would you ever keep an eye on the bacon? I don't want to burn it."

"Yes, ma'am."

Dad and the Priest arrived shortly thereafter, attracted by the smell of pancakes, maple syrup, and bacon. Nuala kissed them both on the cheek, something she had neglected to do to me.

"You both sit at the table. We'll have everything for

you in only a minute, unless your man burns the bacon."

"I will not burn the bacon."

"You've hired a new cook, Mom," the Priest observed. "And she gives orders like a matriarch."

"Just like Ma," I said, referring to Mom's mother, the ineffable and greatly lamented Nell Pat.

"Bossier," said my father, "But unquestionably competent and efficient."

"Yes, Doctor," herself sniffed.

A grand time was had by all at breakfast.

"Out of the kitchen, all of you," she said after we had licked the last plate clean. "Won't I join you on the porch to read your latest work, Derm, after I'm finished here?"

She reminded me of an ad for a miracle cleaning compound—the White Tornado with a brogue.

The porch is really a deck overlooking the lake. Cup of tea in hand, I walked out and sat on the swing we keep there in memory of the days when you couldn't have a front porch without a swing.

Nuala joined me on the porch after about a quarter of an hour later.

"We've become quite the homemaker today, haven't we, Ms. McGrail?"

"Ah, sure, Mr. Coyne." She sat on the swing and sent it spinning back and forth. "Didn't I ask meself what me own ma would do if she were here, and isn't that just what she would do? And your Nell Pat, too, and isn't that a grand picture of her in the parlor? Sure wasn't she the super woman?"

When she was translating Nell Pat's diaries for me in Jury's Hotel in Dublin, Nuala had identified with Ma (as all called our grandmother) so intensely that she claimed she actually heard her voice and received advice from her about a number of matters—presumably including me. I no longer questioned Nuala's psychic propensities.

I had learned, however, that when she fired off three Irish rhetorical questions in a row, she was in high good humor.

"That's very generous of you."

"Now let's see your frigging report."

She rested the document on her bare thigh and examined my face intently.

"Sex is a frigging mystery, isn't it, Dermot Michael?"

" 'Tis all of that."

"Last night our . . ." she paused.

"Embrace?"

She hesitated. "Well, we can call it that, I suppose. Not a very good word."

"What about it?"

"It was holy, wasn't it?"

"I think so."

"Not like the other night—not at all, at all, was it?"

"Woman, it was not."

"Yet we were the same two people, the same two bits of cosmic fluff with the same needs and longings."

Cosmic fluff, was it?

" 'Tis true."

She sighed. "Why was it so different? And don't talk about the difference between love and lust. It was more than that altogether."

"I don't know, Nuala. I do know that I felt terribly guilty the other night and wonderful last night."

"I don't understand it at all, at all."

She sighed again and picked up my second summary of my research on Camp Douglas.

" 'Tis a much greater mystery than what happened to your man's frigging letter."

"After you're finished reading it, I have a short story I wrote, ah, recently. I'd like your reaction to it, too."

"Only after I've finished the serious work of the morning."

Nuala my love,

  Let me begin with two letters:

"*January 18, 1863*
"*My dear mother,*
  "*I'm very sick today. It's terribly cold in the barracks. Eight inches of snow outside. Only a slice of bread this morning, and I could not keep it down. Some of the men are killing rats and eating them. They tell me that rats taste like chicken. I'll never know whether they're joking.*
  "*I'm dying, Mother. By the time you receive this letter, I will be dead. When we marched out of Macon on that sunny day last April, I never thought that I would die of cold and hunger in Chicago nine months later. I was nineteen, I had finished two years of college at Emory. A young woman loved me. I had a wonderful mother and father and a darling brother and sister. I had my Christian faith to protect me. A house full of darkies loved and respected me. I had a whole life ahead of me. I was confident that with the new levy of troops we would capture Washington and drive on New York and force that devil incarnate Abe Lincoln to grant us our peace and freedom.*
  "*Instead of an assignment to the valorous and victorious Army of Northern Virginia, we were sent to the Army of the Mississippi and to that charnel house of brutality, Shiloh.*
  "*We fought valiantly and killed more of them than they did of us. But we were captured and sent here to this antechamber of hell called Camp Douglas.*
  "*At first I was confident that with good health and strength I could survive this place. But I was wrong. My life is flowing away.*
  "*I would like to have come home and lived out*

*my life to its proper length. I would have been
ready to give my life on the field of honor for my
country. It would have been a glory to die of a
musket ball or a bayonet. Yet I was born to die
in Chicago. There is little glory in that.*

*"I have only two regrets. One is Lavinia, and
she knows that regret. The other is that during my
short run of life I have not been grateful or loving
to you and to Father and to my sister and brother.
I took the love of all of you for granted. I am
deeply sorry that I didn't respond generously to
that love every day of my all too short life.*

"Please forgive me.

*"I grow weaker. I have watched how the men
react to someone who will not live to see the next
day. Some walk by pretending that he is not there.
Others stop and smile piteously and encourage the
poor wretch to false hopes.*

*"That is how they treat me today. My strength
fails. I can hardly hold my pencil. I will die before
the night is over. I will see all of you in heaven.*

> *"All my love,*
> *"Your son,*
> *Ralph Pickering*
> *14th Georgia Volunteers"*

I reflect, Nuala Anne, as I read that letter, that but for
the grace of God, there goes Dermot Michael Coyne. You
can tell me whether you identify with poor Lavinia.

Maybe in Paradise we will meet them both.

The other letter, from an officer in the 10th Texas, is
much shorter:

"My dearest Elizabeth,

*"I don't have much longer to live. I think I have
smallpox. Soon they will bring me to the smallpox
hospital from which none return. I'll be buried in
the wretched cemetery behind the place. I will*

never see you and the children again.

"Please forgive me, Elizabeth, for dying so soon and leaving you a widow with three children to care for. I will love you always.

"Your loving husband,
Edward"

Nuala bowed her head after she had read those letters. Her fists clenched, her fingers turned white. I waited for her to explode. However, she said nothing and continued to read, her face grim and pale, her lips tight.

I've tried in my first report to give all the background of Chicago and of the problem of prisoners of war in the early 1860s. Those constitute, I believe extenuating circumstances for what happened. While some guards were cruel and many camp commandants were unconscionably indifferent, cruelty was not a matter of national policy as it was in Japanese, North Korean, and North Vietnamese prison camps during their respective wars with us. While there may have been some deliberate torture, torture was surely not something that the camp commandants demanded.

Yet, from the point of view of many of the men who endured Camp Douglas and survived it, those fine distinctions are irrelevant. Take the case of Private M. J. Bradley of Company G of the 10th Kentucky Infantry who was captured near Pound Gap, Virginia on July 7, 1863 and spent nineteen months at Camp Douglas. He contributed an article to a collection of prison memoirs published by one Griffin Frost in 1867 at Quincy, Illinois. The memoirs, compiled as they were just after the war, have the full flavor of the anger that many of the ex-POWs must have felt. Only Union camps are described, and one has the feeling that, in part, the book is a response to the prosecution of the Confederate officers from Andersonville, a kind of "You were as bad as we were and worse."

Allowing for that perspective and for Bradley's rhetoric, his account is still one of great horror.

He begins by complaining that he and his fellow prisoners were treated at Kemper Barracks in Cincinnati worse than men would treat "mean-spirited curs." Camp Douglas was a little better. "Had we been a lot of horses under their care, we would have been provided for, by having good warm stables, to ward off the inclemency of the blast and with plenty of good substantial food to satisfy the craving of our appetites, but being rebel prisoners we were denied either of these essentials."

At first, he says, friends and relatives of the prisoners were able to provide them with food and clothing, but as the camp grew more crowded, their rations were reduced to a "small piece of tough beef or pickled pork and bread, with occasionally some beans and a little vinegar." They were allowed neither "sugar, coffee, bacon, potatoes or vegetables of any kind." When they complained, they were told that this was retaliation for what their prisoners were suffering in Confederate prisons.

"His Satanic Majesty is swift in excuses and always prompt in furnishing them to his followers, when called upon."

They were compelled to "muster and stand in line every morning whether hot or cold, and there to remain in the scorching sun, the pelting rain or the driving snow, sometimes for hours."

They slept on pine planks without mattresses. They were allowed a blanket for every two men, though "some poor fellows" were left without blankets. They were forbidden to speak after sundown. They were surrounded by guards at all times and spies among the prisoners.

"I may safely say that thousands of my fellow prisoners died of privations—or, in other words—*starved to death!* Murdered by slow torture, being denied month after month even the common necessities—while their fat-fed, well-clothed sentinels mocked our sufferings and laughed at our miseries. O, it was all human nature could endure to see these brave men thus dying of starvation day after day, at the hands of those vile, detestable, unfeeling villains who were rolling in affluence, stolen from the letters of these prisoners whose friends had sent them aid, which they poor, deluded mortals, thought the federal authorities would allow them to receive."

For a time, they were allowed to eat the meat bones that the cooks had cooked until they were so soft that they could chew them. Then these bones had to be thrown into a slop barrel. Some who tried to raid these barrels were shot summarily. Others were punished by having the bone "fastened between his teeth, across his mouth and made to fall down and crawl around on his hands and knees like a dog."

There were worse tortures:

"A piece of timber four feet long had four legs nailed to it and made very much to resemble a carpenter's trestle ten or twelve feet high, was made into what they called by way of taunt and ridicule, 'the wooden horse' or 'Morgan's mule.' For the most minor and almost unavoidable violation of any of the rules and regulations, we were made to climb up as best we could and sit astride of this narrow piece of wood for hours at a time, day or night, hot or cold, rain or snow."

He describes how a plot of crazed men to rush the guards, seize their guns, regardless of casualties, and break out of the camp was frustrated by an informer.

Then a more serious attempt was made to dig a tunnel out of the camp. The plot almost succeeded (as did a much more successful plot a few years before) but was also betrayed by an informer.

The whole camp was mustered on the parade ground and made to stand day after day until the plotters were named. Those who fell to the ground were shot promptly. When the guards found the guilty men they put them in the "white oak" dungeon where many of them died.

"A 'dead line' was drawn around prisons on the inside of the fence enclosing the barracks. Several men were shot by guards along this line, without any provocation whatever. I remember one circumstance in particular, which I do not think I will ever forget; a man who had just come into prison, being very thirsty, and the water having been shut off from us as had frequently been the case, seeing snow lying near the fence on the ground, attempted to pick up some and eat it, when he was shot by the guard without any warning whatever."

Their money was often stolen, he claims, either from their mail or by federal officers searching their few belongings during a daylong outdoor inspection on Sunday, no matter what the weather.

He would have been treated better, he tells us, if he were imprisoned by a group of "woolly-headed Negroes" because there was something in the character of Union soldiers that made them particularly evil.

While Bradley's charges may sound exaggerated, they are all confirmed by other reports and studies. Tens of thousands of dollars of "Confederate funds" (sent by family and friends) simply disappeared. Cruelty was rampant, especially during the later days of Camp Douglas when he was there.

"I don't want to read any more of this horrible stuff," Nuala said and tossed aside my essay. "I'm sick of the whole frigging mess and all them disgusting shite hawks. Dermot Michael, don't make me read any more."

She jumped up off the swing and paced back and forth like an angry lioness.

"You don't have to read it, Nuala love," I said as I gathered up the pages from the floor.

"I don't want to hear a word about your frigging Camp Douglas ever again. Not at all, at all. Do you hear that, Dermot Michael?"

"I do indeed."

Then she sat down and picked up my rearranged manuscript. She started to read again.

"I thought you didn't want to read any more," I said very cautiously.

"I don't. But she's making me."

"Who's making you?"

"I don't know! I don't know!"

I shivered. Was my love thinking she was in contact with the dead again?

However, there was another side to the story; not one which cancels the horrors, but reveals that not all the guards were as bad as the men Bradley describes.

A story from a man named M. J. Vesey of the 14th Mississippi presents a different picture:

"I was a member of Company I, of the same regiment, and my mess of eight men occupied three small rooms at one end of the barracks. We had been drawing rations with the company, but, being dissatisfied, we asked the commissary to allow us to draw our rations separately. He said: 'Well, as you can't *find* anything else to secede from, you want to secede from your company.' However, being a good-natured old fellow, he granted our request. Instead of drawing the black molasses and the brown sugar, we got good vegetables, cabbage, potatoes, etc. instead, and fared fine from then on until we were exchanged.

"Our guards were Mulligan's Irish Brigade, who had been captured at Springfield, Mo., by the Confederates. They were a nice, clever lot of men and never oppressed us. We had in our mess an Irishman named McGrority. Frequently a little Irish guard would come in early with a canteen of whisky and give McGrority and others a drink.

"While Mulligan's Brigade was guarding us, a Lieutenant Morrison had charge of the barracks occupied by the 14th Mississippi. He was as nice and clever a gentleman as I ever met. When his command was ordered South to reinforce Grant before the battle of Shiloh, a number of us prepared and signed a paper setting out how nice Lieu-

tenant Morrison had been to us and asked that, in the
event of his capture, he be treated with consideration.
Among those who signed this paper was a young man
named Billups, a son of Colonel Billups, a wealthy and
prominent citizen of Columbus, Miss. It so happened that
Lieutenant Morrison was captured at Shiloh and sent as a
prisoner of war to Columbus Miss., and he wrote to us of
his experience. After being in prison a few days, he
thought of this letter and showed it to the officer of the
day. The latter borrowed it and showed it to Colonel Billups, who, recognizing his son's signature, went to the
commandant of the Post and procured Lieutenant Morrison's release to his care and then took him to his elegant
home. Colonel Billups had two beautiful and accomplished
daughters, and Morrison wrote us as he was having the
time of his life."

Mulligan (not above corruption charges himself) was replaced by a much more nefarious officer named Tucker.
Vesey notes the change and then, with his irrepressible
sense of humor tells what he made of it:

"While Mulligan was in command at Camp Douglas, a
great number of the good people of Chicago visited us
daily, keeping us well supplied with tobacco, cigars,
shirts, socks, etc. and once in a while smuggled in a citizen's suit of clothes to someone who had procured money
and was anxious to escape. When Mulligan's command
was sent to the front, some six-months troops under the
command of a Colonel Tucker were brought there to guard
us. Colonel Tucker proclaimed that no more prisoners
would escape and no visitors would be allowed without a
pass signed by him, so but few visitors were seen by us
for a while. One day a visitor lost his pass. It was found
by a prisoner and brought to me to see if I could make a
good imitation of it. After practicing for a while, I got so
I could imitate Colonel's signature to perfection. After that,
whenever a prisoner could get a citizen's suit of clothing,

he would come to me and I would give him a pass and he could go out without molestation. Two men from my company, an Ed Liller and a Mr. Lochart, went out on a pass. Just outside of the the gate was a higher tower where people have a view of the prison. The day Ed Liller went out, I saw him at the top of this tower,[1] taking a farewell look at his former prison."

Many but not all of the visitors were opponents of the war and Confederate sympathizers. Many were merely decent human beings.

Among the frequent visitors to the camp were the family of a certain John Walsh, the owner of a cartage company in Chicago and the father of three lovely and "high-spirited" young women who were lace makers.

While some men were killed by the guards (certainly twenty and perhaps forty-five), most of the deaths came from causes over which the guards had no control. Even the good commandants were no match for the constant overcrowding as each new batch of rebel prisoners came in, nor for unhealthy sheds in which the prisons were jammed, nor the disease, especially smallpox (of which more than 1,000 died).

Moreover, the prisoners were also victims of corrupt sub-contractors who delivered rotted food, venal doctors, inadequate medical supplies, sutlers (men who operated a kind of post exchange) who charged exorbitant prices, and a federal bureaucracy that had other matters to occupy its attention.

I have a lot other material, Nuala, my love, especially diaries and letters from prisoners, many of which would break your heart. There is one from a man who spent almost four years in the camp. Each day he records the names of friends who have died. I think to myself that each

---

[1]Presumably, this was the astronomical tower of the University of Chicago.

one of these men had a mother and/or a wife and maybe children somewhere whose lives would never be the same. It makes me want to weep.

What can we do?

I don't know, Nuala Anne; these awful tragedies happened long ago. They cannot be undone. We cannot console the bereaved. Lavinia and Elizabeth long ago joined their lovers in death.

We can remember them. We can remind Chicago what happened where the peaceful lawns of Lake Meadows are today. We can realize how inept and stupid bureaucracies are when they face crisis. We can decry the folly of war. Above all, maybe, we can practice more compassion in our lives. Towards everyone.

I'm sounding more like George the Priest.

I imagine that most of the screams you heard came from the smallpox hospital, the White Oak dungeon, and from the men dying of starvation.

Each death, someone wrote of the 45 million people who died during World War II, was a personal tragedy for the person who died and for that person's survivors. Camp Douglas is small potatoes compared to the Holocaust or the Gulag or the Great Famine. But I am with your friend George Orwell: after the death of the first child, tragedy increases only quantitatively.

May it never happen again in this city and this country. Or anywhere else.

— 6 —

THEN SHE read it through a second time. She put it down on the swing and sighed.

"It's very nicely done, Derm. The comic and the tragic mixed together."

"It resonates with what you experienced last Sunday."

"The tragic part of it. That darling Lieutenant Morrison sent me no messages. Don't ask me how I know he was a darling. I *know*."

"I won't argue. Did he marry one of those beautiful and accomplished women?"

"Of *course* he did. After the war."

She picked up the paper again, thumbed through it, and then put it back on the swing.

"I agree with everything you say about the lessons. I might want to make it a little more explicit that, like your man from Georgia, we should never stop saying thank-you to them who love us and whom we love."

"Right."

"Even though *she* wants me to get involved, I'm not sure why we're in this. You've answered my question about who the men were that I heard screaming and why they were screaming. Maybe that's enough. Aren't these frigging 'bursts' often irrelevant? Sometimes they don't mean anything at all. We drove by that street on the way up to Grand Beach, didn't we, and nothing happened then?"

"We did."

"But we both think that this particular experience is very important, don't we?"

"We do."

"Why?"

"I don't know, Nuala Anne."

"You think the conspiracy is important for both of us?"

"I think it might be."

"We might learn something from it, is it now?"

"Maybe."

"You want me to solve that mystery?"

"I do, Nuala Holmes."

"Go 'long with you, Dermot Michael Watson."

She pounded my arm, more delicately than sometimes.

"And I've got to find that letter," she said as her stubborn jaw took on its most stubborn form, "from your man, and himself going to a play on Good Friday."

"I'll work on it all day Monday and give it to you Monday night."

"Grand! Now, me bucko, let's go over to the tennis court so I can beat the shite out of you again and come back here to help your ma and the other women with lunch."

Even though all my siblings and their spouses own their homes, they tend to come over to our place for meals and to bring the kids to the beach. They cooperate by implicit agreement so that the work is distributed evenly.

"You're forgetting something, Nuala Anne."

"What? . . . Oh, the saints preserve me"—hand to her mouth—"I've forgot to read your story!"

She grabbed it and read it in a guilty hurry. Then she read it again slowly, her face turning crimson the second time around. She grabbed my hand and squeezed it hard. Tears streamed down her face.

"Och, Dermot, isn't it terrible lovely? Don't you keep improving? You really are a friggin' genius, aren't you, now?"

"I doubt it."

"I can understand how you know your young man—though he's not afraid of the cold water, is he? But how do you get inside the woman's feelings? How do you know what it means to her?"

"Maybe I'm just good at getting inside women."

"You dirty-mouthed thing, you! Isn't that just like a man?"

She was smiling when she said it.

She gave the story back to me and, an odd sort of frown on her face, examined my face closely.

"You're going to send it to your editor?"

"Unless you mind."

She waved her hand. "Why should I mind? Isn't the young woman grand?"

"I thought so."

"Dermot . . . ?"

"Yes, Nuala?"

"Do you really understand me that well?"

"Sometimes. Not very often. Maybe I was just lucky in that story."

"If you understand me at a time like that, there's not much point in my hiding from you, is there?"

"We all hide, Nuala. It's part of being human."

"I suppose you're right. . . . Well, I don't care if you see right through me. I kind of like it. It's like being naked, if you take me meaning, and not being afraid."

"I take your meaning."

"Come on, then, let's play tennis."

So we played tennis. She won both sets 6–3, 6–3. Then she beat Prester George 6–4, 6–4. Then my brother Mike (the oncologist as opposed to my brother Peter the lawyer). 6–1, 6–1. My brothers thought it was great fun being beaten by Nuala, but then, they're not as competitive as I am.

She also played the maid-of-all-work role all week-end, giving orders at a frantic clip, but only to men. All the rest of them thought it was very funny.

Moreover she acted as baby-sitter, nursery school-marm, and entertainment impresario for children of all ages, even the two teens that the family had managed to produce. She sang and told stories and led the games.

"You'll be exhausted before the sun goes down."

"I will NOT! I'm young and vigorous, not a worn-out old man like certain people I know."

My mother said to me at one point, in the tone of one who has given long and serious thought to the matter, "I don't think Nuala's quite ready to marry yet, do you?"

"I am unaware that she is contemplating marriage at the present time."

"She's so young."

"Only six months younger than you were when you married the Old Fella."

"Things were different then."

"That is what they all say."

She laughed and kissed my forehead.

"Well, she's a wonderful young woman."

End of discussion.

Before Mass on the dune, after long and serious consultation with His Lordship, Nuala, now dressed in a modest flower-print summer dress—no reference to Galway Hookers this time—taught the congregation to sing an Irish *"Kyrie"* and *"Agnus Dei,"* as she called them, by a priest named Liam Lawton.

"Aren't you a grand choir, now? Sure, won't I have you all talking in the Irish before the summer is over?"

Normally, congregations resent those who impose yet another hymn on them, even in English and even when the day is not a Technicolor masterpiece on the shore of a mighty lake. However, no one could resent Nuala, the pretty and charming music teacher who made everyone laugh. Yet another quickly donned persona.

The little bishop caught my attention and then rolled his eyes. He didn't know the half of it.

Even super-Nuala runs out of energy. On Sunday, just as a Coyne family wiener roast on the beach was winding down about one o'clock, she whispered in my ear, "I'm exhausted altogether. I'm going to bed."

"I warned you."

She kissed my cheek and bounded upstairs.

"You'll never figure that one out, little bro, not in a hundred years, but it will be fun trying."

"Quite the contrary, if I am to believe that one's testimony, I already have figured her out on all important matters."

"Yeah?" he said in a tone of someone who finds the last statement very hard to believe.

"Yeah."

On Sunday morning while herself was bustling around the kitchen I flipped on the TV to watch *Today on Sunday,* something I rarely do. Reading the Sunday *New York Times* is usually enough of a Sunday obligation.

NBC reported yet another art heist in Chicago, this one at the prestigious Armacost Gallery, with the usual tone of faint contempt with which the media view crime in our city—as if crimes never happen in New York. Two Monets which were being exhibited here before the big Art Institute show later in the summer had been stolen the night before. Chicago police suspected that the thieves had found a way to disarm the electronic detection system with a laser beam. They had removed the door of the gallery, taken the paintings off the wall, and escaped out the door. About one A.M., a driver on Huron Street had seen four men rushing out of the gallery with two large objects in their hands, and depart at high speed in an old pickup truck. The driver had then driven to the Chicago Avenue police station to report what he had seen; the police had not been able to apprehend the perpetrators (that last phrase from a captain at the station).

Pictures of the paintings appeared on the screen, both of them of Monet's garden. The driver of the car was interviewed briefly by the anchorwoman, who said it was too bad he was not equipped with a car phone. The man said that he had one, but had not thought to use it.

Poor fellow.

I did not like the sound of this stuff. Could the lads or the pseudo-lads be into art thefts these days? In the United States? In Chicago? Would Gerry Adams tolerate that?

No way those guys could be so sophisticated as to snatch two Monets.

Later I insisted that Nuala phone her mother and father in Carraroe.

"I can't be using your ma's phone for a long distance call."

"You can, woman. The rates are so cheap that they actually pay you to make the call. Besides, I cleared it with the old gal. She said you worked so hard here this weekend that you're entitled to it."

"Grand!" She bounded over to phone and punched the buttons from memory.

"Ma, tis meself!"

Then she spoke to her parents in Irish, a soft, musical, gentle language, at least the way Nuala spoke it.

I was then constrained to talk to her parents.

"Hasn't herself become a wild Yank already?"

"Wasn't she always wild, the wildest of all of them?"

"Aren't you just discovering it, Dermot, you poor boy?"

"Well, I've had my suspicions. . . ."

Then Ma got on the line to sing herself's praises to the sky—a marvelous young woman, a great credit to her family and to Ireland.

"I may vomit," I whispered to Prester George.

"I think we can all manage to get used to her," he replied with a crooked grin. "She'll exhaust us though, won't she?"

"On that subject, big bro, I have no comment whatsoever."

I wondered whether herself would display as much vigor and energy and enthusiasm in bed. No reason to think she wouldn't.

On Monday morning at 6:30, I rolled out of bed to drive her into Chicago so she wouldn't be late for work. She'd wound down by now, I said as I staggered down to the kitchen.

No way. She was in the kitchen producing buttermilk waffles for the two of us.

"Only two for you now, Dermot Michael. You don't want to be putting on weight, do you, now?"

"No, ma'am."

She was content with consuming only one.

Then we piled into my Benz for the drive to Chicago. Leaving Monday morning instead of Sunday night always looks good on Sunday night. It looks bad when, feeling gray and blah, you must struggle with traffic into the city. I expected her to do the sensible thing; relax in the comfort of my car and take a good long nap.

She did no such thing. Instead, she jabbered all the way into the Loop about her job, her plans to go to school in the fall, the excitement of her lessons with Madame, the great fun of the weekend at Grand Beach.

She jumped out of the car when I pulled to up to 123 West Monroe.

"All eager for another exciting day at the office, Nuala?"

" 'Tis a grand life, isn't it, Dermot Michael?"

She leaned over and kissed me solidly.

"Thanks for a brilliant weekend."

Nuala Anne was on a roll.

I drove back to my apartment, straightened out my notes, ignored the temptation for a relaxing morning nap, and set to work on my final report. There was a lot of material to digest into a narrative which tried to present both theories of the "Camp Douglas Conspiracy," a conspiracy in which, one writer said, you can believe only by an act of faith.

I finished it about five o'clock, went to the pool for my daily swim, and cooked myself a hamburger for supper. Junk food is less junk if you eat it at home.

I polished my short story after the hamburger and dropped it in the mailbox on my way up to the Tricolor.

Nuala was into grunge that night—black jeans and a black cropped top which left several inches of delectable midriff open to view. Why the change in public image? Better not ask.

She seemed tired as she sang; she was not at full vitality and energy. Only someone who heard her every time she sang would notice. The crowd was as enthusiastic as ever.

At her first break, she joined me at my table and brushed her lips against mine. She seemed listless and preoccupied.

I made a quick decision to give her only half of the documents in my final report. I'd save the last document and my own commentary until she read the others and had a chance to reflect on them. It would be interesting to see how she would react to one side of the story without even knowing that there was another side.

"Report number three," I said, giving her the manila folder in which contained two different versions of the Great Conspiracy.

"I'll read it tomorrow," she said putting the folder aside.

"You do seem tired," I said cautiously. "Too much kitchen work over the weekend?"

"I said I'd read it!" she snapped.

"I wasn't suggesting that you wouldn't."

"That'll be the end of it, Derm. I appreciate all the work you did because of a silly whim of mine. I really do. This was a long time ago, though, wasn't it? It has nothing to do with our lives today, does it? I'll have to learn to ignore these foolish experiences of mine. They're a waste of time. You have a lot better things to do than being my research assistant."

I became uneasy. Had the child become a changeling? Where had the real Nuala Anne gone?

"That's up to you, Nuala. I've always enjoyed poking around in history. I found enough material for a couple of novels."

"You don't have to work for a living, Dermot, but I do."

"You must always listen not to what a woman says, but to what she means," my father had advised me.

What did Nuala Anne mean?

"And you work very hard and very effectively," I said tentatively.

"That's NOT what I mean."

"I didn't think it was."

"I've got to get back to me frigging harp," she said as she rose from the table. "We must talk when we walk back to my house."

"Yes, ma'am."

Something was up, something serious. I didn't like it.

She carried my manila folder in her right hand as we left the Tricolor and thus avoided my left hand.

Dermot Michael, me lad, you are in deep trouble. What had you done since this morning to upset this one?

"Dermot, I think we shouldn't see so much of one another."

My heart sank. I knew these breakup lines when I heard them.

Uninvited and out of nowhere, the Adversary intruded himself in our privacy.

YOU'VE BLOWN IT, ME LAD. BLOWN IT REAL BAD.

"Shut up," I told him. "I haven't done a thing all day."

To herself I said, "That's your decision, Nuala. I won't argue with you."

"I don't mean we should break up, Dermot. I love you too much to want you out of my life."

That was standard breakup talk, too. Let's go out occasionally. Let's remain friends.

"I'm glad to hear that."

The Adversary had no intention of shutting up.

YOU'RE NOT LISTENING TO WHAT SHE MEANS, ASSHOLE.

"Go away!"

"I mean," Nuala said as she rushed on, "that if we went out once a week or so, would that be all right?"

Nuala the accountant was quantifying the rules of our relationship. Well, that was better than suggesting that we should remain friends.

I almost said that normally that was what we had been doing. However, that would be responding to words and not to meaning.

So instead I said, "Once a week would be wonderful."

"You're not angry at me, are you, Dermot Michael?"

"I have no reason to be angry, Nuala. Once a week would be grand."

"I haven't hurt your feelings?"

"Woman, you have not."

"You seem, well, kind of funny, if you take me meaning?"

"I'm a little surprised, that's all."

"I gave me notice at that frigging pub tonight. Next Thursday will be the last time. I'm sick of them amadons ogling me tits and for twenty-five dollars a night."

"I never liked the place," I said. "Maybe you could try the Abbey. They're always looking for Irish talent."

"I've heard from them. I told them that I didn't want to sing in public any more."

"Now I AM surprised."

"I'll see Madame until the end of July because you've paid her up to then. She's a darling. But I just don't have enough time to spend with her or to do all them friggin' exercises."

Ah, that was it. Not enough time. Welcome to America, Nuala Anne McGrail.

"You really feel under terrible time pressures," I said, hoping that now I was hearing meaning. "Everyone is making demands of you."

"I just can't go on this way, if you take me meaning."

"I do, Nuala. You want to be left alone for a while."

"Not completely alone, Derm. I'd die if that happened."

She must have shifted the manila folder to her other hand because now she was touching my hand cautiously and tentatively. I took her hand firmly in my own. She sighed.

"Never completely alone, Nuala."

"And I'll have to stop coming to Grand Beach on weekends."

I gulped.

"We'll all miss you."

"Your family is wonderful, but I just don't feel like I belong there."

"With all the swells?"

"That's NOT it, Dermot Michael," she said, pulling her hand away. "I'm not a frigging snob."

We turned onto Southport. The dimly lighted street was deserted.

I was losing it. Once again not listening.

"You simply don't have the time for it?"

"A weekend up there wastes four days."

"Four?"

"Friday, because I dash around like crazy to get everything packed on Friday, and Monday because I'm so worn out, especially from the ride in during the morning. I don't have that kind of time to waste."

"You told me this morning that it was a brilliant weekend."

"You're not listening to me, Dermot Michael! It WAS a brilliant weekend, I just don't have the time for any more—not this summer, anyway."

"I see."

"No, you don't." She took my hand again. "It's not you or your family or Grand Beach or anything like that."

"It's time."

"That's it," she said vigorously. "When I think about learning me new job and getting ready for the University of Chicago and then taking me courses, I already don't have enough time. They say that the university is a terrible difficult place."

She'd be the best student in class on arrival, but I'd better not say that until she got her first A.

"It is a demanding school," I said cautiously, for fear that once again I'd be accused of not listening.

"I have to support meself, Dermot Michael, and develop my career. I have to earn money for meself and for my family back in Ireland and Ma and Pa getting on in years. I'm not a kid anymore, and I'm not playing a game. My life has to be serious because the real world is serious."

"It is that."

"Not for someone who is rich like you are. . . . Do you finally understand what I'm trying to say?"

Oh, yeah, I understand. The raise and the promotion and the promise of graduate-school money has scared the living daylights out of you. You're trying to become a responsible, ambitious Yank overnight. God protect you from that because if you're successful, you won't be Nuala Anne anymore.

"I think I do. You're saying that you need more time."

SHE'S SAYING A LOT MORE THAN THAT, GOBSHITE, the Adversary whispered in my ear.

"I know that, you eejit," I responded. "Leave me alone."

"That's it, Derm. I have to concentrate my energies and my attentions, if you take me meaning. It's not you or your family . . . I love all of you. It's me own fault for acting like an a frigging *onchuch*."

Which is a female amadon. Sort of.

Don't argue with her, Dermot. She's terribly wrong. But you'll never talk her out of it. Not now. She'll get over it.

I hope.

"Nuala," I said very carefully, "I've always told you since you came to the United States that you have to be free to be your own self, live your own life, chase your own dreams, seek out your own stars. How can you think I wouldn't approve your decision? We'll miss you at Grand Beach. But your job and your life are too important for you not to chart your own path."

"I knew you'd understand, Dermot." She hugged me. "You're such a sweet and wonderful man!"

No, YOU'RE NOT, said the Adversary. YOU'RE A JERK.

"You will still take me out once a week?" she asked anxiously. "I really don't want to break up with you."

"I'll call you over the weekend and see what night next week you might be free."

"That's such a long time, Dermot."

"Next week?"

"I can't complain. I made the rules, and there it is."

Later I realized that she meant I could phone her before the weekend, even if I couldn't see her. I had overinterpreted the rule.

Well, too bad for her. She had made a decision in favor of loneliness, and that was that. If she wanted, she could always call me. Right?

"Maybe we could have dinner and see that film *The Brothers McMullen?*"

"Wouldn't that be grand? Don't they say that it is a wonderful fillum!"

Which is the way the Irish pronounce that word.

We arrived at the old wooden building. She embraced me and kissed me good night.

"I'll walk up the steps meself. Won't I be moving out of here in a week or so? I'll sublease this place and get meself a nice quiet studio where I can be by myself and do me own work."

What about your friends who can't afford a place to live?

However, I said, "That sounds like a good idea."

Which I have been pushing for a couple of weeks.

She climbed up the stairs with much less than her usual enthusiasm. Probably crying. She made a great sacrifice for her career, and it hurt. Doubtless she was brokenhearted, but proud of her courage.

Bullshite, Nuala Anne, it's all pure bullshite.

You'll have to find that out for yourself.

At the top of the stairs, she turned and waved. I waved back and turned for the melancholy walk over to Clark Street and a cab.

I was hoping the three hard men would show up. I would take great pleasure in stomping them all into the ground.

"Well," I told myself, "it's not all bad. She'll still go out with me. This will take some of the pressure off both of us. Maybe there's even a story in this quasi-breakup."

YOU'RE A DAMN FOOL! The Adversary abandoned his phony brogue. HOW LONG DO YOU THINK IT WILL BE BEFORE YOU BECOME ONE MORE PRESSURE ON HER TIME? SHE'S JUST LETTING YOU DOWN GENTLY.

"You might be right," I admitted.

FROM A SHY CHILD TO A DULL ACCOUNTANT, THAT'S A PRETTY QUICK TRIP.

"Overnight. Less than that."

YOUR FEY GALWAY LASS HAS TURNED INTO A DULL YANK.

"You could put it that way."

AND IT'S ALL YOUR FAULT. IF YOU HADN'T BEEN SUCH A WISE GUY WITH HER BOSS AT THE EAST BANK CLUB NONE OF THIS WOULD HAVE HAPPENED. YOU MADE HER A SUCCESSFUL ACCOUNTANT, SO SHE DOESN'T WANT TO BE A MINSTREL GIRL ANYMORE.

"Minstrel woman."

REGARDLESS. YOU SAW TO IT THAT THEY THREW A BUCKET OF COLD WATER IN HER FACE. THEY REMINDED HER THAT SHE HAD NOT COME HERE TO BE A SINGER BUT TO MAKE MONEY AND EARN HER WAY THROUGH LIFE. BRILLIANT!

"She has the right to that opportunity. She has the right to a career of her own."

AS A SINGER.

"If she *wants* to sing. Now leave me alone."

IF YOU'D HAD THE SENSE TO PROPOSE TO HER ON SUNDAY, NONE OF THIS WOULD HAVE HAPPENED.

"You're crazy."

NO, I'M NOT. WONDERING ABOUT YOU AND TRYING TO FIGURE YOU OUT WOULD BE A STRAIN ON ANY WOMAN, ESPECIALLY A GREENHORN WHO DOESN'T KNOW WHICH WAY HER LIFE IS GOING. IF SHE KNEW SHE WOULD MARRY YOU IN A YEAR OR SO, SHE WOULD BE LESS WORRIED ABOUT HER FUTURE, LESS LIKELY TO FEEL ALL ALONE IN THE WORLD, AS SHE DOES NOW.

"I don't like that."

I caught a cab on Clark Street. The Adversary, usually a free rider, left me.

Did Nuala really feel that way about me? Was my strict insistence on her freedom, which, after all she had merely taken seriously in her revised life plan, leaving me out in the cold, so to speak?

ALL WOMEN WANT TO GET MARRIED! the Adversary shouted at me as he flitted by the open cab window.

"No, they don't!" I shouted after him.

"Sir?" the cabbie asked.

"Nothing, I was just mumbling."

Most women, like most men, did want to marry. Given Nuala's background, surely she wanted a husband and kids. But so young? Was she that insecure, fragile, vulnerable? That much a shy child?

Was there any reason why she could not be her own woman with a husband and a family? Sure, there'd be some constraints, but might not they actually be a help to her?

That was a possibility of which I had never thought.

And, as I told myself after draining a glass of whiskey (Scotch, not Irish), one I didn't want to think about now or ever.

—7—

THE MORNING after my quasi-breakup with Nuala Anne, I woke up groggy and with a bad headache. It was the second Scotch that had done me in. I looked at the clock. Short hitter. Already nine-thirty. What had happened yesterday to make me so unhappy?

Then I remembered: I had lost my Nuala Anne.

Well, maybe not completely.

The Adversary must have recognized my pitiable condition because he did not renew his previous night's attack.

I swung my legs out of the bed and tried to persuade the city of Chicago to stop twirling out beyond the windows of the John Hancock building

What else was I supposed to remember? Oh, yes. I had turned off the phone before I went to bed. I wanted no heartbreaking conversations with her at two o'clock in the morning.

I turned on the phone and sank into the easy chair next to it. It promptly jangled, torturing every nerve in my body.

"Dermot Coyne," I growled.

"Where the hell have you been?"

My sister Cynthia, aka Cindy. In her lawyer mode. With her children and her husband and the rest of the Coyne clan, she was one of the sweetest and gentlest women you have ever met. When she turns litigation lawyer, Cynthia Coyne Hurley, Esq. becomes hell on wheels. Lately she has turned to tax law because she can do that and telecommute. Today she was obviously being the litigator.

"Sleeping."

"Did you see the morning TV?"

The call was coming from her car, a massive and ungainly Toyota van—without which you cannot be a properly certified suburban wife.

"No."

If only my mouth did not taste like I'd swallowed garlic.

"They've taken Nuala."

"Who?"

I was now very wide awake and, if the truth be told, spoiling for a fight.

"My idiot ex-employer, Zack O'Hara, the duly elected State's Attorney for the County of Cook. He has charged that she was involved in the robbery of the Armacost Gallery on Saturday night and conspired at a meeting on Thursday night to commit a felony."

"She can't have been! She was with us at the wiener roast on the beach."

"I am aware of that, little brother. I saw O'Hara's thugs dragging them into Area Six on the tube this morning, a bedraggled and confused crowd of Irish kids, all of them, according to O'Hara's office, illegal aliens. To my horror, there was our Nuala among them."

Our Nuala was it?

"She's not illegal, she has a Morrison visa."

"I suspect that my former employer has not the foggiest notion of who Morrison is or what a Morrison visa is."

"Probably not. . . . Did she call you?"

"No. I'm sure that the cops read her rights rapidfire, so that neither she nor any of the others understood.

I am going down to Area Six to represent her. Do you want to join me?"

"I sure do. . . . Area Six is where?"

"Diversey and Western. Under the bridge. I'm fighting traffic out here on the Ike. Whoever gets there first, wait for the other."

I ran an electric razor over my face, brewed a cup of instant coffee to take with me, washed my mouth with Scope, sprayed myself with cologne, gobbled a couple of Advil tablets, and dressed in jeans and T-shirt. I grabbed the coffee and a raisin roll and hurried towards the elevators.

It is an absolute given that whenever I am in a rush to get to my car, the three elevators I must traverse slow down so as to make the trip as long as possible. Also, there will be repairs on the spiral ramp so there is a long wait before you get a chance to go down the one available ramp, always facing the possibility that the incompetents who are supposed to manage the traffic flow will foul up and halfway down you will meet a car coming in the opposite direction. Then you will have to take the long way around so that you get stuck in the jams in front of the Drake Hotel and, you should excuse the expression, the *Playboy* Tower caused by taxis pulling in and out of the Drake.

That particular hot summer morning, the Fates decreed heavy traffic on Michigan, a jam getting off it, and a monumental tie-up on Diversey.

I was so foolishly impatient with the delays that it was only as I inched across Damen that I remembered to call Reliable Security.

"Yes Mr. Coyne. We tried to call you at your home early this morning and repeatedly thereafter. It's all quite awful. We can't believe that Mr. O'Hara is doing this thing."

"As your record may show," I said, "Ms. McGrail was at Grand Beach all weekend."

"Yes sir, and she did not attend any meeting on

Thursday. After you dropped her off at her house, she did not leave till she departed for work on Friday morning."

"So."

I had not thought of that angle.

"Should we continue to guard her, Mr. Coyne?"

"Yes, indeed. We expect to have her out by the end of the day. . . . By the way, do your people testify about these sorts of things?"

"Certainly, sir. That's in the contract we sent you."

"Fine!"

I was beginning to feel better, but I should have taken more Advil. My head was still pounding, as if I'd been thrown on the mat by a wrestler twice my size. I arrived at the modern police station at 10:30, just as Cindy's van pulled in. We found a place in the parking lot, and Cindy, leading the way like Grace O'Malley storming a fortress of the O'Flahertys, charged into the police station.

A melancholy captain was leaning against the wall.

"Can't help it, Cindy. It's all your friend's show. We didn't pick them up. He's holding them here until he can get an evening news shot transferring them to 26th and California."

That's the County Courthouse and Jail.

We barged into the lobby of the station to encounter a Zack O'Hara press briefing. He obviously was playing it for both the noon and the five o'clock news.

Zack has been running for governor since the day he was elected state's attorney. He cultivates the image of a good-looking square, a bright, plainspoken, straight-dealing prosecutor, tough and honest, with great respect for the law. The faster he talks, the more honest he seems. In fact, he is not very bright but is as devious as they come. He has also has one of the hardest heads that the South Side of Chicago, notorious for its hardheaded Irish, has ever produced.

This morning he was obviously playing two cards:

the solution to the Art Heist gang card and the xenophobia card. The latter was sweeping the country as candidate Bob Dole suggested making English the only "official language" of the United States and Pete Wilson, having been elected governor of California by running against Mexican-Americans, was now running for the presidency on the same platform.

"I received a tip yesterday that there had been considerable discussion at a certain pub called the Tricolor, where known supporters of the Irish Republican Army gather, about yet another offense by the so-called Art Heist gang. There was a meeting at the aforementioned pub on Thursday night to plan the robbery. Our informant was present and gathered the names. Unfortunately he was unable to get in touch with us in time to stop the theft of the priceless Monet painting. However, acting on this information last night, we arrested every name on his list. All of them—each and every one of them—are illegal aliens in this country. We are continuing our investigations and expect to arraign them tomorrow. I am delighted that we have been able to break this case. I assure the public that I will not tolerate illegal aliens of any nationality in this jurisdiction."

Vigorous, concise, blunt. That's our Zack O'Hara.

Questions erupted from the reporters.

"Have you recovered the paintings yet?"

"Not yet, but I have every reason to expect that we will in the very near future."

"Are you convinced that these young illegals are responsible for all the art heists?"

"We are in the process of establishing that at the present time. We expect that we will be able to do so."

"Will there be any more arrests?"

"If more evidence emerges, we certainly will make more arrests."

Cindy whispered in my ear, "He doesn't have a

thing, Dermot. One tip-off from an informant. Unless the kids snitch on each other, he won't even be able to get an indictment. He's going to have to find out where the paintings are."

"Then why all the fuss?"

"If he's lucky, he may find some evidence. If not, he can ship them all back to Ireland and get publicity on that. People will sigh with relief that the country has been freed of dangerous illegals and forget that Zack didn't recover any of the paintings."

"And if there are more thefts while Nuala's friends are in jail or after they're deported?"

"Then he'll have lost his gamble; the media will climb all over him."

"Sounds like a risky gamble."

"You don't know how much Zack likes to see himself on TV. He's really an Irish cement head."

"Republican."

"Zack," a reporter asked him, "does it bother you that there's a possibility that you'll be deporting people from your own ethnic background?"

"Planted question," Cindy said, this time in a stage whisper.

"Absolutely not. My grandparents were immigrants and they came legally. All immigrants should come legally. Those who come any other way have no right to be here, Irish or any other group."

"You'd think," Cindy said aloud, "that he's the State Department and the Immigration and Naturalization Service. He can't deport anyone."

A couple of reporters turned to her and smiled.

"Hi, Cindy," one of them said. "Good to see you. How are the kids?"

They exchanged information about their respective children, ignoring Zack's continuing pontifications.

"He's finishing," Cindy told me. "Let's bait the jackass in his stable."

She strode up to the temporary podium, elbowed

her way through the crowd of flunkies around O'Hara, and said, "Zack, this is my brother Dermot. He writes. I'm here to represent Nuala McGrail."

He nodded to me, as if I were a trivial flyspeck, and glanced at his notes.

"She's one of the perpetrators, part of the conspiracy," he said proudly.

"You mean *alleged* perpetrators, don't you Zack?"

"She's an illegal alien like the rest of them."

"So I heard you say. Your statements are defamatory and in reckless disregard of the truth. Since those statements went out on WGN and hence across the nation, I intend to file a suit against you in Federal Court this afternoon."

"She's an illegal alien," he repeated. "*And* engaged in an illegal conspiracy."

I felt my fists clench. It wouldn't help matters at all if I assaulted this man. But it sure would make me feel good.

"Still the asshole, huh, Zack? She's *not* illegal. She has a Morrison visa."

The state's attorney frowned, as if he didn't know what such a visa was.

"Have one of your flunkies look it up, Zack," Cindy continued.

She had been a top prosecutor under his predecessors, Rich Daley and Cecil Partee. When Zack took over the office, he purged all the senior personnel of what was supposed to be a nonpolitical staff.

"We lifted that visa," he said triumphantly after peering at his list.

"It may surprise you, asshole, but you have no authority to lift anyone's visa. Only the State Department can do that. Moreover, it's a permanent visa, and even *they* can't lift it unless the person has been convicted of a crime. Give it back to her now, or when I go over to the Dirksen Building this afternoon, I'll ask for a court order mandating you to return it."

"She has already committed a crime . . . and keep a civil tongue in your mouth, Cindy."

"You're a fine one to talk about civility, Zack. Would it surprise you to know that Ms. McGrail was at Grand Beach, Michigan, over the weekend, in plain sight of twelve people? On the night in question, she attended a wiener roast on the beach."

"Who are these people?"

"My family."

"I don't care. She still attended the meeting where the conspiracy was hatched."

"No, she didn't," I said.

Cindy looked startled.

"You can't prove that," Zack said, growling at me.

"Yes, I can."

"How?"

"At my instigation, she was being protected by Reliable Security Agency. They will testify that she returned to her apartment on Thursday night after singing at the Tricolor—and by the way, Mr. State's Attorney, it's pronounced Trickcolor—and did not leave till the next morning."

Cindy stared at me with her bright brown eyes wide open in amazement.

"Why did you have her under surveillance?"

I turned to Cindy like someone appearing before a Senate investigating committee.

"Do I have to answer that, Counselor?"

"Of course you don't have to. You may if you wish."

"Because someone had made threats of sexual violence against her."

"I'll look into this matter, Cindy. It sounds pretty thin to me. I'll have Slim come talk to you."

"Aren't I the lucky one! First, I see my client. Then, I warn you, if she is not released by noon, I will carry out all my threats *and* I'll stop by 26th and California for a writ of habeas corpus."

"You know I don't yield to threats, Cindy."

"We'll see about that. Now, I want to talk to my client."

"I'll arrange for that."

"NOW!"

"I said I'll arrange for that."

"Mary Jane," Cindy said to the reporter who had asked her about her children, "is everyone staying around?"

"Sure, we're all supposed to get pictures of the alleged perpetrators being taken off to the concentration camp at 26th and California."

"How soon do I have to call a press conference to get what I say on the noon news?"

Smart girl, my big sister.

"Are you going after Zack?"

"Naturally."

"Most of us will want to do it live. It's a great lead. What's the story?"

"I represent one of the alleged perpetrators. She's got an ironclad alibi. Moreover, she is not illegal but has a Morrison visa which Zack has lifted, a clear violation of due process of law."

"I'll spread it around, Cindy. The guys will love it."

"I thought they might."

A cop appeared, asked Cindy if she was the attorney for Ms. McGrail and conducted us to an interrogation room like those you see on *NYPD Blue,* a walless concrete cell with a wooden table and three uncomfortable wooden chairs.

We waited another fifteen minutes before they delivered Nuala to us.

She looked terrible, if one dares to say that about such a beautiful woman. She reminded me of the pictures one sees of Bosnian refugee women staggering down a road after an air raid—ashen, exhausted, confused. She was wearing shorts and sweatshirt and sandals.

Tears poured down her dirty face at the sight of us.

She ran into my arms and then embraced Cindy.

"Holy Mother of God, am I glad to see you two!"

"I propose to act as your attorney, Nuala. Do you approve?"

"I've been praying all morning that you'd be coming."

"They read you your rights? You had the right to phone a lawyer?"

"The man read us something, but so fast we couldn't hear it."

"Typical," Cindy made a mark on her yellow legal-size notepad, without which lawyers, as everyone knows, cannot travel.

"It was terrible frightening. Late at night. There's a loud knock on the friggin' door, and before we can answer, don't the guards—I mean the police—come rushing in and tell us we're all under arrest. Most of us thought it was a terrible dream—and being summer, none of us are wearing all that much. They tell us to dress and they half-watch us as we do it and say terrible things. Then they drag us down here. And aren't the television cameras grinding away when we get out of their lorry? This disgusting man named O'Hara shouts at us that we're common criminals and will be treated as such, and then they throw us into cells and lock us up. Didn't I think that the friggin' Black and Tans had come to Chicago?"

She collapsed again in my arms.

Cindy reassured her, "I intend to have you out of here shortly after noon. You were at Grand Beach all weekend. You couldn't have been involved in stealing the Monets from the Armacost Gallery. Moreover, you were home in bed when the alleged conspiracy meeting happened on Thursday night. Finally, you are not an illegal alien. I intend to constrain the state's attorney to return your Morrison visa, which he has lifted illegally."

"How will you be doing that?"

"Just wait and see. You'll enjoy it."

Nuala continued to cling to me. I helped her over to a chair, sat down next to her, and took her hand firmly in mine.

My head continued to pound.

"Officer," Cindy said, as she opened the door, "Would you ask Mr. Keegan to come in here, please?"

"Sure thing, Ms. Hurley."

"Slim Keegan"—she turned to us—"is an ugly, slimy, vile mound of flesh who, for some reason, the State's Attorney for Cook County thinks is a genius at negotiation. I assume—and indeed almost hope—that he will stall. Then," she said with a broad grin, "future sister-in-law, I'll put on a show for you that is the equivalent of yours on the tennis court."

Nuala turned purple and refused to look in my direction.

"You may be a bit premature in that appellation, Cindy," I said mildly.

Nuala turned yet more purple. She still would not look at me, but I saw that she was smiling. Good enough for her.

"We'll see . . . ah, I note the advent of the all-wise Deputy First Assistant State's Attorney Keegan. . . . Slim, this is my client, Ms. McGrail whom you have arrested illegally and whose right to due process of law you have violated. The gentleman is Dermot Michael Coyne, who, in addition to being a distinguished and famous literary figure, is also my brother."

"Yeah? What's he doing here?"

"Slim" Keegan was every bit as ugly as Cindy had said, only more so. He collapsed into a chair, which he overflowed, sighed loudly, pulled his already-open tie more open, and glared at me.

"He has certain information that you and your lord and master should take into account before you decide to hold my client any longer."

I yielded my chair to my sister, leaned against the wall, and tried to look ominous.

"Yeah, well, Cindy, I hate to disappoint an old friend like you, but it doesn't look too good for your client. She's an illegal, and she's involved in a conspiracy to rob art galleries. So I say we continue to hold her prior to arraignment."

"Obviously, Mr. O'Hara didn't rehearse our conversation with you. Item: Ms. McGrail is not an illegal, but has a valid Morrison visa which your office has lifted illegally. Item: She was in Michigan all last weekend where she was seen by scores of witnesses, including an auxiliary bishop of this archdiocese. Item: At the time of the alleged theft, she was participating at a wiener roast in full view of at least a dozen adults. Item: When this alleged conspiracy meeting took place, Ms. McGrail was home in bed. I presume that, for an attorney of your perspicacity, I don't have to outline the motions for relief I can enter against your office."

"Who are these people in Michigan?"

"My family."

"Yeah. I'm not impressed."

"If it comes to that, I suspect a judge will be."

"And this proof that she wasn't at the meeting?"

Cindy cocked an eyebrow at me. I took a deep breath and hoped that Cindy's alleged future sister-in-law would not go ballistic in my direction.

"Last week a gentleman approached me at the Tricolor Pub—and please note the proper pronunciation of that name, Mr. Keegan—and made certain vile threats of sexual assault against Ms. McGrail. Since she had worked for, uh, *with* me in Dublin on certain matters and since she was very new in this country, I thought it proper to make sure that she was properly protected. I therefore hired Reliable Security to guard her. It is my impression that the off-duty cops who work for Reliable would like nothing better than to shove certain materials up the various orifices of you and Mr. O'Hara, and therefore will be delighted to testify that Ms. McGrail never left her apartment after returning from her interlude of singing at the Tricolor."

"Yeah?"

"Yeah."

"Who is this guy who allegedly made the threats?"

"Billy Hernon," Nuala supplied the name.

"Yeah? He's involved in this art-heist business, too?"

"Since your boss didn't mention him this morning, I presume you have not apprehended him."

"We'll get him. IRA slime."

"Yeah?"

"Yeah. . . . Tricolor, huh? Cheap, dirty pub," Slim said with a loud sigh.

In fact, it was more than a sigh. His breathing came in heavy and exhausted gasps, doubtless the result of the necessity of dragging his outsize body around.

"The singing, however, is excellent!"

Cindy was laughing, Nuala Anne was looking at me with eyes shining proudly. So I wasn't in trouble.

"You have no probable cause to hold her," Cindy proclaimed like a judge ruling from the bench.

Though seated in a chair, which I thought might break at any moment, his breathing became more labored. Unless he changed his lifestyle, Slim didn't have many years of life left. He should cut down on all his big (well-done) steaks and mountains of mashed potatoes. However, I would not tell him so.

He struggled to his feet.

"I say fuck it all. We'll hold her."

"Any special reason?"

"We gotta check out all this shit of yours."

"You expect to find that my family did not see her at Grand Beach all weekend and that the Reliable Security people cannot verify that she did not go to your precious meeting? You do not believe there is probable cause to release her—and return her Morrison visa?"

"I say we check out all your shit."

"You could release her and if my statements do not hold up, you could then rearrest her."

"Well, we're not going to do that."

"I see. And I say, Slim, that you're on very thin ice in this matter."

"Fuck you!" he said with a noisy belch, and lumbered out of the room.

"Charming fellow," I said.

"Yes, indeed," Cindy agreed.

"This is a friggin' terrible country with men like him and those who pulled us out of bed with hardly any clothes on last night."

"In many ways," Cindy said, "you're right, Nuala. Yet every country has criminal-justice personnel like the ones you have had the great misfortune to encounter today. However, I know of no other country in the world—not even Germany, where they let madmen who cut up teenage tennis stars go back out on the street—where relief from men like that can be obtained so quickly."

Nuala nodded dubiously.

"Wait and see. Unless O'Hara comes up with stronger evidence than he has against all your friends, he'll have to release them in another couple of days, which is more than would happen in your native land, future sister-in-law."

Nuala blushed again and averted her eyes from me. However she didn't argue against the appellation.

PROPOSE TO HER TODAY, the Adversary said, having appeared out of nowhere as he usually does. SHE CERTAINLY ISN'T GOING TO REFUSE. THAT'LL SOLVE ALL YOUR PROBLEMS.

"You gotta be kidding," I told him.

LOOK, ASSHOLE, PEOPLE DON'T MEET THEIR TRUE

LOVES AT THE TIMES THEY THINK ARE APPROPRIATE. THEY MEET THEM WHEN GOD WANTS THEM TO MEET THEM.

"You sound like Prester George."

YOU KNOW I'M AN INTERNALIZED PRESTER GEORGE.

I banished him. He went reluctantly.

Nuala, who naturally was unaware of this internal dialogue with my internalized brother, nodded in agreement with Cindy.

"Sure, isn't that the truth? They can hold you a long time under the Official Secrets Act without making any charges at all. I'm sorry for attacking this wonderful country. I'm not meself this morning."

Cindy glanced at her watch.

"I must go meet my friends in the media. Tell you what, Dermot, why don't you and herself watch television from here?"

"No TV."

"We'll get one."

She opened the door to the concrete room and said to the African-American cop lounging at the door, "Albert, can you do me a big favor? I'm about to have a press conference. Would you be able to bring in a TV set so that my brother and Ms. McGrail can watch the conference?"

"Sure thing, Cindy. I think most of our folks will want to watch in person, so we won't need the set."

Cindy left for her press conference. Albert came in with a small color set, turned it on, adjusted the rabbit ears, and said, "I've put in on Channel 9. It gets the best reception. And they'll certainly carry your sister's press conference. Great lady, your sister."

"Amen! It's good that Channel 9 comes through clearly here. That way you can watch the Cub games."

"They're a little discouraging aren't they, Mr. Coyne?"

"Dermot," I said, "and we must all have faith."

We both chuckled and then he left the room. I turned to face Nuala Anne's inevitable first question.

"What is Reliable Security, Derm?"

"It's a company which provides a wide range of private security services. Does the things cops can't do because they're too busy filling out forms. Nice thing is that most of its people are cops, of both genders, moonlighting part time. So they do the things they would like to do—protect people—and get paid for it, which helps their wives or husbands and their families."

"Isn't that a grand idea?" She nodded her head vigorously. "I suppose we have something like that in Ireland?"

"Securicor, I think."

"And you hired them to take care of me?"

"Your man frightened me a little."

"Wasn't that kind and thoughtful of you, Dermot Michael?"

"I'm glad you think so."

"Sure, at another time, wouldn't I have screamed something terrible about your interfering with me life?"

She grinned up at me, a tentative little-girl leprechaun—and the leprechaun's pot of gold in her smile!

"Maybe that's why I didn't tell you."

"Well, I'm terrible grateful anyway. And Dermot . . . ?

"Some of the times when I'm screaming something terrible and making a gobshite of meself, all you have to do is tell me to fock off and I'll shut up."

"Eventually."

She laughed and threw her arms around me and hugged me ferociously.

"I love you something awful, Dermot Michael Coyne."

The Adversary had been correct. If I had said to her, then and there, something like "Would you ever accept that title, me sister wanted to give you?" we would have left the Area Six lockup an engaged couple.

I simply couldn't take advantage of her present misery. No way. However, I knew now that I wouldn't ever be rejected.

Small help that was.

An anchorperson babbled for a moment; then Cindy appeared on the screen.

"Och, doesn't your sister look beautiful with her pretty face and her lovely hair, Derm?"

"She does, Nuala. But there's more to the show than that."

I had seen Cindy play such games before and had a vague idea of what might happen.

"Good afternoon," she began. "My name is Cynthia Coyne Hurley. I have the honor to represent Ms. Nuala Anne McGrail, who is one of those accused by the state's attorney this morning. I believe that there is a prima facie case that my client could not have been involved either in the Armacost Gallery theft itself or in the alleged conspiracy meeting. In the first matter, she spent the weekend at Grand Beach, Michigan, and was seen by many people through the week, at Mass and in other activities. When the crime was allegedly committed, she was in plain sight of twelve adults and many children on the beach at a wiener roast. At the time of the purported meeting, she was under the protection of a high-quality security firm because of threats which had been made on her physical safety. The agents of that firm will testify that she was in her apartment during the entire time of the meeting and did not leave until the following morning. Moreover, she is a legal alien with a so-called Morrison visa which Mr. O'Hara's people have illegally removed from her possession.

"I have attempted to negotiate with Mr. O'Hara concerning her release. I have so far been unsuccessful. Therefore I will seek a writ of habeas corpus this afternoon. Moreover, Mr. O'Hara has defamed her in reckless disregard of the truth by asserting that she is an illegal alien even though she had a valid visa about which he knew. Since this was done on a superchannel, among other stations, the defamation can be assumed to have been national. Accordingly I will file a suit in the Federal District Court for Northern Illinois, charging that Mr. O'Hara did willingly and maliciously defame Ms. McGrail by charging her with a crime, namely immigrating illegally to this country. Finally, I will also seek an order from the same District Court commanding Mr. O'Hara to return Ms. McGrail's visa, which he has taken from her without due process of the law. I will hold in reserve a damage suit against Mr. O'Hara for false arrest."

Ms. McGrail jumped up and down, clapped her hands, and did a little dance.

"Isn't she a grand woman, Dermot Michael? Ah, don't I wish I had that presence?"

I took a big chance.

"She does law, Nuala; you do song. Both of you have enormous presence when you're doing your thing."

"Law is more important," she said rather lamely.

"Woman, it is not."

"Shush, Derm, let's listen to what herself is saying."

"You ask why Mr. O'Hara insists on holding my client? Beats me. You'll have to ask him."

Bemused smile.

"The other alleged perpetrators? I represent only Ms. McGrail. So far I have heard no evidence to persuade me that there are grounds for even a misdemeanor charge."

"When do you expect your client to be released?"

"Immediately, if not sooner."

"With whom was she staying in Michigan?"

"With my family."

"Why, Cindy?"

"She and one of my siblings cooperated in solving a mystery in Ireland. There is a possibility of a romantic attachment there."

"Humph!" Nuala snorted.

She did not seem particularly upset.

I didn't say a frigging word. Everyone was closing in on me.

The press conference faded away. The reporter told the anchorperson that State's Attorney O'Hara was unavailable for comment.

"*Well*," Cindy said as she dashed back into the interrogation room, "that should do it. What did you think, Nuala?"

Nuala blessed her with a hug.

"Weren't you grand? And isn't it wonderful your family likes me? What would I be doing without you?"

"I was just the first Irish lawyer that got here, Nuala. There'll be a ton of them this afternoon. We've got Zack in a real bind this time."

"Will me friends be deported?"

"I'm afraid so. They are here illegally. But I also think that once they're cleared, there'll be many Irish lawyers figuring out how to get them back in the country legally, which will be a lot better for them."

"You think they'll be cleared?" I asked.

"What do you think, Nuala?"

"Sure the whole frigging lot of them couldn't come up with a good conspiracy if their lives depended on it. That Billy Hernon is another matter."

"Do you know where he is?"

"I'm sure he's out of the country."

"What went on at the meeting?"

"Me friends said that Billy did a lot of talking about special orders from GHQ and the resumption of the fighting and the need to obtain funds by whatever means. He didn't mention any specific plans though."

"There's your man on television."

This time "your man" was Gerry Adams.

"I cannot speak for fringe groups over which we have no control. However, as I've said repeatedly, we have chosen the path of peace. We have suspended all operations. That includes robberies to raise funds. After all that President Clinton has done for us, it would be mad to attempt anything like that. I categorically deny that any of our units are involved in the theft of fine art in Chicago."

"That settles that," I said.

"Wasn't he grand? Sure, if we have peace it will be because of him. And John Hume, too."

The poor shy child was still an excitable nervous wreck. The downs and up of the tumultuous morning had pushed her to the brink of hysteria.

A very young and very embarrassed assistant state's attorney (female) entered the interrogation room.

"Ms. McGrail," she said, keeping her eyes glued to the floor, "here are your papers, including your visa. You are free to go now. We ask, however, that you remain in the vicinity of Chicago. Please sign this receipt for your documents."

Nuala became very formal and self-possessed, another persona flowing into place.

"Of course," she said politely, as she signed the receipt. "Thank you very much. I appreciate your cooperation."

The kid grinned sheepishly and fled the room.

"That was very nice, Nuala," Cindy said. "Very generous of you."

"Sure, it wasn't her frigging fault, was it, now?"

The media people swarmed around us shouting questions as we left the station.

"Do you want to make a statement, Nuala?"

Does a bee like honey?

A new persona slipped into place: Nuala the smooth, charming, gracious public figure.

She waited till the media arranged themselves around her.

"I want to thank Ms. Hurley for obtaining my release and recovering my visa for me. I am delighted that the American justice system works so quickly. I'm looking forward to a good night's sleep and returning to my job tomorrow. I'm also grateful for your support."

"Do you think your friends are guilty?"

"I don't believe that my friends were involved in stealing art."

"Are they illegal aliens?"

"You'd have to ask them."

"What do you think of Mr. O'Hara?"

"He has a very difficult job. All of us make mistakes occasionally."

"Who is the romantic interest in Ms. Hurley's family?"

Bright smile.

"That would be telling, now, wouldn't it?"

Then she ducked away from them and walked Cindy and me around to the back of the parking lot.

"I'll buy you lunch."

"We're not dressed for it!" Cindy protested.

"You won't need to be."

Inside the Benz, Cindy launched into a paean of my lover's performance with the media.

No one in my family seem to comprehend that herself was an actress. Give her a stage—and all the world was a stage for her—and a role to play, and she would rise to the occasion; and she would love the excitement of playing the role. When the role ended, she would revert to her previous persona, on this occasion a disheveled and traumatized shy child.

I had noted that "my" had replaced the "me" of her usual speech and that the brogue had faded. There was enough of it left to be charming, but it was T.C.D.

and not Galway. None of this was cunning or artificial. It was merely Nuala.

I took them to an "ethnic" restaurant on Irving Park, across from St. Benedict's Church. Cindy plowed into Hungarian goulash, while herself nibbled at a hamburger after she had taken it out of its bun.

"Just not hungry, Derm."

"Your privilege, Nuala."

"That goulash thing looks grand."

"I'll bring you back here again. It's where I hang out before Cub games."

Nuala, with the Irish obsession with all things sporting, had been "studying" baseball, though she did not understand it nor why one would be a Cub fan, and themselves on a rebuilding program which started half a century ago.

After lunch I drove Cindy back to her van and turned on Western Avenue.

"Dermot!" Nuala gasped, hand at her mouth. "Me job! Sure, won't they have fired me altogether?"

"I don't think so. What's the phone number?"

I punched it on my car phone. Your man congratulated her, praised her for her courage and poise, and told her to take the rest of the day and the next one off. Nuala was shyly grateful, but hardly a church mouse.

She pecked my cheek when we pulled up to her house.

"Dermot, I'm going to take a shower and have meself a nice nap. May I call you this evening?"

"Woman, you may."

"Will those nice men be guarding me?"

"They will."

"Thank you ever so much."

Another very brief kiss.

She permitted me to open up the car door for her and then dashed up the steps before I could offer to accompany her. At the top, as usual, she turned and waved.

I called Reliable just to make sure they were still on the case.

Then I drove home, swallowed two more Advils, and headed for the swimming pool.

As I swam I wondered whether the new rules which were supposed to govern our relationship were still in force.

I also wondered where Billy Hernon was.

8

ON THE five o'clock evening news, the media people were giving Zack O'Hara a very hard time.

When the network news began, my phone rang.

"Dermot Coyne."

"The seanachie?"

"The very same."

"Derm, would you ever come over to my house for supper? I'll make you a ham-and-cheese sandwich and brew you a nice pot of tea."

She pronounced it "samich," just as we had done on the West Side of Chicago.

"An offer I can't refuse."

"I want to talk about Camp Douglas."

"Grand."

In preparation for this conversation, I opened my file on Camp Douglas and reviewed what I knew about the official side of the "Great Camp Douglas Conspiracy" story.

The principal document and the source of all subsequent history of the Camp Douglas Conspiracy was the text of a long speech by William Bross, an editor of the *Chicago Tribune* and a rabid Republican. It was published in the review of the Chicago Historical Society and represents a paper that Bross read at a meeting of that society on June 18, 1878, thirteen years after the alleged conspiracy. It is titled "History of Camp Douglas," but is, in fact, a history of the purported conspiracy. Until very recently, most historians of the city took his report at face value.

There were some preliminary facts about the case, facts concerning which there seems to be no controversy:

In the spring of 1864, the Confederacy, close to despair because the war was turning decisively against the South, sent a secret agent, one Thomas R. Hines, to Canada. He was to determine whether it was possible to use escaped Southern prisoners in Canada, Confederate sympathizers from that country, and Union citizens who leaned towards supporting the Confederate cause to begin serious war campaigns behind the Union lines. It is argued that Hines had $800,000 in federal money to finance these plans, but since that would have been $5 million in Confederate dollars, the sum may be an exaggeration. The Confederacy also dispatched three "commissioners" to oversee the work of Hines and his agents.

Inside the camp, massive escapes were being planned at the same time. The "supreme council" of the prisoners had organized the camp into "regiments" and "brigades" which were to storm out of the camp after a hundred volunteers, willing to lose their lives in the attempt, overwhelmed the guards on duty and commandeered their guns.

Hines was persuaded that a combination of pro-Confederacy "Butternuts" (downstate Democrats similar to the "Hoosiers" in Indiana and the "Buckeyes" in Ohio), opponents to the war in Chicago, like the Sons of Liberty and the Golden Knights and other "Copperhead" groups and Southern officers smuggled into Chicago might enable him to break into Camp Douglas, free the prisoners, and burn Chicago to the ground.

The plan was communicated by code to the "supreme council" inside the camp, though the links between the two sets of conspirators were thin. The first target day was July 4, when the Democratic National Convention was meeting in Chicago. Why would you burn the city down when a political party opposed to the war was meeting? Would they join the burning of Chicago? Not very likely. Or would they be burned by the liberated prisoners?

The convention was postponed till August 29. The breakout was scheduled for July 20 and then August 29. Again, nothing happened. Hines expected 5,000 Copperheads to attack the camp. At the most he had twenty-five men.

Yet another phase of the conspiracy was allegedly set for the day before the November election. Whether or not that was a real conspiracy is a matter of debate. At that time, however, the prisoners staged their own attempt at a breakout; it was easily suppressed by the guards who had been warned that it was coming.

"Deacon" Bross adds rich detail to this story. He claimed that save for the vigilance of General Benjamin Sweet, the commandant of the camp and himself, Chicago would indeed have been burned to the ground. He begins with the first of the alleged plans to break into the camp at the time of the Democratic convention.

Before the convention assembled I was standing near the *Journal* office then in front of the Tremont House when a friend said to me, "Do you know there are ten thousands of arms secreted in cellars and basements within four blocks of us?" I said I presumed that the rebels have that many hid in different parts of the city. During the afternoon, several similar stories were told by others, and in the morning, thinking General Sweet should know them, I called on him at Camp Douglas. He listened to the fact and suspicions I narrated with great attention; he said he would investigate them and call at my office the next day at eleven o'clock.

I had previously, if any, a mere casual acquaintance with General Sweet, but his close attention and careful analysis of the facts I had given him gave me great confidence in his ability and fitness for the important post he occupied. He called promptly as appointed and I found his entire detective force had been busy all night searching the city through, that they had verified some of our suspicions, and got track of many more. He had, subsequently, trusted men in every Golden Circle of the Knights and by ten o'clock the next day he knew what had occurred and the plans that were made all over the city. Almost every leading rebel that arrived from the South or from Canada was spotted and tracked to his den and could not move, even for the most trivial purpose, but sharp loyal eyes were upon him.

For a week or more I saw General Sweet frequently, and I found that his detectives tracked like sleuth-hounds every scent and rumor to its source, and his plans and the way he carried them out filled my highest ideal of the ability needed to cope with his adversaries, and I therefore soon gave the matter little further care and attention.

On Saturday, August 26th, the Democratic politicians, many of them very respectable gentlemen, with their blowers and strikers, began to arrive. As day after day passed, the crowd increased till the whole city seemed alive with a motley crew of big-shouldered, blear-eyed, bottle-nosed, whisky-blotched vagabonds—the very excrescence and sweepings of the slums and sinks of all the cities in the nation. I sat often at my window on Michigan Avenue, and saw the filthy stream of degraded humanity swagger along to the Wigwam on the lake shore and wondered how the city could be saved from burning and plunder, and our wives and daughters from a far more dreadful fate. Many besides myself would have been in despair had we not trusted in the good providence of God, General Sweet, and the brave boys under him. We knew that he had small squads of men with signs and passwords in all the alleys in the central portions of the city ready to concentrate at the point of danger at any moment.

In the loyal states, and in our own city especially, venomous Copperheads kept up their warfare to the very end. They were bent on letting loose the ten thousand prisoners in Camp Douglas, that they might burn and destroy the city, and thus prevent an election here. And besides, they had lists of scores of our leading citizens whose property and lives could alone atone for the part they had acted throughout the war. General Sweet and his brave officers at Camp Douglas were equally active and vigilant. The appointments at the post were strengthened by every means in his power, so that as small a force as possible might safely guard the prisoners and a large detail might be spared to station in the city at the time of election. Detectives were kept intensely busy to watch every suspicious character that arrived by the cars, and some were sent to Canada to learn from officers there what villainous schemes they were plotting for the destruction of Chicago. Others went to the virulent Copperhead districts in central and southern Illinois and found that large detachments were to be sent here, ready for carnage and plunder, should the prisoners break out, and in any event to vote early and often in the infected sections of the city.

Hence, on the Saturday before the election Tuesday, the 8th of November, General Sweet knew where all the dens of the Knights of the Golden Circle were, and what was going on in them; what gangs were expected from our own state, and what officers were expected from Canada to lead them and the rebel hordes in Douglas in their bloody raid upon the city. To know them was to know how to provide against and defeat them. To be more specific: At first it proposed to let loose the prisoners two weeks earlier, but for various reasons the thing was postponed till the night before the election. During the previous week, delegations began to arrive from Fayette and Christian countries, in this State. Bushwhackers journeyed north from

Missouri and Kentucky. Some came from Indiana, and rebel officers from Canada. But so perfectly had General Sweet made himself master of their movements that in the early morning of Monday, he arrested Colonel St. Leger Grenfel, Morgan's adjutant general, in company with J. T. Shanks, an escaped prisoner of war; Colonel Vincent Marmaduke, brother of the rebel general of that name; Brigadier General Charles Walsh, of the Sons of Liberty; Captain Cantril, of Morgan's command, and others. In Walsh's house, General Sweet's officers captured two cartloads of large-sized revolvers, loaded and capped, and two hundred muskets and a large quantity of ammunition. In his official report, General Sweet says most of these rebel officers were in the city in August, on the same bloody errand that brought them here when arrested. When the officers were secured, General Sweet's boys turned their attention to certain parties of a baser sort. Twenty-seven were arrested at the "Fort Donaldson House"—a base misnomer, of course—all well armed; another lot was captured on North Water Street, and by evening Camp Douglas had an accession of at least a hundred of these wretches. During the day the "secesh" sympathizers telegraphed their friends in the central and southern parts of the State that the trap had been sprung; parties on the way were notified of the fate that awaited them here, and they got off at Wilmington and Joliet; but some fifty who had missed the notice arrived on Monday evening, and were at once duly honored with an escort to Camp Douglas. Some of these visitors had boasted in Vandalia, on their way here, to intimate friends, that "they would hear of hell in a few days," and generally they were of the most desperate class of bushwhacking vagabonds.

The plan, as derived from confessions of the rebel officers and other sources, was to attack Camp Douglas, to release the prisoners there, with them to seize the polls, allowing none but the Copperhead ticket to be voted, and to stuff the boxes sufficiently to secure the city, county, and

State for McClellan and Pendleton, then to utterly sack the city, burning and destroying every description of property except what they could appropriate to their own use and that of their Southern brethren, to lay the city waste and carry off its money and stores to Jeff Davis's dominions. Thanks to a kind Providence, all this was averted.

The degraded rabble, by the way, were Irish Catholic Democrats whom many Republicans like Bross feared even more than they feared Jeff Davis.

Winners write history and losers don't. More than a decade after the end of the war, Bross's account became the received wisdom. In desperation, the South had thrown together a massive plot to seize victory from the jaws of defeat. Southern agents had put all the pieces of this brilliant conspiracy in place, and if it had not been for the ingenuity of General Sweet, the conspiracy would have worked.

I put aside the Bross document and pondered it again. Despite its high-flown rhetoric, it did describe a situation which was consistent with the situation in the North while the War dragged on. Granting some exaggeration, did the story not seem plausible?

There almost certainly was an uprising in the prison on the night of the arrest of the plotters. Captain Shurly, the second in command and no friend of Colonel Sweet, which was his actual rank at the time he smashed the conspiracy, confirms that fact:

In October, 1864, one of the prisoners requested an interview with the commandant of the post, General Sweet. The message was sent to headquarters. In the absence of General Sweet, I ordered the prisoner sent to my office. He told me that for some time there had been an organization amongst the prisoners of war to break out of the prison square—and that one hundred men had taken an obligation to lead the way, to break the fence, attack the guard in rear of camp, and in the confusion that *would* ensue, the 11,000 prisoners taken in charge would escape. He said that at eight that evening was the time appointed—this was about 6 P.M. that the interview mentioned took place. It was a cloudy evening, and dark—looking like rain. After dismissing the prisoner, I started for the prison square. The officer in charge told me there seemed to be an unusual activity among the prisoners—advised me not to go round without a guard. This, I knew, would attract attention, if not suspicion. At this time the barracks occupied by the prisoners were in rows raised on posts, and each barrack contained from one hundred and fifty to two hundred men. I noticed there was an unusual stir among the prisoners in the barracks. After completing the tour, I returned to headquarters satisfied that there might be truth in the statement of my "spy." I at once sent an order to the commanding officer of the Eighth regiment to take post on the south and west of the camp. I ordered the Pennsylvania regiment on the rear of that, and around it. I had notified the officer in command of the guard of what might be expected, at the same time had strengthened the guard by turning out the other two reliefs. The rain began to fall, and it seemed to me that the camp was unusually quiet. The disposition of the troops had been made so quietly that the prisoners had not suspected it. I greatly regretted the absence of General Sweet; but I carried out his plan to the best of my ability. Eight o'clock had scarcely sounded, when *crash!* went some of the planks from the rear fence, and the one hundred men rushed for the opening. One volley from the guard, who were prepared for them, and the prisoners recoiled, gave up, and retreated to their barracks. Eighteen of the most determined got out, but in less time than I can relate it, quiet was restored. I had the Pennsylvania regiment gradually close in from the outer circle of the race course to the camp, and recaptured all of those that had escaped. I think eight or ten were wounded, but they gradually recovered.

I put the two documents side by side. They were the basic primary sources for the theory of the Great Camp Douglas Conspiracy—one written in baroque style and the other in the plain language of a military officer. Something had happened all right, no doubt about it. The captain seemed much less worried about a prison outbreak than the editor. What had actually happened?

I packed the two documents, which I had already given to Nuala along with some commentary of my own, in my briefcase.

I added the final document, the one which in my own head I was already calling "Irish Lace."

9

WHEN I arrived at her apartment, Nuala Holmes, brilliant detective, was wearing jeans, a blue blouse, sandals, a nice scent, and no makeup. She was well scrubbed, and her hair was tied in a ponytail. Her apartment was again as neat as a nun's cell. No nap for her this afternoon.

I resisted an urge to crush her in my arms and hold her forever. Instead, I brushed her lips modestly, once and then, for good measure, again.

Even that transient affection seemed like pure glory. It was, after all, the first time I had been invited to her house for supper.

Hopelessly in love, was I? I'd been in that condition since O'Neill's pub, across the street from St. Anne's Church (C. of I.), down the road from Trinity College.

An old window fan was striving mightily to drag fresh air into the room. It didn't seem to make much difference in either the humidity or the heat.

She placed the ham and cheese—in a fresh croissant—on the coffee table and a pasta salad next to it. Then she poured the promised nice cup of tea. The show was elegant and graceful, winsomeness and sex appeal (however muted) compensating for the sparseness of my supper.

"There's a second sandwich if you want one."

"I'm sure I will."

"And some chocolate ice cream, too."

"I'll need that."

"Didn't I know you would?"

She sat in the easy chair across the table from me and spread a paper napkin on one of her knees.

"I like the salad. Where did you get it?"

She giggled.

"Sure, didn't I make it meself?"

"Just for me?"

"Well, for both of us."

The room was heavy with erotic tension. I shifted uneasily. As tantalizing as the prospect might be, I was not quite ready to be seduced.

Then, with the equivalent of a wave of her magic wand, she dissolved the lustful fog.

"Your man's a gobshite," she said brandishing the complete text of Deacon Bross's paper. "A terrible liar altogether."

"Indeed?"

"Your other man"—she jabbed a finger at Shurly's account—"is telling the truth but not the whole truth."

"So?"

"Where's the second half of this report?" she demanded.

"This is a memoir," I handed the text to her, "written many years later by one Letitia Walsh, daughter of the alleged ringleader of the conspiracy."

"I was wondering when you were going to get to her."

I was taken aback. I had told Nuala nothing about the Irish Lace. How did she know about Letitia?

I shivered as she read the memoir.

My dear children and grandchildren,
Many of you have asked me recently whether your grandfather and great grandfather, Lord have mercy on his soul, was really part of the

Camp Douglas Conspiracy thirty years ago. Some of you have even shown me that terrible article by William Bross, one of the greatest liars who ever lived, in the Chicago Historical Society Journal. *"Deacon" Bross, as everyone called him because of his sanctimonious hypocrisy, dreamed up the "conspiracy" as an excuse for arresting Democrats at the time of the 1864 election. Colonel Benjamin Sweet made the dream a reality, most likely because the Deacon, who was president of the* Tribune, *was influential enough to win Sweet his brigadier's stars. I must note that the Deacon told the story of how he learned about the conspiracy many different ways. The one he narrates in the Historical Society journal is the fourth or fifth version, unlike any of the previous ones.*

You have suggested that I put down on paper the true story of what happened during that terrible summer. I believe that is a good suggestion. The truth should be told somewhere so some people will know what a terrible criminal Colonel Sweet was.

Let me put three questions before you as I prepare to write down the story.

(1) If Granddad was a traitor and a conspirator, why did his cartage company haul the United States mail for years after the war? Why does it continue to haul the mail now, even after he has gone home to Jesus?

(2) If such a terrible crime was really committed, why was he pardoned after only a few months in jail?

(3) Why did Mr. Lincoln, a man for whom I have never had much respect, refuse to believe in the Conspiracy and order one of the men released immediately?

I cannot believe that if Mr. Lincoln had not

been killed by that awful fool John Wilkes Booth
there ever would have been a trial.

I believe all the trouble started because of our
house. When Daddy came home from the Mexican War and left the Army, he built the house at
what is now Ellis Avenue, even before Senator
Douglas, Lord have mercy on him, great man that
he was, bought his huge tract of land along the
Lake. When they built Camp Douglas, its walls
were only two blocks away from our house.

When Daddy built the house, there was nothing
out there at all besides prairie land as far as we
could see in any direction. To the north there was
always a smudge of smoke on the horizon, but
that was all we saw of Chicago. The three of us,
the "three sisters," as we were always called, were
only little girls when we moved out there. Your
Aunts Mary and Margaret, the first a year younger
than me and the second two years younger, and I
loved the house and the prairie. It was a big house
with plenty of room for everyone and lots left
over, even though Mommy and Daddy eventually
had twelve children. We played in the house and
played in the garden and played on the lawns. We
never needed neighbor children because there
were so many of us.

Daddy didn't want any of us growing up in the
city because it was such a horrible, dirty, foul
place.

"We must not pretend it's not there, children.
We must not hide from the truth. But it is one
thing to know about the place and face its sinfulness and quite another to live in it all the time."

In those days I never was quite sure what
Daddy meant by "sinfulness." Later I found out
what he meant and I was quite shocked. I am still
shocked by what men do to women in some of the
buildings in the city.

But we all did travel in on coach every day to St. Xavier's Academy and the Mercy nuns or to St. Patrick's Academy and the Christian Brothers. The city was scary at first, but we quickly got over it and hardly noticed it on rides to school and then back to home every day. We all stayed in school till we were fifteen which is more than most young women did in those days. After we left school, we made lace for sale and helped towards paying for our living expenses. Daddy was not poor, but there were, after all, twelve hungry mouths to feed. At least there was food for us, unlike the poor men in Camp Douglas.

Mom was quite accomplished, as many of you remember. She could sing and play the spinet in the parlor and make drapes and curtains and read to us from wonderful books. All of the girls were taught to be accomplished, too. The most fun for us was when Grandma, Mom's mother, would teach us to make lace. Margaret and Mary and I became enthusiastic lace makers and all of us still are, even if our eyes become a little tired these days. I'm sure you've all heard me say it a thousand times, still I want to say in writing for any young women who might read this memoir in years to come: lace making is a very artistic skill. Once you've learned the basics, you can put into the lace almost any design that you imagine while you're working on it. Lace making is both challenging and rewarding.

"The three of you are all Irish lace," my good and wonderful husband Pat Murray used to shout in his loud and lovely voice. *"Thin and delicate and pretty, and just a little complicated."*

And I would say to him, "Well, Patrick Murray, you've changed your opinion. You used to say I was very complicated!"

And he'd say, "Complicated enough for one man."

I made an Irish-lace gown for our marriage night that he liked. Still does, if I am to believe him.

My mother protested that it was a scandalous garment when I showed it to her.

"Are you saying I shouldn't wear it?" I asked dubiously.

"Certainly not, my dear!"

So you see we were not quite so old-fashioned in those days as you might think.

I suppose I have told you often that I saw your father when I was thirteen years old at a social at St. Mary's Church and fell in love with him on the spot and never stopped loving him. He says the same thing, but I tell him that's his blarney doing the talking.

I am wandering, which is an old woman's privilege.

So we had a very happy childhood. Our mother and father were strict disciplinarians, but their manner was always gentle and reasonable so we did not feel unduly restrained. We sang together and performed musicales and little dramas and made lace. The three of us came to be called "The Irish Lace," which we all took to be a compliment.

Then the war began in 1861 and our lives changed. The Government built the camp almost in our backyard. Daddy said not to worry because the war would be over in a few months.

Daddy supported the war at first. He helped organize Mulligan's Regiment at Camp Douglas itself, because he said that States couldn't be permitted to drop in and out of the Union whenever they wanted. There certainly had to be agreement with the other parties of the contract, meaning the other States. Colonel Mulligan, Lord *be good to him, you may recall was the colonel who, when mortally wounded at Winchester, Virginia, told the men who were carrying him off the field of battle, "Lie me down, boys, save the flag!"*

His burial monument is at the entrance of Calvary Cemetery up in Evanston.

My Pat signed up for that regiment, even though he was only seventeen. "Don't worry, love, I'll be back in three months."

He didn't come home to stay for three years.

As for the slaves, Daddy felt that slavery was evil and wanted it to be abolished. However, he said that the government should buy the slaves from their owners to set them free. A long and horrible war was too high a price to pay, he said, when the matter could be handled much more simply by a financial transaction.

Then the prisoners began to arrive from Fort Donaldson and Shiloh in the Spring of 1862. Daddy would stand in front of our house and watch the men marching into the camp, weary and sick, and shake his head in dismay.

"Brave fighting men," he said. "Look what defeat and capture does to them."

Mommy and Daddy and the rest of us would go over to the camp every week to bring food and clothing to the prisoners.

Once Mommy sent little Dickie, who was only two years old, to carry a coat the last twenty feet between her and a prisoner. The guards thought it was cute and let the man keep the coat. He escaped the next night in a complete suit of clothes that we had smuggled in to him.

"They're human beings," Mommy said, "enemies or not."

The Irish Lace would come home from each visit and vomit because what we saw was so terrible. Still we went over every week, as did many others because we felt so sorry for the poor boys.

As long as Colonel Mulligan was in command, the Union Army did its best. Daddy would say that they were overwhelmed with the prisoners, but they were working hard. He had been responsible for some prisoners during the Mexican War and said that it was a strict rule that they should be treated as gentlemen would treat other gentlemen.

"However," he would add, "we had nothing like these many prisoners."

When Mulligan's Regiment went to the front, and, as you may believe, all my prayers with them, the condition of the men became much worse. Every day we would see several of Mr. Jordan's hearses passing by on the way to the Chicago City Cemetery.

As if to torment the prisoners, some rich men constructed the Chicago Driving Park within a stone's throw of the camp. It was a popular gathering place for these rich men and their ladies who had nothing better to do with their time during the war years. The poor boys in the camp heard the shouts and the laughter of these feckless people every day of the racing season.

Daddy did not believe in racetracks though he enjoyed the racing of horses. As he said, "All Irish delight in racing."

"That place is evil," he told us sternly. "It's not a racetrack. It's an outdoor gambling den with the same fancy women who populate the indoor dens. It is not fair to the prisoners, poor starving devils that they are. It must drive them out of their minds to hear the laughter of those painted ladies and to catch a glimpse of their lascivious bodies."

The Irish Lace pretended to be shocked. However, the next time Daddy was away on business, we dressed in our finest spring frocks and strolled over to the Park. We left after the first couple of races.

"I do not think that we would be very successful as painted ladies," I told my sisters.

"You're more beautiful than any of them, 'Titia," Mary told me. "Those men devoured you with their eyes."

"I was not flattered," I said firmly.

In my heart of hearts, I was a tiny bit pleased to discover that without paint I was more attractive to many men than the painted ladies.

"Those poor women," I continued to my sisters, "are just as much prisoners as the poor men in the Camp."

Daddy stopped talking about the camp, except to become angry on rare occasions and actually swear at the incompetence and corruption of those who were running the camp.

"The men should be turned loose and allowed to find their way home. It would cost the Union less money. Many of them would not want to fight again in this terrible war. Many others would not be able to fight. What harm would be done?"

As far as I can see, no one has ever provided an answer to that question.

Much later, after he was released from prison, Daddy heard about the Confederate camps like Andersonville from men who had managed to survive.

"They were much worse than ours," he would say. "Still, two wrongs don't make a right. Surely the governments involved ought to have been able to arrange prisoner exchanges more readily than they did."

I heard some of the men who were Daddy's friends tell him that he was "obsessed" with Camp Douglas.

"How can I not be?" he would say in that powerful, commanding voice of his. "When I have to look at that hellhole every day?"

We would bring as much food as we could every week to the men and whatever warm clothes we could find. They were so happy to see us. We'd chat with them for a few minutes and try to make them laugh. Then we'd come back the following week and ask for a man who had red hair or who was from Texas or who sang for us and learn that, as one soldier said, "The boys in blue gave him a free ride up to the North Side. One way."

When they would march out of the camp for a prisoner exchange, we would line up and cheer and wave.

"Are you a Copperhead, miss?" an officer from Alabama asked me one day.

"No, sir," I said. "The man I love is in the Union Army. If he is taken prisoner, I hope some kind Southern woman will try to ease his lot just as I am trying to help you."

"I hope he's not taken, miss, and that he comes home fit. If he is taken, I'm sure our women will be as generous as you have been."

Well, that was very pretty, and it was true, too. Still, not enough women tried to help the prisoners on either side. They kept on dying.

Daddy protested to everyone who listened. He even wrote a letter to Colonel Hoffman who was the Commissary for Prisons.

"Hoffman has written back to me," he said one night at supper to all of us. "Good man, honest man, brave man. He says he's doing all he can to help the prisoners, but that General Montgomery Meigs who is the Quartermaster General doesn't want to spend money on rebels."

"God forgive him," Mommy said, pale and angry. "What a terrible thing to say about decent human beings."

"It is terrible," Daddy said solemnly. "I don't know what we can do about it."

"Can't we free them and send them home?" I said. I was always the first one of The Irish Lace to speak up.

"It would take at least a thousand men to do that. What good would it do? Many are too sick even to leave the camp. The others are too tired to walk more than a couple of miles towards home. Where would be the food for them? The Union soldiers would hunt them down, and the people in the countryside would fear them, quite properly so, and kill many of them. That's an attractive idea, my impulsive little redhead, but, alas, it wouldn't work."

I could see that it wouldn't.

Then my Paddy came home on leave and told Daddy how bad the combat was and how many men had died because of stupid decisions by their officers. Daddy was very grim. "I was wrong to think it would be a short war. Nothing is worse than these kinds of losses. We should make peace while some of our young men are still alive."

You can imagine the chill that those words struck in my heart.

During his leave, Paddy and I pledged ourselves to one another. When he left, I thought I'd never see him again. I prayed to God to send him home safe and to protect him from prison camps.

Daddy became involved with a group of men called the Sons of Liberty. They were not Copperheads, but they were opposed to the war. At first, he explained to my mother, he wasn't sure about opposing the war. He was a Democrat, naturally, like all the Irish Catholics in Chicago. He didn't think much of the fanatical Protestant Republicans for whom the Tribune had become almost a bible. They hated Catholics, he said, as much as they hated Rebs.

Then in 1863 after Antietam, which Dad said was the costliest victory in the history of war, Mr. Lincoln issued the Emancipation Proclamation, which freed all the slaves in the South.

Daddy was furious.

"The darkies shouldn't be slaves," he said, his voice tight with rage. "But this is no way to do it. It will prolong the war and make the eventual peace even more vicious than it has to be. The war will be fought out to the bitter end, no matter how many young men are killed. And all of this just to please the Protestant black[2] Republicans in New England."

He became much more active in the Sons of Liberty. Soon they elected him their leader. Mommy was very worried about "sedition."

Daddy denied that there was any question of sedition. "Mae," he said to Mommy, "the Sons of Liberty are not seditious. We do not plan or advocate the overthrow of the Union Government. We do not sympathize with the Confederate cause. We advocate nothing more than the Democratic Party—the peaceful end of this terrible conflict."

At that time there were many secret societies in Chicago, with different attitudes towards the war. The Irish in Chicago were Democrats and hence likely to want the Union Government to convene a peace conference.

"They should be in favor of a peace confer-

---

[2]"Black" does not mean African-American. It is used in the same sense that the Irish also used the adjective to describe certain kinds of Protestants. It could perhaps be taken to mean "fanatical."

ence," I said. "It is our boys who are fighting the war."

Even my beloved Paddy, now an officer with shiny gold bars, in one of his letters right after the battle of Vicksburg (during which the State of Illinois alone lost 14,000 men!) said there ought to be a peace conference.

"There are so many young men dying and to what point?" he wrote. "The Rebs will settle if we let them go. I'm as loyal as any man in the Union Army and I'll fight as long as my country wants me to fight. But now I say let them go. Only I'm not sure that would be enough for the Rebs now. They want to beat us in battle. We hear rumors here that Meade and the Army of the Potomac sent "Ol' Marse Robert" on the run at Gettysburg and that Pickett's Division was destroyed. Some of our officers say that our victories here and there will bring the war to a quick end. I'm not so sure they're right. The Union will think it doesn't have to make peace, and the Rebs will be afraid they will lose everything. It may be too late for peace."

Paddy was right, as he usually is, except when the poor dear has the temerity to disagree with me.

It's hard to explain how the people of Chicago felt during the later years of the war. You could not divide the city into the supporters of the North and the supporters of the South. Opinions went all the way from those who actively advocated the Southern cause (the true Copperheads) to those who wanted to push the war to its end, no matter what the cost (like the Republicans associated with the Tribune) with lots of different shades of blue and gray in between.

I truly believe that the majority in Chicago swayed back and forth between the two sides. When the Union was winning, they wanted victory. When the Union was losing, they wanted peace.

Daddy thought that the Democrats would win the election and that General George McClellan, who had a reputation for valuing the lives of his men, would call for peace. Then, when Sherman captured Atlanta and Savannah, Daddy knew Lincoln would be reelected.

Most of these different shades of opinion had their own secret societies like the Sons of Liberty, for their own protection and support and because, as Daddy said, "Americans love to have secret societies. They make us feel important." Some of the groups advocated violence. The Copperheads wanted to overthrow the government. Some of the black Republicans wanted to kill off everyone opposed to the war.

One day in early 1864 while I was brushing down my pony in the barn, I noticed two large carts that had not been there the day before. Naturally, being who I was (and who I am), I had to know what was inside them.

I pulled back one of the canvas covers and screamed—guns! Muskets and pistols and ammunition. Quickly, I pulled the canvas back over the guns. Gingerly, I peeked under the canvas on the other cart and saw the same thing—more guns!

I leaned against the wall of the barn and, my eyes shut tight, gasped for breath. As soon as I had calmed down, I went to Daddy's library to tell him—I never thought twice about telling him anything.

"Daddy," I said, choking out the words, "There's guns in the barn!"

For a moment he was very angry, "Young woman, you ought to mind your own business! You have no right to be poking around looking *for things you ought not to be looking for!"*

"*I wasn't looking for anything,*" I said, just as bold as ever. "*I saw the two wagons and wondered what was in them. . . . Are they our guns or someone else's?*"

He looked at me coldly for a moment and then smiled, "*They're ours, dear, just in case some of the black Republicans should decide to try to kill some of us Democrats.*"

I gasped again. "*Would they do that Daddy?*"

"*Some of them are crazy enough to try. If they do, they won't get away with it.*"

"*I won't tell anyone,*" I promised. "*Not even Mary and Maggie.*"

"*And especially your mother.*"

"*I promise.*"

He smiled again and patted me on the head. "*Good girl.*"

I kept my promise, but later, when he was in jail, I regretted it. If I had told Mom, she would have made him get rid of the guns, and that odious Colonel Sweet would never have found any evidence against Daddy.

Meantime the hearses continued to come out of the Camp, day in and day out. It had become so much part of our lives, that I often forgot to cry or to pray for the poor dead men.

"*This has to stop,*" Daddy kept saying. "*It has to stop.*"

We continued to visit them every week. In the Spring of 1864, the camp officers turned us all away. Five thousand more prisoners had arrived, making more than ten thousand men in the camp. That many men, we were told, makes it too dangerous for visitors.

"*The horrors are so bad in there now,*" Daddy told us, "*that they don't want anyone to see them.*"

The Union had made some improvements in the

camp, better sheds for the men to live in and running water for the latrines. But there were just too many men for a place that size. Now the hearses were a steady procession every day.

Then one day in May of 1864 there was a knock at the door of our house. Since, for reasons I can't remember, I was the only one in the house, I answered the knock. A handsome young man with curly brown hair and a wide mustache bowed very politely.

"Begging your pardon, ma'am. If it wouldn't be too much trouble, I'd like to talk to Mr. John Walsh."

A chill ran through my veins. The man had a very strong southern accent.

"Come right in, sir," I said, pretending that Confederate officers appeared on our front porch every day and tethered their horses at the gate.

"Who shall I say is calling?"

"Thomas R. Hines."

"I'll tell him, Mr. Hines. Won't you please sit down?"

Heart pounding, I walked upstairs to Daddy's study.

"A Mr. Thomas R. Hines to see you, Daddy."

"Indeed. I'll see him directly. Why don't you bring him up here."

"Yes, Daddy."

"What do you think he is?" he asked as I turned to go back downstairs.

"He is a Rebel officer, Daddy."

He nodded. "This will be our secret, understand 'Titia?"

"Yes, Daddy." I went downstairs.

"Would you come with me, Mr. Hines? Daddy will see you in his library."

"Thank you, ma'am. . . . I hope you don't mind my saying so, but that's a very pretty frock you're *wearing, particularly the lace collar."*

*"Thank you, sir. My sisters and I are lace mak-
ers."*

*I almost said, "Thank you, Captain," because I
reckoned that's what he was.*

"I'm impressed, ma'am."

"Daddy, Mr. Thomas R. Hines."

*"Thank you 'Titia . . . Come in, Mr. Hines. . . .
'Titia, will you close the door when you leave?"*

"Yes, Daddy."

*My heart was in my throat and my knees were
weak. Had Daddy become a Copperhead? Were
we all in danger?*

*Yet Captain Thomas R. Hines did not seem an
evil man. He was probably a very brave man,
fighting and risking his life for a cause he believed
in, just as Captain Patrick M. Murray was doing
the same thing with Sherman in Georgia.*

*I was very confused then. I'll admit I'm still
confused now.*

*My confusion did not prevent me from going
into the room I shared with Mary and Maggie and
hiding in the closet, which was right next to the
library. I had learned long ago that it was an excellent way to hear what was happening in the library.*

*You will think I was a very nosy young woman.
I suspect you might not be surprised. I could never
bear to realize that something important was happening in the house, something which would affect
all of us, and not know what it was about.*

*I made it a strict rule that I would never listen
unless I was pretty sure that Dad and Mom were
talking about us. And especially about me.*

*I will never forget that conversation as long as
I live. I can still smell the two cigars in the library.*

*"Thank you for the cigar, sir, I bring you greet-
ings from an old colleague, General Jonathan*

Grimes. I believe you may remember him from the Mexican War."

"I do indeed. You must give him my very best wishes when you see him again."

"I certainly will, sir. . . . Now if I may get to the matter at hand, I believe you have an interest in freeing men from Camp Douglas?"

"I do."

"I have a similar interest, sir."

"Indeed."

"I believe that I can command a force of 300,000 men for such an endeavor."

"Really? You surprise me, sir."

"My colleagues have talked to a gentleman in Canada who assures me that he has that many men, a good number of them Union veterans. He needs only the money to pay for their movement."

"I see."

"I will not pretend that with an army that size we will not pursue the cause of the Confederacy here in the Middle West in bringing this terrible war to a speedy end."

"I see."

"We also believe that we can seize a Union gunboat on Lake Michigan and turn its armament on Camp Douglas."

"I would tend to be wary of that expectation."

"Perhaps . . . we need from you sir, help in storming the walls of Camp Douglas and freeing the prisoners. I am told that you can produce at least 5,000 men who would enlist in that cause."

"That's absurd, Mr. Hines. The membership of the Sons of Liberty and other more radical groups would not be in excess of 2,000 men. By no means all of them would be willing or able to join in combat."

"I am disappointed."

"Nevertheless, it is the truth. . . . Might I ask

what plans you have to send the prisoners home?"

"Send them home?"

"Yes, sir. It will be a very long walk."

"I would not plan to send them home, Mr. Walsh. I would incorporate them in my army. They would add perhaps 10,000 men to my army."

"Mr. Hines, have you ever been in Camp Douglas?"

"No, sir."

"I have. Along with our mutual friend General Grimes, I have had some experience in judging between men who are fit for combat and those who are not. I tell you sir, that there are no more than 1,000 men in that camp who are fit for combat."

"A thousand will be enough."

"And what will happen when the men are free?"

"We will arm them, sir."

"With what?"

"With arms that will be available to us and arms we will take from the guards."

"If they are so foolish as to give them up instead of retreating and then counterattacking."

"We don't anticipate that will be a serious problem."

"And then?"

Hines hesitated. "There are some who think Atlanta can be avenged."

"You will not find much support for that even among the Copperheads in Chicago."

"I didn't say that's what we would do."

"I have some other questions: What assault positions will be manned, and by whom? Who will lead the various forces? Where will the weapons and munitions be stored? What will be done about the dead and wounded? What kind of escape

*routes will be available? Who will act as the rear-
guard units?"*

"Those things will all be arranged in good time,
sir."

"I see. When do you propose to launch the attack on the Camp?"

"On our national holiday, July 4."

"When the Democratic convention is in town?"

"We anticipate help from many of the partici-
pants."

"Then, sir, you don't understand the Northern
Democratic party very well. I myself am a Democrat. There are very few heroes in the party. Politicians don't make good heroes, and heroes don't
make good politicians. The Democrats are especially unlikely to help if they think you might burn
them and their colleagues in their hotel rooms."

"The date is not definite, Mr. Walsh, nor the
next step."

"I see. . . . Do you mind if I ask, Mr. Hines
where your 300,000 men are to come from? I am
tolerably familiar with this part of the country, and
I am unaware of their existence."

The Reb hesitated.

"This must be in strictest confidence, sir."

"Agreed."

"Jacob Thompson, who is the commissioner
working with me, and I had the pleasure of meeting with Mr. Clement Vallandigham in Canada. I
assume that you are familiar with the gentleman
in question?"

"I am, sir."

"And your opinion of him?"

"I would say that he is an incorrigible boaster.
You would do well not to believe anything he
says."

The Reb said nothing for a moment.

"I thank you for your advice, sir. I will take it

very seriously. You must understand that the Confederacy is desperate."

"I understand. However, that is the precise reason that I believe desperate measures must not make the North's aversion to negotiation even stronger than it is now."

"A point well taken, Mr. Walsh."

"Now, one more thing, Mr. Hines. . . ."

"Tom, please, sir."

"All right, Tom. The city is alive with spies and would-be spies, informers who are well intentioned, and informers who are interested in quick money. The young scamp who is the Commandant at the camp presently has taken money from the vegetable funds and used it to buy information. He tells the gullible of Chicago that he knows everything—all the plots and counterplots, all the conspiracies and schemes and plans. In fact, no one could possibly know them all. Nor would it be useful to know them all. Most of them are not worth a hill of beans. However, you must be very cautious. Your group could easily be infiltrated by one of Sweet's agents."

"I'll take that warning very seriously. . . . Can we meet again soon, Mr. Walsh?"

"At your pleasure, sir. . . . 'Titia, will you please show Mr. Hines out the door?"

I ducked out of the closet, brushed the dust off my dress, arranged my hair, and ran quickly to Daddy's library.

"Yes, Daddy."

"I thought you had not heard me. In any event, will you show Mr. Hines to the door?"

"Of course, Daddy. This way, Mr. Hines."

"I hope, miss, that I'll have the pleasure of meeting you again."

"Perhaps."

"Is this lace throw your work?"

"No, sir. My sister Mary made it. Three of us make Irish lace."

"Very skillful. . . . I bid you good day, Miss Letitia."

Well, he knew what my real name was.

I watched him mount his horse and ride down Ellis Avenue towards the city.

Daddy stood beside me.

"You're a very clever young woman, 'Titia. What do you think of young Mr. Hines?"

"Captain Hines more likely, Daddy."

He laughed and said, "I wouldn't be in the least surprised."

"He's a very handsome and polished young man, Daddy. And doubtless very brave. I'm not sure he's very intelligent."

"As always, you're right 'Titia. He is not quite a fool, but his courage, I think, masks his callowness."

"Yes, Daddy."

"He has a fool plot for freeing the prisoners at Camp Douglas."

"We would be sympathetic to that, wouldn't we?"

"I think so, but he has more grandiose schemes. I don't think he can be successful at Camp Douglas. I know the bigger schemes cannot succeed and that any attempt at them will make matters much worse for everyone who favors peace."

"Yes, Daddy."

"Keep an eye on things that might happen here during the summer and let me know what you think."

"Yes, Daddy."

"Not a word to anyone, especially your sisters and your mother."

"I promise, Daddy."

You may well imagine that I did not sleep that night.

This was about the same time that Colonel Sweet was telling William Bross that there were 10,000 rebel guns in Chicago and that he had everything under his very close supervision. The only guns were the 200 or so in Daddy's carts, and no one was going to storm Camp Douglas or burn the city to the ground with such a handful of weapons.

There were meetings at our house all summer. On two occasions Captain Hines ate dinner with us. He brought along a handsome and charming Englishman named Colonel George St. Leger Grenfel who told many wonderful stories about his past military adventures. He had, if one were to believe him, fought with the English in the Crimean War, with a French cavalry regiment in Algeria, with Garibaldi in South America, and in the Sepoy mutiny in India. They were captivating stories, and I didn't believe a word of them.

However, although all the Walshes had reason for hating the English, we could not help liking him. I think Mary was for a time partly in love with him.

I judged him to be even more callow than Captain Hines, a man who was already listening to himself telling the story about the Great Conspiracy.

I would find a way to sneak into the closet to listen to their conversations. They continued to believe that Copperheads would rise to arms as soon as they struck Camp Douglas. They had no clear military plans. They still thought the Democratic convention would provide them with allies.

The Democratic convention was postponed till August 29 because rumors of the "conspiracy" had spread about the city.

Daddy persuaded Hines and his colleagues to postpone their plan till July 20, and once more to August 16, and again to August 29. New men came to the frequent meetings, Captain Castleman, Captain Cantril, Colonel Marmaduke, Mr. Thompson. They were all very fine gentlemen, but daft, completely daft.

Daddy asked often where the guns were and when the other men were coming.

"I have some guns for self-defense," he said. "They are not enough. They are old and would be of little use, save in the hands of very experienced troops."

Captain Hines would thank Daddy for his observations and continue as though he had not heard them.

"I have here a map of Camp Douglas," he said one night. "I propose that we attack at night from three sides; the north, the west, and the south. As soon as we attack, the prisoners are to rush the guards and overcome them. We will cut the telegraph lines and bribe employees of the Illinois Central to transport us to Rock Island, Illinois. There is no longer a question of burning Chicago."

Even a mere girl like me knew that the plan was daft.

"Tom, that's a good textbook plan, but it assumes that we have experienced troops who are practiced in carrying out the plan, that the prisoners inside can coordinate perfectly with the force outside, that the guards have no hint of an attack, which with so much talk and so many stories in the Tribune *strikes me as highly improbable, and that Colonel Sweet is a fool. A scoundrel looking for a general's star, he may be, but a fool he is not."*

"I appreciate your observations," Tom said gently.

That was his standard response to all of Daddy's criticisms.

"You have scouted around the camp, Tom?"

"To the extent that it is judicious."

"I notice on your map that you do not have the tower of the University of Chicago observatory. It's right here and commands a perfect view of all the camp."

"I see. All right I'll mark it."

"Do you not see the implications of the tower?"

"Tell me what they are, sir."

"Sweet maintains several sharpshooters up there. In case of an attack, he could put a whole company in the tower. They could pick off attackers and prisoners with ease and safety."

"We will take the tower out early then. I'll keep it in mind."

Among the others who came to the meetings there was a certain Mr. Shanks, whom I distrusted immediately. He had a very thick southern accent and was reputed to be an escaped prisoner of war. He was most strongly in favor of immediate action.

"We have to snuff out the fires of hell in that camp."

Daddy did not pay any attention to him. Rather, he kept asking where the arms would come from.

That night after they had all left, I joined Daddy in his library. He looked very troubled. So, by the way, was everyone else in the house. They all knew that something serious and maybe dangerous was happening. But Daddy had told no one except me what was being planned.

"You asked me for my opinion about the men, Daddy."

"Yes, child?" he said, taking off his glasses and looking up at me.

I sat down without being asked.

"Most of them, Daddy, are like Tom Hines. Dreamers and romantics, without an ounce of common sense."

"We share views once more, 'Titia. If I wanted to direct a major conspiracy, I'd want your Captain Murray with me."

"That poor man may have certain serious failings, Daddy. But he is not a fool."

"I won't ask you to specify what those failings might be," he said with a laugh.

"I don't like that Mr. Shanks. He's an informer, Daddy, I'm sure of it."

"I'm not particularly fond of him either, but I don't think he's an informer. He's an escaped prisoner of war and intensely loyal to the Confederate cause. I know soldiers, 'Titia. He's a good soldier."

Daddy was wrong. Shanks was a convicted forger, fraud, bigamist, horse robber, and common thief. He was also an agent of Colonel Sweet. In Daddy's trial, he would add perjury to his crimes.

After he was released from prison, Daddy often said to me, deep sadness in his voice, "If I had listened to you, 'Titia, the trial would never have happened; your mother and the rest of you would not have suffered so much; Mr. Anderson and Colonel St. Leger Grenfel, the twelve men who died of smallpox in prison would still be alive; and Mayor Morris and his wife would never have been separated by government edict."

"That one," I would reply firmly, trying to change the subject, "was no better than she had to be. She used her house recklessly for foolish Confederate plots."

"I could never understand why Sweet need to go after Buckner Morris. He was not connected to any of our conversations. He knew nothing about the so-called conspiracy."

"He needed someone to blame for helping his spy escape from prison," I said.

"Mayor Morris's wife gave him plenty of grounds."

Later I would learn that Colonel Swift had written to his commanding officer asking for permission to arrest civilians, which he needed and which was illegal anyway. In this letter he said that to make the arrests "perfect," he would have to arrest "two or three prominent citizens." Buckner Morris, a former mayor of the city and a former judge, was the perfect target because of his wife. She was more interested in the Confederacy than in her husband.

General Hooker, who was the commanding officer of the whole region, told Sweet that he did not expect any attack on Camp Douglas.

I get ahead of myself.

The guns and the other men never appeared. On August 27, two days before the attack, they met again in Daddy's library. Naturally, I was at my listening post.

"We have heard sad news," Tom Hines reported, "Mr. Clement Vallandigham will not be joining us."

Daddy said nothing.

"How many weapons do you have available, Mr. Walsh?"

"Enough for a hundred men, perhaps."

"And how many men can you provide who will be willing to participate in the attack?"

"No more than twenty five, perhaps as few as twelve. As the father of a dozen children, I can hardly lead such a foolhardy endeavor."

"Nor would I expect you to lead it," Tom said crisply.

Everyone was silent.

"Would you be able to muster more men for an attack on Rock Island or Springfield? There would be no question in such a case of burning Chicago."

"I doubt it, Tom. I warned you from the beginning that, for all the talk in Chicago, I did not think that there were many men who would be willing to risk their lives as you gentlemen have for the Confederacy."

"Or as you have for the poor devils inside Camp Douglas."

"I'm not sure there was that much risk."

Though Daddy sounded enigmatic, I knew what he meant: He never thought that there was a remote chance of an attack on Camp Douglas.

They shook hands, bid each other affectionate good-byes, and promised to get together after the war.

They all bowed over my hand as I conducted them out the door. Tom Hines's smile was very pretty indeed. But I had another captain on my mind.

"They're gone, 'Titia," Daddy said. "We'll not see them for a long time."

"Thank God."

But we would see them again two months later, with disastrous results for all of us. Fourteen innocent men lost their lives. Colonel Sweet earned his star and became General Sweet.

I've often wondered why Sweet did not strike that night. He knew that all the "conspirators" were in one place and that the guns were in our barn. He must have had a list of the innocent men he would arrest as part of the plot. Why not move while he could?

Now I think that Shanks actually believed that there would be an attack and that Sweet therefore waited till the day of the attack. It would have made more persuasive proof that there really was a conspiracy. Maybe, in his own twisted way, he thought there might be a conspiracy. Perhaps he also realized that it was small potatoes.

Later he must have been furious at the lost opportunity.

Captain Hines and his friends provided Colonel Sweet with another opportunity in November on the day before the election. This time he did not wait for more spectacular evidence.

Daddy had heard that the Confederates were back in town. Tom Hines, as polite and respectful as ever, rode out to propose a meeting on Sunday night.

Daddy was busy with a client, and Tom had to wait a few minutes in the parlor. I remained with him, as was polite and proper.

"Would I be correct in assuming, Miss Letitia, that you have a young man in the Union Army."

"I do, Mr. Hines; he's either with Sherman in Georgia or Thomas in Tennessee."

"Dangerous places."

"War is dangerous."

"I have a sweetheart back home in Kentucky. I love her very much. Perhaps I understand how your young man feels. Her name is Amanda, Mandy for short."

"It's a very pretty name in both forms."

I had always been stiff and formal with him, not as friendly as my sisters and my mother were. Still, my heart melted for him.

"We have another problem."

"Indeed."

He looked so tired and discouraged that I felt even more sympathy for him.

"Kentucky, you see, is even more divided on this war than other states. My family and her family have been lifelong friends. Mine is Confederate, as I'm sure you've guessed. Hers is Union."

"How terrible!" I burst out.

"Yes, Miss Letitia, it truly is. We write when we can. We still love one another. I'm sure our families will not be reconciled for a long time, if ever. Yet we plan to be married when the war is over."

"Good for you!"

Then Daddy called for him.

That little exchange saved Tom's life.

The purpose of the Sunday night meeting was to discuss a breakout the prisoners scheduled for the following evening. The Confederates wondered if any Chicagoans would be willing to assist them.

"Gentlemen, do you know that the 196th Pennsylvania has had a station outside the Camp for the last several weeks? It would be impossible to keep a plot like that secret in a prison camp. Ben Sweet will be ready and waiting for them."

Some of the Rebs gasped with horror.

"We did not know it, Mr. Walsh," Tom said somberly.

"Who decided on this outbreak?"

"They did, sir. Our communications with them are very poor. I believe some hotheads led them to think that there would be an attack against Chicago on election day. They are so desperate in there that they want to break out no matter what happens."

"You are unable to communicate with them?"

"Afraid not," Mr. Thompson said. "We've already tried that."

"They will be slaughtered," Daddy said bluntly. "The more men fall, the greater become Sweet's chances at brigadier rank. This is folly!"

"So I understand now," Tom said gloomily. "I must confess you warned us that it would be."

They talked for a few more minutes. Daddy agreed that they could come again tomorrow night in case any of the prisoners might escape and need help going home.

It was a terrible risk. I could not warn Daddy because I was not supposed to know what they were planning.

I didn't sleep one minute that night.

I shivered often because of what Daddy had said about Sweet slaughtering them. But Sweet wasn't there. He was out of the Camp, in command of the patrols which were preparing to round up all of us.

In fact, he was so concerned about a conspiracy that never was, that he did not know about a real—if foolish—conspiracy going on in his own camp. His vaunted spy system was not all that good where it ought to have been good.

Captain Shurly, the adjutant, was in command. Just before sunset on that blustery and fateful day, a Reb came to the Captain, terrified at the slaughter he feared would happen, and warned him. As cool under pressure as Sweet would have been wild, he lined up his troops at strategic points and waited. The Rebs knew the game was up. Still the men who had volunteered to attack the guards did so anyway. Captain Shurly's note to William Bross is, as far as I know, an accurate account of the events.

In our house on Ellis Avenue, we heard a brief round of gunfire in the distance. We waited for more, myself in the closet.

There was no more shooting.

As Captain Shurly said in his note to Mr. Bross, the few prisoners who had escaped were recaptured. No one was killed in the gunfire.

And that was the end of the conspiracy that never was.

When the men in Dad's library realized that the breakout had been a failure, they decided to leave. I scooted downstairs to see them out. There were the usual tedious farewells. Daddy accompanied them out of the house. Then, just as they were mounting their horses, Union troops appeared in the dark and swarmed in from all sides, led by Colonel Sweet himself. As I watched in horror, they surrounded the men with fixed bayonets.

The Colonel, a pompous little popinjay with a voice like a girl, announced that he was arresting them on charges of armed rebellion and high treason. If they did not put up their hands in surrender, he would order his men to shoot.

Naturally, they surrendered. They were immediately bound and taken off to the camp. Daddy was unable to say good-bye to any of us.

Mother and the other children were wailing and crying. Union soldiers, still with fixed bayonets, advanced on our house.

Tom Hines had lingered to say good-bye to my mother and sisters, an act of foolish Southern hospitality. We later learned that Sweet wanted him more than anyone else because he was a man the Union Army could hang without the slightest doubt about injustice.

He knew it, too.

"Can you hide me, Miss Letitia? I would count it a great favor."

All I could think of was the poor girl down in Kentucky. What could I do for her?

"Follow me quickly," I ordered him.

I raced up to our room.

"Hide under the bed."

"What?"

"I said hide under the bed. Do it now!"

*I heard the sound of Union troops on the stairs.
I blew out the candle, threw off my dress, jumped
under the covers, and shut my eyes as tight as I
could.*

*At that very moment, two Union troopers threw
open the door, one of them holding a lantern and
the other a rifle with a bayonet on it. He pointed
right at me.*

*"Pardon us, ma'am," one of them said very po-
litely. "We're searching for Confederate spies and
Copperheads."*

*"In my bedroom at this hour of night?" I pulled
the covers up to my neck. "You really cannot be
serious."*

*I could have been arrested, too. However, that
thought did not occur to me. I was too young and
too naïve to think that I would be dragged off to
Camp Douglas.*

*The soldier with the lantern examined our bed-
room while the other one continued to point his
bayonet at my stomach.*

*"Must you point that weapon at me?" I asked,
as if in high dudgeon.*

*"We've already arrested one woman tonight,
ma'am."*

"Who, pray tell?"

"Mrs. Buckner Morris."

"I trust I don't seem that fatuous."

*"No ma'am." He smiled and lowered the
weapon. "You're not screaming that you're proud
to die for the rebel cause."*

*"My fiancé is a captain in the Union Army,
Corporal. With General Sherman in Georgia."*

*The man with the lantern had searched our ar-
moire, carefully moving each dress to make sure
no one was hiding behind it.*

"Guess there's no one here."

I'll never know why they didn't search under the

190 · ANDREW M. GREELEY

beds. Perhaps I intimidated them. I certainly had tried to do so.

"Sorry to disturb your sleep, ma'am," the corporal with the gun said, and they left the room. They closed the door softly.

I held my breath to make sure they were gone. They rummaged about the rest of our floor and found no one. Someone, however, stole $500 of Daddy's money. We could have used that to hire a better lawyer during his trial. They tramped noisily down the stairs. I waited till I heard the last of their footsteps.

"Are you all right, Tom?"

"Yes, Miss Letitia. I'm powerful—"

"Remain there," I commanded, cutting off his expressions of gratitude which might yet prove premature. "I will go to console my mother. When they have left, I will lead you out of the house."

"Yes, ma'am."

I threw on my robe, slipped out the door, and strolled regally downstairs.

My mother and brothers and sisters were in the parlor with two Union officers, one of them Colonel Sweet who, at thirty-one years old, reminded me of a child, a child with a fever.

Mary and Maggie were harassing the two of them fiercely. Naturally, I joined in.

"I suppose you expect to win a general's star, Colonel Sweet, for this night of infamy."

He turned to me and considered me with his wide, empty eyes.

"I am sure the Union will reward me as it sees fit."

"You have also won yourself a place in the deepest pits of hell."

My family stopped weeping. There was a moment of eerie silence in the room. No one dared to talk to Colonel Sweet that way.

"You keep a civil tongue in your head, young woman, or you'll spend your night in the White Oak dungeon in Camp Douglas with your friend Mrs. Buckner Morris."

"I would be delighted to do that, Colonel, though that fatuous Mrs. Morris is no friend of mine. Wouldn't it look good in your Chicago Tribune that you, an officer who has never seen combat, would imprison and torment the fiancée of a decorated Union officer who at this moment is fighting with General Sherman."

A gasp went round the room.

Colonel Sweet backed down.

"You will take me to your father's study and show me his papers," he said as the flush of anger died from his pasty face.

I noted that the captain with him had a pistol in his hand. The contempt of the rest of The Irish Lace and the wailing and weeping of the Walsh family had evidently left them in fear of their lives.

"I will take you to my father's library, sir. You may examine whatever you wish. I, however, will not assist you."

"Come along, Captain," he ordered. "We'll see what incriminating papers this Copperhead has left for us."

"My father is not a Copperhead, Colonel. Neither is he a poltroon."

Later, when I reported the details of that evening to the good Captain Murray, he burst into laughter at my use of the word "poltroon."

"You certainly must have scared the living hell out of him to be able to get away with calling him that," the good Captain observed. "He was wounded in action at Perryville, so he wasn't exactly a coward."

"He wasn't a hero, was he?"

"Well, from what I've heard, his regiment broke

and ran. If his friends had not obtained his appointment to Camp Douglas there probably would have been an investigation of his conduct. Not a hero by any means, but not a coward, either."

Captain Murray's laughter, however, did not deter him from the rather passionate embrace in which he had imprisoned me, poor dear man.

I had decided by then that this is the way we would have to deal with the Union Army. My sisters agreed and that was the strategy we pursued through the horrors of the trial.

Needless to say, my good Captain, I do not use words like "fatuous" or "poltroon" in my ordinary conversation.

"Only when fighting off the Union Army. Not all of it, I hope."

In response, I rested my cheek against his.

"Not quite all of it, Captain."

Colonel Sweet and his sycophantic officer ransacked Daddy's library. Naturally, they found nothing.

"If my father were truly a Copperhead, you may depend on it, Colonel, he would have left nothing here for you to find."

Each time they discarded a pile of papers on Daddy's desk, I would straighten them out and return them to their proper receptacle. Whenever they moved a piece of furniture, I would move it back to its proper place.

"He was foolish enough to participate in a conspiracy, Miss Walsh."

"No, sir. There was no conspiracy, as you well know. He was, however, foolish to trust your degenerate spy Mr. Shanks."

They both turned and glared at me venomously.

"Shanks is a prisoner, not a spy. He may cooperate with us."

"You may swear a perjurious oath to that, Col-

onel, and yet you will win no one's belief."

That was an accurate prediction. He did perjure himself, as both he and Shanks did often during the trial, and no one believed either of them.

"I told you that you would find nothing," I said triumphantly as they walked out of the room.

They did not have the grace to thank me. Nonetheless, I shouted after them, "You're quite welcome!"

They finally took their leave.

"Do come again!" I yelled as I slammed the door.

Then I set about calming the family and getting them to bed.

"There will be hard days ahead. We must be prepared to fight them every inch of the way."

At that moment, I did not expect to see my father ever again. I felt quite certain that the legal niceties had been brushed aside and that he would be shot or hanged the next day.

I reckoned without the need that both Sweet and the Tribune felt for public approval and acceptance of this ridiculous conspiracy.

Nevertheless, unless I offered the others an illusion of bravery, they would not hold up under the strain we would face in the days and weeks to come.

After everyone was in bed and, I hoped, asleep, I carefully explored the outside of the house in all directions through the windows. There were no brave prison guards of the Union Army in sight. I returned to my own bedroom and whispered to Tom Hines, "Come out very quietly, Tom. I believe my sisters are both asleep."

Noiselessly, he slipped out from under the bed and tiptoed in the dark out the door of the bedroom.

I followed him just as quietly.

We had gaslight in the house, of course, though not in all the rooms at that time. But I risked neither light nor candle as I led him down the stairs and out of the house through the kitchen. A quarter moon shed some light on the yard. It had turned bitter cold. I remembered that my only outer garment was my robe.

Tom laughed softly and then whispered, "Mandy will never believe that I spent part of the night in a bedroom with three beautiful young women and never once had a temptation concerning them."

"You do not flatter us, sir, with that comment."

We both laughed softly.

I conducted him to the barn, helped him to saddle one of our horses, and pointed the path through the dead prairie grass he must follow if he wished to avoid Colonel Sweet's patrols.

He bent down from his horse and kissed my forehead.

"Thank you, 'Titia. I have no understanding of why you're doing this for me."

"A wedding present for Mandy."

"I trust that in God's time you will meet her, and on a much better day."

"You let him kiss you!" Captain Murray would later protest in mock horror.

At that moment, he was caressing me most provocatively, not quite beyond the boundaries of what was acceptable to a refined Catholic girl, but close enough to them. I realized that we must marry soon. It was not that I did not trust him, but I was no longer sure that I trusted myself.

"On the forehead, Captain. I thought it was a perfectly appropriate reaction in the circumstances."

"You saved his life, 'Titia. You realize that, don't you?"

"*Naturally.*"

"*I'm glad you did. Too many men died in the war as it was.*"

I knew that was what Paddy, poor dear man, would say.

The next day we read horrid headlines in the Tribune:

A General Sack of the City Intended—Plunder, Rapine—Fire—Bloodshed in the Streets of Chicago

Based on Colonel Sweet's report, they also described poor Daddy as "General Charles Walsh" when everyone in Chicago knew that his name was John Walsh and that he was not and never had been a general.

I wondered if anyone could believe such nonsense. Most people did not. Rather, they reacted with the sanity of the Times: "*That such an attack was contemplated by half a dozen rebels is probable, but that they could have relied upon any local assistance in the undertaking is wholly improbable.*"

When the dust had settled a couple of days later, everyone saw clearly how improbable the "Conspiracy" had been. Colonel Sweet with his elaborate organization of spies and detectives had managed to arrest fewer than 100 men and found only the handful of weapons in our barn. With these resources, the "conspirators" were to take on more than 1,000 guards and other troops at the Camp and then sack the city?

It was too absurd.

Mr. Lincoln thought it was a bad joke and promptly released several of the prisoners, including Mr. Thompson, who, as the chief commis-

sioner, could well have been charged as the head of the conspiracy.

If Mr. Lincoln, God be good to him, had lived into the summer, no one would have gone to jail.

I note that I have never prayed for Mr. Lincoln before. That has been very unchristian of me.

But, to satisfy the readers of the Tribune and to promote Colonel Sweet's career, it was necessary to go through the motions of a trial.

Daddy and the others were tried by a military court in Cincinnati, thus (as our lawyers pointed out) violating two provisions of the law: Military courts were not permitted to try civilians and the prosecutor was not allowed to transfer the accused from one jurisdiction to another.

However, the law was not important in this trial. All that mattered was the public event and the conviction of as many defendants as possible. It was comic opera, though, as it turned out, deadly comic opera for some of the men.

Daddy had decided that Mommy must stay home with the younger children and that The Irish Lace might come to the trial, "if they wished."

Naturally, we wished. We arrived in Cincinnati in January spitting fire and continued to do so till April, after General Lee had surrendered at Appomattox Courthouse. Both to the swarms of journalists and on the witness stand we said that the General (he had finally received his tarnished star) was a liar, a perjurer, a poltroon, a maniac, a pervert, and (in my words) "a sick, filthy, lying snake."

I also told the court that Judas had been rewarded with thirty pieces of silver and General Sweet with two pieces of gold.

This wild behavior won us the reputation of being "high-spirited and beautiful young women who are intensely loyal to their father." They also won us many approving laughs from the members of the military court and the spectators in the courtroom.

"Keep it up," Daddy's lawyer told us. "You're winning much support for your father. No one is going to vote for the death sentence of the father of women like you."

After he became a lawyer himself, Paddy said that was a strange remark for a lawyer to make during a trial.

"It was not a trial, dear one. It was a farce, an entertainment, a comic opera. All that was lacking was that we three should sing. We actually thought of doing that, too. You've read the reply of Judge Burnett to our lawyers' charges that the court had no jurisdiction. He read the whole thing—all fifty pages of it—out in court, putting most of the spectators to sleep but causing great laughter among the lawyers with its pompous and specious arguments. Even some of the other members of the military court snickered."

"A weak argument," he agreed.

It was not all comic opera, however. Twelve of the prisoners died in jail, probably from smallpox. A Mr. Anderson, a very confused man who had nothing to do with anything, hanged himself in jail. His own crime was muttering some demented threats to the Union in the hearing of Sweet's spies. Daddy did not even know most of the other men, including those who died. Many of them, he told us, were opportunists who had drifted into Chicago at election time because of rumors of violence and destruction.

"Some of them are certainly scoundrels," he told us. "However, they violated no laws and ought not to have been dragged into this pestiferous jail."

We worried that Daddy might get smallpox too, but, praise be to God, he did not.

He worried about us, too. I assume we were in some danger of contracting the disease, but we simply dismissed that as foolishness. We were young and angry and perhaps even "high-spirited" as the papers kept saying. We were afraid of nothing.

Presumptuous little fools, I say of The Irish Lace as I look back on them. But secretly I am proud of their courage and loyalty and happy to have known them at one time.

As the trial dragged on, we became more confident that Daddy would be spared the death penalty. The war was almost over (and would be over before the final verdict), the charges were exposed as the frauds they were, the military court was bored, and the journalists had lost interest.

Daddy's lawyer told us, "There'll have to be some convictions to satisfy the Tribune and the black Republicans in Congress. But the sentences will be light. Your father will be free before the year is over."

Daddy was convicted and sentenced to five years in prison; Colonel Marmaduke was acquitted, as was Mayor Buckner Morris. Mr. Semmes was convicted and sentenced to three years in prison. He was soon pardoned. Mary Morris proudly proclaimed her loyalty to the Confederacy and was banished back to it, which, since the war was over, meant nothing.

Colonel St. Leger Grenfel was sentenced to death, a punishment which shocked the courtroom. He had not been at the meetings at our house those last two nights. The only evidence against him came from Mr. Shanks, who was clearly a perjurer, though a clever one. Daddy said later that the court needed one scapegoat to sen-

tence to death, "to feed the hungry lions at the
Tribune." The judges expected him to be pardoned. They convicted him because he was English and there was little love lost for the English
in the North because of their blatant support of
the Confederacy.

Also, there were no powerful people to inter-
cede for a foreigner.

However, General Sweet, of all people, did in-
tercede for him, perhaps in a rare moment of troubled conscience. The sentence was commuted to
life imprisonment at Fort Jefferson in Florida. It
was a very bad prison, and three years later he
died attempting to escape. Poor man, he was utterly harmless, if somewhat reckless. None of the
real Confederate leaders took him seriously. He
was never able to tell his "conspiracy" stories to
drawing rooms of awed ladies.

If he was not murdered by Sweet and the court,
then murder has never been committed in this
country.

As you know Daddy was pardoned after a year.
The "conspiracy" was quickly forgotten, except by
the people at the Tribune. Mayor Morris died in
poverty a few years ago. His wife, who had never
returned to him after the trial (she was too busy
acting as First Lady to her brother the Governor
of Kentucky), had the decency to try to return for
the funeral, but was prevented by particularly bad
Chicago winter weather.

Captain Hines did return safely to his Mandy,
whom he married at the end of the war. I received
a cordial note from her informing me about the
wedding and thanking me for saving Tom's life.
She also said that, amazingly, their two families
had reconciled.

I replied with equal cordiality and offered expressions of my congratulations and best wishes.

I also said that I hoped we would meet sometime.

Tom became a lawyer, just as my dear Paddy did, and a judge on the Kentucky appellate court. They visited Chicago in 1875 after the fire, and stayed at the new Palmer House. We ate supper with them there and then invited them back to our new home on Washington Boulevard.

Tom had lost some of his curly hair and added a few pounds of weight in compensation. He had matured considerably but still to some extent substituted dash and courtesy for real intelligence. Patrick Murray possessed such an intelligence to an almost alarming degree.

Both couples enjoyed their time together. Mandy, a very pretty little woman, hugged me privately and, with considerable tears, thanked me for saving her man's life.

She showed no signs of jealousy, but there were no reasons for it.

"So you really spent several hours in my wife's bedroom," Paddy demanded, his voice loud as if he were willing to start a fight. But his eyes twinkled and his lips spread in a big smile.

"I did, sir," Tom replied, his eyes twinkling, too.

"I wasn't your wife then," I said, just to keep the facts straight.

"In proximity to her bed?"

"Indeed, sir, about as close as I could get to it without actually being in it, as a matter of fact."

"And herself not fully clothed, either?"

"All I can say is that when we went into her bedroom, she was wearing a very pretty frock; and when she led me out of the house, she was wearing an equally fetching robe."

"Fetching, is it?"

"Pay no attention to him, Mandy," I told her. "He's just acting up."

"I know the symptoms," the pretty little woman replied.

"Aye," I say. "The Lord made them, and the Devil matched them."

"I wonder, sir, if she has ever worn a robe that was not fetching."

Poor dear Paddy could no longer control his laughter.

"A point sir, a point well taken. Now let me put this question to you: Were you able to engage in any speculation about what—if any—garments she was wearing under the robe?"

My face grew very warm. I knew men well enough to know that they cannot help giving way to such fantasies.

"I will hardly be so bold, sir, to speculate on that matter. Again, I'd yield to your superior experience."

"I had everything on, including my corset."

They both seemed very pleased with themselves. They knew that their risqué talk was embarrassing me.

"Ah, yes, Counselor. I will agree I am not unfamiliar with that awkward and totally unnecessary contraption. . . . Now, as I understand the situation, you were without chaperones for some time."

"I think I could agree with that supposition, Counselor. Actually, her sisters came in eventually and, I assume from the noise I heard, disrobed for bed. Naturally, I could not observe this from my, ah, awkward position."

"Worse luck for you," I said, getting my two cents in as I always do.

"And a point to you, Mrs. Murray."

"But then they went to sleep, did they not?"

"I believe so. Certainly they seemed to be asleep when I left the room with Mrs. Murray."

"So you admit that your entire time with this woman in her bedroom, and herself not completely clothed, was unsupervised?"

"Save by the woman herself, sir. And I believe you will agree with me that her supervision is more than adequate in all circumstances."

They both guffawed.

"I'm in no position to deny that, Captain Hines."

"You two stop it!" Miss Amanda ordered us. However, she was laughing, too.

Paddy took up the game, "And thoughts about her were in your mind when you rode off on your return to Ol' Kentuck?"

"That's easy to answer, Captain Murray. I thought she was the second most beautiful, the second most generous, and the second bravest woman in the world."

More laughter.

"I should have left you, Captain Hines, to rot under the bed," I informed him. "And as for you, Captain Murray, I should have left you waiting at the altar rail of St. Mary's Church."

So I got in the last word, as you all know I usually do.

"Nice fella," Paddy said to me after they had driven off in a cab. "You did a generous thing by saving him."

"Impulsive folly."

"Neither of us believe that, 'Titia."

"Indeed."

"Clever lawyer, a lot of fun to talk with, not terribly deep."

"I knew that eleven years ago."

Our dinner took place the year after General Benjamin Sweet died suddenly of pneumonia at the age of forty-one and was buried up at Rosehill

Cemetery on the North Side. All of us went to his funeral mass and to the cemetery.

He was a lawyer, I learned after the war, and had been a member of the Wisconsin legislature. He volunteered as soon as the war started. He was a very ambitious man and had schemed to stir up trouble for his Commander in the Wisconsin infantry and then for Colonel DeLand who had been his superior at Camp Douglas. He had been wounded in action at the battle of Perryville, Kentucky. So he wasn't a poltroon when I accused him of being one. His wife had died young in a train accident, leaving him four young children, whom he raised himself. His eleven-year-old daughter Ada lived with him in the camp and once helped a prisoner to escape. He had cleaned up the camp and the prisoners, but cut the rations on his own, and no more than anyone else did he cope with the lack of medical care and supplies.

He sent his children to St. Xavier Academy, though none of them were in class with any of us. He became a Catholic on his deathbed.

But before that, after the war was over, he would come to social affairs at the academy. So we encountered him. The Irish Lace cut him cold.

Daddy did not.

"Good evening, Ben," he said to the general one night at the annual benefit ball for the academy. I remember the day very well because Paddy and I had just that day moved into our new home in the North Division just two blocks away from the river, or the North Side as you call it today.

"Good to see you looking so well, John," the general replied, his face red with embarrassment.

"I wish you continued good health, Ben."

Even then the general did not look well.

I was not to be outdone by Daddy in my Christianity.

"Good evening, General; it is good of you to come to the ball."

He bowed ceremoniously. "Marriage certainly becomes you Mrs. Murray."

"Thank you, General."

I felt sad for him since he had lost his wife.

At subsequent events, Daddy chatted amiably with him. Occasionally, I would say a word or two to him, always with my very best smile. After a little while, it was not even difficult to smile at him.

"Mrs. Murray," he said to me at a subsequent ball when Daddy and Patrick were talking to other people, "May I ask you a question?"

"Certainly, General. I promise no answer however."

"I wondered often where you hid Captain Hines when we raided your house."

Pretending to be unflustered, I looked him straight in the eye and said, "Under my bed, of course."

He nodded solemnly.

"That was very clever of you, and, as I presume you know, very dangerous."

"He had a sweetheart in Kentucky whose life I did not want to see ruined."

He nodded sadly.

"In the end it was just as well. I tried to save St. Leger Grenfel and as you know now I both succeeded and finally failed. I would not have been able to save his."

"So I understand, General."

We bowed politely to one another and he took his leave.

After he died, he was charged with being involved in bribery in the Chicago Federal Pension Office of which he had been the director. No one I know doubts the charge.

He was a much more complicated man, I must

assume, than we had thought in 1865. He had his own share of sufferings. I no longer judge him because I have come to believe that only God judges—and He much less harshly than we do. I mourn his death as I mourn the death of every fellow human. May God have mercy on his soul.

That is my story. I hope, beloved children and grandchildren, that you have enjoyed reading it and have not laughed too much at what a fierce young woman I was back in those days. You may read my story in comparison with that of Mr. Bross and judge which you believe.

I am confident that you will decide that the "Great Camp Douglas Conspiracy" was a conspiracy that never was. Deacon Bross played a very old game: You dream up a conspiracy and then you take credit for opposing it. General Sweet showed some signs of regretting his lies. The Deacon never did. I don't think he knows the difference between truth and falsehood.

I hope that someday the story I have told you will come to public attention so that everyone will know the truth about the "Camp Douglas Conspiracy." Now, however, is not the time.

I wish I had saved the letter Mr. Lincoln sent me when I wrote him about the trial. It would prove that what I say was true. However, I did not think much of him in those days and put the letter somewhere, but never could remember where. Later on, I realized how important it was.

In conclusion, I love you all very much, and I thank God every day for you and my wonderful Captain Murray and for all the graces in my life.

Letitia Walsh Murray
Lace Maker

There it is, Nuala Anne. I'm sure you will like 'Titia. She reminds me of certain other young Irishwomen I have met in my life.

A few additional observations:

Someone recently discovered a letter from Sweet to General Hoffman asking permission to pay Shanks $100 a month for a year to reward him for his work as he "detected and identified the presence of some of the officers and prisoners engaged in the conspiracy." There is no record of Hoffman's approval, but presumably Shanks was paid. This letter confirms the claim by Letitia Walsh that both Shanks and Sweet had perjured themselves at the trial.

Most of the writing after the war about the "conspiracy" reflected the opinion of the *Tribune* and William Bross. Letitia's memoir was never published. However, recent writers like Chicago's George Levy in his fine book *To Die in Chicago* (1994) finds the same weakness in the Great Conspiracy theory that she attempted to explode in her memoir—though Levy did not have her memoir available. He comments that it requires an act of faith to believe in the "conspiracy." If we are to judge by Letitia's words and by John Walsh's subsequent successes, not many people believed in it after the war despite the propaganda of the *Tribune* and its allies. Perhaps the historical record has been clarified because now both sides have told their story—long after anyone but a few historians, and you and I, bother to care about it.

Despite our sympathy for "The Irish Lace", you might want to consider that our memoirist is curiously vague about the weapons stored in her father's barn. The records show that the Union troops took away 142 shotguns and 349 revolvers that night, along with 13,412 cartridges and 8 bags of buckshot. This is a small arsenal, though it probably would not have been enough with which to storm the camp.

John Walsh's claim that the weapons were merely for the protection of the Sons of Liberty and Chicago Democrats against riots by Republicans may seem a little thin.

That is for you to judge.

I'll be fascinated to hear your opinions about all of this and how it might have relevance to us.

Dermot Michael Vincent Coyne
Aspiring Seanachie

10

"SOMETIMES I frighten myself," Nuala said with a shiver. "I don't like it at all, at all."

"More voices, Nuala?"

She hugged herself as if she were walking down a dark street on a cold winter night.

"Wasn't this the first house they lived in, Dermot Michael?"

"Who lived in?"

" 'Titia and her Paddy. Doesn't one of my colleagues at work look up the old censuses for the fun of it? And didn't he tell me that this house was built right after your Civil War? And didn't the 1870 census list the people who lived in it as Patrick Murray, Attorney at Law, and Letitia Walsh Murray, Lace Maker—and themselves with two children already?"

It was my turn to feel the winter winds that had swept into Nuala's little apartment.

"Nuala, that's—"

"I know it is, Dermot, but here's the memo he sent me."

There it was—on Arthur Andersen stationery in neat computer type: a hint of a voice from the past.

In response to your question about the house in which you live on Southport, the first owners were a Captain and

Mrs. Patrick Murray. He was an officer in the Union Army during the Civil War and she was a famous lace maker. Her father was alleged to be involved in the famous Camp Douglas Conspiracy.

"I wondered whether this old house might be source of my visions. So didn't I ask your man last week if he could look it up, and didn't he send it over here this afternoon?"

"That's why you phoned me?"

"Well," she blushed, "didn't I want to make supper for you, too?"

"You think there's a connection between the fact that the two of them sat together in this room a century and a quarter ago and what you felt out at 31st Street?"

"Slept here, Dermot. Before they split this poor old place up into two apartments, this must have been the master bedroom."

She hugged herself again.

For a moment I felt pure terror, a sense of the uncanny enveloping me like a vampire's cloak. I wanted to get out of that room, then and there.

"So we'd better listen to her."

The voice was that of Nuala the matriarch: the matter was settled, and that was that.

"I like the woman," she said as she lifted my third report from the floor next to her chair and arranged it on the coffee table beside the teapot.

"Letitia?" I said stupidly.

"Isn't she the brave and clever woman? Doesn't she tell nice little secrets about her sex life to titillate her readers and win them even more to her side?"

"You noticed that?"

"Doesn't she say that she knew the same feelings when she was their age and that she still does? And, sure, didn't she show it to himself before she gives it to anyone else to read?"

"Do you hear her voice as you read it, Nuala, like you heard Ma's voice when you were translating her diary in Dublin?"

"Och, don't you know that I do?"

I shivered. More of Nuala Anne's spooks.

"And weren't them Irish Lace trio a powerful bunch?"

"They were indeed."

"Sure she cuts things a little fine when it suits her purpose, like never telling them or us how many guns her father had stashed away in the barn."

"She did that."

Nuala lifted my text and weighed it in her hand, as if measuring the truthfulness.

"She's telling the truth—mostly, anyway. I think she was never quite sure what her daddy was up to and didn't want to speculate."

"There were not enough guns in the barn to break open the camp—not without a serious risk of failure. John Walsh was not the man to try something like that."

"And, besides, they had nowhere near enough men, did they, now?"

"They did not."

"Do you want to know what I think?"

"Naturally!"

"Well, won't you have to wait till I make another ham-and-cheese sandwich for you?"

"I guess so," I said, as she grabbed my plate and bounded out to the tiny kitchen.

In a few moments, she bounded back, sandwich on a new plate. As she put it on the table, she ran her hand quickly along the side of my face. I gulped.

"Well, now, where was I? Och, wasn't I about to tell you what I think?"

"Woman, you were."

"I *think* that your man was so obsessed with the prisoners, poor men, that he would have led a break-in—and himself the father of twelve!—if there was a good chance to free them and send them home, and if there were not eejits dreaming about burning down Chicago. She suspected that, but had no proof and was not going to put her suspicions down on paper because that friggin' gobshite Bross had already roused enough suspicion. So your man listens to Hines and his crowd because he thought this might be a chance to get the prisoners out. He quickly realizes that they are frigging amadons altogether, and maybe dangerous, too. Still, he hangs on because doesn't he think there might be a last chance to free the prisoners? He hangs on a little too long and gets caught."

"He would have stormed the camp with the small amount of weaponry at his disposal?"

"Not with the Hines bunch, because they are a bunch of shallow dreamers with no knowledge about how to do it right. With the right people at the right time, and himself knowing about tactics from his years in the army, sure I think he would have done it, wouldn't he?"

"How would he do it?"

"Maybe a quiet attack in the early-morning hours when everyone is asleep. He tells no one of the plans except the men who are in on the plot. And they're the kind who don't talk. He doesn't tell the prisoners either, because he knows there are spies all over that place. He and his people sneak up at night, overpower some of the guards, and most of them probably sleeping anyway. Then don't they sneak into the camp, disarm more of the guards, throw open the gates, and tell the prisoners to run for it?"

"Risky."

"He's a brave man with strong principles. He's ready to take a chance to end the suffering in the camp, and who is to say he's not morally right? Wouldn't we praise Germans who broke into the concentration camps and freed as many of the prisoners as they could?"

"I see your point."

"Except he's a frigging eejit, and himself with twelve children."

"He probably figured that he and his men could slip away in the darkness as soon as they opened the gates and before the boys in blue knew what was happening."

"And he had enough weapons so they could maybe get themselves home to the South, but not enough to burn down the city."

She peered at me anxiously, hoping I would not ridicule her theory.

I had learned my lesson in Dublin. When Nuala Anne, girl detective, was on a roll, you let her roll.

"Makes sense."

"So, don't you see, Derm, that was another conspiracy that never was?"

"Is the woman mad at you for figuring it all out?"

"Certainly NOT! Doesn't she believe that now it's time for the whole truth to be told?"

I shivered again. I had yet to figure out how much of this talking with dead people was just Nuala's West of Ireland mysticism and how much of it was real. Probably the question was irrelevant, anyway.

"I'm sure she would."

"Would *you* have stayed under her bed, Dermot Michael?"

"That's a very personal question, Nuala Anne. If I had a Miss Amanda waiting for me home in Ol' Kentucky, I think I would have, though the temptation would have been strong to engage in other activities. I wouldn't have wanted to mess with her if she decided to fight me off."

"And herself half in love with him anyway."

That shook me up. "Really!"

"Sure isn't that obvious? Halfway through the story,

she starts to call him 'Tom.' At that silly age, a woman might be truly in love with her soldier boy. But he's a long way from home and might never come back. And this young man is right there and very nice and very darling. And you're lonely and your emotions are volatile, as they are at that age. In a way aren't you happy to see him riding off through the prairies in the dark because that removes the temptation? Sure, she half loved him, poor child. Not that she ever would have been unfaithful to her Paddy, if you take my meaning."

"I do indeed, Nuala. Her love for Hines was a delightful and somewhat wicked fantasy, and she enjoyed it and would not permit anything to come of it."

"That's true enough," she sniffed, "though it's a man's way of putting it, isn't it, now? Still you're a man, and it's all right for you to put it that way."

"I miss a few of the emotional nuances?"

"Just a *few* of them! I'll be getting your chocolate ice cream now. One or two scoops?"

"Three."

She returned shortly. It looked to me as if there were four scoops of ice cream. I didn't complain. Herself had brought on a very delicate half-scoop on her own plate.

"She was more than a flighty girl, Nuala. After all, she was older then than you are now."

"Just barely, but how else would I know her emotions unless I was capable of the same feelings meself?"

"You're the one who should be the writer."

"Haven't I told you often, that I'm an accountant?" she said with a warning frown.

"Woman, you have!"

The frown vanished.

"Still and all," she continued, "wasn't he a pleasant memory in the back of her brain, though she had no illusions about him? And wasn't your man wonderful that night at dinner?"

"Paddy Murray?"

"And himself telling her that he didn't mind and that it was all right for her to have that memory?"

"Yeah, he seems to have been a pretty impressive guy."

"Wouldn't he have to have been?"

"Yep."

The ice cream was delicious, probably because now I was fully out of my hangover.

"So there were lots of conspiracies going on at the same time; her daddy's, the Rebels, Colonel Sweet, the prisoners, the *Tribune*, and maybe a lot of other amadons in town who were up to no good or waiting around for someone else to be up to no good. So what was the 'Great Camp Douglas Conspiracy,' the one that never was?"

"What was it, Nuala?"

The ice cream was disappearing at an alarming rate.

"Wasn't it an accidental combination of all of them which took on a life of its own and ran out of control? Wasn't it just what might happen in a city divided by the war, uncertain about the slaves, teeming with rumors, and desperately afraid? Why can't your historian fellows see that?"

Explained that way and with such eloquence, it did seem like a reasonable explanation.

"Because none of them are as perceptive as you are, Nuala Anne McGrail."

"Go 'long with ya!" she said, with a pleased smile.

Like I say, I had learned my lesson in Dublin.

"Well," she continued, "I'm sure herself thinks it's time the whole story be told. Otherwise, why would I be finding out about Camp Douglas? So you'll have to write it up, won't you, now? Maybe in one of your stories."

"Her document is in the archives, Nuala Anne."

"What good is it doing there?"

"A point well taken. . . . All right, I see the makings of a historical novel in this stuff. I've always wanted to write about the Civil War."

"And we have to find the letter."

"From your man in the White House?"

"The very same. A. Lincoln himself."

"But doesn't she say that she lost it?"

"Mislaid it. Now she knows where it is. She expects me to find it. She needs that to clear her father completely."

"Nuala, they're both in heaven. . . ."

"That doesn't mean they're not interested in seeing that the truth is told."

That was a highly idiosyncratic theology, but who was I to argue?

"How are we to find it?"

"Keep looking for it."

"All right," I said to humor her. "I'll keep looking for it."

"Just like we looked for your man's gold in them mountains."

"Right."

It was a very different story than that of Roger Casement's gold, but I was not about to argue. Not in what once had been Letitia Walsh's bedroom.

"Now do you want to know how it fits to our problem today?"

"I didn't know that was the way you were thinking."

"Sure, why else would I have dragged you over here on a hot night like this?"

She poured me a third cup of tea. She did not, however, offer me more ice cream.

"Och, this is too cold. I'll go out and boil some more water."

"Fine."

She returned after turning on the electric teapot on her minuscule sink.

"Sit down, Dermot Michael. I want you sitting when I explain it to you."

"Let me hear about it."

"Well," she said, drawing a deep breath, "won't I tell you now?"

And she did, pausing in mid-narrative to bring in the fresh water for our tea. After ordering me to let it steep for a minute or two, she poured more tea for each of us and went on with her theory.

It was wild, mad, improbable—and probably accurate.

"Am I right or am I wrong, Dermot Michael Coyne?"

"It all figures, Nuala. Makes sense. But how do we ever prove it?"

"I want to become a temporary employee of Reliable Security. Then you and I can solve the mystery of a conspiracy that never was."

"You want me to get us credentials as private detectives?"

"Well," she said shyly, "wouldn't it be nice if you did?"

Back to my Dermot the Spear Carrier guise.

"What about your job?"

"Didn't they offer me a couple of days off to recover from me trauma?"

"OK," I said, swallowing my male pride, "Tell me what we're going to do."

So she did.

It was a crazy solution to the art thefts.

Only it didn't sound crazy when she explained it to me.

Not until she said, "Herself thinks it's the right solution."

"Who?"

" 'Titia, naturally. She knows all about conspiracies that never were."

I didn't know whether Nuala was joking. I didn't want to know.

— 11 —

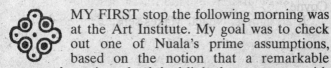 MY FIRST stop the following morning was at the Art Institute. My goal was to check out one of Nuala's prime assumptions, based on the notion that a remarkable woman, long since dead, had linked our mystery with her own. Several times as I walked down Michigan Avenue, I told myself that I was out of my frigging mind for believing that Letitia Walsh was pointing out a solution to our mystery.

However, spear carriers do what they are told to do.

I give the Art Institute (never, absolutely never, in Chicago called simply the "Institute" the way the University of Chicago is normally called the "University") some money every year, as I do the Lyric Opera and the Symphony because I figure I should. I hang around over there occasionally, probably less than I should. You tend to take the really good places in your home city for granted because they'll always be there.

I knew a man in the administration of the Art Institute who was happy to see me at 10:30.

"How are the preparations for the Monet show coming along, Edgar?" I began.

"Splendid, Dermot. It will be the biggest Monet exhibit ever. Probably the biggest there ever will be for a long time. We're planning a lot of special events. I hope you'll be able to attend some of them."

"I will indeed."

"You know that the young people have attributed a special meaning to the word 'Monet'? I must say that it's a remarkably erudite slang word."

"I've heard some of the teens in our family use it. It's not exactly a compliment, but I haven't caught the allusion."

"It means"—he grinned sheepishly—"that the person looks great from a distance, but when one comes close, one notices that the person is all mixed up and confused."

"It *is* remarkably erudite for adolescents."

One of which I was not so long ago. Some in the family would say that my adolescence had ended only recently, if it had ended at all.

"We can only hope that the popularity of the word will attract them to the Art Institute for the exhibition. We will not be lacking for people, heaven knows. Yet we would love to attract young people. I'm sure that Monet would appeal to their romantic instincts."

"As they do to mine."

We were both dodging around the subject of the theft at the Armacost Gallery. He must have assumed that I had heard about it and was curious. Whether he knew about Cindy and Ms. McGrail was another matter. He didn't seem to be the kind who watched a lot of television.

"We'll be sure you get a brochure about all the events that our sponsors are free to attend."

"Thank you."

By the middle of August, I would be sick of Monet, and never want to see one of his canvases again.

As is generally known, the Irish like to approach matters indirectly and at the end of a conversation, over dessert, perhaps, or when one is saying good-bye at the end of the night or as one is walking out of a room. So I was uneasy about jumping into the reason for my visit directly. Genes or culture or both constrained me not to do it. Yet I had to.

"Were those canvases that were stolen from Armacost to be part of the exhibition?" I asked very cautiously.

If Edgar was surprised at my uncharacteristic bluntness, he did not show it. However, he answered me uneasily.

"Well, no, Dermot. Actually not. They did not offer them to us. That's understandable. They might very well want to keep their canvases distinct for fear that they would be lost among so many others. After all, a Monet is a Monet, so even an early and somewhat dubious painting still may be worth millions. Moreover, they may attract potential buyers who are in Chicago for our exhibition."

"I see. . . ."

"As you no doubt realize, Monet destroyed many of his canvases because they did not achieve his own standards of excellence. The existence of the two paintings over at the Armacost became known only recently."

"You have not asked to exhibit their canvases?"

"No, Dermot, we have not."

"And if they had offered them to you?"

He hesitated again.

"This is a very delicate area, Dermot."

"So I understand."

"It has never been the Art Institute's policy to, ah, disparage the holdings of a commercial gallery, especially one in Chicago. Our worlds are rather different, you know. Moreover, the Armacosts have been very generous to us."

"So I understand."

"Moreover, we hardly are in the police business. If someone asks us about a piece of art, we would normally be very hesitant in offering an opinion."

"I'm sure you would."

"Nonetheless, in the present circumstances—"

"Which are a little different from ordinary circumstances."

"You will not quote me?"

"Certainly not."

"Or involve the Art Institute?"

"No way."

"Well, let me show you the latest catalog from the Armacost."

He rose from his desk, opened a file cabinet, and rummaged through it.

I watched the cars moving down Monroe Street towards the lake—a wondrous, shimmering light blue mirror. I was to meet herself at the Chicago Yacht Club at the foot of Monroe Street later for lunch.

Finally Edgar removed a catalog from the cabinet.

"Here we are, Dermot. You'll note the Monet picture on the cover."

"Yes, no water lilies."

It was, in fact, a painting of a boat anchored in a body of water under marvelous thunderhead clouds.

"Sainte Adresse, I'd guess," I continued, showing off just a bit. "It's quite lovely, isn't it?"

He opened a drawer in his desk, pulled out a color photograph, and shoved it across his desk.

I looked at it and compared it with the picture on the cover of the Armacost catalog.

"They certainly look similar, Edgar, though a lot of Monet's paintings look like one another. The man loved to paint the same scenes."

"Not *that* similar."

"Ah?"

"He never actually repeated himself. There were minor variations. That's natural, when you stop to think of it. He was a different man on a different day each time he painted the garden. Actually, it would have been very difficult for him to repeat himself."

"I see."

"We are quite confident of the provenance of the ones we will exhibit. The other is a beach scene from the same period. It is from the gallery of a private collector of unimpeachable integrity who would not have been fooled by an imitation. They have never been exhibited before."

"Ah!"

"Naturally, we do not intend to make any comparisons. There might have been some controversy with two versions of the same scene hanging in Chicago at the same time. But we assume that the Armacosts would remove their paintings from display. We certainly wouldn't have created the controversy. Some of the art critics may have, to say nothing of the media."

He spoke the last word with great distaste.

"The Armacost catalog would still be available?"

"Yes, indeed. I do not see how the controversy could have been avoided."

"And these two"—I flicked open the cover of the catalog to look at their second painting—"are fakes."

"Yes, Dermot. But very clever imitations, masterfully done by someone who had studied Monet very carefully and believed that the two paintings we will exhibit would never be seen in public. Doubtless he had seen the originals at some time and remembered very clearly what they were. More than likely, he managed to photograph them secretly."

"Would the Armacosts have been able to detect the fraud?"

"Our experts here could have looked at the paintings and seen nothing wrong with them. If the Armacosts were wise, they would have brought in one or two of the world's truly great Monet experts. I don't think they would have been fooled. However, as I have said, it is a very, very ingenious copy. Imitations like these have a considerable value in and of themselves."

"Insurance companies?"

"Unless they brought in the same one or two of the best men in the world, they would have insured as if these canvases were valid paintings by the master. We have no way of knowing."

"How much would the imitations earn in the open marketplace?"

"Once they were known as imitations? Oh, perhaps a couple of hundred thousand dollars each."

"And if they were thought to be authentic?"

"Millions. Indeed, at a Sotheby's auction with Arab oil barons and wealthy Japanese collectors, perhaps tens of millions."

"I see."

"I beg you, Dermot, not to draw any conclusions from this. It is altogether likely that neither the Armacosts nor the thieves were aware of these facts. The imitator, if he is still alive and knows where his canvas is, might have read that the originals were to be exhibited and was afraid of being trapped. Anything might have happened."

"Indeed."

"None of this may have any relationship to the theft at all."

"Was it known that your collector was permitting the exhibition of his canvases?"

"Indeed it was. It was big news in the art world because he was known to have ten Monet canvases. Pictures of some appeared in the European papers, most notably, the Sunday *Times*—of London, naturally."

I didn't think it was the *Chicago Sun-Times,* the remote descendant of 'Titia's paper.

"No pictures of these two?"

"Not insofar as I am aware of it."

"Yet, if the insurance company sees that your exhibit has almost exactly the same canvases, they may be reluctant to pay out the claims of the Armacosts."

"That is altogether possible. However, in the ab-

sence of the Armacost canvases, it would be difficult—
if not impossible—to prove that they were not original. A world-class expert could confirm that ours were
original, but he could not really make any judgments
about those that had been stolen. . . . Incidentally, I assume that there was actually a theft. Did not a passing
driver see the frames actually being carried out of the
Armacost Gallery?"

"He certainly did."

Which of course meant that he certainly claimed
that he did.

I shook hands with Edgar, promised him my total
confidence, and took my leave.

Before I had left the John Hancock Center for the
Art Institute, I had called Reliable Security and asked
them if I could talk to the head of the company.

"Casey," said a flat cop's voice at the other end of
the connection.

"My name is Dermot Coyne . . ." I began.

"I know who you are Mr. Coyne," he replied with
a pleasant laugh. "I'm kind of a shirttail relative of the
bishop for whom your brother works. I also know
about our protection of your, ah, young woman."

"We would like to meet with you, Mr. Casey. My,
ah, young woman has some ideas about the art-gallery
thefts."

"Could we have breakfast tomorrow morning? Coffee shop of the Ritz-Carlton?"

"Fine. Er, I believe she would like to work for you
on this case. Volunteer."

"Indeed?" he chuckled. "I look forward to meeting
her in person. She has a smooth television persona."

"That's only one of many."

I then told him about how, in her detective persona,
in Dublin and Galway she had solved the mystery of
who had killed Michael Collins, the great Irish revolutionary leader.

"I certainly look forward to meeting her," he said,

duly impressed. "Eight o'clock too early?"

"Not at all."

Outside it was hotter, and curtains of humidity were growing thicker—and it was still mid-June. It looked like a long, hot summer.

Nuala had called me early in the morning and said that she was fine and that she was going to work so "they won't give me job to someone else. I'll ask them for the days off."

"I have set up a breakfast tomorrow with the head of Reliable."

"Mike Casey? He's a famous artist, too, you know. Relative of the bishop."

"Of course."

Naturally, I didn't know. I knew about Casey the painter, but I didn't know that he had a security firm on the side. Ah, Chicago!

"Can we meet for lunch?" Nuala continued. "We can compare notes. I'm going to talk to one of me friends at work who knows something about the art galleries."

"Chicago Yacht Club at noon?"

"Grand! . . . Where is it?"

"The foot of Monroe Street. You walk out of your office, turn left, and walk till your hat starts floating."

"I won't be wearing a hat, but I take your point."

"See if you can get an extra half-hour off. They might give you that because you came in today."

"I'll ask, Derm, but I don't know for sure—not after I ask them for the next two days off."

In my mind there was no doubt that the young accountant from T.C.D. could get anything she wanted at that company.

I ambled over the Illinois Central tracks, as we still called them, though the I.C. no longer used them. I adjured myself to remember that until she had gone to Trinity three years ago, Nuala Anne had never been out of County Galway, and not even to Galway City very often. She had grown up an area where Irish was still the first language, part of a backwater that history had left behind. Indeed, she could watch the world on a telly, but that was not quite the real world, was it, now?

Foreign travelers had come to their farmhouse, often on big buses, to drink their tea—and probably be told that this was a typical Irish-speaking family in one of the most picturesque districts of Connemara. She had owned a bicycle but not a car. Her parents had used a donkey cart. She herself had admitted that she would have attended U.C.G. (University College Galway), and "Sure, there's nothing wrong with that at all, at all. Isn't it older than U.C.D. (University College Dublin)?"

Hadn't she, like a true eejit applied for the Trinity scholarship, but only because her ma and da had urged her to? When she won it, wasn't she horrified? She did not want to live in a terrible big city like Dublin at all, at all. She had planned to return home and work in Galway City. But then she learned about the Morrison visa program and the possibility of a job at Arthur Andersen. So she entered her name in the lottery, and hadn't she won it?

Again she didn't want to go to America. Hadn't all her brothers and sisters already left home? Wouldn't her parents be left alone way out in Connemara? Yet didn't her ma and her da urge her to take the job? And didn't she think that they'd be needing money as they grew older, and herself wanting to contribute to their needs?

And, Dermot Michael, you didn't have anything to do with it at all, at all and don't you go thinking you did!

Not even a little bit?

Well, maybe just a little bit.

So she was utterly unprepared for Chicago and its big buildings and the professional-class family that had absorbed her as one of their own on arrival, to say nothing of being hauled off the Area Six lockup.

And she'd been here for only two months!

No wonder she drifted from one persona to another with practiced ease.

No wonder she was homesick.

No wonder she felt like a greenhorn!

She *was* a greenhorn, albeit a gorgeous and self-possessed one.

I slouched into the yacht club some five minutes before noon, demanded a diet Coke from the bartender, and took a whole dish of their great popcorn.

Knowing herself, I looked out the door about a minute before twelve. Sure enough, there she was, standing patiently in the sunlight, waiting for the light to change. She was wearing a light green summer dress with a white belt, nylons, pumps, and, as best as I could tell, a touch of makeup.

What a beautiful young woman!

WELL, the Adversary, said, trying to join me, ISN'T SHE YOURS NOW FOR THE ASKING?

"Go away. I'm working on a mystery."

He slunk away.

Nuala crossed the Drive when the stoplights changed. On a hot summer day with a nice dress, she was not about to hurry. Greenhorn that she was, she didn't know that you had to rush to get across the street before the lights changed again.

So a line of northbound cars could not jump the instant the light changed.

Some boor in a Buick New Yorker beeped at her. She turned in surprise and smiled at him. He beeped more insistently.

I wanted to break his neck.

She turned and looked back at the skyline. She stood there for at least a minute, gazing in awe and admiration at the city.

Then she strolled gracefully into the club.

I met her at the door.

"Glory be, Dermot Michael, isn't this a brilliant place? Look at that skyline and look at all them glorious boats? Can I go out and look at them?"

Every eye in the club followed us out on the deck. A big motor cruiser, at least fifty feet long, drifted by, followed by the powerful blue-and-white boat of the Chicago Police, and then by a sail boat, of the sort which, in a few weeks, would race up to Mackinaw.

"Dermot!" she whispered, "What lovely boats!"

"Aren't they ever?"

"You don't have a boat here, do you Derm?"

"The family has one up in New Buffalo, Michigan, a few miles down the road from Grand Beach. That's why they let me belong. Actually, I joined because of the pastry."

"Go 'long with you," she said, tapping my arm in a gentle reprimand. "You do sail, though, don't you, Dermot?"

I remembered the Galway Hooker T-shirt.

"Sometimes. I'm about the only in the family that still likes it. They're all into windsurfing."

"Sure, I've never done that."

"I'd be glad to teach you and also to let you crew for me on the *Grania*."

"Named after the pirate princess, I suppose?"

"Who else?"

We went back into the club. I ordered another diet Coke for her, sat down a chair, and pushed the popcorn bowl in her direction. She dipped into it with her long, slim fingers and pulled out a huge handful of popcorn.

"Am I not perishing with the hunger, and on a hot day like this, too?"

"Eat all the popcorn you want. We'll go to the table in couple of minutes."

"Could I be taking some of this along for the afternoon, or is that a dumb greenhorn question to ask?"

"Not at all. I'll ask them to put together a package for you."

Actually I had never seen anyone do it before, but why not?

I stopped at the desk and bought her a Chicago Yacht Club sweatshirt (dark blue and gold), a T-shirt (red with the club's semaphore seal on it), and a cap (white).

"You shouldn't be doing this for me, Dermot Michael Coyne."

"And what would your ma say if she heard those words coming from your mouth?"

"She wouldn't say a thing, Dermot, because she'd know I didn't mean it. However she would insist that I thank you very much and, maybe, kiss you."

Which she did.

We sat for a few moments while I finished my Coke and Nuala "destroyed altogether" the bowl (large) of popcorn.

"You're looking much better today than you did yesterday."

" 'Tis only the makeup," she said with one of the all-purpose West of Ireland sighs. "I'm still a little frazzled. I didn't sleep much. . . . Now, isn't that a glorious buffet? I see what you mean by the pastries. And such lovely views! Ah, isn't this an exciting place to eat!"

"How did they react when you came into the office today?"

She blushed.

"Ah, sure, didn't they act like pack of eejits, and themselves cheering and clapping their hands and me boss saying I should have used the extra day off and insisting that I should take two hours off for lunch."

"And they all wanted to know who the romantic interest is?"

"How would you be knowing that?"

"Human nature to be curious about that subject."

"Well, it's none of their friggin' business."

"You didn't tell them that."

"I did not," she replied, sticking her nose up into the sky. "I said that all the speculation was terrible premature. . . . They all know who you are, by the way, and they all say you're a fine man. Didn't my boss say that you really are a grand fella and very bright, too?"

"Yeah."

"He even said that you're very perceptive with women."

"Calumny! Now let's go and collect our buffet and get down to work. If we don't eat wholesome food now, I'm afraid I'll have to get another bowl of popcorn."

Mr. Foster, the maître d', led us over to a table next to the window which looks out on the harbor and was not near any of the other luncheon patrons.

Nuala sat at the table for a moment, asked if I would ever buy her a glass of red wine, and dashed for the buffet. After I ordered two glasses of cabernet sauvignon, I joined her at the buffet. She was filling her plate as if she expected a food shortage in Chicago that afternoon.

" 'Tis grand, Derm, super, brilliant."

Which are the three favorite words in the vocabulary of the Irish. Even the Irish speakers when they are talking in their own language, will often say "did fockin' brill."

That's the super superlative.

"I don't want them to take any of this away before I have a chance to eat it."

I took her salad dish, assured her that the meat and pasta would not get cold, and herded her back to the table.

"Well, your appetite has come back, Nuala Anne."

"This is the first real meal I've had since dinner at Grand Beach on Sunday. I'm perishing with the hunger."

We sat at the table. The wine was served. Nuala took time away from wolfing down the salads she had collected, and toasted me silently. I returned the toast. Then she dug into the salad plate with renewed gusto.

"Well, Ms. Holmes, what did you find out?"

"You first, Dr. Watson."

I reported on my conversation with Edgar.

"Aren't all the conspiracies even more complicated than I expected—and kind of like all that were going on in Chicago a hundred and thirty-one years ago?"

She finished off the very large piece of smoked salmon and then continued working on her salad plate.

"Do you know what the slang word 'Monet' means?"

"Sure. Everyone knows that. It's someone who looks great from a distance, and then is all jumbled and confused and messed up if you get close to him . . . or her. Even we greenhorns know that. Now what do you have to tell me?"

I felt very old, close to retirement.

"You were right about your key prediction. There is indeed something funny about those canvases."

"Didn't I tell you there would be?"

Several members of the club and their wives came to our table; purportedly to say hello to me, but actually to meet herself. Some of them didn't even know about the drama at Area Six yesterday. She responded to them graciously and told everyone how "wonderful altogether" the food at the yacht club was.

I reflected that even though I was receiving something of a reputation—in very limited circles—for my stories, Nuala would always be the first to get attention when we appeared in public. Nor did she need a few sound bites on TV to attract interest.

So be it.

We returned to the meat and vegetable table. Didn't Nuala sweep through that table like a Viking—roast beef, ham, mashed potatoes, two kinds of pasta, and just "a small bit of chicken."

"Am I disgracing you altogether, Dermot Michael?"

"You're entitled to as much as you want, Nuala Anne, and yourself hardly eating a thing all day yesterday."

Back at our table, and with another glass of cabernet, Ms. Holmes turned to her report.

"Well, didn't your man tell me everything I wanted to know without asking why I was interested and himself suspecting all along why?"

"And he said?"

"He said that the art business in Chicago was in frigging terrible shape. People don't like modern art anymore and most of the galleries have contracts with artists who do only modern. He said that the last recession dried up demand and that the recovery is also slower in the luxury markets then other markets. The galleries in River North, says he, have high rents to pay and not many customers anymore. He also says that a place like the Armacost or Richard Gray's Gallery in your building are still doing well enough, but the others are living on the edge, even though their books look pretty good. It's the big inventories that are doing the trick on them."

"So, did he think they might turn to theft of their own work to collect insurance?"

"He said that there were easier ways to collect. Like arson. There are a lot of very accomplished arsonists in Chicago who would leave no clues at all, at all."

You learn something new about your city every day.

"He did say that he's fairly certain the insurance companies will pay eventually, but not without a fight that will take a long time. He says he could hardly believe that Wayne Armacost would do anything like that."

"Uh-huh."

"He said that the big office-building boom in Chicago ended about five years ago. Architects and developers had bought many modern paintings to decorate walls and lobbies and such like—there's one in the lobby of your building. Now they aren't building any new buildings and won't for a long time. The rents in River North are going up, and restaurants and high-price specialty stores are replacing the galleries. It's hard times over there."

"I didn't know that."

"It fits my theory perfectly, doesn't it?"

"It sure does."

"Don't you see, Derm, me love, that the gobshites could have waited inside till they saw a car coming and then dashed out into the street to make it look like a theft?"

"Pretty wild possibility, it seems to me."

"That's what happens when several conspiracies come together and men and women are desperate. That's what we learned from 'Titia."

"Well, I know what my task is for tomorrow."

"Tomorrow evening, I have another idea on which we can cooperate. . . . Now let's try some of those pastries."

"The Linzer torte is wonderful."

So she took a slice of Linzer torte, a dish of dark chocolate mousse, and a large piece of apple pie with whipped cream.

I was content with the Linzer.

"And our buried treasure, Ms. Holmes?"

"One thing at a time, Dr. Watson. It will turn up. I know it will."

All right. I know my role.

We finished eating at 12:50.

"Don't we have tons of time, Derm? Let's go over to Mr. Daley's Ferris wheel."

I aged several more years. I didn't like heights, and I didn't like rides. While I had not eaten as much as Nuala Anne, I could easily vomit at the top of Rich's

Ferris wheel. Humiliate myself half to death. I was too young to be such an old man.

There was no way out, however.

I hailed a cab and we rode up to Navy Pier.

"What a brill place, Dermot. Can we come back here again and look at the grand shops and museums and the lovely walks?"

"Certainly," I said, already feeling queasy.

The line waiting for the wheel was, alas, short. We slipped into our car, which we had all to ourselves, before one o'clock.

The wheel doesn't move very fast. You can easily climb on it while it's running. In fact, it never stops moving till the end of the day, so you have to get on a car while it's easing along the platform. Herself flew in without a second's pause.

I had a more difficult time and stumbled in on my second try. Nuala didn't notice because she was too busy screaming.

She screamed, shouted, laughed, hugged me, and clung to me as we spun around slowly. Normally, I wouldn't ignore such gestures, but I was so frightened by the height and so queasy from the motion that I hardly noticed.

Unlike the windows in my apartment, the doors in the Ferris-wheel cars could open. Therefore, my acrophobia concluded, they WILL open.

I concealed my woes from Nuala, who was so busy with her cries of glee that she wasn't paying much attention to me, save as a guarantee of stability.

When our car reached the very top of the wheel, I thought I would lose everything—my lunch and my nerve.

However, the revolution of the wheel continued; the ground rose to meet us, however slowly.

Nuala shrieked joyously all the way to the ground, loving every second of terror.

I really am too old for her. Maybe I was born too old.

When we eased up to the platform, I stood up on very shaky pins. The attendant opened the door from the outside, I tried to step out of it but the ground was tilting and swaying and shaking.

Nuala simply shoved me out.

"Och, Derm, wasn't it brilliant!"

"Dead friggin' brill."

"Thank you so much. And won't your man be unhappy with you if you don't ride on his carousel?"

"What man?"

"The Lord Mayor, who else?"

"We don't have Lord Mayors in this country, Nuala Anne, only mayors—and how would he know that I didn't ride his merry-go-round?"

"Well, sure the next time I see him," she hesitated and then continued, "somewhere or the other, won't I tell him?"

So Grand Beach was still under interdict.

"You never would!"

She had cleverly guided me to the ticket office for the merry-go-round. I still wasn't quite sure where the ground was, so I had followed her trustingly.

"Yes, I would. Here it is now. Just one ride, and then I have to get back to me office."

With unsteady hands, I bought two tickets. We waited for the merry-go-round—which is its proper name no matter what they call it in Europe. Even before it stopped to pick us up, my stomach was rumbling and churning.

Nuala bounded on to a white horse. I climbed gingerly aboard Ol' Paint. The music started, the machine began to move and then spun forward at an altogether rapid rate.

My young friend was vibrant with the thrill of riding around in circles, her black hair streaming behind her, eyes dancing, face glowing, thin dress pressed against her body.

She was a wonderful sight. I figured that if I kept my eyes on her I wouldn't vomit.

Maybe that helped. I climbed off Ol' Paint when the merry-go-round finally clanked to a halt, convinced that I would be sick for the rest of my life. But vomit I did not.

Of course herself took no notice of my condition.

"We must find a cab and hurry back to my office," she warned me. "Ah, there's one, Derm!"

She waved her hand and yelled. The cab stopped. Nuala jumped in and dragged me after her.

"122 West Monroe," she told the driver. Then she leaned back in her seat and recounted all the terrors and delights of our midday adventure. The jerking forward and braking of the cab as the driver wrestled with early afternoon traffic through the Loop was almost a repetition of the rides.

"Here we are, Derm," she shouted exultantly. "I'm five minutes early."

I helped her out of the car.

"I think I'll walk home."

"Pay the man, dear."

"Yes, of course. Sorry."

I gave him a ten-dollar bill and waved away the change.

"Would I be right in thinking, sir, that the young lady enjoyed those rides more than you did?"

"She is too young for me."

"I very much doubt it, sir. . . . She's very attractive."

"I've noticed that, too."

I walked over to the Richard J. Daley Civic Center, found a convenient men's room, and left my lunch as a tribute to His Honor's new Ferris wheel.

Then I walked back to my apartment and collapsed into bed. The only way to deal with vertigo is to sleep it off. Even in my sleep the wheel continued to sway and the merry-go-round to turn.

I was awakened by the phone which I had forgot to turn off.

"Dermot Coyne."

"Are you all right, Dermot?"

Herself.

"I'm fine, Nuala. Why not?"

"You looked kind of peaked. Some of me friends in Dublin, great big strong amadons like yourself, used to get sick something terrible when we would ride the beach Ferris wheel down in Bray. Sure, there's no disgrace in that. We're all born with different inner ears, you know. If you get sick on them friggin' things, you should have told me."

I lied. I said a barefaced and total falsehood.

"Occasionally I get a little dizzy. Nothing more than that. I had a wonderful time watching you enjoy yourself. Anything that makes you hug me that often has to be good."

"There's no disgrace in being dizzy, Dermot Michael Coyne."

"Yes, ma'am."

"Well, I was thinking about our project."

"Ah."

"I don't think we should talk about it on the phone. So I wonder if I could take you to supper tomorrow night?"

"How can I pass up an offer like that?"

"You know the restaurants around my office."

"Have they taken you to the Italian Village yet?"

"They have not, but I hear it's a brilliant place."

"I'll pick you up at your office at five, and we'll walk over. I'll drive you home afterwards."

"Grand!"

"You doing OK, Nuala Anne?"

"Much better, Dermot Michael, much better. By tomorrow I'll be me old self. Are you sure you are OK?"

"Couldn't be better."

Another lie.

If our relationship had a future, I must tell her the truth about everything. She'd figure it out if I didn't.

Ugh.

I SWAM the next morning. I had to be in good condition to persuade this cop-turned-painter that Nuala and I were not over the top.

It might be hard because I was not perfectly sure that we were not over the top—and maybe 'round the bend altogether.

The swim helped, but every time I closed my eyes, the wheel swayed and the merry-go-round sputtered.

A few minutes before eight, I walked into the Ritz-Carlton coffee shop—on the eleventh floor of Water Tower Place, as was the lobby and the Carlton Room where I had taken herself to supper, it seemed like a hundred years ago.

A tall, handsome man in his early sixties, with iron gray hair and an innocent face, stood up. Sean Connery with hair. I grinned and he grinned back.

"Mr. Coyne?" He held out his hand and smiled genially.

"Dermot." I shook hands with him.

"Mike," he replied.

He was impeccably groomed in a charcoal gray three-piece suit, a blue shirt, and a dark blue tie. He was about as unlike your Hollywood private eye as any man could be. We chatted for a few moments about the heat and the Cubs. Like me, he was a long-suffering Cub fan; he had been alive in 1945, the last year the Cubs had won the pennant, a half-century ago.

Promptly at eight, Nuala appeared, today in somber gray suit, her hair knotted in a bun, and wearing her phony glasses.

I ordered raisin bran, an English muffin, and tea.

He ordered toast and coffee.

Nuala ordered most everything on the menu. She turned on all her charm for Mike Casey. It worked. It always did. How could anyone so lovely and intelligent be crazy?

Just wait till you hear her.

"Perhaps we should get down to business, Dermot."

"I think Nuala will present our case."

In terse and succinct declarative sentences, Nuala summarized my research on the Camp Douglas conspiracy.

At first the former police superintendent—as I had learned he had been—listened politely. Then he leaned forward, coffee cup in hand, and absorbed every word my beloved was saying.

"Fascinating," he murmured.

"So you see," Nuala said, "It was a conspiracy that never was. There were lots of trivial conspiracies—the *Tribune*'s, Colonel Sweet's, Captain Hines's, poor St. Leger Grenfel's, John Walsh's, Clement Vallandigham's, the prisoners' in the camp—but none were serious in the sense of having any chance of ever happening. So the Great Camp Douglas Conspiracy never was."

"That's the way it is with a lot of alleged conspiracies," Mike Casey said with a nod of his head.

Then she told him about Letitia Walsh Murray, who had lived in the house she lived in now.

I think the cop-turned-painter shivered, just as I had.

"Very interesting," he said. "My wife was once involved in something like that."

"Irish?" I asked.

"What else? You two will have to meet her."

"Well, don't you see now how the art-gallery theft at the Armacost is the same thing, a conspiracy that never was?"

Her first interrogative sentence in several minutes.

Very slowly, Mike Casey put down his coffee cup and gulped.

"To be perfectly honest, Ms. McGrail—"

"Nuala."

"I don't quite see the connection."

"Well, aren't there a lot of conspiracies—one perhaps at the gallery, another with the terrorists, another with the state's attorney, one with the real thieves?"

"Are there?"

"There are," she said firmly. "And the real conspiracy never was."

"Indeed?"

"It's only an analogy," she continued. "But if you take Camp Douglas as a model and apply it, you come up with very interesting results."

"Do you now?" he said, resting his chin on his fist.

"You do."

Then she explained what she thought had happened.

He did not ridicule her theory, nor even express any doubts about it. He merely listened thoughtfully and then nodded his head.

"You might be right, young woman. It certainly fits what we know about, especially when we take into account Dermot's research on the Monets. . . . So you two want to sign on as temporary employees as well as clients of Reliable? Why not? Only promise me you'll be careful."

We promised solemnly.

"I'll make a few calls to clear the way for you. You'll

want to talk to the man who saw the thieves fleeing the Armacost, won't you?"

Indeed we would.

We waited for him in front of the elevators. The tireless fountain continued to spit water, producing a noise which Nuala described as, "Doesn't it sound like a herd of cattle pissing on rocks?"

Once heard, the metaphor is never forgotten.

The "beautiful people"—the only kind you see at the Ritz-Carlton—bustled back and forth from the elevators. An idea for a story about a hotel like this percolated through my brain. I dismissed it quickly: The only reason for the story was to use Nuala's metaphor.

Herself had drifted off to the women's room.

"We're in luck," Mike Casey said. "Our man is a banker in Mount Prospect and will be happy to talk to you."

"Could I ask a small question, Mike?"

"Sure."

"You don't think this is crazy?"

"I think it's worth a shot. . . . You plan to marry that extraordinary young woman?"

"My family thinks I will."

He nodded and smiled.

"She's an accountant?"

"Yes."

"Anytime she wants a job as a detective, she's got one at Reliable. She has the green thumb."

In my car I explained to the Woman with the Green Thumb what Mount Prospect was—a suburb that wished Chicago would go away.

"Doesn't it strike you as interesting that our man from Mount Prospect, and himself a banker, would be driving on Superior Street that late at night?"

"People from out there," I replied, "aren't aware that Chicago exists. It's like another country to them.

They go by O'Hare and they start looking for Allan Quatermain with his elephant rifles."

"Not like your River Forest people?"

"River Forest is an old suburb," I responded. "It's even has a lot of Democratic voters. To your point, however: It does sound very strange. Why Superior Street? You can't get to the Expressway from there. Maybe he was at the Hard Rock Cafe and became confused."

"To tell you the truth, Dermot, he doesn't sound like a Hard Rock Cafe type."

We turned into a massive traffic jam on Ontario Street and inched forward towards the Kennedy Expressway ramp. I described to Nuala the history of the Suho (Superior, Huron, and Ontario) art district as we passed along its south border. Back in the middle 1980s, most of the galleries were forced off of Michigan Avenue by rising rents, a great misfortune for the attractiveness of the Magnificent Mile. They migrated west to the lofts at the edge of the Loop and transformed the neighborhood from a nascent slum to a smart and fashionable place. Some galleries built new structures, others worked marvelous transformations of the lofts. Then, having made the area chic and a definite "must-visit" in Chicago, the galleries were faced with another wave of rent increases which were forcing them to move again or close or, if the galleries owned the building like the Armacost did, to consider renting them to bistros and restaurants and tony bars and nightclubs. In some arenas of life, nothing fails like success.

As we edged our way towards the Kennedy Expressway, I tentatively proposed a theory to explain her contact with Letitia Walsh.

"I assume that since she lived and loved and cried and laughed and raised children in that house, there would be a lot of psychic vibrations from her life still lingering there."

"Why wouldn't there be?" she replied indifferently. "Dermot, why are there so many cars?"

"It's just an ordinary morning in Chicago. . . . So you move into the house and your psychic sensitivities pick up those vibrations."

"Why wouldn't I?"

"Among them is a concern for truth and for her family's reputation, as we saw in her memoir."

"Why wouldn't there be?"

"So that explains why you hear the screams and see the bodies and know about the letter."

"Sure, Dermot Michael, if you need an explanation, that's as good as any other, isn't it now?"

So much for science.

The Kennedy Expressway was a mess. "Fifty minutes to O'Hare," the radio reported with no exaggeration. Our ride to the bank at Mount Prospect required a solid hour, and when we stepped out of the Benz in the shopping plaza, we encountered a solid wall of humidity. I wished I was on the beach over in Michigan, preferably in the company of a gorgeous young woman with long black hair in a skimpy swimsuit. As it was I had to put up with her during one of her attempts to appear dowdy.

The bank seemed to be running very smoothly. It was only slightly less quiet than a mausoleum. Everyone smiled politely at us. In Chicago that's against the rules. An extremely pretty woman with a slender waist and gorgeous legs, in her late fifties or early sixties, greeted us and led us to the president's office. I introduced myself as Mr. Michael McDermot from Mr. Casey's office, showed him our credentials and, as an afterthought, presented Ms. McCool, my assistant.

Our strategy, laid down by herself, was that I did all the talking and she took notes. She did not want anyone to remember her from her brief television appearance.

Mr. Whelan, an overweight man with gray hair, a

frowning face, and nervous hand gestures, said he
would be happy to cooperate with us. Not surprisingly,
he was the same man who had been interviewed on
Today Weekend.

He assumed that we were working for the insurance
companies, an assumption which we neither confirmed
nor denied. The theft of such priceless art was a terrible thing. What you have to expect in a city, of
course; but still terrible.

What had he been doing in Chicago?

His brother had just survived heart surgery. He and
his wife had spent the day with the sick man's family.
He had sent his wife home earlier in the evening. Finally the doctors had told them that the worst was over
and it was safe for them to return to their homes.

"I became tangled up in that rabbit warren of streets
down there. Can't understand why anyone wants to
live in a place like that. I figured if I headed west long
enough I'd find the expressway."

Bad strategy. If he continued west on Superior, he
might still be there. Since he didn't call it the "Kennedy Expressway" or simply the "Kennedy," he was
probably a Republican. (You can recognize Democrats easily, too: They use the real name of the Congress Expressway from the Burnham plan instead of
calling it the Eisenhower, a name Republicans im-
posed on Chicago without asking us.)

And then?

"I was driving slowly west, I stopped at the stop sign
on—what is the name of that street under the L
tracks?"

"Orleans," I suggested.

"Right. It was quite dark there under those tracks.
Foreboding I might say, the kind of place where a car-
jacking might occur. I crossed the street. Suddenly
these men rushed from a building, five of them, four
men carrying these large frames, two for each, and the
fifth man directing them. It all happened very quickly,

faster than a similar scene in a film would take. At first I thought it was all unreal. They threw the frames in the back of an old red pickup truck and drove off at high speed. The police were displeased with me because I could not recognize either the make of the truck or the license number. I told them that it was absurd to expect that I would in the dark."

"You drove over to the Chicago Avenue station?"

"Yes indeed. I was dead tired, and I wanted to get home as quickly as possible. The building from which they had fled was an art gallery, and I felt that it was my civic duty, even in a lawless city like Chicago, to report what seemed to be another art theft."

"How did you find the station?"

"I remembered from the television that there was a Chicago Avenue police station. I calculated that Chicago Avenue was to the north of me. I turned right at the next corner and drove up to Chicago Avenue. Fortunately, my dead reckoning was accurate."

Like Lindbergh crossing the Atlantic! He fiddled nervously with his letter opener—Waterford crystal—as he talked. There was something a little false, a little phony about him. Maybe I just don't like Republicans all that much—and people who describe one of the most interesting neighborhoods in the world as a "rabbit warren."

"I saw the blue lights and turned in that direction. I must say that the Chicago police were quite indifferent to my presence until I used the words 'art heist.' That seemed to awaken them."

"They tend to be very busy down there on Saturday nights," I said smoothly, as if I were there often on Saturday night.

"Yes, that is true. There were a lot of unsavory people in the station that night. Later I learned that the most unsavory appearing were policemen—and women!"

"Detectives, no doubt."

"I suppose so. . . . In any case, they finally permitted me to report the crime; an officer told me that they would take care of it and that I might go home. As far as I could determine, no one seemed inclined to take any immediate action. I must say that, as a taxpayer, I was disturbed by their apparent incompetence."

"Not like *NYPD Blue*—eh, Mr. Whelan?"

"Decidedly not."

His frown became deeper as he talked.

"Now let's go back to the crime scene itself. Can you tell us whether they ran out while you were still at the stop sign, or crossing Orleans, or actually next to the Armacost Gallery?"

Whelan paused; he tapped his letter opener and looked down thoughtfully.

"To the best of my recollection, I had just finished crossing the street and was about at the sidewalk on the other side. It all happened very quickly."

"I quite understand. . . . Do you think it is possible that men could have been waiting inside the gallery until a car would appear because they wanted someone to witness their flight?"

Whelan rested his letter opener on the desk and stared at it thoughtfully.

"That's a very interesting question. It's altogether possible that is what happened. They *did* emerge in quite a rush. Why would they do that?"

"There are any number of reasons, sir. The criminal mind, as I'm sure you realize, is often quite twisted."

I hear a sound from my assistant which could have been a suppressed laugh.

"Yes indeed, Mr. McDermot."

"Did you notice whether the door of the Armacost Gallery was open when you went by it?"

"I had ample time to observe that it was wide open. I stopped there to determine what I ought to do next."

"No lights on?"

"None at all. The place was as dark as a tomb."

"Have you ever visited any of those galleries in the Suho district, Mr. Whelan?"

"No, I have not. I go into Chicago as little as possible. I find that, despite the claim, it is not a city that works. Moreover, I do not like this 'modern' junk at all. I much prefer realism, especially hunting and fishing scenes."

He nodded in the direction of a syrupy canvas on the wall depicting a fisherman and fish staring at one another, the latter still in the water.

I asked the key question, one which the tapping of a pen on notebook next to me suggested I had delayed too long.

"Did you actually see the paintings—I mean, the canvases themselves?"

He puzzled over that one.

"It all happened so quickly. However, I have the impression that the paintings were either covered, or I was seeing the back of the frames. For a brief second or two, they were illumined by my headlights. I have no recollection of any colors."

We thanked him, shook hands, and left the bank.

As we struggled through the wall of humidity, Nuala asked me, "Would the cops at Chicago Avenue really respond that indifferently?"

"In a district like that late Saturday night and early Sunday morning, cops are tired, jaded, and confused. Some of them, not all of them by any means, are dumb. You could walk in off the street and tell them that the Pope had just been shot in Holy Name Cathedral and some guy would make a note and tell you that they'd take care of it."

As the Benz, its blessed air conditioner functioning flawlessly, cruised down the Northwest Toll Road towards the Kennedy, Nuala asked me another question, "What did you think of your man?"

"He's a Republican and in addition to that, I didn't like him. Otherwise he was all right."

"You don't think he'd be the kind that would be involved in an art heist?"

"Who knows? I don't think so."

"Neither do I. . . . Still they were waiting for him, weren't they? They wanted a witness."

If her theory was right, they did indeed want a witness.

Our next stop was the Armacost Gallery, a big new brick building with large picture windows on Superior Street just west of Orleans.

There were three viewing rooms on the first floor, each arranged tastefully and elegantly with thick beige carpet, soft indirect lighting, and attractive salespersons who spoke in hushed whispers. The walls and the pedestals displayed an incredible variety of art subjects, some of it very lovely and some of it gosh-awful.

I felt as if I were in church or a funeral home or maybe a suburban public library.

I whispered to Nuala, "The difficulty with stuff like this is how you know the good stuff from the junk."

"The good stuff is the stuff you like; the bad stuff is the stuff you don't like. That red-and-gold sunburst by Catherine Collins over there is good. That hideous black-and-green thing called 'High Rise' is grotesque. Anyone who hangs that in their parlor is a geek."

The second room displayed older pieces—a Picasso, a Mondrian, and a Jackson Pollock among others. Two blank spaces on the north wall marked the former location of the missing Monets.

"You could look right in through that picture window and see the two paintings, couldn't you?" Nuala murmured softly.

"Yep, they were sitting there just waiting to be taken."

"Kind of silly, with all the thefts going on in town, wasn't it? And everyone knowing that the thieves had a way of zapping the security systems. Asking for a break-in?"

"Maybe. And you gotta wonder why they didn't take the Picasso and the Mondrian."

I pointed at the two paintings.

"I like Mondrian."

That settled that.

The third room contained more representational work. A few years ago, the Armacost would not have bothered with such stuff. Representational art was out, and too bad for Wyeth and Hopper. Now the market had changed and the Armacost had changed with it, though perhaps reluctantly.

There were no fishing and hunting scenes and nothing syrupy like Mr. Whelan's canvas. Some of the canvases, like two misty nudes by Catherine Curran, proved that you could make powerful statements with representational or quasi-representational works. Idly I wondered whether Ms. Curran, who also was some kind of relative of the little bishop for whom Prester George worked, would want to paint Nuala. Maybe she could capture the shy whimsy, the vulnerable strength, the mystical wisdom of my love.

Applying her criteria that what you didn't like was junk, there were also some junk canvases in this room, too: a hideous nude prostitute, which I deemed pornographic, a couple of exhausted racing dogs, a little girl who had been shot by a street gang. They all made statements, which was all right, and appealed for action, which was all right, too. They did not, however, incite the viewer to either compassion or hope.

"You like this one?" Nuala asked me, still sotto voce.

She pointed at a misty scene of the new Navy Pier at night with the Ferris wheel radiating magic light.

"Great," I said fervently, despite my unfortunate experience with the wheel.

"Oh, Dermot . . ."

"Michael."

"Such an eejit I am! . . . But look, isn't it your man the painter?"

She pointed at the signature which said: "Michael Patrick Vincent Casey."

"Can I help you sir?" one of the attractive (female and blond—probably authentic) attendants asked us.

"Mr. Michael McDermot and his assistant to see Mr. Armacost."

"Oh, yes, Mr. McDermot. Wayne is expecting you."

Wayne, huh? Aren't we the informal ones around here.

We were conducted up a spiral staircase to the second floor.

The corridor was lined with offices where men and women were working on computers and other men and women were trying to complete a sale.

It reminded me of the office wing of a car dealership—maybe, given all the tony people in the offices, a Lincoln or Cadillac or, in these days, an Infiniti or Lexus dealership.

At the end of the office an open door awaited us. So Wayne Armacost was a man whose door was always open.

"You may go right in, Mr. McDermot," the attendant said and nodded with a faint perfunctory smile at herself, again to her dumb clerk persona.

Wayne Armacost turned off his computer and stood up to greet us, a tall slender handsome man with white hair, a white goatee, and a faintly English accent (though he had been born in Chicago). He was wearing gray slacks and a white dress shirt with the neck open and the sleeves rolled up. The smile on his thin face was pleasant enough, though his hard brown eyes suggested irritation. With his supple posture, his hooked nose, and the appearance of wisdom provided by his white hair, he might, outfitted with a toga, be an important senator in ancient Rome.

He shook hands vigorously and summoned his wife

Julia from an adjoining office. She was definitely someone to catch and hold the male eye—younger than he was and in her light gray sweater and slacks curvaceous in a Junoesque way. That style of woman was out of fashion now—regrettably, I always thought.

We sat at chairs around his desk, chairs and desk the creation of some modern type. They looked comfortable until you sat in them. Slim Keegan would have destroyed one of them immediately.

Nuala took out her notebook and faded into the background.

"I'm ready to be as cooperative as I can," Wayne Armacost said, leaning forward over his desk. I want to see justice done in this case as well as recover our canvases. I am not at all persuaded that those unfortunate young immigrants would have been capable of a crime of this sort. More than likely, the theft is the work of highly skilled professional art criminals from the Continent. The sophistication of their laser beams which wipe out the security protection suggests men and women of quite superior proficiency. The fact that the various security companies have been unable thus far to develop countermeasures indicates that the thieves are hardly youthful amateurs."

"Do you expect them to be captured?"

"Hardly. I assume that they chose Chicago because of the concentration of galleries in one place, though that does perhaps improve the possibility of their capture. Such men—probably from Eastern Europe, I would guess—will not be greedy. They will commit their last crime fairly soon, I would expect, and then vanish without a trace."

He spoke with the practiced weariness of someone who, in the last couple of days, had repeated this analysis frequently.

"Wasn't it an invitation to theft to leave them hanging on the wall where everyone who looked through the picture window would see them?"

"In retrospect, it may seem so. However, everyone knew that the gallery had those two canvases. We might have attempted to hide them if our insurance company had so ordered. However, they did not. In addition, with the upcoming exhibition at the Art Institute, we stood an excellent chance of selling them. As much as we would hate to lose them, their sale would have been an enormous advantage to us in this rather difficult time in the art marketplace."

"Surely the insurance companies will pay you for the loss."

"Eventually," he said with a grimace, "and after much snooping and haggling and at a level much less than the pieces would bring on the marketplace today, especially since the Art Institute exhibition will increase the interest in Monet's works enormously. Their loss is a terrible blow to us; certainly not a deadly blow, but nonetheless one which will cause us great discomfort."

"I wonder that you did not take more effective security precautions."

He shrugged, suggesting some of the acute discomfort he was feeling.

"Actually, we had twenty-four-hour guards here, just in case, until the week before the break-in," he said wearily. "The insurance companies recommended a new device to add to the security systems of all the galleries in this district. You might have seen the stories in the press about these units. They were very costly, indeed—especially for a gallery with such an elaborate system as we have here. Yet their laser beam overcame our protection units and shorted out our system, apparently with a single blast. Julia deals with the insurance companies and is much more effective with them than I am. I am much too trusting. She was also the one who arranged for the purchase of the two Monet canvases and verified their provenance. I don't know what I'd do without her."

He touched her arm gently. A faint flush of pleasure raced across her face; her breathing quickened for a second or two. Then, just as quickly, these signs of instant sexual arousal disappeared. She really loves him, I thought; and he knows how to turn her on.

"Would you like to see what their laser blast did to our security system?"

He rose from his chair and opened a neatly carved oak cabinet on the wall behind him, perhaps once a valued antique. Inside it, however, there was an elaborate maze of wires and circuits, most of them burned out.

"You see what they did; somehow they introduced a current which ran through the whole system virtually instantaneously, before it could activate any alarm either in the building or at our security agency or at police headquarters."

I stood up and peered at the mess inside the cabinet which still emitted the acrid smell of burnt-out circuits.

"Yeah," I said. "Pretty powerful blast all right."

"You may, if you wish, check all the other boxes in the building. They're all in the same condition. Even the lines to our more expensive inventory and the beams across the two stairways were burned out."

"Could the laser blast have caused a fire?"

"It didn't, neither here nor in any of the other galleries that have been robbed. So they must use a device which destroys the network so quickly that fire cannot occur."

"Didn't it affect your computers?"

"No, not at all. They are on a separate electrical circuit. We had trouble with our telephones the next morning, as have some of the other galleries that have been robbed. I should mention that the insurance investigators, who are considerably more thorough than the police, think that the blast which hit us could have been substantially stronger than those that struck the other galleries. Having been warned by the media of the new units which had been added to the security systems, they developed countermeasures. In effect, they called our bluff. The articles in the press were supposed to frighten them off. Instead they were merely a challenge to their ingenuity."

"So now . . . ?"

"Now we and most of the other galleries are back to twenty-four-hour guards. It is costly, but the insurance companies insist. For us it is rather like locking the barn door after the horse has been stolen, if you understand my meaning."

He moved uneasily in his chair, anxious to get rid of us and get on with his work.

"You would not have exhibited those two paintings in the Art Institute show?"

"Hardly. They would be lost over there. Here they are unique. We considered it when the Art Institute approached us, but we declined regretfully. Naturally, they understood."

A patent lie. We had caught him in a lie, and an unnecessary one at that.

"Now, Mr. McDermot, if there are no more questions," he moved as if to stand up and dismiss us, "Julia will be happy to show you around the gallery. You may stay as long as you like and look at anything you want to."

We shook hands with him and followed Julia out of the office. She had listened to our questions and his answers with an expressionless face and a motionless body. An Eastern European woman, perhaps. No Celt or Latin could possibly have accomplished such a feat of immobility.

She gave us catalogs, on the cover of which I noted with interest was the Mondrian. The inside cover displayed the Jackson Pollock. Otherwise, the catalog looked the same as the one I'd seen at the Art Institute and carried the same title: "Armacost Gallery Summer 1995."

You can print new catalogs pretty quickly. Still, why the rush to change? Probably didn't mean a thing.

Julia gave us the red-carpet tour. We entered every room in the building, including the washrooms. She described the works of art, explained the temperature-control system, opened the blown-out security boxes, and indicated where the lines which had been shorted had protected the most costly paintings. She also praised work which I did not like and indicated lack of enthusiasm for the Mike Casey and Catherine Curran works.

"They are pretty, of course, but they are not very earthy, don't you see? A little too much Celtic twilight to please the discriminating art lover—is that not the case?"

I didn't see, and it was not the case, but I didn't argue. What the hell was wrong with Celtic twilight, anyway?

"You would like to see the downstairs, perhaps? It is where we store our canvases. Naturally, we cannot exhibit everything at the same time. But if you do not have time . . ."

We assured her that we had time.

The basement, as I would have called it, was cooler than the ground floor and seemed to be quite old. Its stone walls were painted a dark brown. It contained perhaps a half-dozen rooms, each with neat cabinets in which canvases—sometimes in frames, sometimes stretchers—could be stored.

Julia explained that, when the demolition company had torn down the old warehouse and uncovered the foundation, Wayne had been delighted with the battered basement. Its thick stone walls were precisely what was needed for storage and workrooms. The architects said the foundation was as good as new, so the gallery had been built on top of it.

She conducted us through the storage rooms and opened the two safes in which their more precious canvases were stored. She stood aside as we casually examined some of them.

Two Jackson Pollocks, I noted. This place was rolling in expensive art.

We turned a corner and entered a large workroom area—stretchers and frames and tools and worktables, all in a workroom arranged for a portrait. Against the south wall stood an ancient coal-burning furnace painted red and black.

"Naturally, we don't use that," she explained. "Wayne, however, with his remarkable eye for such things, realized instantly that it was a classic. So naturally we preserved it."

I remembered my grandfather's stories about stoking the coal furnace early in the morning and shuddered. I spotted behind the furnace, leaning against the wall, a stack of large frames without canvases in them. Brand-new frames.

Julia and I continued our tour while Nuala Anne ducked over to inspect the frames.

Out of the corner of my eye, I saw her quickly tilt the frames from against the wall. I caught a glimpse of a square iron door, maybe four feet high, probably to a coal bin to which it had been connected by an automatic stoker of the sort Pa had described to me. Nuala pulled the door. Naturally, it was locked.

Julia did not seem to have noticed Nuala's departure from the grand tour. If our suspicions were correct, Julia would have been suspicious of any unusual snooping in this part of the basement.

Nuala, who became quite invisible when she wanted to, couldn't have been away for more than fifteen seconds.

Julia led us to the door of the gallery and showed us the blown-out box on the wall across from the door. It was a mass of melted wires and circuits.

"We assume that this is where the blast hit first because the greatest damage is here," she said.

"Obviously," I agreed.

"And you can see the marks on the door frame where the door was removed. It was done very quickly."

"Obviously," I said again.

We thanked her. She graciously invited us to return. Nuala and I walked down Superior towards Orleans, where we had parked the Benz in a crowded multi-level parking garage.

"You see anything down there?" I asked her.

"Did I ever! Behind a pile of picture frames, I found an old iron door, probably linking the furnace to a coal bin. It was locked."

"Just like you said there would be; a safe hidden somewhere behind something else."

"I was not quite right, Michael. It wasn't a safe, though I suppose there might be one inside."

"Maybe a big one. You're too young to remember. My grandfather told me once that coal bins, especially for a warehouse, tended to be pretty big. It's probably sealed up from the outside now. Too bad."

An attendant brought our car and we headed north and turned left on Chicago Avenue, the same route that our Republican friend from Mount Prospect had followed.

"You caught his one lie?" Nuala asked me.

"Yeah. The Art Institute never approached him."

"Couldn't we get the cops to search it?"

"Sure, they could get a warrant if they had any reason to believe that there was something down there. What reason do we have, except your young woman's excellent insights?"

"None that I can think of."

"That laser blast of theirs could just as well be caused by someone who turned off the system, jammed a screwdriver into that main box at the door, and then turned the system back on. I've seen things like that done before."

I parked the car in the John Hancock Center garage. As Mike Casey had invited us, we walked over to Oak Street and the Reilly Gallery. It turned out that the Caseys, Mike and his wife Annie, lived in the Hancock. She was an attractive woman in her early sixties at whom I had nodded and smiled often in the elevators.

They were very much in love with one another. I was promptly identified as the brother of "that nice young priest over at the cathedral."

I didn't say that George was not all that young anymore. If I had, I would not have been served a tall glass of raspberry kiwi herbal iced tea, which was the best thing for thirst quenching since pink lemonade, along with a large plate of homemade chocolate-chip and oatmeal-raisin cookies.

Naturally Ms. Casey and Nuala bonded almost instantly.

The gallery was smaller than the Armacost and much more charming, a place where you felt you could talk in your natural voice. Mike Casey's and Catherine Curran's work were displayed prominently, both festivals of Celtic Twilight. The latter's misty nudes were overwhelming. Dead focking brill. I'd have to ask the Priest if he thought she would want to paint herself.

We reported our efforts for the day.

"I'd never trust her," Annie said decisively. "He's pretty square. She's a devious conniving woman. Loves him though, at least as far as you can tell. Might stop at nothing to protect him."

"They're in trouble?"

"You bet they are," she said. "Huge mortgage, big inventory, high expenses, and very slow sales. They're not going to fold like some of the other Suho galleries but they might be forced to rent that place and move farther west into the barrio."

"You folks don't seem to have any trouble," I said.

"We are just the opposite: small gallery, no mortgage, low expenses, no prejudices in favor of art that only the critics like, and strong sales. That's why we didn't run from Michigan Avenue when everyone else did. As long as my husband and his cousin keep turning out their works, we'll flourish."

"When I heard the story of the Armacost theft last Sunday," Mike Casey observed, "I smelled something. Thieves that are smart enough to blow out a security system don't dash out in front of an oncoming car. They do exactly the opposite; they wait till there's *no* car coming. I don't know what's taking them so long to search the place, except they may not have probable cause yet. There's plenty of reason for the insurance investigators to be suspicious. I expect the cops are waiting till they catch the heist ring and find the pictures."

"The Armacosts think they may be an East European gang of specialists," I said. "Pretty soon they'll cut and run."

"They might at that, particularly if they think someone else is trying to steal their thunder. Former Russian Black Berets, maybe. A lot of them have turned to spectacular crime. Still, they better be careful. The local guys, the ones out on the West Side, think this is *their* territory. They're not likely to take kindly to someone cutting in on it without asking permission. The old guys are pretty tired now, but the young bloods might take this one into their own hands."

I swallowed two more oatmeal-raisin cookies.

"Aren't you folks worried about someone raiding your place?" I asked.

"We have a couple of my friends watching it every night," Mike said, with a wink at the word "friends."

"Just off Michigan Avenue is pretty safe," Annie added. "People coming out the movies at the Esquire, kids like you, Dermot, roaming around. Although there's a new nightlife clientele over there, it's not like this part of town."

"I don't roam," I protested. "I sleep. I'm old."

"Terrible old altogether," Nuala agreed.

They laughed at me. They didn't know what happened to me on Ferris wheels. Or merry-go-rounds.

"Mr. Casey," Nuala asked, "do you think you can find us the architects' plans for that building? I'd like to know what that coal bin looks like."

"Give me a ring first thing in the morning, seven o'clock or so. I'll see what I can do. They have to be registered somewhere—zoning commission, most likely."

"Good. Come on, Dermot, before you spoil your supper with all those cookies."

Again much laughter at Dermot's expense.

"No lunch. Besides, nothing ever spoils my supper."

I grabbed three more cookies as we left the Reilly Gallery.

I swam, took a shower, and dressed in a lightweight dark blue suit with thin white threads running through the cloth. You're having supper with a rising young Arthur Andersen type, you dress for it.

Mike Casey phoned me just as I was preparing to leave.

"I have the plans for that building, Dermot. Don't ask how I got them. I'll see you and Nuala at the Ritz tomorrow morning. Annie will come along. Seven-thirty?"

"Grand!"

I told myself that, after a long hot and exhausting day, the evening was likely to be relatively quiet. I would merely listen to her observations and her new theories, tell her about breakfast with the Caseys, and come back to my apartment for a good night's sleep.

Was I ever wrong. Again.

— 13 —

NUALA WAS waiting for me at the Italian Village, charming the maître d' and the waiters. She was dressed in a nicely fitted black suit, a silver blouse with its own tie, and moderate heels. She wore a touch of makeup and had done up her hair in a gently upsweeping bun. The successful young accountant must appear chic—at the cheapest possible prices.

"My don't we look handsome tonight?" she began.

"If I'm going out with a successful young accountant, I have to look the part, don't I?"

Her eyes dancing with mischief, she considered that.

"No, Dermot, you look quite nice, but you don't look like an accountant. I don't think you could ever look like one even if you tried, which I don't want you to do."

"Then what do I look like?"

She pondered again.

"Well . . . like a movie actor or television personality, or maybe a successful young venture capitalist."

"Not like a seanachie."

"Hmm . . . maybe an Irish-American seanachie."

We both laughed, she touched my hand. I told myself that if I were careful for another day or two, the old rules would be back in place.

I was wrong, but this time it wasn't my fault. Or hers.

"Nuala, I lied to you yesterday."

"Sure, I never lie to you, do I now? Only deceive you a little bit now and then." She put her hand over mine and added, "What did you lie about?"

"I am afflicted with both acrophobia, vertigo, if you want to call it that, and an inner ear which objects violently when I spin around in circles."

"Now, didn't I suspect that yesterday, and didn't I ask you, and didn't you say that you felt fine?"

"That was the lie."

"But why ever lie about something as unimportant as that?"

"I didn't want to spoil your fun."

"Sure, you wouldn't have spoiled it, at all, at all. Wouldn't I ride those frigging things by meself?"

"I know."

"You thought I'd laugh at you?"

"No."

"Then, why ... Och, don't I understand? Real men don't have bad inner ears! That testosterone thing again."

"Maybe."

"And why are you telling me the truth now?"

"I felt guilty. I shouldn't ever lie to you, Nuala Anne."

"Sure, Dermot, you're a grand man. That's why I'll always trust you. ... What should I eat at this super place?"

I ordered a bottle of expensive Barolo and two fettucine bolognese. We finished the pasta and most, but not all of the wine. I was cautious with it because I would be driving back to her house.

"Dermot Michael, don't you have grand taste in wines?" she said, savoring the last sip of the Barolo. "And won't you spoil me altogether for all your cheap wines?"

"I'm glad you like it. Now, over our spumoni, tell me what we do next."

"I couldn't eat a bit of anything else. Don't be ordering that spumoni for me."

"You really think those paintings are in the coal bin, Nuala?"

"Either there or somewhere else in the building. If I were them, I'd try to smuggle them out, but that's a risky business."

"Do you think both of them are involved?"

"I'm not sure. It's hard to tell. They're both pretty strange sort of folks, aren't they? Can we search the coal bin?"

"Not without breaking the law, which would be dangerous around an art gallery these days, and besides not the sort of thing we should be doing. If we can find out a little more, maybe the cops will search it for us."

She nodded.

We lingered over coffee and chatted happily. Then Nuala adjourned the meeting.

"We have another little task after dinner," she said. "We can do it on the way to my house. It'll take only a minute."

"Grand," I said, feeling very proud of myself for the way I had handled the dinner.

In the public parking lot she practically assaulted me with a passionate embrace and a wave of passionate kisses.

"Wow! Nuala Anne, what was that all about?"

"Ah, nothing much at all, at all! I just love you a great frigging lot tonight."

"Remind me always to order Barolo!"

"I'd like that," she giggled.

"Where to, me love?" I asked her as I paid at the entrance of the lot.

"Lakeview, wherever that is."

"Kind of an unsavory neighborhood."

"1413 West Hollywood."

"Very unsavory. . . . What is it?"

"Isn't it your man's basement apartment?"

I made a good guess as to who my man was this time.

"Billy Hernon?"

"None other."

"Woman, you're daft altogether!"

"No, I'm not. He's out of town now. If he's there, we won't go in."

"You want to break and enter?"

"I want to do no such thing. I want to use this key and enter."

She dangled a key chain with two keys in front of me.

"Where did you get that?"

"Didn't me pal Aisling slip it into my hands before I left your police station?"

"Did she say why?"

"She said that she never trusted that gobshite for a single minute. So she lifted his key in case anyone wanted to search his place without breaking and entering."

"What do you expect to find there?"

"Isn't it the clearest thing in the world, Dermot Michael? The frames from the Armacost Gallery!"

Right! The clearest thing in the world!

Most of the buildings in the neighborhood were vast apartment buildings, five or six stories high with twelve apartments on each floor. Not as bad as public housing perhaps, but not very attractive anymore—though in the 1920s they had been elegant places to live. Their cousins on Lake Shore Drive were highly prized condominiums now.

I parked a block beyond the building in a spot barely big enough for the Benz. A short distance ahead of us was the Rosehill Cemetery, where General Benjamin Sweet was buried. We hiked back to the corner where the building stood and prowled around looking for 1413. Several highly dubious characters appeared out of the gloom and stared menacingly at us. They must have taken a look at me and decided that they'd rather be safe than sorry. I was terrified that we might bump into Billy Hernon or one of his friends.

There was so little light in the courtyard that I had to feel the numbers to find out where we were.

"Here we are, Nuala: 1413."

"It's dark and scary, Dermot Michael."

"Do you want to wait till morning?"

"Certainly not . . . here's the key."

"You're shivering."

"I'm perishing with the heat and quaking with me fear. . . . There's no sign of life in that basement apartment, is there?"

"No lights, anyway."

"It's too early for that gobshite to go to bed. . . . Open the door, Derm."

"Yes, ma'am."

I fumbled around and finally got a key in the outer door. I turned it one way and then the other. The door would not open. I tried the other key. It fit, too. I turned it to the right and pushed. No dice. I turned it to left and pushed again. The door sprang open and I tumbled into the equally dark lobby, which smelled strongly of urine.

"It took you long enough," Nuala grumbled.

"Did you want to open it?"

"I'd have been scared I'd drop it."

The next step was to figure out in the darkness which of the two doors led to the basement apartment. If I'd had any sense at all, at all, I would have remembered to bring a flashlight from the car. I tried the first key on the door to the left. It opened easily—to stairs going up.

"Wrong door," I whispered.

"How do you know?"

"Because the stairs go up. The basement stairs should go down."

"But couldn't they go up and then go down?"

"Nuala," I said, "have you ever been in an American apartment building like this?"

"I have not."

"I have, many times. Are you willing to concede that I might have some expertise in the matter?"

"Fair play to you, Derm," she said with a giggle.

I fit the key in easily enough. It wouldn't turn either way.

I tried the other key, the one that opened the outer door. It turned easily and opened on a dark, dark stairwell. I listened intently for noise.

Nothing.

"I'm going down first, Nuala. You grab my belt and follow me down. Quietly."

"Yes, Derm."

She stumbled only once and made a terrible racket in the process. Nuala was good on stairs only when she bounded up and down them.

"Be *careful!*" I snapped.

"Sorry, Derm."

We reached the bottom of the stairwell. I put out my hand like a blind man and felt ahead of me. I touched a wall and felt to the left and to the right. No door. I felt around the wall and reached another. I continued groping till the wall yielded to a door. Neither key would fit in the door.

Nuala was silent. Good for her.

I probed back in the opposite direction and found another door. As an expert on American apartment buildings, I should have known that there are often two basement apartments.

This time the key fit perfectly and the door opened easily. A bit of light from one of the outside lamps bathed a segment of the floor with a pale glow.

The room smelled of stout and whiskey and cigarette smoke. No noise. I stood in the doorway and listened for the sound of breathing. Nothing.

The glow of light revealed a mess of takeout food cartons on the floor. Still no noise.

I probed around walls inside the doorway for a switch and found one on the right side. It was one of the old push switches. I pushed, and a single light went on and flickered as if it were not sure that lighting the room was worth the effort.

"Glory be to God! Would you look at the place! Isn't it a filthy mess altogether?"

Empty cans and bottles were strewn all around. Food cartons littered the floor. Urine traces marked the walls. They had smashed the small television set and broken up the furniture. Deliberate wanton destruction.

"Whose apartment is this, Nuala?"

"Two lads who went home for their holidays and left it to your man."

"They'll be a little surprised when they come back. . . . Careful, Nuala, don't leave fingerprints on anything."

This after I had smeared the outside walls with my own prints. The FBI, however, did not have my prints.

"Yes, Dermot."

"I don't see any frames."

"They're here—I'm sure they're here. Let's find them!"

There was not much to search—a bedroom, two small closets, a filthy bathroom thick with unbearable stench.

No sign of the frames.

"I don't know, Nuala—" I began.

"The bathroom, Dermot Michael! Let's go back there!"

We went back. Tissue in hand Nuala turned on the light. No more than forty watts.

"Behind the shower curtain, Dermot Michael. I know they're there!"

With my elbow I pushed back the curtain and peered into the dingy shower stall.

Sure enough! Two frames! On the back of the one closest to me was the stamp I had seen earlier in the day: "Wayne and Julia Armacost Gallery."

There was nothing in them. They seemed brand-new, never used.

So she had been right.

"What do we now?"

"I'll just run out and get Joannie."

"Who's Joannie?"

"The officer who guards me at night. Aren't we great pals?"

She bounded up the steps and out the doorway, making enough noise to wake up the dead, should there be any such in the building—as there well might have been.

Using the tissue she had given me as she raced out, I pushed open the buttons on the ledge of both the outside door and the door at the head of the stairwell, so that Nuala and her "pal" could get back in.

Actually there were two "pals," Joannie and Bert, two young cops, the former African-American, the latter Asian, probably Thai.

Nuala introduced them both to me as if we were at a formal ball. Bert, she told me, was the one who watched me often at nights.

She showed them the Armacost frames.

"What do you think we ought to do?" I asked.

"Someone should call the cops," Joannie said with a chuckle.

She removed a pair of latex gloves from her purse and picked up a phone which rested precariously at the edge of a broken chair.

"Dial tone," Joannie said with a nod of approval.

She punched in some numbers.

"Captain Culhane, please," she said, mimicking the voice of a dowager who might have lived in the Edgewater Beach Apartments before they closed. "All right, *Commander* Culhane, if that's what you call him. . . . I am sorry. I have some important information about the Armacost robbery. I must talk to Commander Culhane. If you don't put me through to him, I will be unable to provide the information."

She winked at us.

"Ah, yes, Commander Culhane, listen carefully as I will not repeat this information. You should send some of your officers to apartment B-R—that's Basement Right—at 1413 West Hollywood. In the shower stall of the apartment you will find two frames from the Armacost Gallery. Nice to talk to you, Commander."

She hung up and giggled softly.

"We all better get out of here. If I know John Culhane, and I do, he'll be here himself in ten minutes."

"At the most," Bert agreed.

Joanie wiped off the door handles, put the safety locks back on, and led us out of the apartment.

"You're going to take this darling girl home, aren't you now, young man?" she demanded of me, in a mock Irish brogue.

"You bet."

"I didn't think you'd use a place like this for a tryst, Dermot."

"Tryst, is it now?" I replied. "Woman you gotta be out of your frigging mind!"

We hurried back to the Benz, Nuala holding on to my hand for dear life.

At the car we encountered three of the young local dubious characters, all with their baseball caps on backwards in the prescribed manner, inspecting the car with considerable interest. They looked up at us suspiciously but did not back off.

I didn't need this new aggravation. I grabbed one of them by the neck and lifted him off the ground.

"You fucking bastards, get the fuck out of here or I'll kill all three of you."

I threw the terrified kid to the ground. The other two turned tail and ran. The guy on the ground scrambled to his feet and sped away after them.

"Dermot, you're a desperate man!"

Her teeth were chattering despite the humid night air.

"I should have run after the other two guys and knocked their heads together."

With difficulty, I maneuvered the Benz out of the cramped parking spot, turned left at the next street, and headed back to the Drive.

"I was terrified out of me frigging life, Derm," herself informed me after we turned on to the Drive, "from the time we went into that courtyard and until just now when we entered this brilliant road of yours."

"And look at the lights of the city, Nuala," I said, extending my arm round her holding her tight.

She was still trembling.

"Aren't they glorious, like flights of angels bringing us home."

"Nice metaphor."

"Dermot, if there's one thing I can't stand in a woman, it's nagging. I was a terrible nag back there in that smelly place. I'm sorry. I'll try to never do it again. I promise. If I even say a single word that sounds like nagging, you'll remind me of my promise?"

"Woman, I will!"

"Promise?"

"Promise to make you keep your promise?"

"Yes."

"OK, I promise."

She sighed happily.

"You're the bravest and kindest and sweetest man in all the world, Dermot Michael Coyne."

"Have you just found that out? And you might add tiredest, too."

"Most tired," she corrected me.

We both laughed, confident that we had solved much of the mystery, and confident, too, that we were picking up some of the preliminary skills required for a sustained relationship.

"There's four conspiracies, Dermot," she said later as I cruised down Fullerton towards Southport.

"Four?"

"The Art Heist gang, the Armacost Gallery, Billy Hernon and his crowd, who were playing their own game, and Mr. O'Hara."

"That's right. There are four. And just like the Camp Douglas conspiracies, they almost ran out of control and created a conspiracy that never was."

"I don't think it's all over yet."

I walked her up the steps to her apartment, insisted on inspecting it to make sure there was no one lurking in the shadows, and gently kissed her good night.

"Aren't you the friggin' genius, Nuala Holmes?"

"Dermot, I love you more than anything else in the world."

The words slipped out of my mouth before I could stop them.

"And I love you, Nuala, with all my heart and soul."

I figured, as I collapsed into bed at the John Hancock Center, that we were playing under the old rules again. That would involve certain problems, but I was so proud of me woman and meself that I didn't mind.

THE 6:00 A.M. news on WFMT, the Chicago Fine Arts Station, reported that there had been another gallery robbery during the night, at the Grenada Gallery just down Superior Street from the Armacost Gallery. This time, however, the alarms worked. Nonetheless, the criminals removed several valuable works of art from the gallery before the police arrived.

The gallery, the persnickety announcer informed us, was only two blocks away from the Chicago Avenue police station.

Oh, boy, I thought, this is going to really stir up trouble.

I forced myself down to the pool to limber up for the day. I would need a long weekend at Grand Beach, hopefully with Nuala present, to recover from this whole mess of conspiracies, past and present.

Though I was at the coffee shop of the Ritz promptly at 7:30, Nuala and the Caseys were chatting amiably at a table. She was, I could tell, acting the sweet young immigrant child this morning, one of her more authentic personae, though all of them were authentic in some fashion.

She was wearing a light summer dress with a floral print. Perhaps she had observed that her female colleagues dressed for the heat these days instead of for professional image. The thin dress clung to her figure in several appropriate ways. The bra beneath it must also be pretty thin because one could observe the slight hint of nipples beneath the dress. Lascivious thoughts swirled around in my head. Do women dress this way, I wondered, without realizing it, or do they do it deliberately?

I figured that the answer to that was pretty obvious.

"You look lovely this morning, Nuala Anne," I said, kissing her cheek.

"Sure, and aren't you the sweetest boy in all the world?"

"Maybe."

We talked for a few moments while we ordered and the waitress delivered raisin bran and English muffins and dry toast and fruit salad and three pots of tea.

"I talked to my good friend Commander John Culhane of Area Six this morning," Mike, whom Nuala had completely captivated, began the serious part of the conversation.

"Ah," Nuala said, feigning indifference to this information.

"He tells me that an anonymous caller last night told him that there were two unused frames from the Armacost Gallery in a basement apartment on West Hollywood."

"Isn't that interesting," Nuala said.

"It was the apartment of your good friend Billy Hernon, judging by the papers scattered around. They have a warrant out for his arrest."

"That's a good idea," I said as I slopped raspberries over my two packages of raisin bran and drenched them both with cream, "He's a dangerous man."

Nuala and I pretended as best we could to be surprised by this development.

He was not deceived for a moment. Naturally not. After all, it was a couple of his part-time employeess who had helped us.

"I told you to be careful," he said with a frown.

"Dermot is a very careful man," Nuala said fervently.

"But sweet," Annie Casey added with a wink.

"Very sweet," I agreed.

"I also have here"—he reached into a small briefcase on the floor next to his chair—"a copy of the revised plans for the Armacost Gallery."

He placed the plans on the table and turned over three pages.

"This revision was made after they decided to save the old basement. You'll note that the coal cellar was preserved. It's a fairly large room, extending several feet out of the building and under the sidewalk towards Superior Street. There was probably a coal slide fairly close to the street."

"Interesting," I murmured. "It's sealed now?"

"It would appear so. The only entrance seems to be the one from the basement. Observe, by the way, that there's a design for a safe in this diagram."

"Isn't there now?" herself agreed. "I suppose your commander man realizes that the new security unit worked last night?"

"Yes, he did. I think I can say that he has a pretty clear picture of what went on at the Armacost Gallery that night. Incidentally, Nuala, I presumed your permission to tell him about these plans and share them with him."

"It was an eejit scheme altogether," Nuala observed. "How could they have trusted a gobshite like Billy Hernon?"

"Why did he tip the police that you and your immigrants were the thieves?"

"Because he's an evil man who loves to hurt people," Nuala replied. "I suppose that he had wrecked the apartment where he hid the frames?"

"I understand that he did," Mike said without batting an eye.

Had Nuala come close to suggesting that we were in the apartment? Neither she nor Mike seemed to care.

"Why did he hide the frames instead of destroying them?" I asked, as Mike put the plans for the gallery back in his briefcase.

"He'll come back to blackmail the Armacosts and collect more money from them," Nuala replied. "He's a nasty man, Mr. Casey, a nasty man altogether. He enjoys nothing more than watching people suffer."

"He's also a stupid man," I added, "or he wouldn't have involved you and your pals."

Nuala nodded solemnly.

"I wonder if you both would have lunch with the Commander today? He's very eager to meet you. With your permission, Dermot, I'll reserve us a room at the Berghof at noon."

"He won't arrest me again, will he?"

"No, Nuala, he certainly will not."

"You know where it is, Nuala?" I asked.

"Haven't me colleagues told me?"

So it was settled. Nuala went off to work, Mike to his canvases and I to the East Bank Club for an intense morning workout.

John Culhane was a trim man of medium height with wavy brown hair, rimless glasses, and a solid, honest face. He looked more like a priest than one of the best cops in the city.

"I want to apologize to you, Ms. McGrail, for what happened to you in my district the other morning. I assure you that it was not my officers who were involved. The state's attorney, as usual, did not observe the appropriate etiquette of informing us and asking for our cooperation. His behavior was deplorable."

"Aye," Nuala agreed, "He's not a very nice man."

"I wonder if you could explain to me how you were able to solve this puzzle."

"Ah, sure, there was nothing to it at all, at all. I

asked meself who would have been the informer—the false informer that is—who told the police. Sure, didn't it have to be that gobshite Billy Hernon. That explained why the raid on the Armacost Gallery seemed so clumsy compared to the others. Then I says to meself, why would anyone hire Billy. Well, says I to meself, what if they want to pretend to be victims of them Art Heist fellas and wouldn't they be wanting to make it seem that the thieves were carrying the Monets out of the gallery. So don't I figure they wait inside for a driver and then rush out? Maybe someone is still in the gallery to make sure they don't steal the real paintings. Or maybe they have already hidden them. You wouldn't want your man to know where something valuable is hidden unless your're a complete amadon."

"I see," said Commander Culhane, his eyes wide.

"So I says to your man"—she patted my arm—"look for a place where they might hide the paintings. And doesn't he find it just like I knew he would?"

She was giving me credit for her discovery.

"Why did they want to arrange the theft? Did they need the money?"

"Doesn't everyone need money? Maybe they wanted to collect the insurance money. Or maybe there was something funny about their paintings and they didn't want others to find that out during your big exhibition at that Art Institute place."

Culhane nodded solemnly.

He would be even more impressed when he later found out that Nuala had described perfectly the motive for the crime. The little imp had summarized the results of my excursion to the Art Institute without tipping her hand that she was doing anything more than guessing—or "theorizing."

"Do you think both Wayne and Julia were involved?"

Like so many others, myself included, Commander

Culhane stared at Nuala with wide eyes, hardly believing that Ms. Holmes was for real.

"I do not. I think she did it because she loves him desperately and wanted to protect him. Your man tells me that she deals with the insurance companies, and she arranged for the purchase of the two Monet things. She'll probably, uh, take the fall for him. Love does strange things to people, Mr. Culhane."

This was a new bit of "theorizing" to me.

"It sure does, Ms. McGrail. . . . Her fall is not likely to be a very long one. We'll give her a chance to confess and then to plead. She may not have to do any time or no more than a couple of months. No one has been hurt by her scheme."

"Except me pals."

"That's true," he sighed. "However, their lawyers will get delays on the expulsions, and eventually things will work out. No one hates Irish illegals."

"Their skins aren't dark enough," I said.

"Too true," Culhane agreed. "It's crazy, but it's the way the country is just now."

"We think we're closing in on the Art Heist gang," he continued. "We expect to arrest them soon. We'll discover that they do not have the Monets, unless Ms. McGrail's suppositions are completely wrong—which I do not for a moment believe possible. Then, armed with this diagram and the empty frames, we show up at the Armacost Gallery with search warrants which we have prepared beforehand."

"You'll be having someone watch the gallery so that they can't slip the paintings out at night, won't you, now?"

After a slight pause of surprise, the commander replied, "Of course. We certainly will. . . . Ms. McGrail, if you ever want to be a detective, would you please give me a ring?"

"Och, I'm too much of a coward to think of doing that. Isn't it accounting that suits me perfect?"

"I very much doubt that."

"I suppose," I said in a characteristically Irish style of question asking, "that our friends out on the West Side are not happy about someone trespassing on their turf?"

"I don't suppose they are," the commander agreed in a typical Irish response to such a question.

So it was the Outfit who had tipped off the Chicago cops about the Art Heist gang.

We left the restaurant and went in our own direction. I walked with herself back to her office.

"I guess that's that," I said.

"I wish I thought so, Dermot Michael. They haven't caught Billy Hernon yet."

"True enough."

"And wasn't that woman a stupid gobshite to involve herself in such a foolish conspiracy? I wonder where she met him? Probably at some bar."

"As we learned from reading about Camp Douglas, people can do very dumb things when they get caught up in conspiracies."

"*Well,* thank God, I'm not a conniver or a schemer."

"Certainly not!"

I kissed her briefly.

"Won't I be calling you tonight, Derm?"

"Grand."

I went back to my apartment and worked on a number of my stories. I would send a bunch off to my usual editor. Maybe I could even find a novel about a young man in love, a man caught between raw physical hunger and respect for the young woman.

Unfortunately, I had no idea how the story would end.

So I began a story about Letitia Walsh Murray, Lace Maker.

I turned on the five o'clock news and discovered that controversy was again swirling around the cement head of Zack O'Hara. He had announced early in the afternoon that he had turned nine illegal immigrants over to the Immigration and Naturalization Service which, in turn, had deported them to Ireland. He had thus sought deftly to turn attention away from his mistake of arresting them as the Art Heist gang and focus instead on his resolute integrity in expelling illegal immigrants of whatever nationality.

The media, however, had found out about his plans and filmed the Immigration agents pushing the Irish kids, in chains and looking woebegone and confused, out of the Area Six station and jamming them into a van which was too small to hold them all.

Other clips showed the agents herding them through O'Hare and on to a Delta plane bound for Atlanta and then Dublin.

"O'Hara's Chain Gang!" was the teaser on one station.

All hell broke loose. The lawyers for the immigrants, serving pro bono, bellowed that Zack had ignored the habeas corpus writs which had been handed down in the morning and that the immigrants were entitled to due process in appealing a deportation order. The Irish consul said that he was "surprised" that the American authorities had not permitted him to speak to the young women and the young men. "Expert" lawyers told the cameras that O'Hara's action was "extraordinary." One even accused him of covering up his mistake in arresting them in the first place, because it was now evident from the continuation of the crime wave that they were not involved.

"How could he believe for a moment that such inexperienced greenhorns could perpetrate such sophisticated felonies? I would be surprised if those young men and young women would ever want to return to a country where such a Fascist has so much power."

The guy was clearly a Democrat, and more power to him!

Parents for whom some of the young women had worked as nannies were incensed.

"She was so sweet to the children and so kind. She loved to play with them. She was little more than a child herself. They adored her. It's not fair that they do this to her."

No, nor was it fair that routinely Polish and Hispanic nannies would be treated the same way. Finally it was not fair that their employers pay the immigrant nannies and handymen below the minimum wages. But the media, faced with a choice between two paradigms—illegals expelled and O'Hara's brutality—went for the latter.

Then O'Hara himself appeared again at a live press conference at the County Building across from the Civic Center.

"I think the sympathy for these criminals is misplaced. They committed the crime of entering this country illegally. By so doing and by taking jobs to which they were not entitled, they deprived American citizens of employment to which they were entitled. I think the sympathy should be directed towards those Americans, especially African- and Hispanic- and Asian-Americans who are unemployed and perhaps living off welfare, because of the greed of such criminals. If the United States as a nation cannot maintain and protect its borders, then we cannot maintain our national identity."

It was a valiant try. He had played the race card and the welfare card and the xenophobia card. He would win some people over with those cards. The imagery of nine young people in chains at O'Hare would remain with the citizenry of Chicago (those who watched television) for a long time. Many of the same people would have cheered enthusiastically if the deported "criminals" had skins of a somewhat darker hue.

Nor would there be much outcry if those darker-hued people were deprived summarily of their due processes, as in fact happened every day.

Would a mother who was paying substandard wages to, let us say, a nanny from India praise her in the same words that these mothers were using to praise the deported Irish?

Not hardly.

However, illegal immigration was not in O'Hara's jurisdiction. He could turn such immigrants over to the INS for appropriate action. They, in turn, would have to follow the appropriate legal processes. The expulsion of these "alleged perpetrators" looked very much like a conspiracy between Zack and Immigration to cover Zack's ass. I was willing to bet that lower-level personnel at Immigration, zealous to do their job, had made the decision to collect the young Irish people and throw them out of the country as a routine matter without consultation with their superiors. Didn't they do such things in cooperation with the local authorities every day?

I could see the editorials in both papers the next day. Yielding to the popular xenophobia, they would lecture their readers sternly about the need to protect the nation's borders and to maintain a firm definition of national identity. However, they would add, even illegal immigrants in this country have the right to due process of law. State's Attorney O'Hara had acted wrongly in violating that right.

Neither editorial would mention the self-evident truth that when you had a labor demand on one side of a border and a labor supply on the other side, there would be illegal immigration if the potential workers were denied access to legal immigration.

The last TV clip presented us with an Irish-American "activist." I didn't know there were any such. The activist was an oversize woman in the middle years of life. She announced a Committee for the Chicago Nine which would devote itself to securing the rights of the allegedly illegal immigrants and to finding a way by which they could return to America and remain here permanently if they wished.

Nothing succeeds like failure.

No doubt the legal battles would go on for years. Then a higher court would rule that the rights of the young people had been violated and that the federal government must grant them appropriate hearings. With luck they could return to America while these hearings and appeals dragged on. Meanwhile, some of them would be granted visas and return legally and others would find jobs and perhaps marry in Ireland and would not want to come back. By the time the lawyers were finished, maybe in five years, the outcome would be moot and the media would have long since lost interest. The final appeal would be reported in a two-paragraph story at the back of the local-news sections of the papers.

And Zack O'Hara, Fascist or not, might well be Governor of the State of Illinois. O, happy thought!

Thank God that Nuala has a valid Morrison visa and can't be shipped out in similar summary fashion, I prayed.

I was, as it would turn out, unduly optimistic.

The phone rang. I knew who it was.

"I know Nuala, I know: It's friggin' awful."

"They're not criminals, Dermot Michael. They're not. Weren't they just looking for jobs? And weren't they just taking jobs no Americans wanted? If that's against the law, the law ought to be changed!"

She was sobbing as she talked, close to hysteria but not yet over the line. Basically, she was right. Some of her "pals" had come looking for jobs, some of the others on a lark, still others curious about what Yank land was like. Yet the law had to be changed. There was not a chance of that as long as the fires of xenophobia were burning brightly and the Republican candidates were pouring gasoline on the fires.

"You're absolutely right, Nuala, absolutely right."

"What can we do? Whatever can we do?"

"All that can be done is being done. Eventually, those that want to come back probably can. It may take a lot of time, but they'll be let in one way or another. A lot of people will take on their cause. When they come back, they'll be legal and safe, just like you."

"It's not right that I should stay and they can't. Maybe I should go home, too, in protest."

"It's absolutely not right," I agreed, trying as always to hear what she meant and not just what she was saying. "It won't help things for you to give up your job in this country. We have to make it easier for them to come to America if they want to and find work here if they can."

"They just wanted to be Americans!" she wailed. "What's friggin wrong with that?"

"Nothing at all, Nuala Anne, nothing at all. It's what my grandparents wanted, and what O'Hara's ancestors wanted, and what the ancestors of all us American-Irish wanted. And none of us are too careful about learning how they got in. These are the kind of people who made American great. As are you. We need people like you, Nuala Anne. We need you. Don't leave us because a few of us have behaved horribly."

She stopped sobbing. Sniffles replaced frenzied gasps.

"You don't really need me Dermot Michael, not at all, at all. You're just saying that because you're such a sweet man. Why ever would your United States of America need me?"

"You mean Yank land."

She giggled.

"I don't use that slur word anymore."

"We need you for the reasons we need everyone who has the courage and ambition to immigrate. You're hardworking; you're intelligent; you're charming; you're dedicated. If we don't get an influx of people like you in every generation, this nation will go to pot like France and England and Germany."

"You're a darling man, Dermot Michael, even if that's not the truth."

"Woman, damn it all, it is the truth."

"Well, maybe. Just a little bit."

"Didn't your man offer you a job today? He thinks he needs you. You're doing us a favor by coming to his country."

"I'll always be Irish, Derm," she said dubiously.

"Who said you had to be anything else? We don't want you to change a thing, even your friggin' gobshite language. If you change we might send you back. You only add a few things and become Irish-American or American-Irish—take your pick."

"Not a friggin' Yank?"

Another giggle.

"Yankees, young woman, are your frigging New England Protestants. There's nothing wrong with being that, if that's what one is. It is absolutely impossible for you to become one of them."

"Now I'm crying because I love you so much."

"I love you, too, Nuala Anne."

So we both cried a little and she said, "I'll need a couple of days by meself to mourn and pray, Dermot."

"Take all you need."

I was reasonably pleased with myself. I had listened pretty well to what she meant. I was progressing. I'd slipped again and told her I loved her, but that was surely the truth. She was entitled to some time of silent grief and prayer, wasn't she?

Somehow, however, I felt uneasy. Was I missing something important?

—15—

THE NEXT morning I worked feverishly (you should excuse the expression) on my stories about young love and young passion and how the two relate to each other. Naturally, I didn't permit myself to think through what that relationship should mean to me.

I turned on the noon news.

The broadcast began with clips of a shoot-out.

Cops hiding behind police cars were banging away at a two-story wooden house, newer than the one in which Nuala lived, somewhere in the city. Someone from inside the house was banging back.

At ten o'clock this morning, the anchorperson told me, the Chicago Police Department stormed a home in the Jefferson Park area on the northwest side of the city where they believed the Art Heist gang was hiding. Two Chicago police officers were wounded by gunfire from inside the house.

One of the wounded officers was an African-American woman.

The clip changed to police firing a barrage of tear gas into the building. The guys inside were in real trouble now. You shoot a cop, you're practically dead.

The police, the anchorperson continued, opened fire with tear-gas grenades and ordered the gunmen inside to surrender immediately.

Yet another clip showed three men with their handkerchiefs over their faces charging out of the house, guns blazing in a fury of pops. All three of them fell to the ground.

Three gunmen charged out of the house, the anchor went on, and fired at the police. The police returned the fire, killing one man and wounding two others critically. Three others surrendered.

A clip showed three terrified men coming out of the house, hands over their heads. The cops swarmed all over them with handcuffs.

"We understand that in the basement of the house the police found many art treasures which fit the descriptions of those taken by the Art Heist gang. Now we have Commander John Culhane of Area Six, whose detectives broke the case, live with Andrea Smith from Jefferson Park."

John Culhane was wearing a flak jacket and a helmet. He appeared tense and distraught.

"First of all, Commander, how are the two police officers doing?"

"I understand that they are both considered 'serious,' but that they both will recover, thanks be to God."

"Did you expect to encounter resistance?"

"We were ready for it in the sense that we were all wearing helmets and flak jackets. Art thieves usually have no taste for gunfights. These guys were different. One of them waved a sheet from the second floor. Our advance team was moving into position when they opened up. If it wasn't for the flak jackets and the helmets, they'd be dead."

"Are you certain that they are the Art Heist gang?"

"It would seem probable that they are since we found many works of art that were reported stolen from the galleries."

"Who are they?"

"We're not sure yet, Andrea. None of the survivors

speaks English. They appear to be from Eastern Europe. Some of them may be Russians."

"Are they former members of the Black Berets, as people are saying around here?"

"They may be. We're looking into that."

"How did you learn of their whereabouts?"

He smiled thinly.

"Good detective work."

And a tip from the Outfit. The Wise Men must have figured that it was safer to let the Chicago cops dispose of these foreign intruders. The Outfit is as xenophobic as anyone else. As American as pumpkin pie.

"Did you recover the priceless Monets from the Armacost Gallery."

"We are still examining the artwork we have recovered."

It doesn't take much examination to spot a Monet. That meant there would be a raid on the Armacost Gallery this afternoon before Paula and Wayne figured out what Culhane's remarks meant.

Why not go over there and see what happened?

I walked over to Superior Street in shorts and a T-shirt and found myself a ringside seat.

Just as I arrived at the corner across the street from the gallery, a half-dozen patrol cars and a couple of plainclothes cars roared up to the gallery. Cops poured out, guns in their hands. No risks of being shot without warning this time.

A couple of television trucks pulled up, and camera persons and journalists tumbled out.

The cops, led by a man in civilian clothes who, from my distance, looked like Commander Culhane, pushed their way in the door. A TV crew tried to rush in after him. A couple of determined cops blocked their way.

Then there was a wait, presumably while they searched the basement for the Monets. I wandered across the street and stood among the journalists as if I belonged. Seanachies have some rights, don't they?

After a half-hour, two women detectives appeared, one holding each arm of Julia Armacost. She was wearing handcuffs and sobbing. Poor woman, she'd look awful on the five- and ten-o'clock news. Wayne was right behind her, seemingly stunned.

John Culhane appeared, and the media flocked around him.

"All I can say at the present is that we have found the alleged Monets in a safe in an old coal bin the basement of the gallery. It would appear that they never left the gallery. We are holding Ms. Julia Armacost, and we are not holding Mr. Wayne Armacost."

He caught my eye and, with an almost-invisible flick of his head, signaled me to follow him. He murmured something to the uniformed officer at the door, who greeted me with the same flick of his head.

They must teach these gestures at the Police Academy.

John was waiting for me.

"I want to show you the coal bin."

"What went down here?"

"She broke down as soon as we demanded the key to the coal bin. She wanted to protect her husband from an exposé of the fake Monets. She had arranged to purchase them in Europe, asked an expert to evaluate them, and then bought them cheap from the crooks who were trying to sell them. They were insured only for their values as imitations, which I gather is still considerable. She says she intended them as ornaments for the gallery, and that she expected no one would ever buy them. If anyone did, she swore she would tell them the truth. I kind of believe her. When she heard about the Monet show, she was terrified. Someone suggested this Billy Hernon to her, and you know the rest."

"Who will charge her?"

' "Probably the feds. They'll charge her and the Art

Heist gang. Your good friend Zack wants no part of this anymore. Her lawyers will plea, and she'll get off with a year, less time off for good behavior. The husband is standing by her."

"The joke is that the fake Monets and the love story will attract more people here than the supposed real ones."

Culhane twitched his eyebrows. "Yeah, you're probably right. It's a crazy world, Dermot."

"Don't forget about Billy Hernon. He's the bad one."

"We won't . . . you want to see the coal bin?"

"You bet."

We went down to the basement, through the storerooms, and behind the red and black furnace. The iron door was ajar. The commander bent low and crawled into the coal bin. I followed him.

We both stood up, and he flicked a light switch. Two powerful floodlights came on and illumined the bin, which had been plastered and painted and looked as modern as the rest of the gallery. Against the far wall, where the coal chute probably had been, stood a very serious-looking safe, bright and shining and formidable. The door was open.

"They were both in here," he said. "Beautiful. I couldn't tell them from the real thing. I'll take her word that they are imitations."

"Most people couldn't tell the difference, either."

"Your young woman was right on."

"John Culhane, in matters like this, she always is."

I went back to my apartment and, since I had been solemnly forbidden to call Nuala at work, returned to my stories.

On both the five- and six-o'clock news, the commander mentioned Nuala by name as the one who had solved the case. "If she ever gets tired of being an accountant, we'll have a job for her at Area Six."

The feds were going to take the case against Julia

Armacost. The United States Attorney said that so far she had been very candid and very cooperative, and naturally that would be taken into account.

My phone rang.

"Is this the famous celebrity detective?" I said on picking it up.

"Och, Dermot, he shouldn't have mentioned me name at all, at all, should he?"

Translated, that meant she was delighted.

"You deserve all the credit, Nuala, especially after all you've been through."

"I won't be able to show me face at the office tomorrow, will I now?"

"I imagine you can work up your courage and do it just the same."

"Wasn't it grand, Dermot Michael, altogether grand!"

Having gone through the motions of protesting, she was now free to delight in it. She added, "They'll still have to haul in that gobshite Billy Hernon."

"They'll get him eventually."

"I hope so. . . . Can we get together tomorrow night?"

"I was hoping you'd ask that. . . . Sure we can!"

"I'll call you from work in the late afternoon, and you can tell me where you'll meet me."

"Grand!" I replied.

She didn't say she loved me, and I didn't say that to her.

There was still another conspiracy working that we hadn't thought about.

I BEGAN to worry about Nuala when I had not heard from her at a quarter to five. I called her office, despite the threat of permanent interdict reserved to the Holy Father himself.

"Nuala didn't come in today, Mr. Coyne."

"Did she call in?"

"No. It's not like her. She's always super responsible."

"You called her?"

"Yes, we did. There was no answer. We kind of think she slept in and was entitled to it."

"Thanks."

I then punched her phone number.

A long ring and no answer.

I called Reliable. They patched me through to Joannie.

"Joannie, have you seen Nuala?"

"No, Mr. Coyne. I have been around all day, but she didn't come out of her apartment after Mass. I figured she wanted to escape all the celebrity."

"She didn't call her office and she didn't call me and she doesn't answer the phone."

"My God!"

"Did you see her go into the house, Joannie?"

"Not exactly, Mr. Coyne. I stayed behind to light a

candle. She always runs across the street to her apartment; she's rushing all the time."

"Check the apartment and call me back."

In five minutes, she was back on the line.

"She's not in there. I'll try to find out where she is. I'll be back."

Billy Hernon, I thought. He's got her. I'll tear the bastard apart.

I called Area Six. John Culhane was still in his office.

"Billy Hernon's got Nuala."

"He's not in the country, Dermot. What's happened?

I told him.

"It sounds more like our friend Zack O'Hara. I'll check with those assholes at Immigration."

He called back in fifteen minutes while I planned how I'd deck Zack O'Hara.

"I was right. They lifted her this morning, took away her visa, and shipped her off on Delta. That's against the law."

"That doesn't seem to matter."

"Your sister can get a writ ordering them to return her. That should be no problem. Then she can file a huge damage suit. They can't do this to her."

But they had.

That morning when Nuala came out of St. Josephat's, still in her running clothes, two Immigration agents picked her up, handcuffed her and dragged her into a car. The took away her Morrison visa, which she always carried in her purse. They held her in the tank at the Federal Correction Center at the south end of the Loop, still handcuffed, till noon. Then they took her to O'Hare and put her on the 3:15 Delta flight to Atlanta and the 6:15 flight to Dublin. They removed the handcuffs only a few minutes before the Dublin plane took off. She was already over the Atlantic before I knew she was missing.

Everyone would say in the days and weeks ahead that they can't do what they did. But somehow that didn't seem to mean anything.

Ten minutes later, Joannie called with new information. Her voice was strained with grief.

"Two people actually saw these men in a government car kidnap her. They didn't want to say anything to anyone about it because they figured, if it was the government, it was all right. . . . It's all my fault, Mr. Coyne. I'm so sorry."

Though I was very angry at the woman, I held my tongue. It was not her fault at all. In this country, no one grabs women coming out of church in broad daylight. Except the government. Not even the Outfit would dare do that.

"It wasn't your fault, Joannie," I said. "No one could possibly have expected them to pull a trick like that. Don't blame yourself. We'll get her back."

"Thank you, Mr. Coyne," she sobbed. "Thank you."

I called Cindy.

"Hurley residence," said a very polite little boy voice.

"Marty, this is Uncle Dermot. . . ."

"Hi, Uncle Dermot."

"May I speak to your mother?"

"Just a moment, Uncle Dermot. I'll see if she's home."

"Hi, Dermot! The little rascal never lets anyone talk to me without clearing it with me first. Too much television, I think."

"They've lifted Nuala," I said.

"What? Who?"

"Immigration. Presumably with the help of Zack O'Hara. More likely at his instigation."

"Is she down at the Federal Correctional Center?"

"She's on her way back to Ireland!"

"They can't do that!"

"Cindy, they *have* done it!"

"They won't get away with it. I'll have her back inside of a week, at the most. When does she get home?"

I ran the numbers through my head. They didn't come out right.

"Let me see, the plane probably gets to Dublin between nine and ten tomorrow morning their time. If they left her any of her money, she'll ride the bus into the city and take the train to Galway. The bus and the train will take between four and five hours. Then she'll have to take another bus from Galway out to Carraroe. They don't run very often."

"Can't her parents pick her up?"

"Cindy, all they have is a bicycle and a donkey cart."

"They really are poor?"

"Very."

"So what time will that be?"

"Maybe six o'clock their time. Noon our time."

"Damn, I can't go into Federal Court with a petition till the day after tomorrow. I'll have to interview her first."

"What will you ask for?"

"An order mandating the State Department to return her Morrison visa and an injunction to the INS to cease and desist their harassment of her. We'll get her back, Dermot, never fear. They can't get away with it."

That's what everyone kept saying.

"Can I direct-dial to her house?"

"It's a modern country, Cindy. Even the people who own nothing more than a donkey cart can direct-dial anywhere in the world.

The McGrails had such a phone because I had installed one when Nuala came to America and persuaded the Irish Ministry of Post and Communications to send the bill to me every month.

"What is it?"

I told her.

"I'll call her at noon our time."

"Let me call her first. She may need some persuasion to fight back."

"Hell, Dermot, whether she wants to come is up to her. We still have to make them give back her visa."

"Fine, but I'd better talk to her first. I'll call you."

"OK. Tell her we can't let them get away with this."

"Is this routine for them?"

"Sure. They pick up a Mexican or a Pole or an Asian in one of their sweeps and the man or woman has a green card. They think the person has gone back to the native land and then come in here illegally a second time, they take the card and ship him home. They don't need to have much proof. Often they don't need *any* proof. The poor guy doesn't know any better. In his life, government is always arbitrary. No one bothers to tell them that they have a right to a lawyer and an appeal to an immigration court."

"And they get away with it?"

"They're protecting their country's borders, little bro—who cares how? Pick up something like a Morrison visa, that's pushing their luck a little far. Now get some sleep."

"Sure."

Instead of trying to sleep, I put on walking shoes and, in T-shirt and shorts, walked north along the lakeshore as far as Loyola University and then walked back, maybe fifteen or sixteen miles. I returned about midnight, dehydrated and exhausted, took a shower, and slept a few hours.

Everyone in the family, including Prester George, called to promise me that they would get her back.

"We'll get the cardinal to issue a statement condemning them," he said. "We'll go after them tooth and nail."

The Priest is as fierce a fighter as I am when he gets his Irish up.

Tom (psychiatrist) said that the action was the kind that concentration-camp guards used to pull in Nazi Germany. His wife Tracy, a woman with her own very successful public-relations firm, told me that she had spoken to Cindy and that she would launch a national campaign on Nuala's behalf.

They all said that the opposition couldn't get away with it. I was not so sure. I'd seen enough xenophobia in the country in the last two years to realize that it was a magic potion for demagogues.

Promptly at high noon, I punched in the number of the little cottage in Cararoe.

A familiar voice greeted me with a burst of musical Irish words.

"Nuala?"

She continued to speak the language of the Gaeltacht.

"It's Dermot," I said. "Would you ever mind speaking English?"

"Glory be to God, Derm, how did you know where I was?"

"Commander Culhane found about what was done to you."

"I just this minute came into the house. I'm destroyed altogether. Me ma and da haven't come in yet. Won't they be surprised!"

"Did they take your Morrison visa, Nuala?"

"They did, Derm," she said with a weary sigh. "They kept me in handcuffs from right after Mass in the morning till the plane left Atlanta, twelve hours later."

"Don't worry about it, Nuala. First thing tomorrow morning, Cindy is going to go into a federal court with a petition demanding that the State Department give you back your visa and that Immigration readmit you to the country."

"I'm tired of fighting them, Dermot, and I'm tired of a country where they can do such things to you because you're a foreigner. I don't want to come back. I'm so tired and so mixed up, I just want to be left alone."

I had been afraid of that reaction.

"That's a decision you must make for yourself, though if you decide to stay there, you'll disappoint a lot of us and break a few hearts, mine included. However, you have to let us fight them if only to prevent them from doing what they did to you to others. Let us get your visa back, and then make up your mind."

"I don't know, Dermot. It's been a terrible three months for me. I don't think I belong over there. I know I don't. I belong here in Cararoe."

"Cindy will call you in a few minutes. Promise me that you'll talk to her."

She thought about it, sighed, and said, "I'll always talk to Cindy, Dermot."

"I love you, Nuala Anne."

She sighed again. "I love you, too, Dermot Michael."

I called Cindy on her telecommute line.

"Dermot, Cindy. I just talked to her. She's a wreck, exhausted, battered, jet fatigued. She's tired of fighting. As we knew they would, they lifted her visa. She said she'd talk to you."

"I'll call her right away and get back to you."

A half-hour later, Cindy called back.

"I had a hard time with her, Dermot. She is, as I hardly need tell you, a very strong-minded young woman. Those bastards traumatized her. I think we'll go after them with damage suits—the head of the Chicago office and the whole INS. Anyway, she agreed to at least tell me what happened and let us fight so she could come back if she wanted to. That's only fair, she says. It was a hard fight to get her Irish up."

"I know."

"Anyway, she did let me interview her and she did give me all the facts I need. I'm going into the Federal Court in the Dirksen Building tomorrow morning and asking for emergency relief. We may have her visa back by the end of the day. Tracy has scheduled a press conference for ten o'clock, and we intend to go after the whole lot of them."

It was a hell of a press conference.

Cindy started out by saying, "The right to due process of law was inherent in the human condition. The framers of the Constitution had merely made it explicit. The whole history of American jurisprudence left little doubt that the right to due process belonged to everyone who lived within our borders. We are not—and never have been—a country which yields to its police agencies the power to abrogate the right to due process. When they do so, immediate action must be taken. The rights of any one person, immigrant or native born, citizen or legal resident, are the rights of everyone. When any of us lose a right, all of us do. When the storm troopers violate Ms. McGrail's rights, they violate the rights of all of us. Everyone who hears my voice was violated yesterday, when government-paid storm troops brutally seized Ms. McGrail in front of St. Josephat's Church after the morning Mass. What sort of country are we, anyhow? Are we a country in which innocent young women are kidnapped in front of their churches, held without benefit of legal counsel, and expelled from a country in which they have every legal right to be?

"There can be no doubt that under some circumstances the government can lift the visas of those who are not yet citizens. It can do so only when it permits them legal recourse, first to immigration courts and then to the federal judiciary. There are enough cases to leave little doubt of that. I have already cited several score of them in my brief.

"Even if Ms. McGrail were guilty of some heinous

crime, she would still have a right to a hearing. However, no charges have been made on the public record against her. Of what was she guilty? She is a hardworking employee of Arthur Andersen, a lovely vocalist, a delighted and dedicated Chicagoan. Everyone who knows her will sing her praises. What can she possibly have done?

"I will tell you what she has done, gentle persons: She has shown up our state's attorney and wannabe future governor by solving the mystery of a crime that, in his cement-headed stubbornness, he was unable to solve, save by arresting a group of totally harmless immigrants. Doubtless, Mr. O'Hara will deny this. Nonetheless, we propose to prove that the men who kidnapped Ms. McGrail were in fact Mr. O'Hara's agents working inside the Immigration and Naturalization Service.

"I presume these agents and their supervisors will plead that they expel people like this every day. If that be the case, then the harm done to the rights of all of us is enormous. There are perhaps times when clearly invalid or forged or doctored green cards may be lifted. Even then, the people so sanctioned have the right to appeal of which they are often not informed. But Morrison visa? There can be no question of the validity of that visa.

"Therefore, I am initiating the following actions:

"In a few moments I will go into a Federal Courtroom and ask for emergency relief in the form of an immediate order to the State Department to reissue a visa to Ms. McGrail. Tomorrow I will file suits in the Federal District court for Northern Illinois seeking damages of one million dollars against each of the following defendants: the Chicago director of the Immigration and Naturalization Service, the State's Attorney of Cook County, the Immigration and Naturalization Service as a corporate body, and the two agents who kidnapped and brutalized her."

Thus did the firestorm start. Tracy saw that it continued to burn.

The story made national television that night—all four networks—with a clip of Nuala's statement on her first release, denials from the state's attorney, a statement from the Chicago Director of the INS that for the moment he was standing by his agents and from the INS office in Washington that they were awaiting a local investigation.

The decisions by the latter two to defend their bureaucracy were serious errors. They could have put out the firestorm then and there by ordering that the visa be returned to Nuala. But in times of crisis, bureaucrats don't do good things. Rather they do the things they do well.

On local TV, the mayor, the cardinal, the presiding partner of Arthur Andersen, the priest from her parish, and Commander John Culhane spoke in praise of Nuala.

None of this was by chance. Tracy had created a powerful first impression that would be hard to replace, even if she had done nothing else. As time went on, she did much more.

We had bad luck, however in the Federal Court for the Northern District of Illinois.

"We drew the worst possible judge, Dermot. Thomas Winthrop Manley. He is a supercilious, egotistic, fussy, mean-spirited Republican."

In my family it is the last word which is the worst of them all.

"Will he rule against us?"

"You can't tell what he'll do. He loves to think that he has an acute legal mind and that he develops brilliant new legal theories which transform the shape of American law. The Seventh Circuit slaps him down every time, but he keeps on trying."

"We don't necessarily get justice?"

"Maybe not here. Most likely in the Appellate

Court. No guarantees. The system usually works. But it's not perfect. Sometimes it works slowly and sometimes not at all. I think we'll win, but the hatred of foreigners in this country is so strong just now that I can't be certain."

My parents, George, Tracy, and I sat in the back row of the courtroom. The press filled up every seat in front of us. At the door, Cindy spoke with the recent law-school grad who was the United States attorney for this emergency motion.

"We're not inclined to fight this motion, Ms. Hurley. The boss thinks the whole business is disgusting. You can never know what old T.W. will do."

A short, pompous man with a perpetual sneer listened to Cindy's argument for a time.

"That's quite enough, Counselor," he cut her off with a wave. "This is not a press conference. I have read your petition and find it hastily done and improperly documented."

"Your Honor, this is an emergency petition. I beg you to consider the substance of the case, the horrendous violation of the Constitution, and the savage violation of this young woman's rights."

"You are not a priest, Ms. Hurley nor are you likely to ever be one. Nor am I a Catholic. Please do not preach at me. *I* am the one who determines in this courtroom what is an emergency and what is not."

Cindy bit her lip to control her anger. Then she said with a smile, "I take exception, Your Honor, to the suggestion that I will never be a priest. About that only time can tell."

There was a titter in the courtroom. Judge Manley glared us into silence.

"Ms. United States Attorney, do you have an argument to make on this matter?"

"The United States, Your Honor, does not wish to dispute this motion."

"Madam, there are very important points of constitutional law involved in this case. I order you to appear in this same courtroom a week from this day at the same time and offer the best possible argument that the legal wizards at the office of the United States Attorney can prepare against Ms. Hurley's motion."

"Yes, Your Honor. Thank you, Your Honor."

"Do you understand, Ms. Hurley?"

"Yes, Your Honor." She choked back her temper so that she might honor the requirements of ritual. "Thank you, Your Honor."

I wanted to go up the bench and break his nose.

The media rushed outside and were waiting for Cindy as she strode out.

"What are you going to do, Cindy?"

"This afternoon I am going to file an emergency appeal in the Seventh Circuit."

That appeal was promptly denied on the grounds that a mere week's delay would not cause a grave injustice.

The newspaper headlines the next day announced:

Judge Denies McGrail Appeal
Circuit Court Agrees

Both television and the newspapers carried pieces which recounted the reaction of law professors. Generally, they were on Cindy and Nuala's side. As a professor from University of Chicago put it, "There is a dictum which says that if the law says that, it is a fool. If Judge Manley said that, he is a fool." However, in the interest of balance, they were also able to find someone who would say that Tom Manley was a brilliant constitutional lawyer and he might have something very important to say.

I went home furious, confused, and determined, though I had no idea what to do. So I went over to an electronics shop in the 900 North Michigan Mall (also known as the Bloomingdale's Mall) and bought a tape deck which would record in both European and American format, so I could send Nuala the tapes of the television news.

Tracy arranged for Cindy to appear on the *Today* show by satellite from NBC Towers in Chicago. Bryant Gumbel was very sympathetic. Cindy described what Nuala was like and how she had been treated. "Makes you wonder about this country, doesn't it?" Bryant observed. "I'm sure justice will prevail in the end."

Cindy then delivered a terse version of her lecture that if one person was denied a right, all of us lost some of our rights. She had no comment to make on Judge Manley. She said that she regretted the Seventh Circuit's decision. "Justice delayed is justice denied. In a case like this, even a week's delay is a serious violation of justice."

I called Nuala after the *Today* show and told her about what had happened.

"Would you ever send me my harp, Dermot? It's still in my apartment."

"Sure. I could bring it over."

"Please don't. I'm confused something awful."

"All right. I'll send over the tapes of the television. Cindy was wonderful on the *Today* show."

"Was she now?" she said, displaying a few signs of life. "I'd love to see it, but, Derm, we can't play American tapes on our little VCR."

"Woman, don't I have here a machine that will record our programs in your format?"

"That's impossible, Dermot."

"I'll send over the tape, and you can see what I mean."

"Wouldn't that be wonderful!"

"And my other things. They're not much. Maybe your ma could pack them up for me."

"She will, I'm sure, but she'll be very sad while she's doing it."

"Thank you, Dermot Michael."

"May I call you every day?"

"Please, Dermot, not for a while. I'm confused something awful. Cindy will keep me posted. When I'm back here in my own snug little world, I realize how out of place I am in America. I have to think it out, if you take my meaning."

"Certainly. You call me whenever you want."

"I will, Dermot Michael. I truly will."

"You can reverse the charges."

"Och, I'll never do that because aren't you paying for this phone anyhow?"

We both laughed, rather hollowly, and bid each other good-bye without any exchange of affection.

I sat on my easy chair next to the phone, my head sunk into my hands.

The Adversary took advantage of my discouragement.

IF YOU HAD ANY BALLS, YOU WOULD GET THAT HARP AND FLY IT OVER TO HER. BUT NO, YOU'RE A WIMP. YOU LET HER PUT YOU OFF WHEN SHE NEEDS YOU THE MOST.

"I don't feel like arguing."

I GIVE UP ON YOU. YOU DON'T DESERVE MY TIME AND ENERGY.

"Fine!"

She did call me once after she received her harp.

"It arrived fine. Dermot. A little out of tune, but harps are always a little out of tune. Thank you."

"You're welcome."

"Aren't you folks having a grand time on the telly. Good on you. I half-wish I was there to see it."

"I totally wish you were here to see it."

Tracy's publicity blitz went on in high gear. The *New York Times* carried a front-page article about her and an editorial which blasted Judge Manley's decision and the Seventh Circuit's decision to delay an appeal. Such an editorial would have no impact on Manley, but it would serve as a warning to the Seventh Circuit that, should there be an appeal, the world was watching them.

A British TV team traveled to Galway to interview Nuala. Herself was wonderful. She turned on all her piquant charm and praised the city of Chicago for all its marvels, the skyline, the lakefront, the parks, and, naturally, Mr. Daley's Ferris wheel. She praised Mr. Daley, too. He was a "grand man" and didn't she see him every Sunday during the summer at Mass?

The Brits were sympathetic, but one of them fired a fast pitch at her.

"Doesn't it make you wonder about the American legal system, however?"

"I'm sure justice will be done eventually," she replied calmly.

"Yes, but how long will it take?"

"A lot less time that it takes to get out of your jails in the North if one is held under your Official Secrets Act."

They steered away from that subject.

PBS in Chicago played the whole half-hour. That was after one of our stations sent a crew over there to a do a special on her. She was even better than she was with the Brits, playing now the role of Nuala the comic-opera heroine. She told a couple of wonderfully funny stories about Zack O'Hara, mimicking his square-jawed, angry integrity.

Then they asked her to sing something.

"Och, now, I'm out of practice altogether, but don't I have here my Celtic harp made in America, if you please. I guess I'll have to sing if you force me to do so."

She strummed the harp carefully.

"Sure, isn't it out of tune, but then aren't your harps out of tune all the time?"

"At least she didn't say 'friggin' harp,' " Prester George said with a cackle.

We all laughed, even my mother despite her injunction, "Shush, George."

I'm not fey, not in the slightest but I knew what she was going to play before she began. The tears rolled down my cheeks as once more she told all of us and especially me about the bittersweet story of Molly Malone.

We were all of us crying, on both sides of the Atlantic.

"You're a gallant woman, Nuala Anne McGrail," said the interviewer, and herself an Irish-American woman.

"Ah, no," Nuala replied. "I'm only an Irishwoman."

"Every judge in the Seventh Circuit will see that program!" Cindy crowed. "They won't dare turn us down."

"Manley?"

"I'm sure he doesn't watch television."

I sent the tape of the program over to Galway, along with a note which said:

> *You were great on Channel Six. Wonderful. Everyone cried and said how terrible proud of you they were.*
>
> > *All my love,*
> > *Dermot*

No answer. Again I was tempted to fly the Atlantic. However, I didn't.

The brief the United States attorney filed was a terrible mishmash of contradictions. Due process was an inviolable right, but it was not clear that the present case fell under that right. Legal immigrants were certainly protected under the clause, but perhaps not in the same way as American citizens, though maybe they were not really exceptions.

"I'm not going to file a reply," Cindy said. "This is nonsense."

Judge Manley seemed to agree in court a week after our first appearance.

"I note, Ms. Hurley," he said, fussing with the papers on his bench, "that you have not replied to the brief of the United States attorney."

"How can I reply, Your Honor, to a brief that ignores the principle arguments in my petition. It's a disgrace."

"On that point at any rate, Ms. Hurley we agree completely," he said with a sneer. "Counselor, I would be inclined to hold you in contempt of court if I didn't realize that you are at the mercy of the best thinking of those legal birdbrains who staff the office of the current United States attorney. I suppose once again I'll have to straighten out the mess you people have created."

He yawned.

"I suppose I can reach a decision in this matter within a week or ten days."

Cindy said nothing as we left the courtroom.

To the waiting press, she said, "I do not expect justice in Judge Manley's court."

In the meantime the accusations in her damage suits created another firestorm. She had established links between the state's attorney's office and the two agents who had kidnapped Nuala. Both had relatives, a wife in one case and a brother in the other, who worked for the state's attorney. Moreover, she had found witnesses who testified that these two men had been seen entering the state's attorney's office late in the afternoon on the day before Nuala was snatched.

"They'll settle," she predicted to me confidently. "The day after Manley is reversed."

"When will that happen, Cindy."

"Before the middle of July."

"Five weeks after she was lifted!"

"I know, Dermot, I know."

To keep my sanity, I devoted my energies to remodeling Nuala's apartment, painting it, and replacing all the old furniture. My mother advised me since I was helpless in such matters.

I had bought the whole house. The other renters were moving out on October 1. The building could be restored to its original status as a two-story home and converted into a spacious urban town house. A new neighborhood was emerging here. St. Josephat's Parochial School was just across the street. It would be a nice place to raise a family. Any family.

I had called Nuala to ask for her permission to begin remodeling.

"I bought the house, Nuala Anne, because I was afraid that someone else would tear it down to make room for a modern town house. The apartment beneath yours is vacant. The lease is up on yours at the end of the year. The house should be preserved."

"She'd be grateful, Dermot."

I did not want to ask who "she" was.

"I was thinking of remodeling the apartments and wanted your permission."

Actually, I was thinking of temporarily restoring her rooms so that they could quickly be converted into a master bedroom and three other bedrooms. The first floor would become the first floor of a home, furnished to remind one of its origins, though with larger rooms, more bathroom space, and better electric wiring.

"Sure, I don't live there anymore, Dermot. It's not up to me. I know you'll make it a nice place to live."

I listened for whispers from Letitia Walsh Murray, Lace Maker. Perhaps she would tell me something about the missing letter from A. Lincoln. Maybe she had left it somewhere in this home of mine. I heard nothing.

In the first week of July, Judge Manley delivered his opinion. In effect, he argued that the right to due process was not absolute. Had not the Nazi spies during the Second World War been executed without due process? Had not the Japanese been ordered to relocation camps at the same time? Did not Abraham Lincoln himself suspend the right of habeas corpus? Did not the Union Army violate that right in the case of the notorious Camp Douglas conspirators?

Ought one not to conclude therefore that under some circumstances that the interest of the larger society constitutes a right which exceeds the due-process right? Is not the massive violation of our borders by immigrants such a circumstance? Is not the threat to our national identity from this invasion as critical as if a foreign army were invading us? Does not the government have the right to act vigorously and immediately to stop this invasion? Is it not possible to derive a legal theory that tells us that the behavior of the immigration-control agencies might safely be left to their own internal supervision in the present crisis? Does not a too-rigid application of the due-process clause leave the nation at the mercy of this foreign invasion? This court therefore believes that the too-rigid enforcement of the due-process clause without any attention to other rights, including the nation's right to reasonable measures of self-defense, and denies the plaintiff's petition.

Cindy demanded an immediate emergency hearing before the Seventh Circuit. Her request was granted, and a panel was appointed. But "immediate" does not necessarily mean immediate in the American courts. One of the judges was away on vacation. The hearing was postponed till the last week in July, six weeks after Nuala had been lifted.

The media attention had diminished, but Tracy kept up the pressure. A few columnists and some editorial writers embraced Judge Manley's theory. A Republican presidential candidate contended that at last someone in the federal courts was talking sense on immigration. Other candidates said they tended to agree in general with the judge but they didn't think it ought to apply in the case of this remarkable young woman.

The President, for his part, insisted that Nuala was just the kind of young person the United States needed. The two agents and the Chicago Director of INS were transferred to Texas. The head of the INS admitted that the behavior of the Chicago office might be seen to be improper.

The Irish media went crazy with anger at the American courts, but no one in this country paid any attention to them.

Most editorial writers took the position that, while immigration was indeed a serious problem, the means used in this case were unjustified and much too drastic.

Fear of the xenophobes muted much of the protest. Even the American Civil Liberties Union refused to become involved. The editor of the Jesuit magazine *America* accused the ACLU of cowardice and denounced Judge Manley as an unreconstructed nativist bigot.

Meanwhile lawyers for the state's attorney and the INS talked settlement.

"They're offering $50,000. We've cut our demand to a half-million."

"What will she get?"

"Something around two-fifty. We'll have to agree to keep the settlement secret. By the way, the U.S. attorney told me that the Feds want to settle, too, but they can't till we get a decision, somewhere or the other, up the line. In the end we'll get about the same from them. We'll probably end up with around a half-million, and they'll think they're lucky. Nuala will enjoy some financial independence."

"She gives away all her royalties on our book based on Ma's diaries."

"All of it?"

"Half to a trust fund for her parents, the rest to Irish

charities. Maybe she'll keep some of this, but I wouldn't bet on it."

"Interesting young woman . . ."

"How's herself doing?"

"She doesn't call you?"

"Nope."

"Don't blame her, Dermot. She's going through hell."

"I'm not blaming her, Cindy."

"For all her poise and seeming sophistication, she is the product of a lifestyle that in many ways is a hundred years in the past."

"I know. I've been there. I have the T-shirt and the baseball cap."

"These last two months have been hell for her. She's brilliant when the media venture to Cararoe. The rest of the time, she's tired and confused and depressed. Her mother says she's not eating much. We have to finish this shit soon to protect her from a breakdown. There's a limit to how much pressure anyone can take."

"Is she working?"

"She has a job in an accountant's office in Galway City. They pay her one-quarter of what Arthur did. The other people in the office ridicule her constantly."

"The Irish are great for kicking someone when they're down," I said bitterly.

"She'd never do that to anyone."

"No."

"I don't think we'll get her back, Dermot. Too much has happened."

"At least we must see that she has the right to return if she wants to."

"We'll do that, Dermot. Believe me."

I didn't quite believe her. I had known all along that no legal system is perfect, yet I still believed that ours worked most of the time. Now I understood that, like all systems, it was gravely flawed by its inability to take into account what stupid, venal, and ambitious men and women might decide to do. You received justice in America if right was on your side *and* if you were lucky.

Nuala had been very unlucky.

— 17 —

ON A hot Tuesday morning in early July, the phone in my apartment rang. It was herself.

"Are you remodeling the whole house, Dermot Michael?" she began.

"I am. I hope to turn it into a home, like the one herself lived in, only a bit more modern."

"Have you been in the basement?"

"Woman, I have not. I looked into it once and it was a terrible mess."

I began to shiver, expecting to hear another voice from beyond the grave.

"I think there might be an old closet down there underneath the steps—just a tiny thing. Boarded up. I noticed when I was down there to wash some things that there should have been a place beneath the stairs, but there wasn't."

Her voice drifted off into silence.

"You expect me to look down there when I get a chance?"

"No, Dermot Michael Coyne. I expect you to go over there this instant and look. Right now!"

"Yes ma'am."

I caught a cab up to Southport. No wasting time getting out of the building when buried treasure was at stake. I wondered how Nuala Anne knew that today the workers were going to clean out the basement and begin working on a family room.

When I arrived, I saw them loading rubbish on a large dump truck.

"The basement was full of shit," one of them said to me. "Newspapers from a hundred years ago in an old closet that they had sealed up."

"Where are those papers?" I asked frantically.

"We put them in the Dumpster," he replied. "Anything wrong?"

"I have to search through the whole mess. There might be buried treasure in there."

"Buried treasure!"

They were very helpful as I searched through the withered and rotting trash, looking for an old letter, as I told them. However, I had to look at every piece of trash myself. I wondered, as I searched, how much of it would be of interest to the historical society. I tried to separate the worthless from the valuable.

But I found no letters.

I went through everything again.

Still nothing.

It had to be there somewhere. Otherwise, why would Nuala have called me?

I'd search the trash all day and all night if necessary.

"Here's the *Chicago Times* from 1871," the foreman said. "All about the fire, which came within two blocks of this place."

I glanced at it, flipped through the pages, and handed it back to him. Then I reached for it again.

Were there two pages sticking together?

Carefully, very carefully, I opened them. There, sticking to one of the pages, was a piece of stationery, brown with age, worn at the edges, its ink dry and smudged:

The White House

Apr. 14, 65

Letitia Walsh
Lace Maker
Chicago Illinois
Dear Miss Walsh,

*I agree with the observations you made in yours
of the 5th ins. I thank you for them. I must let
the trial run its course. However, I promise you
that when it is over I will grant pardons to
everyone.*
Yrs.
A. Lincoln
President

With trembling fingers, I carried the buried treasure
up to Nuala's apartment. Nervously, I punched in the
numbers to Cararoe. Her mother answered the phone.
"It's Dermot, Mrs. McGrail. Is herself there?"
"Isn't she asleep, Dermot? It's eleven o'clock here."
Had I been searching for all those hours?
"Wake her up. It's important."
Then—in a moment—herself on the line.
"You found it, Dermot, did you now?"
She was sleepy, but excited.
"Woman, I did!"
"I knew you would. Aren't you the greatest treasure
hunter in all the world?"
"I think the title belongs to you. . . . Should I read
it to you?"
"That would be nice."
I read it.
"A nice man, your A. Lincoln."
"He was all of that."
"Thank you for calling."
"Nuala, it belongs to you. It's worth millions. You

found it."

"No, you did. I don't want it. Not at all, at all. Now, can I please go back to bed?"

I was prepared for her refusal. So I made a proposal about how to deal with the treasure.

"That's a grand idea," she said. "Brilliant!"

"We'll have to test it, of course, and put it in some protective container."

"Grand. Good night, Dermot."

The line went dead. I glanced at the phone. She might have said something more than that I was the greatest treasure hunter in all the world.

Well, she didn't.

After all, it was late in County Galway.

I called George at the cathedral.

"Incredible, little bro. Let me check with my friend Ralph, and I'll phone you back."

He was on the line in ten minutes.

"Tomorrow at nine. . . . It belongs to herself, naturally."

"Naturally."

"What does she want to do with it?"

"I told him."

"Sounds like her."

The next morning, the expert's office felt like the sanctuary of the cathedral during the elevation of the Sacred Host. We were all solemnly quiet as he carefully unwrapped the old issue of the *Times*.

He and George gasped as he saw the letter.

"The last words he ever set on paper," he said softly. "Worth millions. A last act of compassion before his death. We'll have to test the paper and the ink and the handwriting, of course, but my preliminary reaction is that it is authentic. Authentic beyond any doubt."

"You'll piece it together and protect it from any further decay."

"With utmost care . . . Is it yours, Mr. Coyne?"

"No. It belongs to a young woman."

"What does she intend to do with it?"

I told him.

He smiled. "She must be a remarkable young woman."

"All of that," George agreed. "All of that."

— 18 —

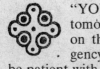"YOU CAN come into the court with me tomorrow as a clerk, Dermot," Cindy said on the day before the "immediate, emergency" hearing. "Don't punch anyone. And be patient with me. I'm planning a tirade. I want their decision tomorrow. No delays while they write an opinion."

The hearing was around an impressive oak table in the Everett McKinley Dirksen Federal Building, a much more informal setting than a regular courtroom, but still one subject to rigid rules of conduct. The three judges sat at one end of the table: An African-American man who was presiding and a white man and woman, the last no older than Cindy.

They greeted us cheerfully and informally at first. Cindy introduced the young U.S. attorney around whose head the case hung like a millstone, and me.

Then the presiding judge said, "Perhaps we may begin." A pall of formality and ritual descended on the room.

"You may assume, Counselor," the presiding judge informed Cindy, "that we have read your petition very carefully, as well as the responding brief of the United States attorney. We will now hear oral arguments. We will grant time for arguments and rebuttals till twelve o'clock. I hope we may be able to adjourn in time for lunch."

"Your Honors, I would be remiss in my obligation to my client if I did not make this initial observation. If the Seventh Circuit had not been remiss in its duty when I first moved for relief, we would not be here today."

The presiding judge stirred uneasily.

"I don't think we can accept that charge, Counselor. We can accept the fact that if a different decision was made in June we would not be here."

"We sought emergency relief, Your Honor, and we did not get it. Six weeks is far too long for an emergency. Justice delayed, I would remind you, is justice denied."

"It is our responsibility to decide what is justice in this case."

"I put it to you, your honors, that when I am finished you will understand, if you do not do so already, that there was a prima facie case for justice in June and that Seventh Circuit ought to have recognized it."

The judge sighed, nothing he could say would satisfy this outraged Celtic warrior goddess across the table and he knew it.

I thought I saw a flicker of a smile on the face of the woman judge.

"Perhaps you might begin your oral argument now, Counselor."

"I begin with the words of an English political philosopher of the last century, Lord Acton: Power corrupts, and absolute power corrupts absolutely. I put it to you that the district court in its decision offers absolute power to a government agency which has often used its authority, as we all know, to behave with appalling lack of humanity in its treatment of poor and unfortunate men and women."

Then the tirade began. With biting sarcasm and often furious anger, she attacked Judge Manley's ruling.

With soaring patriotic rhetoric, she praised the due-process clause as perhaps the most noble judicial principle in the history of the species. She decried the current nativist xenophobia that dared to call those noble words into question. She dismissed the arguments about the suspension of the principle at certain times as aberrations for which we should hang our heads in shame instead of citing as a precedent for further violations of elementary human justice. She did not attack Zack O'Hara, nor praise Nuala.

The three judges listened with considerable interest because Cindy was a show and a half, a brilliant, passionate performer of the sort that they would not ordinarily encounter in an appellate hearing.

Sometimes they smiled; occasionally they laughed. My sister, of whom I was immensely proud, was on a roll, and no one could stop her.

I wanted to punch someone.

The woman judge winked at me twice.

"The plaintiff is a remarkable young woman, Your Honors," she said, winding down, "with much to offer to our society. However, I am not here to argue from that fact. Even if she were an unattractive and vicious woman with whom we would not want ever to share a meal or invite into our homes, even if she were a prime candidate to have her visa lifted, even then she would have the right to a hearing, to appeal, and to turn to the judicial system. If the Immigration and Naturalization Service has reason for its action, let it bring charges against her and let her defend herself however she can. The issue here is not whether the plaintiff will make a good American. The issue is whether she was inadmissibly deprived of that possibility. I do not ask you to rule that she be permitted to continue to live in America, I merely ask that you mandate the State Department to renew her visa so she may return to this country and defend herself against whatever charges may be made against her. I also ask that, if the Immigration and Naturalization Service does not have such charges, you will enjoin it to cease harassing her. That seems to me to be a very minor request on which you can rule today. I ask you to do so in defense of one of our most sacred rights."

I wanted to get up and cheer.

I still wanted to punch someone.

"Well," the presiding judge said, clearing his throat, "we have just heard a very eloquent plea. Do my colleagues have any questions?"

They did not.

"Neither do I. Does the United States attorney want to present an oral argument?"

He began to write on his inevitable legal-size yellow pad.

"No, Your Honor I do not. Originally, as you know from the record, we did not intend to oppose this petition. We were ordered to. We have presented our best arguments in two briefs. I have been instructed to say that I have nothing to add to those briefs."

"Well, I see that we may even have an early lunch."

He passed his yellow pad to his male colleague. He read it carefully and nodded his head. The presiding judge than handed it over to the woman. She added a carefully written line.

I was sure we had won. Cindy continued to frown, her anger not yet cooled.

"Well," said the presiding judge genially, "I believe we can make an oral ruling now and direct compliance this afternoon. We will provide a written ruling with appropriate citations in the near future."

He cleared his throat, adjusted his glasses, and began to read the decision:

"This court reverses the decision of the Court for the Northern District of Illinois and rejects its arguments as fatuous. It directs the Department of State either to retrieve the plaintiff's visa from the Immigration and Naturalization Service or to issue a new one immediately. We also direct the Immigration and Naturalization Service either to begin action against the plaintiff within a reasonable period of time or to cease and desist its harassment of her. In any case we enjoin that Service not to prevent her return to his country."

"Thank you, Your Honors," Cindy said, biting her lip so as not to cry.

There were congratulations all around.

"You see, young man," the presiding judge said to me, "there is justice in this land of ours."

Not wishing to be churlish, I said, "I never doubted it."

"Proud of your sister, Mr. Coyne?" the woman asked me.

"Dazzled."

"Will she come back, do you think?" the third judge asked Cindy.

"I'm not sure. I'm afraid she won't. What do you think, Dermot?"

"She'll come back because she knows she belongs here. Eventually."

I was surprised by that insight.

"Did you get any material for your stories?" the presiding judge asked.

"If I use it, I'll be violating Cindy's copyright."

They all laughed.

In the corridor, Cindy and I hugged each other and cried with joy.

We were not out of the woods yet. A spokesperson for the passport service announced that it would take several months to issue a new visa because all the paperwork would have to be done over.

She changed her mind the next day, reportedly after a furious call from the White House. The papers from the previous application would be adequate. A new visa would be sent to Ambassador Jean Kennedy Smith in the afternoon diplomatic pouch.

The next day the ambassador journeyed to Cararoe, met Nuala and her parents, and presented her with the visa and a ticket to Chicago via Manchester on American Airlines. The airline had upgraded her to first class.

Nuala smiled shyly, thanked the ambassador, introduced her parents, and offered Ms. Smith an afternoon cup of tea. She accepted the offer, drank the tea, ate the homemade scones, complimented the McGrails on their tea service, and took her leave.

"When will you be home, Nuala?" a television journalist asked her.

"This *is* home," Nuala said politely. "I don't know that I'll ever go back to America, much as I like it."

I decided that enough was enough. I would fly to Shannon, drive up to Galway, and carry her off with me.

I was saved that task. Your man called her and pleaded with her to come back to America. Some of his ancestors were Irish. America needed young people like her from all over the world. We would miss her badly if she did not give us another chance. She would have two homes; one in Chicago and one in that lovely spot out there in Galway. The mayor of Chicago had spoken to him not an hour ago and asked him to convey his urgent invitation that she come to her other home. Just one more chance, Nuala Anne.

Who was "your man" this time? Come on, you know.

Being who and what she was, she could not refuse his request for forgiveness.

So she came back to the United States, confident, I suppose, that all the conspiracies had been put to rest. But there was one more conspiracy with which to contend.

19

NUALA'S HOMECOMING was solemn high, a beloved celebrity coming home. The new Chicago director of the INS greeted her at the plane, apologized for the "misunderstandings," stamped her visa and her customs form, and carried her small bag to the immigration room. The INS agents in the room cheered for her, shook her hand, and hugged her. Those of us who were waiting in a tight little circle in the back of the room joined the cheers. Herself was wearing a short-sleeved powder blue summer dress with the usual white belt *and* a white hat with a blue ribbon. She carried her harp in her left hand.

"She's acting like the frigging Queen of England," I whispered to Cindy who was standing next to me.

At the door, Her Majesty warmly acknowledged the welcome of the mayor, the cardinal, the little bishop, the presiding partner of Arthur, her boss, and the Coyne clan. She hugged the latter appropriately and, I thought, reserved a special hug and kiss for me at the very end of the line.

"Ah, 'tis yourself now, is it?"

" 'Tis."

She sighed and I sighed, too.

The persona was smooth but with cracks around the edges. She was wearing more makeup than she usually did and she had lost weight. Herself had been through emotional hell and was covering the effects up with an actress's aplomb. The show must go on.

To the waiting media, she said, "I'm so happy to be home in Chicago again. God willing, my stay here will be a little longer this time. I'm grateful to all those who helped me to return."

Simple and sweet.

We carried her off in a limousine to her redecorated and refurbished apartment on Southport Avenue. A caterer had laid out an elaborate buffet. Cindy proposed a toast with a glass of Barolo.

"Nuala Anne!"

"Nuala Anne!" we all echoed the toast.

Tears formed in her eyes as she sipped the wine.

"Yourselves!" she said in voice that cracked as she spoke.

She was still wearing the hat, which the women at the party praised mightily.

A duo played a violin and a viola as we ate and chatted. Nuala consumed only a bite or two.

" 'Tis yourself, woman, that should eat a little more. Or won't you wither away to a shadow of your former self?"

"Won't I be making a daily pilgrimage to the 31 Flavors over on Southport?"

"It will take more than that."

She touched my arm lightly. "It'll be all right, Derm, now that I'm home. . . . 'Tis yourself that's responsible for me new apartment?"

"Me ma, mostly. I helped a little."

"Then you'd be responsible for them terrible naked women on the walls?"

"Aren't the two of them nude, not naked?"

"Och, and aren't they lovely—kind of mystical, if you take me meaning?"

"Celtic Twilight. She wants to paint you."

"Ah, Dermot, sure, I couldn't do that at all, at all!

Wouldn't I be terrible embarrassed altogether?...
When?"

"Dermot is too modest," my mother insisted. "Most
of the ideas for redecorating were his. Doesn't he have
good taste?"

"Sometimes."

We all laughed.

I guided her over to the framed picture of the letter
to Letitia Walsh, lace maker.

She nodded and smiled.

"Buried treasure indeed, Dermot Michael."

Nothing more.

I thought or at least hoped that I had been restored
to my former role in her life.

No such luck.

On the phone the next day, she said bluntly, "Derm,
I think we should break up for a while. I need time to
take everything in."

My heart skipped a beat and my stomach and throat
tightened.

"How long?"

"No time limits."

"You're the boss Nuala Anne."

That was that. August, which started in a couple of
days, would be a hot and long month.

HAVEN'T YOU LOST HER ALTOGETHER? the Adversary said to me.

"Drop the phony Irish brogue," I told him. "You're
no friggin' good at it."

I played tennis; I played in a Grant Park softball
league (sixteen inch), as every young man of my age
must do; I messed around with my stories; I began a
novel about a man with a broken heart; I went to the
movies.

Movies are my way of escaping from reality, always
have been.

The novel moved along pretty well. My agent said
that, if I kept it up, it would surely be published. No

one, I thought, will want to read a novel in which the man loses his love because he's a stupid eejit.

The family asked no questions and never spoke about herself in my presence, except when I asked Cindy about the suits. Not even the Priest.

One night in the third week of August as my twenty-fifth summer dragged to a miserable, self-pitying end, I took a taxi down to the Fine Arts Building (where Madame reigned in her studio) to see *The Brothers McMullen,* a film about three Irish brothers from New York (and hence very different from us Chicago Irish) made for $25,000 by a kid only a year older than I was.

It was grand, super, brilliant. If Nuala and I were ever reconciled, I'd have to take her to see it.

I walked back to my apartment despite the 85-degree heat. I was envious of young Mr. Burns, who had written it, directed it, and played the leading role. He was a frigging genius and himself only a year older than meself. I didn't resent his success. Rather, I was angry at my own mediocrity. I possessed all the money I needed for the rest of my life and through no fault of my own. (I'd gone long when I should have gone short on a huge order. The market opened limit up the next day and I made $3 million, whereupon, since I was as bad at trading as I had been at everything else, I retired.) Yet I had not done anything with my life. I was a dilettante writer who fooled around with writing but had yet to do anything important. I'd wasted the whole last year mooning over a woman and lost her anyway. It was time for me to settle down and get serious.

Having lost in the comparison of myself with Ed Burns, I toppled into my easy chair with a stiff glass of Bushmill's Single Malt to kill the pain. What was the film about, besides a comparison between you and your man?

The message was simple enough and Burns made it

clear enough: Once you find your true love, never let her go. A Catholic message pretty clearly, even if Ed Burns was only dimly aware of it: Your true love is a sacrament of God.

I stirred uneasily in my chair. The real difference between the characters in the film and me was that I had let my true love, my sacrament of God, slip through my fingers. I was a frigging eejit.

I hadn't heard from her in weeks. No one had. She had dropped out of sight. I had gathered from Cindy that the two suits were inching forward towards settlement, and from Tracy that she had flatly turned down television appearances and record contracts with the comment, "I'm an accountant, not a singer."

Stubborn bitch.

She was, however, determined to escape the celebrity role, and that was healthy, wasn't it?

As an extra precaution, I had put Reliable back on her as soon as she returned from Ireland.

She was still my true love, and I had let her go too easily.

I grabbed for the phone and punched in her number.

"Hel-lo."

"Nuala?"

"Dermot?"

" 'Tis."

"Brigid, Patrick, and Columcille, wasn't I sitting here staring at me phone and meself trying to work up the nerve to call you?"

"Why?"

Put the ball in her court.

Her voice took on its crafty, scheming, conniving tone.

"I suppose you've been to see that Monet thing, haven't you?"

"I've had had more than enough of your man for one summer."

"Would you ever like to take me over there?"

"That puts the matter in a different light."

"Well, isn't me firm having a dinner party there, and haven't I got two tickets, and don't I need a date?"

"Do you now?"

"I do."

"Well, I might be able to fit it into my schedule. Black tie?"

"Isn't it now?"

"I suppose I can arrange that, too. When?"

"Ah, isn't it tomorrow night, Dermot Michael?"

"Tomorrow night!"

"Viewing at five, drinks at six, dinner at six-thirty. Don't your accountants like to go to bed early? Would you ever pick me up about four-thirty?"

"Kind of short notice, Nuala Anne."

"I was afraid to call you, Dermot Michael."

She sounded so frightened and so sad that I took pity on her.

"For you, Nuala, I'll always be available on short notice. Four-thirty tomorrow it is."

"Thank you Dermot."

Had I recovered my true love? With no effort on my part? Why did I get all the lucky breaks? Well, this time she doesn't get away.

Such were my thoughts when I pushed the bell at the top of the solid stairs, with which I had replaced the old rickety ones.

"On time as usual, Dermot Michael," she said as she opened the door. "And isn't yourself looking handsome tonight, in your black tie and everything?"

I gulped and gaped and gasped.

"You're the one who looks handsome, Nuala Anne."

"I like it so much when you look at me that way, kind of hungry like."

"Starving."

Powder blue was still the color, a full-length gown, thigh slit as high as it dared to go, no shoulders, precious little back, a generous view of breasts, and a shimmering and sheer cape of the same color edged with a touch of gold.

"Why the harp?" I asked as I took her arm and led her down the stairs.

"They asked me to sing and said they'd give me two free tickets. It's a benefit banquet and, sure, I didn't have one thousand dollars for me meal. So I'm singing for me supper. . . . You don't mind, Dermot, do you?"

"Why should I mind?"

She was a sensation at the Art Institute. Naturally. Men and women both, like me, gulped and gaped and gasped.

She introduced me as, "This is me young man, Dermot Michael Coyne. He's a seanachie. That's Irish for a storyteller."

Her young man, is it now?

A couple of Arthur's folks asked me what county in Ireland I was from. I replied each time in flat Middle Western 'Mercan,' 'County Cook, a little village called River Forest.' "

The canvases were overwhelming. The man was truly a friggin' genius. Some of them even distracted me from looking at Nuala.

The champagne was superb, the food excellent, the conversation sprightly, considering that the guests were accountants or computer consultants. Unlike Judge Manley, they read the *New York Times.*

Then came the singing.

Nuala Anne sat on a dais at one end of the banquet room and tuned her harp.

"For them as don't know me or don't recognize me in this fancy and shocking dress, I'm Nuala Anne McGrail and, despite appearances, I'm a junior accountant with the firm, and I'm learning a lot about computers. I also sing, as a matter of fact and—you should forgive the plug—I'll be singing at the Abbey Pub on Wednesday nights after Labor Day."

General laughter. She had disarmed them completely. Performer persona.

Then she began to sing—from her diaphragm.

In Dublin's fair city,
Where the girls are so pretty
I first set my eyes
On sweet Molly Malone.
She wheeled her wheelbarrow
Through streets broad and narrow,
Crying "Cockles and mussels,
Alive, alive, oh!"

Alive, alive, oh!
Alive, alive, oh!
Crying, "Cockles and mussels,
Alive, alive, oh!"

She was a fishmonger,
But sure 'twas no wonder,
For so was her father and mother before
And they both wheeled their barrow
Through streets broad and narrow
Crying, "Cockles and mussels,
Alive, alive, oh!"

Alive, alive, oh!
Alive, alive, oh!
Crying, "Cockles and mussels,
Alive, alive, oh!"

She died of a fever
And no one could relieve her,
And that was the end of sweet Molly Malone,
But her ghost wheels her barrow
Through streets broad and narrow,
Crying, "Cockles and mussels,
Alive, alive, oh!"

> *Alive, alive, oh!*
> *Alive, alive, oh!*
> *Crying, "Cockles and mussels,*
> *Alive, alive, oh!"*

She wouldn't look at me as she sang.

She sang three more songs, two lullabies, and a lament and then finished up with "Paddy Reilly."

Tumultuous applause.

"Remarkable young woman, Dermot," said the man who sat on the other side of her empty chair. "You're very fortunate."

"That remains to be seen!"

She returned, I stood up to hold the chair for her.

"Your voice is in top form tonight, Nuala Anne."

"Shouldn't it be now, and meself seeing Madame every week?"

"Ah?"

"She'll be sending you the bills at the end of the month."

I felt that someone was tightening the lasso around me.

Why shouldn't she? After all, wasn't she my true love?

"Will you come up for a minute or two, Derm?" she asked me as I eased into a parking place in front of her house.

"Sure."

What next?

If she dragged me into bed with her, I couldn't refuse, could I?

Nuala wouldn't do that. She'd try something even more effective.

I felt no sense of impending doom as I climbed the steps with her.

Inside the apartment, she directed me to a chair, whirled off her "Dracula Cape" as I called it, and brought two small glasses of Bailey's Irish Cream.

" 'Tis only a drop because don't you have to be driving home?"

Then she knelt at my knees and said, "I ask your pardon, Dermot Michael, for the terrible person I've been to you all summer."

"You don't have to kneel, Nuala," I said trying to pull her off the floor.

"No, Dermot, you keep saying I am an actress and this is the part I have to play. I confessed to Father before Mass this morning, and now I must confess to you."

I gave up my attempt to lift her from the floor. She folded her hands on my knee.

"I've been terrible to you, Derm. There's no excuse, none at all, and I know you've already forgiven me, but I still have to explain."

"All right."

I caressed her face and her throat and her neck and her shoulders and her chest and her back and the tops of her breasts with chaste and gentle fingers. Well, pretty chaste.

"Don't stop that, Dermot. Please don't stop it."

"If you say so."

"This wonderful city overwhelmed me. I tried to absorb everything. You were overwhelming, too much altogether—big and strong and sweet and kind and smart and nice. I said to meself, this man has captured me and I'll never get away from him and never be able to be meself or even think for myself. And then I said, I must be free of him, or I won't be able to cope with all the other things I had to cope with. I lost the run of meself altogether. You, do understand, don't you Dermot Michael?"

"I do."

"Then, when I returned here and broke up with you, I thought me poor heart would break. One morning, 'twas only last week, I woke up and said Nuala you're a friggin' eejit. He's only your nice young man Dermot, poor dear fella, who is no problem at all, at all. You don't have to cope with him. The only thing to do is to enjoy him. You've got to get him back and then never let him go away."

"You appear to have succeeded."

My fingers rested on the top of a breast, slowly tracing delicate circles.

"You do understand, don't you, Derm?"

"Totally."

"And you do forgive me?"

"Whatever there is to forgive, I forgive . . . still let me say something. I hope you try to have more respect for yourself and your instincts and your talents than you do now. I won't argue with you about what you've said because that would be a churlish male response to such an appealing plea. Yet I could make a strong case—one that's pretty reasonable to me—that you have behaved with regard to your poor, nice young man with considerable skill, all things considered."

My fingers found her other breast and traced designs on it. Nuala drew a quick breath—of pleasure, I hoped.

"I won't disagree with them words . . . and you won't mind if I come to Grand Beach for your bank holiday?"

The schemer again.

I pushed her dress a little lower and removed enough of the minimal bra to reach a nipple. I possessed it with my lips. It rose to meet my demand. Then I paused to rejoice in the glory of her lovely young breasts. They were more wonderful than my constant fantasies about them.

"Here we call it Labor Day weekend, and I'd mind if *you didn't* come. I'll tell Mom in the morning."

"Och, Dermot, I told her today!"

I took her in my arms and rocked her back and forth. I loved the schemer persona almost as much as all the others. Then I lifted her from the floor and grabbed her bare shoulders firmly.

"Listen to me, Marie Phinoulah Annagh McGriel, don't you ever try to run away from me again. The next time I'll run after you and drag you back by your long black hair!"

"Wouldn't that be an fascinating sexual experience now!"

She rearranged her dress, sat in the chair on the other side of the coffee table, and toasted me, "Dermot!"

I returned the favor. "Nuala!"

"Weren't you doing some wicked things to me?"

"You said I shouldn't stop!"

"Och, they weren't *that* wicked!"

We talked for a few minutes, reveling in a barrier overcome.

Then she said with her best County Galway sigh, " 'Tis time to go home, Dermot."

" 'Tis," I said, rising and sighing myself.

We kissed each other lightly and she opened the door.

In the dim light, I saw the last conspiracy at the bottom of the stairs. Billy Hernon and two flunkies, all of them with switchblades in their paws.

"We're going to fuck her all night long and make you watch!" Billy crowed as he began to ascend the stairs, "Then we're going to cut the two of you up, so that no one will ever want to look at you ever again."

20

"GOOD EVENING, Billy," I replied. "It's nice to see you again."

The whole world seemed to decelerate into a leisurely crawl. I saw each movement unroll in slow motion. I knew exactly what I would do. I guess they call the phenomenon "flow," or something like that.

Calmly, as if I had all the time in the world, I moved Nuala behind me. I told her to go inside and close the door, though I knew there wasn't a chance in the world that she would do that. I waited patiently for them to get two-thirds of the way up the stairs. Their blades were gleaming in the light coming from the doorway. "About now," I said to myself.

"I don't think I want you climbing any higher," I said to them.

Then—quite deliberately and with utter confidence and serenity—I threw myself at them in a movement which our coach at Fenwick had urged even the defensive players to practice—an illegal and immoral action called the cutback block.

I heard a scream in the distance as I floated through the air towards them. Herself, no doubt.

Then I hit them at knee level. Not bad for someone who had not done a cutback for nine years.

They tumbled down the stairs, crashing and bumping and tumbling as they were supposed to do. Their screams of surprise and pain blended with Nuala's cries of rage.

Since I had known what I would do, I grabbed a rail halfway down, spun to my feet, observed the tangled mess of screaming men at the bottom, and jumped on them. No chances taken this time, and no mercy shown.

In the slowest of slow motions, I stamped on fingers, kicked knives away, broke noses, kicked groins, and broke another arm or two. I was aware that a wailing she-demon had joined in and was bashing heads with a lawn chair.

Banshee-like wail.

Then a courteous womanly voice said to me, "It's all right, Mr. Coyne. We have our guns on them."

Who was this woman?

Joannie, naturally, and with Bert right next to her. Reliable was reliable this time.

I desisted from my berserking, came out of my trance, and said, quite calmly, "It was good of you to come, Joannie, Bert."

Nuala rearranged her dress, which did not seem to have been damaged, and clung to my arm. Half of the squad cars from Area Six arrived from all directions. The local priest emerged from the rectory, holy oils in hand. Cops swarmed over the injured perpetrators. Commander Culhane appeared in an unmarked car.

"Do you work twenty-four hours a day, John?"

"Dear God, Dermot, you guys made a mess of them!"

"Never mess with Grace O'Malley," I replied. "*Or* her champion."

Then the letdown hit me. My muscles turned to water. My breathing came in gasps. My bladder threatened to flush. My body shook. I would have fallen on my face, save for Nuala's grip on my arm.

However, one might just as well bluff it out.

"That was not a half-bad cutback block, was it, Nuala, dear?"

Herself was crying and laughing and crying at the same time.

I wanted to kick the wounded and battered Billy Hernon in the face. However, the berserking was over, wasn't it?

John insisted that the cops take me to St. Joseph's Hospital. The ER folks pronounced me undamaged, save for scrapes and bruises. I bussed my love good night, told her I would see her at Grand Beach on the weekend, and drove home under my own power.

The next morning every inch of my organism ached. I was too old for berserking, much too old.

Then I thought of Nuala's delicate skin and cool breasts and delicate nipples and decided that I was not too old at all, at all. There were certain things which I had to do. I must get out of bed and do them.

Mom drove up to Grand Beach to prepare for the weekend on Thursday. Nuala Anne, to whom Arthur had granted an extra day off, went along. I pleaded the obligation to my softball league and the need to get the stiffness out of my muscles and the likelihood of some beer taken as reasons for traveling on Friday morning.

I arrived with the sunrise. Mom's Buick was not in the driveway. Likely the two of them had gone to the store at the break of day.

Thinking about a nice nap, I walked up the stairs. As I ambled along the corridor on the second floor, I noted that the door to what had become "Nuala's room" was open.

Herself was inside, brushing her hair in front of a vanity mirror and wearing the most revealing white lace lingerie. Irish lace, I thought as I admired her.

She became aware of the presence of someone.

"Dermot!" she yelled. "You're violating me privacy."

She hugged herself protectively

"Woman, I am not. Wasn't the door open?"

I took the brush out of her hand and drew her into my arms and kissed her.

"Are you trying to seduce me Dermot?" she asked uncertainly not altogether sure whether she should resist me.

"Woman, I am not, and with me mom coming back any moment now."

"Oh," she said and relaxed into my arms. "What are you doing, then?"

"I'm admiring and caressing you. Do you object to that?"

"No."

My fingers traced designs just as they had the other night, though now their ministrations were able to extend to her belly.

"That's nice, Dermot. You're so delicate with me."

And then, in sudden awareness, she protested, "I don't have anything on at all, at all."

I held her at arm's length and drank her in.

"You do too, woman. Irish lace."

"The lace is French. . . ."

"And what is inside is Irish."

"Do you intend to admire me all morning?"

"Would you object?"

"No. But I would like to beat you at tennis if you ever find time for it."

I slipped a finger beneath a thick lace bra strap and drew my designs down to a breast. Then the other one. I eased the straps gently off her shoulders and lowered the cups of the bra.

"Dermot," she sighed deeply, as I caressed her breasts with my tongue.

Then we heard Mom's Buick and disengaged from one another. We both giggled. I restored her bra to proper order and helped her on with her robe. Then

I scooted down the corridor to my own room. She quietly closed the door to hers.

I beat her 7–5, 7–4 at tennis. She was furious.

"You were practicing for the last two months," she accused me.

"Woman, I was."

"That's not fair!"

"Why not?"

"Because it's not—that's all!"

Then she laughed and kissed me and said, "You played powerful well, Dermot Michael. But I'll beat you the next time."

"That will be as may be."

As we walked back from the tennis court, she said, "I suppose you know that herself is painting me?"

"I did not. Catherine Curran?"

"The very same."

"How's it going?"

" 'Tis strange standing naked, uh, nude with someone else looking at you all evening long. I suppose I should get used to it, if I'm going to marry someone."

"In five or ten years?"

"Right. Then after a while it becomes liberating, and you don't mind it at all, at all. You even kind of like it."

"Really? What's the painting like?"

"*Well*"—she drew a deep breath—"if you ask me, it's too candid altogether. It embarrasses me a little. She says she's only celebrating me youthful vigor and strength."

"Bodybuilder?"

"No, silly," she said tapping my arm. "Nothing like that at all, at all."

"When do I get to see it?"

"Forty years from now, when all your passions have died."

"I hear they last a lot longer."

"I hope so."

I was drafted for kitchen duty on most of Friday. Nuala's door was firmly closed. We skied and sailed on much of Saturday, and herself proved a skillful crew.

I figured that this would be the right day.

That evening the family celebrated Tessa's newly announced pregnancy with congratulations and champagne. Calculating back from the due date, I figured that Tessa had been no more than one week pregnant when herself had told me the "secret." She nodded at me and then stuck her nose in the air when the advent of the new Coyne was officially announced. I was not about to bet that it would be a girl.

I suggested to Nuala that we take a walk along the beach. She looked up from her mystery novel. "Don't you ever get tired, Dermot Michael Coyne, and ourselves perishing with the heat all day?"

"Nope."

"All right!" She put a marker in the book; no turned-down pages for this child. "If I have to, I have to."

She in her bikini and I in my trunks, we walked a couple of miles in the light of the full moon, kissed each other frequently in the process, and then sat on the sand in front of my family's house, quietly happy in each other's presence.

Now.

"I suppose me family is telling you that you will surely get a ring by Christmas."

"I know nothing about that, at all, at all!"

She stuck her nose up in the air as she does when she's mortally offended.

"And they're guessing that we might marry sometime next spring or summer."

"That will be as may be. I frankly couldn't care less."

"All I'm trying to say is that there will be no ring for you at Christmas, at all, at all."

"That is of no interest to me."

"Christmas is too long to wait."

She snorted, not taking me meaning.

I took the little box out of the pocket of my swim trunks.

"I did, however, find this on the beach."

She frowned suspiciously. "What's in that box thing?"

I flipped it open.

She recoiled from the sight of it. "Praise be to all the saints in heaven, Dermot Michael, that's the biggest jewel in all the world!"

"Do you want to hold it?" I took the ring, the diamond on which was big enough, if not exactly the Hope Diamond.

She drew back farther from me.

"Wouldn't I drop it in the sand?"

"Would you want to try it on your finger, just for a moment?"

"Only for a moment," she said and held out a trembling ring finger.

I held her finger steady and slipped the ring on it.

Herself turned the ring around and around, admiring it in the moonlight.

" 'Tis brilliant, Dermot, look at the way it glitters in the moonlight."

"As brilliant as the blue in your eyes."

"Go 'long with ya!"

"Are you going to give it back to me now?"

"Not in a million years."

She hid her hand behind her back. I pretended to fight her for it.

Then we fell into each other's arms and talked about love and such matters.

"Here or in Ireland, Nuala?"

"If it's all the same to you, I'd rather it be here and bring me ma and da over. My sisters and brothers who live in Seattle and Long Island and San Diego and Philadelphia could come, then."

She'd done some thinking about the matter, hadn't she? Women do.

"Christmas?"

"It would be terrible hard to find a time for a Mass, then."

"Is Thanksgiving too soon?"

"It would be crowded then, too."

She removed her left arm from my embrace and admired her engagement ring in the moonlight.

"When?"

"You'll say I'm a schemer and a conniver and a plotter."

"I've told you that I like you that way. It took me awhile to realize you were just like Ma."

"Well," she said and hesitated.

"Well, what?"

"Didn't I talk to the little bishop at the cathedral and your man being there anyway, and didn't he say that there was an open time on the second Friday in October at five o'clock in the evening, and didn't I ask him to pencil in our names!"

She was indeed like Nell Pat.

I scooped her up in my arms.

"What are you doing, you big oaf?"

"I'm going to show the rest of me family the ring I found on the beach with a woman in it."

What happened to the Good Friday letter to Letitia Walsh, lace maker, from A. Lincoln? Can't you look at it in the lobby of the National Archives in Washington? Doesn't the inscription say that it was donated by a certain person to the United States of America in gratitude for its generosity to Irish immigrants?

— NOTE —

THE CAMP Douglas documents which Dermot cites in his reports to herself are drawn from historical records, except the memoir written by Letitia Walsh. The arguments she uses about the conspiracy theory, however, are those of contemporary authors, most notably George Levy's excellent 1994 book *To Die in Chicago: Confederate Prisoners at Camp Douglas, 1862–1865*.[3] I rely especially on Chapter 14, "The Camp Douglas Conspiracy of 1864." Readers of this story who wish to learn more about Camp Douglas should read *To Die in Chicago* (Evanston Publishing Company, Evanston, Illinois 60201). Another very useful book is *Dark Lanterns: Secret Political Societies, Conspiracies, and Treason Trials in the Civil War,* by Frank L. Klement (Louisiana State University Press, 1984). Professor Klement was the first "revisionist" historian to argue conclusively that all of the "conspiracies" were frauds and that all the "treason trials" were violations of the elementary human rights of innocent men, whose only crime was to oppose the war.

Letitia's character and her family life flow from my own imagination, based on a line I read about the "high-spirited and beautiful young women who were lace-makers" who fiercely defended their father before the Cincinnati military tribunal. Alas, I can't remember where I read the line.

The letter from A. Lincoln is fictional. However, he did not believe in the Camp Douglas conspiracy and

---

[3]The only full book written about Camp Douglas since 1865.

would doubtless have pardoned the alleged conspirators if he had survived the attack at Ford's Theater. Needless to say, I accept Nuala Anne's balanced judgment about the conspiracy.

(Will Nuala and Dermot really marry one another on the second Friday of October? That would be telling, now, wouldn't it? But, God willing, they'll be back again in a story to be called *Irish Whiskey*.)

Grand Beach—A. Greeley—Priest
  September 19, 1995